WORD
OF HONOR

WORD

OF HONOR

A Peter Wake Novel

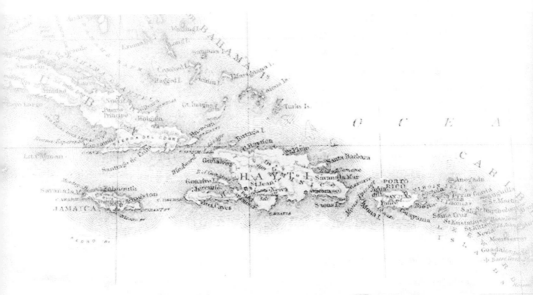

ROBERT N. MACOMBER

Naval Institute Press
Annapolis, Maryland

Naval Institute Press
291 Wood Road
Annapolis, MD 21402

Library of Congress Cataloging-in-Publication Data
Names: Macomber, Robert N., date– author.
Title: Word of honor / Robert N. Macomber.
Description: Annapolis, Maryland : Naval Institute Press, [2020] | Series: The honor series | Includes bibliographical references.
Identifiers: LCCN 2020025994 (print) | LCCN 2020025995 (ebook) | ISBN 9781682475386 (hardback ; alk. paper) | ISBN 9781682475393 (ebook) | ISBN 9781682475393 (pdf)
Subjects: LCSH: United States. Navy—Officers—Fiction. | Wake, Peter (Fictitious character)—Fiction. | Spanish-American War, 1898—Fiction. | United States—History, Naval—19th century—Fiction. | GSAFD: War stories. | Historical fiction.
Classification: LCC PS3613.A28 W67 2020 (print) | LCC PS3613.A28 (ebook) | DDC 813/.6—dc23
LC record available at https://lccn.loc.gov/2020025994
LC ebook record available at https://lccn.loc.gov/2020025995

♾ Print editions meet the requirements of ANSI/NISO z39.48-1992 (Permanence of Paper).
Printed in the United States of America.

28 27 26 25 24 23 22 21 20   9 8 7 6 5 4 3 2 1
First printing

*This novel is respectfully dedicated to a brave man
I was honored to call my friend:*

INSPECTOR KEITH SAUNDERS, QPM

CID/D&CP

Dear friend of thirty years, stalwart comrade in the
neverending fight against criminal evil,
fellow author of history, kindred adventurous soul,
and one of Great Britain's finest sons.
May Keith and his beloved wife, Wendy,
rest in peace among the beautiful green hills of Devon.
I miss them.

An Introductory Word with My Readers

American naval officer Peter Wake, fictional hero of the Honor Series of historical naval thrillers, has had a far from dull existence, so while writing this newest volume of his memoirs, I thought perhaps both new and longtime readers, the famous "Wakians," might appreciate a simple timeline of his life experiences.

I'll also take this moment to remind readers that the endnotes at the back of the novel contain even more information on Wake and the places and people he encounters in the story. There is a research bibliography for those who wish to delve further into this fascinating period of history.

Timeline of Peter Wake's Life from 1839 to Early July 1898

1839—June 26. Wake is born into a seafaring family on the coast of Massachusetts. His father, a third-generation sea captain, owns four schooners in the coastal cargo trade. At age six, Wake begins attending Stonehead School. His favorite subjects are history, geography, and geometry. He does not do well in theology, music, advanced mathematical theory, and philosophy.

1852—At age thirteen, Wake goes to sea in one of his father's schooners to learn seamanship. At his mother's insistence, he still attends Stonehead School one semester a year.

1855—Wake is promoted to schooner mate at age sixteen. He stops attending Stonehead School that year and stays at sea full time. He does continue his reading of history, which becomes a lifelong interest.

1857—At age eighteen, Wake is promoted to command of a schooner and sails the Atlantic Coast from Nova Scotia to Virginia.

1861—The Civil War begins. Wake's father pleads with him to remain a draft-exempt merchant marine captain rather than enlisting. By 1862 his three older brothers, Luke, John, and Matthew, are volunteer U.S. naval officers in the war.

1863—In May, Wake loses his draft exemption and receives notice to report to the Army, which has suffered terrible losses. His father counsels him to join the Navy instead, where he "can at least live cleanly." Wake volunteers and is commissioned as an acting master. Sent to Key West, he is given command of the small sailing gunboat *Rosalie*. Wake operates on the southwest Florida coast and in the Bahamas against blockade runners, and his success quickly gains him promotion to acting lieutenant. Irish-born boatswain's mate Sean Rork joins *Rosalie*'s crew, and the two men become lifelong best friends (as depicted in *At the Edge of Honor*, the first novel of the Honor Series).

1864—Wake chases Union deserters to French-occupied Mexico, marries Linda Donahue at Key West with Rork as best man, and engages in raids against Confederates on the Gulf coast of Florida (as depicted in *Point of Honor*).

1865—Wake's daughter Useppa is born at Useppa Island. At the chaotic end of the Civil War he is assigned a postwar mission to check on ex-Confederates in Puerto Rico, where he discovers a wartime nemesis (as depicted in *Honorable Mention*).

1867—Volunteer officers are dismissed after the war. Most eagerly go home, but Wake stays in the Navy with a regular commission as a lieutenant at Pensacola. His son, Sean, is born that year.

1869—While on a mission to stop an American former naval officer–turned-pirate on the coast of Panama, executive officer Wake relieves his morphine-addicted captain of duty and is subsequently charged with mutiny. He is acquitted of the charge, but his professional reputation is tarnished. Rumors about what happened will persist for the rest of his career (as depicted in *A Dishonorable Few*).

1874—While Wake is involved in questionable political-diplomatic incidents in Spain and Italy, a married French woman enters his life.

Wake faces personal and professional perils in Italy because of her but is saved from disaster by Jesuits. Later, he rescues the woman and other French civilians in North Africa, is awarded the Legion of Honor by France, and is promoted to lieutenant commander (as depicted in *An Affair of Honor*).

1880—Wake embarks on his first naval espionage mission during the South American War of the Pacific (1879–83) and ends up hiding with refugees in the Catacombs of the Dead in Lima, Peru. There, he cements his lifelong relationship with the Jesuits. He is awarded his second foreign medal, the Order of the Sun, by Peru. Before Wake can return home, his beloved wife, Linda, dies of cancer in Washington, and he sinks into depression. In the aftermath he plunges into his work, helping to form the Office of Naval Intelligence (ONI), America's first foreign espionage agency (as depicted in *A Different Kind of Honor*).

1883—On an espionage mission to French Indo-China, Wake befriends King Norodom of Cambodia, is awarded the Royal Order of Cambodia, and is promoted to commander. During the Battle of Hué, Rork loses his left hand to a sniper's bullet, and a French navy surgeon fits him with a unique prosthesis. After returning home, Wake and Rork buy Patricio Island in southwest Florida and build bungalows there for their annual leave (as depicted in *The Honored Dead*).

1886—Wake meets young politician-writer Theodore Roosevelt and Cuban patriot José Martí in New York City as he begins an espionage mission against the Spanish in Havana, Tampa, and Key West. His deadly twelve-year struggle against the Spanish secret police in Cuba and Florida begins, as do lifelong friendships with Martí and Roosevelt (as depicted in *The Darkest Shade of Honor*).

1888—While on annual leave, a search for a lady friend's missing son in the Bahamas and Haiti evolves into a love affair and an espionage mission against European anarchists. Wake's shadowy relationship with the Russian secret service, the Okhrana, begins. He proposes marriage to his lover and falls back into depression when she rejects him (as depicted in *Honor Bound*).

1888—During a mission to rescue ONI's Cuban operatives from Spanish custody in Havana, Wake is designated "a friend of Masonry" by Martí and forges a lifelong working relationship with Freemasons. Barely escaping the Spanish secret police in Cuba, he manages to save the lives of the men he was sent to find and liberate (as depicted in *Honorable Lies*).

1889—Wake is sent on an espionage mission to the South Pacific in an effort to prevent an impending war between Germany and America at Samoa. He is successful, but only by using regrettable methods. He is awarded the Royal Order of Kalakaua by the Kingdom of Hawaii and gains the gratitude of President Grover Cleveland, but he is ever afterward ashamed of the sordid methods he used in Samoa (as depicted in *Honors Rendered*).

1890—Wake learns that his 1888 love affair had produced a daughter, Patricia, who is growing up in Illinois with her maternal aunt, his lover having died in childbirth. Though the aunt despises him, he offers financial support to his estranged daughter, hoping to eventually meet her.

1890—Wake leaves ONI espionage work and thankfully returns to sea in command of a cruiser. This same year, his son, Sean, graduates from the U.S. Naval Academy and begins his own career.

1892—Wake has a love affair in Washington, D.C., with Maria Ana Maura, the widow of a Spanish diplomat. At the same time, he is brought back into espionage work on a counter-assassination mission in Mexico and Florida during which he saves Martí's life. Afterward he returns to sea in command of another cruiser (as depicted in *The Assassin's Honor*).

1893—Wake is promoted to captain, and Rork to the newly established rank of chief boatswain mate, in April. In May, Wake marries Maria at Key West in a double ceremony with Useppa and her Cuban fiancé, Mario Cano. The now famous Martí attends the wedding (as depicted in *The Assassin's Honor*).

1895—Wake's dear friend Martí is killed in action fighting the Spanish at Dos Rios in eastern Cuba on May 19.

1897—Wake ends seven straight years of sea duty with orders to become special assistant to the new assistant secretary of the Navy, his longtime friend Theodore Roosevelt. Together they prepare the Navy for the looming war against Spain.

1898—Roosevelt sends Wake inside Cuba on an espionage mission against the Spanish as the tense confrontation before the Spanish-American War boils over. He is in Havana Harbor when the *Maine* explodes. Presumed dead, Wake sets a trap later that night to kill his longtime archenemy, Colonel Isidro Marrón, the head of the Spanish secret police. After war is officially declared several months later, Wake leads a coastal raid, poorly planned by politicians in Washington, against the enemy in Cuba. The Spanish overwhelm his force, and although wounded, he employs effective but shockingly brutal tactics to save his men and accomplish the mission. Once again his actions bring censure from Washington politicians, the New York press, and senior naval officers. He recuperates from his wounds in Tampa, nursed by Maria (as depicted in the first novel of the Honor Series' trilogy about the Spanish-American War, *An Honorable War*).

1898—After Wake recovers, he is assigned to the U.S. Army as a staff officer and sent back inside Cuba to be the liaison to the Cuban Liberation Army in eastern Cuba. Wake is reunited with Roosevelt, now with the Rough Riders, during the jungle and hill battles around Santiago. Maria arrives in Cuba as a Red Cross volunteer and nurses the sick and wounded in a filthy field hospital. Wake is present at the naval battle of Santiago as a prisoner on a Spanish cruiser. He survives the battle and is subsequently rescued by Sean, now a lieutenant (as depicted in *Honoring the Enemy*, the second novel in the Spanish-American War trilogy).

Word of Honor, the final novel of the Spanish-American War trilogy of the Honor Series, finds Wake in command of the *Dixon*, a large passenger liner converted into an auxiliary light cruiser, on blockade duty along the southeastern Cuban coast. Fate has other plans, however, and Wake will face unanticipated dilemmas and a carefully planned trap set for him by his longtime political foes.

With a man like Peter Wake, during a period like the early twentieth century, anything is possible. So settle into your chair and get ready for action and intrigue in the Spanish-American War and Wake's role in it.

Robert N. Macomber
The Boat House
St. James, Pine Island
Florida

Preface

War has many unintended consequences for both the victor and the vanquished foe, and also for the uninvolved neighboring countries. Some such consequences emerge when least expected or appreciated.

This personal account is a cautionary professional tale of what happens when those consequences overwhelm the plans of the winners. When the celebrations end and the unforeseen responsibilities begin, doubts appear. America, with her new empire of colonies around the world, must now bear the inevitable cost in blood and treasure to subdue, maintain, and defend the inhabitants of those colonies. Inevitably the salient question will arise: Is it worth it?

Regarding the war with Spain, this question remains unanswered. I fear we won't like that answer when it does arrive. Not all victories end up being pleasant, or even honorable.

This installment of my memoirs describes my contributions to America's devastating success in the war against Spain, and the resulting changes it brought to the country. It also explains how I became a pariah to some in power at Washington, for amidst the jingoist cacophony I was a dissenting voice.

But I believed then, and still believe, that dissenting voices expressing cogent views can eventually resonate inside even the most fervent of the closed-minded. Such voices steadily gain in volume until they are finally noticed, listened to, and understood. This is not a painless process, however, and the dissenter must be prepared to face the utter ruthlessness of his opponents, in my case the denizens of Washington. They choose their moment and method for revenge well. The trap was sprung when I least expected it.

But this memoir is not about them. It is about a man making decisions in war, and about the value of that man's—and his nation's—word of honor.

Rear Adm. Peter Wake, USN
Special Aide to the President
Washington, D.C.
26 June 1908

1

The "Conversation"

Room 247, State, War, and Navy Building, Washington, D.C.
Thursday, 10 October 1901

IT HAD BEEN A PLEASANT morning thus far. That should have warned me. Pleasant mornings in Washington seldom last long.

"Thank you for coming, Captain Wake. Please sit down," the admiral said as I walked into the small conference room. "I believe you know everyone." Though his words were polite, there was no warmth in his tone. Neither he nor the other two men in the room offered to shake my hand.

My amiability evaporated. I scrutinized Rear Adm. Theodorus Pentwaller's stern face, somewhat distracted by his outlandish and outdated muttonchop sideburns. He looked distinctly uncomfortable as he gestured to the lone vacant chair on the unoccupied side of the polished cherrywood table.

I'd assumed my summons was to provide an update on the General Board of the Navy's contingency plan to defend against a potential Imperial German Navy seizure of a base in the Caribbean or attack on our territory. My work on the project was nearing completion, and such an update to Admiral Dewey would have been a routine matter.

But Dewey wasn't in the room, and the atmosphere was anything but routine. It was ominous.

The rear admiral sitting beside Pentwaller, Jonathan Caldhouse, looked equally uncomfortable. I'd known both men for several years, but only to nod to in the building's passageways. Both were older men who had won their laurels back in the Civil War as lieutenants, and neither had commanded a ship in more than a decade. Both had retired about eight years earlier but were among the small group of captains and admirals reactivated during the war with Spain to handle the Navy's administrative tasks and free younger officers for sea duty. Pentwaller and Caldhouse were the last of those men still serving, assigned to occasional special assignments from the Secretary of the Navy. Rumor around the building had it that these "quaint old boys" would be leaving soon.

The third man on the other side of the table, a newly promoted captain whom Pentwaller introduced as Phineas Percy Smith, was at least ten years my junior. "Captain Smith is currently on temporary duty at the Bureau of Supplies and Accounts while awaiting new orders and has asked to be present during this discussion," Pentwaller added. Smith's silver eagle insignia were still shiny—no salt air tarnish there. I'd vaguely heard his name before but didn't know him personally. He'd recently arrived from a staff billet in the European Squadron. Unlike the other two, he looked pleased to be present. No, it was more than pleased. A predatory sneer was plastered on his face, which was devoid of the tan or wrinkles of a man who'd stared at distant horizons at sea.

"Ah, yes, well, thank you for coming by this morning, Captain Wake," mumbled Caldhouse, ending with his typical nervous chuckle. "This, of course, is not an official inquiry of any sort."

Not an inquiry. Really? Well, there's the first lie, I decided. It certainly appeared to be an inquiry, official or otherwise, from my side of the table. Then I had another, even more unsettling thought. *No, this is an ambush.* Though anger was building inside me at the duplicitous nature of my summons, I kept my words and tone respectful. I needed time to assess what the hell this was about.

To Pentwaller I said, "Sir, is there a problem of some sort? I was led to believe I should stop by to answer some staff questions about the status of ship repairs at the East Coast yards, as was discussed at the last General Board meeting. Or perhaps defenses against possible German action in the Caribbean. The messenger made the summons sound minor."

I turned to Caldhouse. "And thank you, Admiral, for clarifying that this isn't an official board of inquiry. That, of course, requires three commissioned officers equal or senior in rank to the subject and a designated judge advocate as a recorder. I see three officers, but I don't see a recording officer. So I must conclude some emergency is at hand."

"Oh, well, no, Wake, there is no emergency," Caldhouse answered hastily. "Not at all. That issue about ship repairs can wait for another time. Likewise, the Germans. No, this is merely a *conversation*. You see, Secretary Long has heard some disturbing information and asked us to chat with you about it—something that happened back during the war with Spain. We're hoping you can shed some light on the matter."

I pondered that. *Why would the Secretary of the Navy ask these two admirals to have a "conversation" with me about something that happened three years ago? If he wants to know something, why not ask me himself?*

Politics, of course. There is always a political factor when cabinet secretaries are involved. I knew John Davis Long, having served directly under his assistant secretary, Theodore Roosevelt, from April 1897 to March 1898. Secretary Long was a career public servant with a sterling reputation for honesty. But he was also sixty-three, afflicted with various ailments, and tired out. His heart wasn't in the Navy and never had been. Everyone knew he would be leaving soon for his beloved home and garden in New England.

Did this come from Dewey, then? No, he would've done it himself. From the president? Maybe. But which one—the new one or the old one?

Caldhouse kept furtively glancing at his fellow rear admiral as if waiting for a cue. Pentwaller, the senior officer in the room, cleared his throat to get my attention. He made a show of studying the cover of a thin dossier on the table in front of him. The cover was labeled "CAPT. P. WAKE—1898 Caribbean Operations."

Finally, Pentwaller said, "Yes, Captain Wake, this is just a conversation about that disturbing information. Nothing official."

During all this, Captain Smith sat silently, his eyes locked on me as if examining a strange insect he was intent on squashing.

"And exactly what sort of disturbing information would that be, Admiral?" I inquired, ignoring the captain's open disdain. By now, I already suspected the topic. No wonder the admirals were uneasy. It wasn't the sort of thing the Navy, or the president, wanted the public to know. Especially after the unseemly Sampson-Schley controversy over which one of those senior officers should get public credit for the crushing naval victory at Santiago. That ridiculous feud was still the talk of Washington salons, press reporters, and armchair pundits around the country.

Caldhouse began anew. "Ah, yes, well, Captain Wake, three years ago, back during the war with Spain . . ."

He was interrupted by Smith, who was clearly out of patience with his seniors' cautious demeanor toward me. "Look, Wake, we want to hear exactly what happened down there, and what excuses you might have for doing what you did."

Rear Admiral Caldhouse gasped at Smith's discourtesy. Pentwaller shot Smith an angry glance. "Captain Smith, let us remember that this is in fact a *conversation* with Captain Wake, not an official board of inquiry, and certainly not a court-martial. I expect you to show the courtesy due to another officer."

Smith realized his error and nodded quickly to the admiral. "Yes, sir. I was just speeding up the, ah . . . conversation . . . in order to get to the heart of the issue." He glanced down at the pocket watch in his hand. "You see, sir, I have another meeting in an hour—with a *congressional* delegation."

Pentwaller leveled his eyes at Smith. "Then you will be *late* for your congressional delegation, Captain Smith. And since I happen to know your 'meeting' involves a tour of the Navy Department for a few newly appointed interim congressmen and will be led by a staff lieutenant, I also know your presence there is not crucial. This conversation will take as long as deemed necessary by *me*, and that just might be awhile."

Pentwaller abruptly turned his attention back in my direction. "Captain Wake, we would like to better understand your observations and decisions as commanding officer of the cruiser *Dixon* in the war operations around the Caribbean Sea during the summer of 1898."

That absolutely confirmed my suspicion. I now knew exactly why I'd been summoned and had a very good idea who was behind it. So be it. The very best defense against dark perfidy is the glaring light of truth, no matter how uncomfortable it may be, as these officers were about to learn. The admiral was right. This was going to take awhile.

"Very well, sir," I acknowledged politely. "Where do you want me to begin?"

Pentwaller said, "Let's start with when you took command of *Dixon*. When and where was that?"

"Six bells in the forenoon watch, on Monday, the Fourth of July, 1898, sir. *Dixon* was with the fleet lying a mile off the beach at Siboney village in Oriente Province, eastern Cuba."

Caldhouse produced a notepad and scribbled something with a pencil. Smith just sat there studying me. Pentwaller nodded absent-mindedly as he gazed out the window.

He was looking at the White House next door, the front of which was still draped in mourning black. The oak trees in the presidential park hadn't begun to show their autumn colors this early in October, but the first norther of the season had blown through and left the air refreshingly crisp. Washington's notoriously hot and humid summer weather had ended.

The cool, invigorating air was so very different from that horrific summer in Cuba three years earlier, with its suffocating heat and diseases, and the bloody battles I'd somehow survived.

"Ah, yes . . . I recall that July fourth up here in the capital," Pentwaller mused while still staring out the window, a faint smile on his lips. "It was a very special day in our Navy."

He looked back at me. "Please describe your impressions of the ship and crew that day, Captain Wake."

The ship. My mind flashed back to that first hectic day on board *Dixon*.

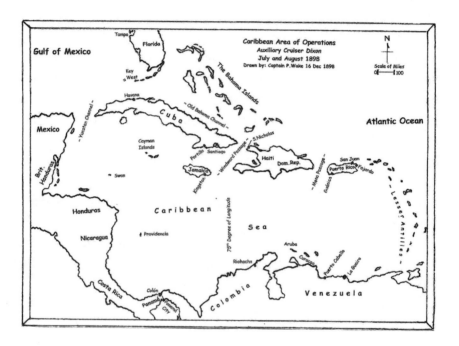

2

The Ship

Cruiser Dixon, *off Siboney, Southeastern Cuba*
Monday, 4 July 1898

THE NOONDAY HEAT WAS stifling. In the shade of the wheel-house, the navigator looked up from the calculations he'd scribbled in a notebook resting on the chart table, studied his pocket watch, and announced, "Captain, I deduce it to be noon, right ... *now*. Our position is latitude 19° 50' 17" N, longitude 75° 42' 12" W."

"Mark it so in the log, Quartermaster," I ordered from where I stood at the aft end of the wheelhouse.

Several things happened simultaneously. The quartermaster of the watch acknowledged the order and began scribbling the data in the ship's logbook. The officer of the watch ordered the boatswain of the watch to pipe noon. The boatswain's pipe immediately rose and fell in the ancient wail. The quartermaster's mate struck the ship's bell eight times, notifying all on board *Dixon* that it was now high noon and a new watch was beginning.

I'd been on the ship for two and a half hours, in command of her for only one. Her previous captain had departed. Everyone around me was a stranger, but the daily ritual was familiar. The incoming officer of the watch walked over to me and reported the precise latitude and longitude of *Dixon* along with her course, zero-nine-five degrees; her speed, four knots; and miles steamed since yesterday at noon, sixteen miles. He also reported the wind and sea conditions, nearby ships' identities and courses, and *Dixon's* remaining coal bunkerage, amount of ammunition, and the sick bay count.

But aside from the usual observance of noon, the day had a special meaning. It was the 122nd anniversary of our nation's birth.

It was also the day after the greatest American naval victory in our history, only fifteen miles from where *Dixon* floated on the languid Caribbean swells.

A booming rumble began three miles astern of us and progressed up the line of ships. It started with Admiral Sampson's flagship, *New York*, huge battle flags streaming from her masts as she steamed slowly east along the coast toward Siboney. Within seconds, explosions reverberated along a hundred miles of the Cuban coast as the American warships present—from those near Mount Turquino in the west to those at Guantánamo Bay in the east—began the long salute of twenty-one guns.

Dixon's crew was ready for our part. All hands manned the rails, still in their dress whites from the change-of-command muster. The call to come to attention, then the salute, was first sounded by a Marine's bugle, then bellowed by the senior petty officer of the ship, Chief Boatswain's Mate Sean Rork, newly arrived like me. Every man on the weather decks faced the approaching flagship and saluted.

A gray-bearded chief gunner's mate, every bit as old and gnarled as Rork, was in charge of rendering the ceremonial gun salute honors. Standing at the forward Driggs-Schroeder rapid-fire 6-pounder gun on the starboard side, he growled out the traditional five-second timing chant between blank shots.

"If I wasn't a gunner, I wouldn't be here. *Fire* one." *Boom!*

His gun crew ejected the spent casing and slammed another into the gun's breech.

"If I wasn't a gunner, I wouldn't be here. *Fire* two." *Boom!*

The gun crew yanked out the spent casing and put in the next round.

It went on and on. When the final gun sounded, Chief Rork called out the end of the salute, then the dismissal of the off-watch.

A naval militia lieutenant—half of *Dixon's* officers were Maryland naval militiamen—smiled at me from across the wheelhouse and offered, "An auspicious start to your command, Captain!"

Cdr. John Belfort, my second in command, glared at the youngster, who obviously had more social experience in Baltimore than naval experience at sea. "Mr. Kushnet, I believe the signal halyards are tangled. See to it and report back."

Kushnet, quickly realizing his error in trying to hobnob with the captain, blurted, "Aye, aye, sir," and fled to the signal deck. The second-class yeoman beside him never cracked a smile, but his twinkling eyes told me that that little anecdote would be all over the lower deck by supper.

Belfort turned to me, quietly saying, "Sorry about that, sir. Some of them are still green. They've got rank but little experience. And, of course, since they never went to the academy—"

He stopped in mid-sentence, his eyes wide with near panic, then hurriedly added, "Oh, I beg your pardon, sir. I meant no disrespect or insult."

"Quite all right, Commander. I know what you meant, and you are right. The Naval Academy teaches them how to conform to naval tradition *before* they report to the fleet. Because I didn't attend the academy, I had to learn all the Navy's do's and don'ts in wartime at sea, and many times got in trouble for my ignorance. Mr. Kushnet strikes me as a quick study. He'll learn fast."

Belfort relaxed a bit. "Yes, sir. I think he will."

I lowered my voice. "And by the way, Commander, please understand that I expect you to be candid with me at all times. Never hesitate to give me bad news or to suggest solutions that might not be in accordance with naval tradition. Frequently, *untraditional* tactics win battles."

He nodded. "Aye, aye, sir."

Though no one else in the wheelhouse could hear the details of our conversation, they could see it was serious. To show them their new captain was not dissatisfied with anything he'd seen so far, I smiled and announced, "Well, that was the grandest national salute I've ever experienced, men, but it's time to return to our patrol station duties now. Come right with standard rudder to circle onto our new course, Commander Belfort. Steady the helm on course two-six-zero. Make revolutions for eight knots. You may pipe the off-watch to dinner. Please advise all division heads that I will inspect the ship at four bells. I am leaving the bridge now and will be in my cabin."

Belfort acknowledged the orders, and the ship's routine took over as *Dixon* heeled slightly to port on her turn to starboard. She steadied herself on the west-southwesterly course back toward Santiago. As I descended the ladder, I heard the boatswain's mate of the watch call out that the captain was off the bridge. I smiled, knowing the junior officers could now whisper their impressions of their new captain to each other.

Around us were dozens of other ships—an impressive array of transports, cargo ships, and warships that had assembled for the invasion of eastern Cuba. It felt good to be back at sea in a command of my own and to be part of that giant effort and its success. It felt even better to be removed from the perilous miasma of the Cuban jungle and depressing incompetence of the senior Army leadership ashore. I remembered my father telling me in 1863 to fight the Confederates by joining the Navy. There at least I could use my seamanship skills and live cleanly until battle. Those poor souls drafted into the Army regiments ashore lived and died in filthy camps before even seeing an enemy. He had been right then and was still right now.

In the course of my career I have commanded seven war vessels, from tiny sailing gunboats to large modern cruisers. My captaincy of *Dixon* began with the usual experiences common to new ship commands, no matter the size. There is always the officers' anxiety, the senior petty officers' scrutiny, the seamen's curiosity, and my own intense awareness of everything and everyone around me. A mutual evaluation, based on first impressions, rapidly unfolds between the new captain and the crew. I liked what I saw on *Dixon*.

Undeniably she had her faults, but she also had some unique assets, for she was unlike the usual American warship. In fact, *Dixon* wasn't a traditional warship in any sense of the word. The 12 officers and 224 men on board weren't a traditional crew, either. Perhaps that is why my new ship intrigued me so much.

From her launching at Newport News, Virginia, in 1893 until her purchase by the U.S. Navy in April 1898, *Dixon* had been a passenger liner on the Morgan Line's New Orleans–Havana route, with occasional transits to other Caribbean ports. Her passengers traveled in grand style.

First-class passengers resided in complete luxury, with every conceivable amenity available at their beck and call. Even the second- and third-class travelers were treated well. Soon, the Morgan Line became known as the preferred way for the aristocracy, tourists, and businessmen from middle and southern American states to get to exotic Cuba and the West Indies from New Orleans, especially during the northern winters.

Then the war with Spain erupted. Fun and profits disappeared. During the naval mobilization frenzy in the spring of 1898, the Navy purchased the liner and she became the cruiser *Dixon*. Over the next six weeks she was hastily converted from a conveyance devoted to safety and gaiety into a machine assigned to danger and war.

Her official naval designation was a relatively new one, borrowed from the Royal Navy. *Dixon* was an auxiliary, or "light," cruiser. The luxurious amenities from her former life were removed, and the ornate public areas were transformed into functional spaces. Ammunition magazines replaced luggage and cargo holds, large-caliber guns were placed on the foredeck and afterdeck, and secondary gun emplacements were installed along the old first-class section's newly reinforced side promenade decks. Second- and third-class passenger accommodations below the main deck became additional crew berthing spaces, with some of the room left over intended for troop berthing, if needed.

At over 6,000 tons, *Dixon* was the largest ship I'd ever commanded. By way of comparison, the largest ship in the entire Navy when I'd joined thirty-five years earlier, in the midst of the Civil War, was only 4,100 tons. My first command, a small sailing gunboat, was barely bigger than one of *Dixon's* launches. At 405 feet in length and 48 feet in the beam, with a draft of 20 feet and only a single screw, *Dixon* would be hard to handle in the tight quarters, currents, and winds the coming coastal operations would present.

Her armament consisted of two Mark 3 six-inch guns—one placed forward and the other aft of the superstructure—accompanied by ten Driggs-Schroeder rapid-fire six-pounder guns, five along each side of the ship. She also had two Colt machine guns on either side of the upper boat deck just aft of the bridge. Though she was no match for a regular cruiser or battleship, this weaponry gave her enough bite to counter any torpedo boat or gunboat. Her disappointing top speed of only eighteen knots was a serious liability, for some of her sister converted auxiliary cruisers could do twenty or more. The enemy's torpedo boats, my main worry, especially at night, could do more than twenty-four knots.

From a personal point of view, one of *Dixon's* unique assets was my cabin. It was enormous and still quite well appointed—almost embarrassingly so. It was easily the most sumptuous quarters I'd ever had in the Navy and the equal of Admiral Sampson's in his flagship. I wasn't alone in luxury, for *Dixon's* officers' quarters and wardroom were also very comfortable. The petty officers' berthing and mess were twice the size of the usual Navy accommodations. Even the crew's berthing deck spaces were better than the naval norm, and included modern lavatory plumbing and ventilators.

I was somewhat worried about *Dixon's* ability to sustain battle damage and continue fighting, something true warships are designed to do. There was nothing I could do about that structurally, but I did intend to train her crew extensively in mitigating and controlling that damage.

The primary question for *Dixon* was the same as for any warship in any navy: How would she perform in actual battle? That crucial factor would be determined by the men on board.

3

The Men

Cruiser Dixon, *off the Coast of Southeastern Cuba*
Monday, 4 July 1898

A WARSHIP IS FAR MORE than steel and wood and guns. She is, first and foremost, the sum total of her officers and men, and their skills, confidence, and commitment to the mission. *Dixon* had been at sea barely a month in her new role, but her crew had already achieved a remarkable degree of cohesion and efficiency by the time I came on board. This I completely attribute to her original Navy captain, an old friend from my days in naval intelligence, who had moved on to more prestigious duties and rank after his command of this ship.

Dixon's officers and men came from diverse sources. The senior officers were mostly regular Navy, while many of the junior officers came from the Maryland naval militia. Her enlisted crewmen were a combination of recent Navy recruits, longtime Maryland naval militiamen called to active service, and salty old regular Navy petty officers.

During the voyage from Norfolk to Cuba, all hands had drilled continuously for every potential type of combat or contingency, from squadron battle formation to landing force skirmishes. Though they were still unbloodied by battle with the Spanish enemy, they clearly felt ready for a fight.

I'd received a brief description of the officers from my predecessor. My own impressions formed quickly that first day and over the next week. Their personalities, abilities, and deficits covered the spectrum.

Cdr. John Belfort, U.S. Naval Academy (USNA) class of 1878, was *Dixon's* executive officer, responsible for the day-to-day operation of the ship. A short, trim-bodied, hawk-nosed fellow from Tampa, Florida, Belfort sported heavy brows over serious eyes. He was constantly in motion around the ship, checking on everything and everyone. He rarely smiled, a reflection of the enormous pressure on an executive officer to keep a warship in fighting condition and always ready to respond to the captain's orders. Belfort fulfilled that role well. He was efficiently attentive to the ship's operational details and, as far as I could initially tell, fair in matters of discipline.

Next in seniority was the chief engineering officer, Lt. Cdr. Jameson Sheats, USNA class of 1884, a plump fellow from small-town Ohio with an obvious passion for things machine driven. Sheats had a dry sense of humor and was not shy about offering his witty opinions on matters ranging from cuisine to politics. Belfort confided to me that he wondered if Sheats had a secret stash of liquor to fuel his comic airs.

Sheats' senior assistant, and his opposite in personality, was Lt. Ian Campbell, USNA class of 1889, a dour Scot born in Glasgow but raised in New York City. With his permanent frown and emaciated frame, he seemed almost as much a machine as the iron beasts he tended. The "black gang"—the men who operated *Dixon's* boilers and engines— grudgingly respected his abilities but resented the cruel sarcasm he constantly directed at them. Campbell was no leader, and I resolved to pay close attention to him.

The gunnery officer was Lt. Cdr. Bodiford Biggs Pinkston, a South Carolinian and 1878 USNA classmate of Belfort, and the grandson of a famous Confederate war hero. Those who met him learned those three things within the first five minutes. Pinkston was a bear of a man who gesticulated grandly while speaking and who delighted in the trigonometry and physics of gunnery. *Dixon*'s guns were his children, and he took great pains that they would not be found lacking. His assistant, Lt. Tom Wundarn of Texas, USNA class 1887, showed intense diligence in following orders but little initiative in giving them. There was something more there—an uncommon deficit of enthusiasm about his mission and his naval career. He was listless, or possibly morose, and I thought him also worth careful attention.

Lt. Robert Gerard, USNA class of 1891, a sharp-minded young man born and raised in Key West, was the ship's navigator and first lieutenant. His skin was the light tan color of weathered teak, an unusual complexion bequeathed to him by Bahamian forebears from the islands of the Abaco chain. I wondered if it had led to discrimination by the naval aristocracy; if it had, he didn't show resentment. Gerard was a quick thinker and a natural seaman, a product of his upbringing in his family's salvage business on the treacherous Florida reefs. The petty officers respected him. I thought he had real possibility for senior advancement in the modern Navy and was curious to watch him further and see if my initial assessment continued. We needed men like him.

The ship's supply officer was a thirty-five-year-old Maryland naval militiaman, Paymaster Lt. Godfrey Shalby. Like the other militiamen, both commissioned and enlisted, he'd been activated into federal service for the duration of the war. His family were merchants, and evidently politically influential in Baltimore. Mannerly, fastidious, and with no experience afloat beyond Chesapeake Bay, I suspected his ten years in the militia had been more for the social connections than a commitment to the nation's naval reserve forces. He appeared far too comfortable, almost lackadaisical, in his post, and I wondered if he was passing off his duties to his subordinates.

Shalby had two assistants, also Marylanders, and both of them set off my internal alarms. Thirty-seven-year-old Paymaster Lt. Mike Kilmarty was the officer in charge of stores, materials, and equipment.

Irish born, he was a publican back in Baltimore, and he entertained the wardroom with uproarious tales of his sexual prowess and amorous conquests. In addition to bragging about himself, he constantly spouted complaints about the Navy. A short, bandy-legged fellow, he'd been in the militia for four years. Kilmarty openly stated that he'd joined only for the monthly weekend drills that allowed him to escape his overbearing wife.

The commissary officer, in charge of our food and attendant supplies under Shalby, was Paymaster Foster Kennedy. A twenty-four-year-old from Baltimore, he'd joined the naval militia because his father told him it would be good for the family's livery business. He was hopelessly lost when it came to the critical function of obtaining and maintaining provisions. Shalby didn't seem to be helping him, and in fact had ridiculed him openly in the wardroom several times.

The signals officer was Ens. Ross Barnett from Montana, USNA class of 1895. Barnett had the slim, wiry physique and quiet manner of a cowboy. He was adequate in his job, but it was obvious he really wanted to be a gunnery officer, for he spoke of nothing else and made it clear that he thought signals were a waste of time. An explanation of the importance of signal communications from his captain might remedy that, but on the other hand, I fully understood his urge to be a gunnery officer. I liked that. It showed gumption.

Because of *Dixon*'s size, we had several additional members of the wardroom. The assigned chaplain was Jim Reeher, a Methodist minister recently transferred to the Maryland naval militia from the Florida militia. Always squared away, Chaplain Reeher was the first shipboard clergyman I actually trusted not to cause trouble. He had done a Navy hitch as an enlisted man years earlier and knew full well how little sailors thought of "sky pilots," an attitude he did his best to overcome with humor and genuine interest.

We also had a fifteen-man Marine detachment under the command of 2nd Lt. James Ostermann, USNA class of 1896, a pleasant, friendly Iowan who was assisted by an irascible old sergeant incongruously named Monk.

All in all, *Dixon*'s officers were the usual combination of achievers, slackers, and unsteady youngsters, with a couple of borderline bad cases. I'd seen men change at sea, most for the better, some for the worse. Only time would tell how each of them would shake out.

I hoped it wouldn't take a battle or storm to find out.

4

Rork

Cruiser Dixon, *off the Coast of Southeastern Cuba*
Monday, 4 July 1898

THERE WAS ONE MAN on board who was also new to *Dixon* but certainly not new to me. I'd known Chief Boatswain's Mate Sean Aloysius Rork for thirty-five years. Against naval tradition regarding fraternizing between officers and enlisted men, we were best friends.

A lanky six-foot-four and clean-shaven, with the ropy muscles and swaying gait of a longtime seaman, Rork was the very image of the old salt tar, with squinty gray eyes and defiantly long gray hair worn in a braided sailor's queue, an old-fashioned style not seen in the Navy for thirty years. Rork might be old, but then as now, he certainly was not feeble. The mischievous lopsided smile he usually wore could switch to a fearsome glare in a heartbeat. Woe to those who failed to heed that visual warning, for soon afterward it would transform into a maniacal mask. At that point, talking was over and violence was inevitable. But those moments were rare.

A voracious reader of history, pretty good one-handed (more on that shortly) harmonica player and percussionist, philosophical raconteur, cook of no small degree, and aficionado of classical Spanish music and

Cuban rum, Rork was truly one of a kind—a "lower-deck Renaissance man," our mutual friend Theodore Roosevelt once called him.

Rork had been a shipmate afloat and ashore since our initial service together in my first command, a small sailing gunboat on the coast of Florida during the Civil War. We'd served together on many ships and missions around the world since then. Over time, professional shipmates became the best of friends. Seven or eight years older than me—he maintained that his birth records had been destroyed in a parish hall fire back in Wexford, Ireland, and therefore he was conveniently uncertain of his exact age)—Rork was about sixty-six in 1898. That was well beyond the newly mandated retirement age of sixty-two for a commissioned officer or noncommissioned petty officer.

Such naval personnel regulations did not worry my friend one bit. He had bureaucratic connections any admiral would envy but never have. Rork's pals among the Navy's petty officers, especially yeomen clerks at headquarters, quietly ensured that his estimated age would be conveniently misplaced, misunderstood, or missing in the relevant personnel documents.

Rork, out of consideration for my position, kept all this duplicity from me, merely mentioning with breezy ease, "Ooh, never worry about such a wee little thing, sir. The lads at headquarters know what they're about. So, if there's not a problem, why run it up the halyard? Ye've far more important matters to be cogitatin' upon for Uncle Sam's blessed Navy."

Uncle Sam's Navy was Rork's home. As a young able seaman on a British sailing packet, Rork had jumped ship in Boston Harbor to escape a brutal Liverpudlian mate and joined the U.S. Navy in early 1861. Though he seldom lacked female company when ashore, he'd never found a wife. It was not due to lack of searching. He'd proposed to several, but none wanted the life of a naval spouse. Only recently he'd fallen madly in love and received an agreement to his proposal, only to be cruelly jilted by his fiancée just a month before the wedding. Grief from that loss had taken a deep toll on my friend, something hard for me to watch.

For twenty years, Rork's shore base in between ships or missions had been a garret across the street from the Washington Navy Yard. He also shared ownership with me of a small island on the lower Gulf coast of Florida where we went when on our annual leave. My family became his family. He considered my daughter Useppa and son Sean (named after him) his own niece and nephew. They in turn adored their Uncle Sean.

Rork, in addition to being a skilled seaman and reliable confidant, possessed rare skills and assets that had proven very handy over the years. He was a shrewd judge of character, able to size up true motives and capabilities at a glance. Though so far he'd been unable to convince a woman to spend the rest of her life with him, he could and did use his Gaelic wit and charm to beguile women all over the world from all cultures to spend a night or two with him. That proclivity had more than once obliged me to haul him out of trouble with sobbing young ladies and their irate families.

In addition to feminine company Rork has another fondness—rum. That, too, has led to problems over the years, but he is doing better in his old age. His drinking bouts are less frequent now, with far fewer casualties. Sober or drunk, Rork is very dangerous in a close-quarters fight. In addition to being a crack pistol shot with his right hand, he bears an extraordinary weapon on his left arm.

In 1883, at the Battle of Hué in the Empire of Vietnam, Rork was wounded in the left forearm by a marksman's bullet intended for me. Three days later, after the inevitable tropical infection and gangrene had set in, French navy surgeons were forced to amputate the arm just above the wrist. Afterward, skilled French machinists fashioned a leather-and-steel appliance to fit over the stub. This appurtenance included a six-inch marlinspike of high-quality steel with a needle-sharp point capable of penetrating any material weaker than iron or steel; craniums are easy. The spike is a terrifying inducement during interrogation and an efficient killer in the dark of night.

This deadly device is artfully concealed by a hollow false hand made of India rubber. The hand, beautifully crafted by the French workmen to appear utterly real by matching its paint with his skin color, complete with tiny hairs and wrinkles drawn on it with ink, has its fingers curled around an opening large enough to grasp the handle of an oar, a belaying pin, or a rum bottle.

The fake left hand has been lovingly repainted each Christmas since 1884 by one of Rork's lady friends whom he usually finds perambulating outside the Washington Navy Yard's Latrobe Gate in the evening hours. Rork is particularly proud of his rubber hand and the spike underneath, and he isn't hesitant about using it should events deteriorate to that degree.

The friendship between Rork and myself is unconventional in the Navy, to say the least. Commissioned officers, who are by law considered "gentlemen," do not fraternize with enlisted petty officers, who are not so deemed. Behind our backs, both sides have muttered about the easy amity between us when we are off duty. Among the officer corps, our friendship has fed the gossip that I am not of the sainted naval aristocracy and thus cannot be fully trusted in delicate social or political matters. I have also been accused of undermining naval discipline. None of their carping matters, though, for I always produce inarguable results on my missions.

Rork faces more uncomfortable consequences of our friendship. A persistent rumor among the petty officers claimed that Rork was a bootlicker promoted by favoritism who had forgotten his noncommissioned brethren. But woe to the member of the petty officers' mess in a station or ship who dares to say that openly. Rork can and will back up his personal honor with his still mighty right hand. Vague word regarding such conflicts occasionally made it up to my level, though Rork always downplayed it as mere "give-an'-take" in the "goat locker," the sailors' term for the senior petty officers' quarters.

Assigned as *Dixon*'s chief boatswain, Rork stood deck watches like all the other boatswains. For him, too, it was a change for the better after weeks ashore in the Cuban jungle enduring hardship and Spanish bullets while living in the mud and insects and heat. Although he was now away from all that, I was still worried about Rork, for that perilous time had exacted an obvious cost on my old friend's health and stamina.

His weakened constitution was further exacerbated by a new bout of recurring malaria. His stump was inflamed from a jungle infection. He had pain in his elbows and knees. The arthritis in his good right hand had become worse, and he still experienced the debilitating effects of dysentery. Anxious at his diminished physical condition, I had nearly forced his retirement but relented. Without the Navy his life would not have been worth living. I hoped some sea time would help him recover from his ailments and reinvigorate his usual vitality.

That had always worked in the past.

5

The "Conversation"

Room 247, State, War, and Navy Building, Washington, D.C.
Thursday, 10 October 1901

CAPTAIN SMITH HAD BEEN fidgeting with his fingers while I'd been relating my observations. When I finally paused, he let loose. "Upon your assumption of command, you found no signs in the records, or by report of the previous captain, of any blatant misfeasance among your officers, correct, Captain Wake?"

"Correct," I replied evenly, sure that he was setting some trap.

"I see. So, any *subsequently* made allegations of misfeasance against them would mean their conduct changed once *you* took command, is that also correct?" He leaned slightly forward, keenly awaiting my reply.

Both admirals were watching for my reaction. Obviously, the three of them knew something I didn't know at that moment. Something profoundly negative.

I took in a breath and remained calm. "I don't know what hypothetical situation you are talking about, Captain Smith. If you have a specific allegation, please inform me so I can address it and we can stop wasting everyone's time."

Pentwaller interrupted to change the subject. "We *will* follow up on that, Captain Wake, but first I want to hear about the mission *Dixon* was given during the evening of July fourth."

A routine mission on my first night as *Dixon*'s captain that became anything *but* routine. I wasn't surprised that they'd heard about what happened. You can't keep something like that under wraps for long. Word had gone through the fleet at Cuba within hours. "Yes, sir. Well, that mission actually started out normal enough, but it ended up a bit bizarre."

6

A Ghost in the Night

Cruiser Dixon, *off the Coast of Cuba, West of Santiago*
Monday Night, 4 July 1898

I N THE MIDDLE OF MY FIRST AFTERNOON on *Dixon*, just as I was beginning my inspection tour of the ship's divisions, we received a flag signal from Admiral Sampson. Starting just after sunset we were to patrol alone along the coast to the west. There, we were to look for Spanish warships, blockade runners, or shore batteries and either capture or destroy them.

I smiled when the signalman reported our orders, for I instantly thought it the perfect assignment: independent patrol and freedom of action. All hands on board apparently agreed, for they turned with determination to preparing the ship for the mission. By sunset all was ready, and as soon as night descended over Cuba we got under way and steamed west.

For the first few hours, nothing of note occurred. I spent most of that time going over division reports in my cabin abaft the bridge. Administrative paperwork is a boring but important chore that I always have to force myself to accomplish. In this instance, I found several relatively minor items worthy of further inquiry but decided they could wait until the next day.

"Captain's on the bridge," announced the quartermaster of the watch when I returned to the red glow of the night lanterns in *Dixon's* wheelhouse. Conversations stopped, and everyone became studiously busy at the helm, the binnacle, the chart table, at the watch bill on the bulkhead, or peering intently out to sea for the enemy—activities that didn't involve attracting attention from me, the new captain, an unknown man who'd come on board that very morning and now completely ruled their lives. I walked over to the chart table to study our position. The quartermaster, who had been standing there, nodded respectfully and slid away.

"Good evening, sir," Lieutenant Gerard, the officer of the deck, offered quickly as he came in from the starboard bridge wing, trailed by Ensign Stark, the junior officer of the deck. Putting a fingertip at a small penciled circle on the chart, Gerard made his report before I had to ask.

"As of four minutes ago, our position is here, sir, five and one quarter miles south of the Cuban coast, ninety-one miles west of Santiago de Cuba, and thirty-four miles east of Cabo Cruz. No ships are in sight in any direction, sir. Ship's course is due west. Speed is seven knots at 125 revolutions.

"I recommend we alter course left ten degrees to two-six-zero in order to maintain our distance offshore," he continued, "since the shoreline will begin to trend a bit more west-southwesterly. On the coast, the nearest village is Portillo, which bears northwest at five miles. The town of Pilón is five miles farther west of that. No lights are visible at Portillo, but we do see some lights at Pilón."

I noticed he pronounced the names in the proper Spanish style. Without pausing, he went on to the other subjects expected in his situation report. "Wind is a light land breeze, and seas are calm with a small swell from the southeast. Sky is clear along the coast, with a cloud bank over the mountains to the north and east. Moon is almost full but hidden in the clouds over Mount Turquino on our starboard quarter. It should emerge from those clouds anytime now, though."

And that should silhouette us quite nicely for any Spanish shore gunners, I reminded myself. I went out on the starboard bridge wing and looked up at the break in the clouds over the mountains, gauging we had maybe another twenty or thirty minutes of darkness.

When I returned inside, Gerard resumed. "Engineering watch reports all is well. Boilers one, two, and four are lit and pressure in each is at normal range. Engines and shafts are operating with no binds or leaks. The anthracite in coal bunker six is being used and our funnel is showing no embers. The ship is under port and starboard watches. All lights are doused and the ship is darkened. Interior and exterior watertight hatches are closed. Duty gunners and ammunition handlers are at their stations. Repair parties are manned. No men from the watch are reported hurt or sick. Lookouts are doubled and have been changed every hour. I just sent coffee around to the duty watch. Captain, the watch is fully manned and ready."

Just as Gerard ended his report, the quartermaster's mate struck the ship's bell forward of the wheelhouse seven times. The middle watch would come on duty in thirty minutes, at midnight.

"Very good, Mr. Gerard," I replied. "I think I'll take a turn around the ship. There shouldn't be any American vessels in this area tonight. Notify me if any ships are seen. Carry on."

"Aye, aye, sir," the lieutenant replied.

As I headed for the after hatchway, the topside starboard lookout called down.

"Bridge there! Possible ship, bearing three points off the starboard bow, by the coast to the northwest. Range is about six miles. Heading west along the coast, but can't tell the speed. It's the dark shadow passing in front of some lights on the shore, sir."

All heads in the wheelhouse, except the helmsman's, swiveled to the starboard bow. Gerard and his ensign dashed out to the bridge wing. I joined them as Gerard raised his binoculars.

"Well, Mr. Gerard, what do you see?" I asked.

"Not a thing, sir. Wait! Yes, there it is, the form of a ship passing in front of the lights of Pilón in the distance. Must be heading west out of Portillo. Maybe a mile offshore. Fairly good size, bulky, like a freighter.

Maybe two thousand tons. Doesn't *look* like a warship but could be. The lookout's wrong on the range. At least eight miles, sir."

"May I have a look, Mr. Gerard?" I said, amused that after rendering such a perfect status report earlier, he'd forgotten the common courtesy of offering the binoculars to his captain when an enemy ship was in sight.

"Oh, of course, sir! Very sorry, sir," he said, his worry clearly showing in his voice.

"Quite all right, Mr. Gerard. Now, what do you propose we do about that ship?" I quietly asked.

He rattled off the standard procedure. "Sound general quarters, alter course to intercept from astern, ring up flank speed, and ready the boarding party with the launch. When in range, light her up with the searchlight and fire a blank warning shot with the forward secondary starboard gun, sir."

"And what if that ship doesn't comply and stop?"

"Fire one shot into her foredeck, sir."

"But we can't hit that area if we are astern of her. What then?"

For a split second, I could see him inwardly cursing his previous answer. Then he calmly said, "Hit the stern to get the rudder and steering gear, sir."

"Very good, Mr. Gerard. Please sound general quarters *quietly*. Increase speed to full. Keep the ship darkened and the lookouts focusing elsewhere also. I'm not yet convinced that vessel is just a freighter. The Spanish still have gunboats and torpedo boats in Cuba. This could well be a trick."

Within forty-five seconds of the muted alarm sounding, Belfort showed up on the bridge. Gerard briefed him on the situation. Then Belfort came out to where I stood on the bridge wing staring at the dark shape far ahead. Below us, the last of the forward main gun crew arrived at their stations. The final reports of stations manned echoed through the wheelhouse.

Belfort turned and reported to me, "All stations are fully manned and the ship is ready for action, sir."

I clicked my pocket watch and held it up close to my eyes.

"Five minutes and eleven seconds. Good time for 224 men to muster to general quarters," I told Belfort.

"Thank you, sir. They're much faster than when we started out a month ago. What do you think of that ship, sir?"

"A bit of a ghost, isn't she? I can barely see her, but I've no doubt she's Spanish, trying to quietly creep out of Portillo under cover of darkness. Probably a freighter, but she could be a gunboat out of Manzanillo on reconnaissance. I want to approach her as stealthily as possible, so they don't see us and slip into Pilón. There's a Spanish gun emplacement there, with two older-model Ordóñez 5.9-inch guns."

By the dim glow of the red battle lanterns emanating from inside the wheelhouse I saw surprise flash across Belfort's face. *He's wondering how I know about the Spanish guns. I've never told him what I did when I was ashore with the Army.*

But Belfort submerged his curiosity and instead announced his assessment of the situation. "Extra boilers are being brought on line and should be ready soon, sir. We're now at twelve knots and accelerating. Should be at eighteen knots within another three to five minutes. If the chase maintains its current course and speed, which I'd guess at eight knots, we'll be in effective gun range in fourteen minutes. We'll be inside searchlight range in twenty minutes, and then she won't be a ghost ship anymore. We'll be directly alongside in twenty-eight minutes. But by then we'll also be well within range of those Ordóñez 5.9-inchers. They can reach about four miles in accurate fire."

"Quickly calculated, Commander. Well done," I said, without adding that his estimate matched mine. Then I set about some other computations. *Hmm. We'll have to wait until we're within searchlight range. Or do we?*

Several factors were at play here. The mystery vessel was in a war zone and showing no lights, and there were no American ships reported to be in this area except *Dixon*. That made her a target. Our forward 6-inch gun could take her under fire right then if need be, but with the target so indistinct, we probably wouldn't hit anything.

If we waited until we were within searchlight range, our guns would be no match for the shore-mounted Spanish guns, even those older ones, which could use our searchlight as a target and weren't under the disadvantage of shooting from a moving gun platform. I had no doubt they could, and would, hit us after a couple of ranging salvos. For a large ship like *Dixon* to come alongside and board the ghost ship under the fire of those Spanish guns would be difficult, at the very least.

Nonetheless, one thing was clear. Whether it was a freighter or a gunboat, we had to stop that ship before she got any closer to Pilón. *But how?*

In that instant an idea came to me.

7

Geometry

Cruiser Dixon, *off the Coast of Cuba, West of Santiago*
Early Tuesday Morning, 5 July 1898

"COMMANDER, WOULD YOU be so kind as to have 'Guns' join us?" I asked, using the Navy's nickname for every ship's gunnery officer. "Also, prepare the steam cutter for launching. I want her boiler fired and ready straight away."

With his second surprised look of the evening Belfort left to comply with my orders. He returned in seconds with Lieutenant Commander Pinkston beside him. I gestured out into the gloom ahead of us.

"Commander Pinkston, the standard firing rate for the Mark 4 6-inch gun is three rounds in two minutes, correct?"

"Yes, sir," he drawled.

"My question is this: Can you put two 6-inch rounds in, or very close to, that distant vessel within one minute of our firing off a blank warning shot from the starboard forward secondary gun? The timing will be crucial."

This was certainly not normal naval protocol, and his initial expression showed it, but he recovered quickly and said, "Yes, sir. Our best gun-layer is on the forward 6-inch. We'll put the first round within two hundred feet of the target. The second one will be even closer."

Even in broad daylight that feat would be difficult, but Pinkston sounded confident. I continued my line of thought. "Very well. Commander Belfort, what is the estimated speed of that ship?"

"Relative bearings now confirm nine knots, sir."

Damn. I was hoping for less. Nine knots made my idea far more dangerous. "And what is the maximum speed of our steam cutter when fully loaded with men?" I asked.

"Eleven knots in calm conditions, sir," Belfort answered with a growing grin. "Like tonight."

"And how many sailors can the steam cutter carry?"

"A dozen fully armed and equipped men, not counting the three-man crew. The steam cutter can also carry one of our Colt machine guns mounted on a pedestal in the bow."

"That could be very useful. Very well, here's the plan, gentlemen," I said, launching into a detailed explanation of how the enemy ship was going to come to us—or more precisely, to our men in the cutter. Soon they were both grinning. They rushed off to make all ready, for there wasn't a lot of time.

Seven minutes later, *Dixon* slowed. Down on the main deck, I shook Gerard's hand as he went over the side into the puffing steam cutter just before she was lowered away.

"Remember, Mr. Gerard," I called down. "With her moving at nine knots it won't be easy and you'll get only one chance for the grappling hooks—make it count."

"Aye, aye, sir. We'll get on board and in control of her before they know it."

The cutter's coxswain knew his business. In seconds, the cutter was chugging off on an oblique course that would put it between the coastline and the ship ahead of us; soon it was out of sight.

Dixon rapidly resumed her full speed, but not on a course directly toward the other ship. Instead, I headed her west of southwest, bearing off to seaward, slightly away from our prey. In twelve more minutes we accelerated to full speed, with the mystery ship bearing just forward of our starboard beam, about four miles off. She also was only three miles from the anchorage—and those Spanish guns—at Pilón. In order to maintain our firing angle on the target, I reduced *Dixon's* speed to nine knots so that any missed shots would go forward or over the ship and slightly away from the cutter as it got closer.

Our new position was outside the range of the enemy shore guns but within our range of the ghost ship. Fortunately, our run at full speed in the darkness, and the attendant foamy white bow wave, apparently had gone unnoticed. The ghost ship's course continued steadily westbound along the coast toward Cabo Cruz, twenty miles distant. Once arriving at that cape, she could either go north fifty miles to the Spanish-held port of Manzanillo or sixty miles due south to Montego Bay in neutral British Jamaica. And, of course, at this point the ship had the option of simply running into Pilón if her captain became alarmed.

According to my mental calculations, the cutter was approximately one and a quarter miles astern of the target ship's starboard quarter. It was gaining on her, but slowly. We would have to wait another three anxious minutes.

At the appointed time, when I judged the steam cutter would be close in to the vessel's starboard quarter, I gave the order from which there was no return.

"You may fire the blank warning and briefly illuminate our flag, Commander Belfort."

Bang! A cloud of acrid smoke rose from the main deck as the searchlight lit up our battle ensign, the largest American flag on the ship. Every binocular and telescope on the bridge nervously focused on the other ship. As I expected, there was no change in her course or speed.

Belfort called up to the upper deck. "Lookout, has that ship stopped, slowed, or altered course?"

"Bridge, there! That ship is still steaming at the same speed on her course, sir!" shouted the lookout.

I counted slowly to thirty, enough time for the other ship to iden-tify us beyond any doubt, then said to the quartermaster, "Let the log reflect we have followed international law and the unidentified vessel in this war zone has violated the naval blockade. She has not complied with our efforts to stop her. You may turn the searchlight onto the target, Commander Belfort, and fire two rounds for effect at the target. Please remember to have the gunners aim forward of amidships. Then you will cease fire and the searchlight will be doused."

The command to open fire was passed to Pinkston, who spoke into the voice tube connecting him with the forward gun crew. The searchlight showed a dark gray freighter-like form in the distance, but no detail. Three seconds later the still night was shattered.

BOOM! A ten-foot-long tongue of orange-yellow flame blasted out of the forward 6-inch gun. I'd closed one eye to protect my night vision and kept my mouth open to mitigate the concussion, but the gun was located just forward and below the bridge, and the effects were more substantial than I'd expected. A moment later a second *BOOM!* erupted from the foredeck. The cone of light illuminating the other ship instantly disappeared.

There was no explosion from a hit. "Where's the fall of the shot?" I asked Biggs, who was peering through the night telescope.

Biggs reported back in a monotone, "No hits or splashes observed, sir."

"Too dark to see the splashes from here," I said. "But I'm sure they saw them on that ship. That's what's important."

"Bridge, there!" shouted the lookout. "Target ship is turning northward toward the coast. She's heading for those shore lights in the town."

Belfort nodded slowly. "Right to where the steam cutter should be."

"We'll know soon enough," I said.

Several pinpricks of light flashed, followed seconds later by a staccato series of faint pops rolling across the black water.

"The Colt machine gun," Belfort reported.

"Good. That confirms she's a freighter, not a gunboat," I said, inwardly breathing a sigh of relief. Gerard was not to attack if the ship was a gunboat, for he'd never be able to overwhelm her crew with only twelve men.

The wait for the expected signal from Gerard was nerve-wracking. I tried to appear composed in front of the dozen officers and men around me on the bridge, cognizant of their furtive glances my way.

Damnation! What is taking Gerard so long?

"Bridge, there! That ship has slowed and is turning to port. Red lantern over blue lantern showing. The ship looks like she's headed out to sea!"

"By God, they've actually done it, sir!" exclaimed Belfort—with a little too much amazement in his voice, I thought. After all, my plan wasn't *that* far-fetched. The executive officer had the biggest grin I'd yet seen on him. "Congratulations! It was a brilliant plan, sir!"

"Thank you," I replied. "But Gerard and his men did the dangerous work and get the credit. We just arranged it."

There were smiles and handshakes all around. I felt the pleasing sensation of my reputation rising among my new subordinates and shipmates. The celebration was premature, however, for that precise moment was when the full moon suddenly chose to emerge from the cloud cover.

Instantly, as if God above had switched on a giant cosmic searchlight, the sea became a silvery glitter and the Cuban mountains and coast were defined in varying shades of gray. The other ship was now clearly visible to us—as was *Dixon* to the shore batteries.

"Oh, hell," groaned Pinkston. "They're still in range of the Spanish guns."

8

Confusion

Cruiser Dixon, *off the Southeastern Coast of Cuba near Pilón*
Early Tuesday Morning, 5 July 1898

THE FREIGHTER WAS ABOUT three miles away and heading toward us, her bow wave gleaming white in the moonlight, when another problem arose. Tiny flickers showed high up on the ship, then a bigger flash. That could mean only one thing. Gerard wasn't in control of the ship yet. We had to help.

"Hard right rudder. Come up to full speed ahead on course zero-zero-ten, Commander," I ordered Belfort, "and call away another boarding party. Rig all the fenders and mats we've got over the starboard side. When we get close, we'll circle around to port and bring our starboard side directly alongside her. Alert the engine room—our speed will need to diminish fast."

Before Belfort could reply, a large flash erupted from the artillery battery at Pilón. Then another. White towers of mist rose in the air a hundred yards astern of the freighter. Someone on *Dixon*'s bridge swore.

Dixon heeled to port as her bow swung to starboard and steadied just to the right of the approaching ship. I turned to Belfort. "Commander, open a slow rate of fire with the forward 6-inch gun on that shore battery. Keep the firing times varied to harass them. I know we can't hit them directly at this range, but maybe we can slow down the gunfire a bit."

Pinkston's men went into action, periodically firing toward the Cuban coast, the rounds going almost directly over the oncoming freighter. On board that ship there were no more small-arms muzzle flashes, and I allowed myself the momentary hope Gerard had finally gotten everything in hand. Then, with a sickening sensation in the pit of my stomach, I realized the lack of rifle fire might mean the opposite: The freighter crew had captured or killed *our* men.

Two more guns flashed ashore, the splashes fountaining up very near the stern of the freighter. The Spanish were walking their gunfire right up her wake to her hull. It was only a matter of time before they hit her. *If Gerard has captured her, why isn't he zigzagging to throw the Spanish gunners off?*

As the steamer grew larger and better defined in the forward wheelhouse window, I estimated the closing speed between the two vessels at around twenty-five knots and increasing. Figuring out the rest of the mathematical evolution, I concluded we would pass each other in less than six minutes.

But passing each other wasn't the plan. I had to get men on her. Putting *Dixon* into a circle to port at exactly the right moment and then coming in alongside the freighter would be a dicey maneuver—in effect, a controlled collision. I had never handled *Dixon* in close quarters, though, and the officer on board with the most time in her, Belfort, had less than two months' experience with how *Dixon* turned, slowed, and handled when close to another vessel.

"Commander, have you ever turned this ship tightly at full speed?" I asked him as steadily as my pounding heart would allow, for my watch showed I would have to begin the turn in ninety seconds.

"Once during training in the open ocean, sir. The radius was half a mile. It's shorter, of course, at lower speeds. Never done it at any speed with *Dixon* in close proximity to another ship, especially at night."

Very well, I'll have to do this myself. It was now thirty seconds from my hastily estimated turning point. Our position would be about half a mile from the other ship. The timing would be very tight. *Better to start the turn too soon than too late*, I decided. *First to the right to get sea room, then circle to the left and close on her.*

"Very well, Commander, right standard rudder. Swing her twenty degrees to the starboard and hold steady momentarily on that course. Stand by for rapid course and speed changes as we start and then complete the circle."

My commands were duly echoed, and *Dixon* leaned over to port as she turned to starboard, away from the freighter's bow. Our forward gun traversed to keep firing on the shore battery. I was relieved when the freighter continued on her due south heading. If she had turned to keep steering for us, it would have been a sign they were trying to ram us.

It was the moment to complete the initial maneuver. "Very good. Now left full rudder, come left in a circle until reaching one-eight-zero, and hold steady on that course."

Dixon listed to starboard as her bow swung in the other direction. Less than a mile away, the freighter charged along, still without navigation lights showing. Two more splashes, one very close to the freighter's port side, showed the shore gunners had the freighter's range and bearing. I knew shrapnel from those near hits would be raking the freighter.

"Any sign of our men on that ship?" I asked Belfort.

"No men visible on her deck, sir."

"Status of the boarding party on our main deck?"

"Boarding party of fifty sailors and Marines under Lieutenant Conner and Chief Rork is armed and ready along our starboard main deck."

Rork? Why the hell is he in the boarding party? Damn him! He's still a sick man. He'd volunteered, of course, as he usually did when there was rough work to be done. I suspected he was making a point of proving his stamina and strength to me. Belfort saw my reaction and paused, but I let it go, saying nothing. Rork could take care of himself.

Belfort continued. "All starboard secondary guns are retracted, and hatches are closed. All the fenders and large mats we've got are hung over the starboard side, sir. The second Colt machine gun and nine of our sharpshooter-rated seamen are ready along the upper boat deck to cover the assault."

Dixon straightened back up when her circle ended and steadied on a due south heading. We'd lost speed during our turn, so the freighter was slightly ahead of us and to starboard by a few hundred yards. We began to recover our speed, slowly forereaching on the ship. I scanned her port side, but no lights or men showed. Gerard's cutter wasn't being towed astern.

The steam cutter must be on a painter line on her other side. Or Gerard and his men might not even be on the freighter anymore. We'll soon know. "Now comes the truly hard part, gentlemen," I said aloud. "Commander, reduce revolutions to make ten knots. Have the helmsman steer by sight to bring the bow into her port side just aft of her bow wave and forward of her bridge. When we get within thirty feet, grapple her fore and aft and haul in with the capstans. At that point we will disengage the shaft and act as a drag on the freighter. Good so far?"

"Understood, aye, sir."

"Good. The boarding party will assault when you are sure the ships are lashed and Lieutenant Conner can get our men over to the freighter without falling between the ships. Sharpshooters will fire on any man on the freighter's decks who is not in an American uniform. And now, please sound the collision alarm."

As the steam whistle shrieked out the collision alarm, another Spanish artillery salvo arrived from the shore, this time very close to us as well as the freighter. A piece of shrapnel thudded into the wheelhouse's forward bulkhead. Belfort looked at me for orders.

The forward 6-inch gun was no longer in position to fire at the coast. Belfort glanced aft, and I knew what he was about to ask.

"No, do *not* have the stern gun fire," I said. "I don't want to give the Spanish an aiming point. We'll concentrate on the boarding for now."

According to the bridge clock, it took thirty-eight long seconds to close the distance. I could now tell the steamer was small, half our size. She was iron hulled and shabby, at least twenty years old, but I couldn't make out a name or nationality. That she was American or European built was apparent, but beyond that I could discern nothing.

"Hold on, men, and stand by for collision!" declared Belfort. Everyone in the bridge grabbed something solid.

Shouts went up from the grappling parties along the starboard deck as the hooks sailed across to grasp the other ship just before we made contact. Between the hulls, waves surged up to the main decks, drenching the boarding party waiting to board the freighter.

"Disengage engine shaft," I ordered. The engine telegraph clanged and the deck suddenly stopped vibrating. Our forward velocity instantly dropped.

A new Spanish artillery volley landed, one close aboard each side of the two ships, hunks of shrapnel thumping into the hulls and ricocheting off bulwarks. Somebody on *Dixon*'s foredeck screamed in pain.

"Steady on, men," I said. "Get ready for the impact."

The first contact was surprisingly mild. Then came the screech of metal grinding on metal as our hull surged forward along hers, lurched to a stop, and rocked back over to port. The quartermaster's mate fell off balance into the gunnery officer, who cursed aloud. *Dixon* bounced away, then rolled back to starboard for a harder crash into the freighter. The forward capstan whirled the bow line taut. A second later the stern was secured alongside the freighter.

"Now, Mr. Conner!" Belfort called down to the main deck.

Conner shouted, "Boarders away! Follow me, men!" A deep primal roar, the sound of warriors for millennia, rose over the wash of the seas and continuing crash of the hulls. Four dozen Bluejackets and Marines leaped down onto the steamer's deck as our sharpshooters peppered away at the freighter's wheelhouse from above.

Belfort and I were on the starboard bridge wing. Other than buckled plates along the gunwale, I saw no major apparent damage to *Dixon*. The two ships were rapidly slowing and heading more to the port—evidently the freighter's shaft was still in ahead gear and she was steering southerly, but she wasn't correcting for our drag on her port side.

The boarding party split into three sections to search the freighter's forecastle, the superstructure amidships, and the engine room hatch aft. A moment later, I suddenly realized it was quieter, for the Americans' shooting and yelling had ended. Only the scraping hulls and seas could be heard.

Something was vastly wrong. A voice on the signal deck above me muttered, "What the hell?"

I looked at Belfort, who was plainly confused as well. He pointed toward the other steamer's wheelhouse. "Captain, I don't understand . . ."

I didn't either. No men were in sight anywhere on the other ship.

9

The Captured Freighter

M Y ANXIETY OVER THE condition of our men—the reader can imagine my dire thoughts—disappeared seconds later when the freighter's wheelhouse door opened and Conner yelled over to me.

"Gerard and his men are all alive, sir! Bringing them back now."

The men of *Dixon* cheered as Gerard and his men, some of whom were badly bloodied, appeared on the steamer's main deck. Helping hands got them up the Jacob's ladder to our deck, where the doctor's assistants waited to take the wounded down to sick bay. Conner and Gerard reported to me on the bridge wing.

Still out of breath from all the excitement, Conner began. "Steamer is secured and totally ours, sir. According to her papers, she's Spanish, named *Paloma*, with a crew of twenty-three. Her log says she came out of Portillo tonight, bound for Jamaica, and then from there bound back to Cádiz in Spain, which she left for Cuba back in late May. She arrived at Portillo four days ago, which must've been right after our squadron's last patrol through this area. Her crew are gone—took French leave when they saw *Dixon* coming for 'em."

He took in a quick breath and surged on, "The engine appears to be in working order, and I've got two men down in the fire room to keep her boiler fireboxes stoked. I've got a man at the helm and the cutter coxswain on the bridge. She's making slow headway, maybe four knots."

Conner fairly vibrated with excitement as he continued. "And Captain, you won't believe what she's carrying. I've got Chief Rork guarding it now. Nobody'll get past *him*. Mr. Gerard can fill you in on what all happened with his boarding party and to our steam cutter."

Gerard, obviously exhausted, shot Conner a nasty look. Belfort interrupted with a significant point. "Captain, we've got to get both ships apart, up to speed, and out of enemy range."

The Spanish guns punctuated his point with another straddling salvo. A hail of shrapnel thudded along *Dixon*'s port side. One metal shard ricocheted into the wheelhouse, barely missing the quartermaster's mate. I reflexively touched the scars on my face, caused by Spanish shrapnel two months prior.

"Indeed, Commander," I quickly acknowledged a bit self-consciously, then turned back to the lieutenant.

"Mr. Conner, you are the prize officer in charge of the steamer. Take ten men from your boarding party and return the rest to *Dixon*, then cast off and get her under way. We'll join you five miles directly due south of here in forty-five minutes. Mr. Gerard, remain right here. You'll present your report in a moment. Commander Belfort, open fire with the stern gun once we are free of the freighter, then get *Dixon* under way to the south at full speed with random zigzags."

Conner dashed out, and Belfort passed along my orders. Once the two ships untangled, *Dixon* fired at the Spanish shore battery and sped up to south. Another Spanish salvo exploded astern of us, right where the ships had been rafted together minutes earlier. The boatswain's mate of the watch and the signalman exchanged relieved glances.

The Spanish artillery ceased firing after that, as did our stern gun. I returned my attention to Gerard. At my suggestion, the doctor had given the lieutenant some coffee laced with medicinal whiskey. He was looking better already.

Belfort joined Gerard and me at the chart table. The others on watch around us cocked an ear our way to hear the lieutenant's story. "All right, Mr. Gerard," I said. "Kindly elucidate what precisely happened tonight, the casualty report, and where our steam cutter is."

He let out a slow breath. "Ah, yes, sir. That freighter didn't quite turn out to be what she seemed. We got into position just like you planned, sir—moving up between the steamer and the coast at Pilón. Then *Dixon* opened up on the steamer, and sure enough, she turned to starboard to run in toward shore. Steamed right up to us, just like you figured she would. In the dark and confusion, no one saw us send our hooks up and get on board.

"That part wasn't easy at all, sir, with the steamer doing every bit of nine knots trying to get away from *Dixon*, and the cutter banging into her hull the whole time. Damn near lost some fellows right there and then, but we didn't."

As he paused for a breath, I could visualize the scene. The boatmen hurling the grappling hooks and lines up, then hauling them taut. A seaman, probably a former topman used to climbing up rigging, pulling himself up to the main deck and then leaning over to hoist up a small Jacob's ladder. Then the boarding party climbing up the swaying ladder as the cutter's coxswain tried to keep it from swamping as it was dragged alongside the freighter. And all this perilous effort being done in the dark, waiting for the Spanish to see them, recognize their vulnerability, and shoot them down.

Gerard took another gulp of coffee and returned to his report. "Well, once we all finally got up on her main deck, which didn't have any men that I could see, I took five men to the wheelhouse and the rest went down into the engine room. They caught the engine crew by surprise, but up on the bridge, we weren't so lucky.

"Turns out the officers had pistols. One of them shot at us, and we had to shoot two of them. Neither's dead. After that, we rounded up everyone and put them in an officer's cabin and put two of our men on the door. At least I *thought* we'd rounded up everyone. Didn't have time to check the holds. Turns out, half a dozen Spanish soldiers and an army officer were down in the forward hold guarding part of the cargo, and they were well armed.

"I knew none of that, of course, because I was busy getting her turned around and headed out to sea. Just after I sent you the light signal and I was thinking we'd pulled it off, those half dozen Spanish fellows from the hold charged up to the wheelhouse and surprised *us*. Had a bit of a shootout, and three of my men were hit; none of them killed, thank God. The soldiers captured us topside, freed the Spanish crew from the cabin, and then went down and surprised our men below at the engines. They got all of us together and put my men in the same cabin we'd just put *them* in."

Gerard didn't like telling that last part. I nodded with sympathy, for I'd been captured twice by the Spanish in Santiago only a week earlier. I gestured for him to go on.

"Yes, sir. Well, right after that, the Spanish shore guns started shooting at the freighter. I guess they were thinking the Americans had captured her, so it was best to sink her. That got the Spanish captain really angry. I was standing next to him on the bridge. He couldn't steam out to sea because *Dixon* would sink him, and he couldn't steam into Portillo or Pilón because his own countrymen would sink him.

"So, he's standing there cursing his own side, then all of a sudden he laughed and said he would fool *both* countries. Next thing I knew, the Spaniards shoved me inside the cabin with my men. I listened at the door to figure out what they were doing next. That's when they lowered their boat, used our steam cutter to tow it, filled both boats with all their men, and headed for shore in the darkness."

"When *Dixon* came alongside and Mr. Conner arrived on board, we were all still locked in that damn cabin and the ship's wheel was lashed. She could've gone on for hours, 'til the coal in the fireboxes ran out. And that's what happened, sir." With a rueful sigh, Gerard straightened up and looked me in the eye. "Very sorry it got fouled up by us getting surprised like that, sir."

I waved away his apology. "Not your fault. It could happen to anyone. You only had ten men, plus the cutter crew. If we'd known about the soldiers we wouldn't even have tried it. But I believe you've left something important out, Mr. Gerard. What was the cargo that needed half a dozen well-armed soldiers to guard it?"

"Oh, sorry, sir! That's the good part. Mostly, the cargo's Cuban coffee and sugar, plus some personal stuff rich planters were shipping back to Spain. But there's also gold bullion in the forward hold. About ten crates of it. The Spanish captain told me about it when he locked me up. Said he wasn't a bit happy about carrying the ill-gotten gains of some corrupt Spanish politicos out of Cuba to safety. Made him a target for every pirate in the area."

An hour later, as *Paloma* and *Dixon* wallowed near each other well offshore, Gerard and I personally inspected the bullion, now being guarded by four Marines and Sergeant Monk. Each crate contained ten crudely formed bars. Except one. It had been pried open and held only seven.

"Never seen that much gold in one spot, Mr. Gerard. Have you?"

"No, sir. Hell'uva friggin' sight, ain't it?"

"Quite. And now you know why the Spanish captain laughed and said he'd fool both countries. I think one of the bars went to the soldiers, to keep them quiet. Probably one to his crew for the same reason. That left one just for him. You know what? I rather hope he made it. Ill-gotten gains from corrupt officials. I'd call that poetic justice."

Gerard's assessment wasn't so philosophical. "And plenty of prize money left for us, sir!"

I smiled at his hopeful expression. Under the old prize law, which hadn't been used since the Civil War, the captain of the capturing ship got the biggest share. I'd gotten *some* prize money during that war, but not as much as I thought I was entitled to. It seemed there were always legalities to reduce the share distributed to the officers and men who actually did the work. Still, it was pleasant to think I might get some again.

"Maybe, Mr. Gerard. But remember, it will be up to an admiralty court to adjudicate the capture and then disseminate the proceeds. The nearest court is in Key West."

He nodded. "I know that court well, sir. My family's appeared before them on wreck salvage cases for decades. They'll be fair. And I could sure use that money."

With those agreeable prospects in mind, and after a final warning glance at Sergeant Monk, Lieutenant Gerard and I returned to *Dixon* and got on with our respective duties.

Early the next morning, *Dixon* returned to the fleet with the captured freighter astern of us flying an American ensign above the Spanish one. I immediately sent a report with the details to Admiral Sampson on board his flagship, *New York*.

In less than an hour, ten of *New York*'s Marines were sent on board *Paloma* to guard the bullion, accompanied by a Navy prize crew from the battleship. The expectant atmosphere on *Dixon* diminished somewhat as "sea lawyers" in the crew suggested the flagship's sailors would either steal the gold outright or try to claim it.

Meanwhile, the admiral sent his own report to Washington via the telegraph station ashore at Siboney, which was connected to the long-distance underwater cable near Guantánamo Bay. The answer arrived that afternoon, an astonishingly fast turnaround time for the stodgy bureaucrats who normally took days or weeks to decide and reply to far more important matters.

I received a summons to the flagship that afternoon. *Dixon*'s decks were crowded with concerned onlookers as I headed off in the rowing cutter. Once I was in Sampson's stateroom, he complimented me for the innovative capture, then dashed cold water on any hopes among *Dixon*'s men for prize money.

He explained that the Navy had learned at the beginning of the war that the owners of many Spanish merchant ships had sold their ships to companies in neutral nations to preclude their seizure by the

Americans, if caught in the war zone. *Paloma*'s owners in Spain were among them. *Paloma* had been officially Dutch since May.

I remembered Lieutenant Gerard's report. The Spanish captain's words and actions seemed to indicate that he didn't know his ship had become neutral property and thus was not liable to forfeiture. If he had, he would've protested Gerard's actions but taken his chances in an American admiralty court.

Then I had a second thought: *Or did he know the ship was now neutral? Was the ship's sudden departure from port and our subsequent capture an opportunistic ruse allowing him to purloin the gold? After all, it was only three bars out of a hundred. How would his Spanish masters ever know? And why would the Americans care?*

With a sympathetic smile the admiral announced the decision of the political authorities in Washington. They did not want to alienate neutrals at this point in the war. The steamer and her cargo would be taken to Jamaica, the nearest neutral port, and turned over to her new owners. Except for the bullion, that is, because it had not been listed on the cargo manifest. It would be treated as "found money," taken to Norfolk by the first returning warship, and put into the U.S. government's treasury. Found money on a neutral ship was not subject to prize law.

Sampson clapped me on the shoulder. "Good try, Peter. Sorry it won't work out for you and your men." Then he invited me to the formal dinner he was hosting that evening on his flagship for the ship captains under his command. Invitations were being delivered to the squadron's other captains as we spoke. The dinner was to celebrate the fleet's great victory over the Spanish fleet several days earlier and the repatriation from Spanish captivity of Lt. Richard Hobson. The lieutenant had been the heroic leader of a doomed attempt to block the channel into Santiago with an old cargo ship a month earlier.

"I expect to see you there," he said. "I think my captains deserve a celebration."

After the disappointing news, I wasn't in the mood. I also detest formal naval dinner functions. But a captain cannot decline such an invitation from an admiral, so I dutifully muttered the reply he expected, "Aye, aye, sir. Thank you."

Returning to *Dixon*, I met with Belfort and Gerard and gave them the bad news about our captured ship and the gold. Belfort muttered something under his breath.

Gerard just shook his head and said, "Well, sir, it looks like that damned Spanish captain was the real winner of this battle."

10

The "Conversation"

Room 247, State, War, and Navy Building, Washington, D.C.
Thursday, 10 October 1901

UP UNTIL THIS POINT in my narrative, my audience of three had been attentively listening. The two admirals smiled slightly at the part about prize money. They well remembered when it was a significant factor in a naval officer's career.

Captain Smith simply snorted and said, "So you didn't get prize money, Wake. Let's move on to that celebration dinner, when you attempted to attack a fellow officer who was your senior."

The two admirals frowned at the captain. He ignored them, intently awaiting my reply.

"That is not true," I said flatly to the admirals. "I have never *attempted* to attack a man. I either attack him or I don't."

"But you *wanted* to attack him, didn't you?" asked Smith, his eyes shining with anticipation of my answer.

"Of course," I said simply.

Self-satisfaction lit up his face as he slapped the table. "Ah-*ha*! I knew it! You carried a grudge against Captain Dimm even then."

At that precise moment, I had the urge to attack Capt. Phineas Percy Smith. *One light smack on his nose would do it. Get the blood flowing to gag his obnoxious mouth.*

Instead, I calmly replied, "But I *didn't* attack that officer. He wasn't worth the effort. And he had no business being there at all. The dinner was a victory celebration for those who had actually served at Cuba and fought in the battle. He wasn't at the battle and had only arrived on the coast a few days earlier. Just another blowhard with epaulets."

"I find that remark both facetious and offensive," barked Smith.

With another hard glance at the captain, Rear Admiral Pentwaller intervened. "Enough, Captain Smith."

To me, Pentwaller said, "Kindly carry on with the chronicle of your war command of *Dixon*, Captain Wake. What happened next?"

"Actually, sir, what happened next was that very dinner Captain Smith just brought up."

11

Celebrating Victory

Adm. William T. Sampson's Flag Mess, Battleship New York,
off Siboney, Cuba

Tuesday Evening, 5 July 1898

IT WAS A JUBILANT OCCASION. Everyone on *New York*, commissioned and enlisted alike, was ecstatic with the flush of victory and the safe return of Lieutenant Hobson and his men. In the admiral's opulent flag cabin, the other captains and I were shown to our chairs at the magnificently laid table. My companions were excited, knowing it would be a memorable evening.

Formal dining-in evenings, most especially that one, are not intended to be an ordeal, of course. But as posh and well deserved as it was, this entire affair was overshadowed by the weather. It was damned hot in the cabin. How could it be anything else in the tropics in July?

For the next hour, thirty-one naval officers—senior fleet staff and commanding officers of many of the warships in the fleet off Santiago—sat elbow to elbow at the long table, sweating profusely in their white dress uniforms, in order to celebrate the recent naval victory over the Spanish in true naval fashion. The cabin's few ports were open, but no cooling breeze entered through them to stir the thick, humid air. I felt like ripping open the choker collar of my uniform; my skin underneath was drenched with sweat and rubbed raw. It was hard even to breathe. My intention to try and enjoy the evening faded. Within minutes my enthusiasm had dwindled to stoic resolve to endure and then escape as soon as I could.

In spite of the stifling atmosphere, the admiral's staff put on a feast worthy of the occasion. *New York*'s finest blue-and-white linen and best china, silver, and crystal graced the table. Moving quietly among us on the thick carpet, the stewards, sweating even more than we officers, provided a carefully choreographed dinner service, course by course. I supposed they'd been practicing all afternoon.

Positions at the table were determined by seniority, a system de rigueur within the rigid aristocracy of the Navy. Officers with the least rank and seniority sat the farthest from Admiral Sampson, who ruled from the head of the table. As a captain with five years' seniority within my rank, I was seated about midway down the table among the other cruiser commanders. Out in the figurative hinterlands to my right were the gunboat and torpedo boat commanders. Closer to the admiral were the exalted battleship captains. Each of these three clans conversed mainly among themselves, for naval officers are expected to remain within their social boundaries. Except for one man, that is.

The loud fool seated to my immediate left was constantly trying to engage the senior officers to his left with absurd banter. At first I thought he was drunk, but then I realized it was just blatant sycophancy. His superiors were neither amused nor patient, but he kept right on trying. I knew instinctively that this insufferable fellow was going to be a source of trouble for me, though how I could not yet fathom.

How did I know this? My answer is simple. More than thirty years of naval service had made me familiar with his type. The fleshy pink face was devoid of the sunburn and crinkled eyes common to veteran seamen who have peered into sun, storm, and dark of night. The soft hands had never hauled a line and had seldom gripped a bulwark in a heavy sea. The carefully coiffed, oiled, and perfumed blond hair was a style more often seen on flamboyant theater actors than naval warriors. The brash nasal voice had never said a prayer over his own dead sailors.

The fellow had rank, but his deportment showed neither professional confidence nor command presence, and I doubted he had much maritime skill. The Navy has its full share of these specimens—the ones who take no chances and then insidiously ridicule those who do and fail, or openly fawn over those who succeed. Politics is their forte, gossip their weapon, anonymity their shield, and arrogance their marker. They are consummate experts in the use of all of it, without risk or responsibility, in their endless pursuit of advancement.

Unfortunately, I was stuck there next to him until the dinner ended. Knowing there was no way to escape what I was now sure was coming, my already sour mood worsened. I studiously ignored him as I awaited the inevitable.

At this juncture I believe a word of explanation to the reader is in order. I do not use the man's real name in this account. He deserves no recognition, good or bad. Instead I call him Capt. Reginald Dimm—a name fitting in all respects.

And now, back to the victory dinner. After a condescending "Hello" and the obvious instant appraisal that I wasn't worth his time, Dimm ignored me altogether while continuing his quest for career enhancement on more fertile ground. He bored the senior officers with loud stories of his prowess at sea, tales that sounded rather overstretched to me, even by Navy standards. Judging by the expressions on Dimm's intended audience, they thought so as well.

From the nonstop monologue, delivered with grand gesticulation and the incessant use of self-superlatives, I learned Captain Dimm was captain of the auxiliary light cruiser *Bronx*, recently arrived from New York. He was charged with guarding the invasion's transports and freighters off Siboney. It would seem that in the execution of his duties he had single-handedly deterred the Spanish fleet from attacking his vulnerable charges, thereby saving the invasion forces, and consequently the entire war.

When the targets of this crowing at last, and rather pointedly, turned their attention elsewhere, Dimm never missed a beat, switching his attentions to the unassuming fellow across the table, who was finishing his dessert. That poor soul was the fleet staff engineering officer and slightly junior to Dimm. The engineer soon heard all about Dimm's exploits while serving the previous year in the European Squadron. Most of the adventures appeared to revolve around his encounters with exotic ladies at soirees on the Riviera casino coast. After enduring this twaddle for ten minutes, Dimm's new target abruptly excused himself to visit the head.

When the dessert plates had been taken away, Rear Admiral Sampson rose from his seat at the head of the table. Everyone, including Dimm, grew quiet. Clearing his throat, the admiral surveyed the table, fixing each man in turn with hooded eyes set in a thin, taciturn face tanned and crinkled by decades on the ocean. Tall and trim, the very image of the old warrior seaman, he began by thanking every officer and man in the fleet for overcoming the Spanish in the battle. The address was mercifully brief, as is Sampson's norm, and ended with a solemn reminder that the Navy had more work yet to do against the foe, not only in Cuba but soon in Puerto Rico as well. And after that, perhaps even on the coast of Spain itself.

It was a serious speech about war. There was no applause or cheering when he concluded. Even Dimm knew enough not to applaud. Instead, the assembled officers rendered a chorus of respectful "Aye, ayes." Afterward, the admiral bid us stay and relax for a while before returning to our ships. Explaining he had to "compose some rather important communiqués for Washington," he nodded pleasantly and exited through a paneled door into his private quarters farther aft. Everyone remained standing as his flag lieutenant–secretary, clutching several thick dossiers, trailed the admiral out.

After the admiral departed, my colleagues quickly dropped back into their seats and, unrestrained by Sampson's somber presence, resumed the celebration with even more enthusiasm. The atmosphere in the cabin, already oppressive from the tropical heat, soon became thick with cigar smoke. The buzz of conversation got louder and more animated as the last round of the port wine was consumed, accompanied by deep-throated guffaws and good-natured slaps on shoulders. It became even harder to breathe in the stench and noise. I felt a headache coming on.

No longer having anyone of importance to talk to, Dimm played absentmindedly with some crumbs he'd spilled on the table. *Perhaps I can escape his attention,* I hoped as I looked in the opposite direction for someone, anyone, else to talk with. *Just another few minutes and this will be over. Then I can excuse myself politely and head back to my ship.*

But it was not to be. Out of the corner of my eye I noticed his brow furrowing in some new intense thought as he shot sidelong glances at me. Seconds later, he turned to face me directly, but without the pleasant camaraderie he'd displayed to his betters. Indeed, Dimm's face showed utter disdain as he leveled an accusatory finger toward me. "*Now* I recall why your name is familiar, Wake."

12

From Annoying to Awful

Adm. William T. Sampson's Flag Mess, Battleship New York,
off Siboney, Cuba

Tuesday Evening, 5 July 1898

*H*ERE IT COMES, I thought with an inward groan. *The old
rumors surface again. Manifestly false, of course, but just too
delicious to fade away.*

Dimm's piggy little eyes narrowed even more. "You're that officer
who mutinied back in sixty-nine and got off at the inquiry. Destroyed
your career, though, and you ended up doing paperwork at a naval
intelligence desk for years, with some sordid skullduggery on the
side. Not the type of work a naval officer and gentleman would do, of
course, but I suppose you had no choice by then."

He was totally wrong on all of that, not that it would have mat-
tered to him. I was about to enlighten him with the facts when he
harrumphed and pounded the table.

"Well, I see our little Cuban adventure got you back to sea! Guess
the Navy needs everybody they can get these days," he sniffed. "Welcome back to the real Navy, Wake. Do try to do better this time. By the
by, whatever happened to your face? Needs some attention."

The engineer officer across the table returned, looking openly relieved he'd been replaced as the object of Dimm's conversational efforts. He quickly began speaking with an officer seated on his other side, leaving me to suffer alone. I couldn't blame him.

Meanwhile, Dimm leaned in toward me with a superior sneer as he awaited my reply, which he apparently assumed would be some apologetic excuse for my past deeds and my presence here tonight. But Dimm had picked the wrong man at the wrong time.

That was when the vision of putting my fist into his solar plexus flashed through my mind. It stayed there awhile as I thought it through. A jab to the solar plexus would shut him up for quite a long time. I'd just embrace him in a comradely manner and laugh loudly to cover the gasp of air leaving his lungs. *No one will notice except maybe the engineer, and he won't tell.*

My left hand reached for Dimm's shoulder, pulling him even closer to me as if to share a good joke. But just as I tensed my right fist out of sight below the table, I noticed the fleet's flag captain furtively beckoning to me from the far end of the table, followed by a nod toward the passageway. Then he stared knowingly at me for a moment. It was both a summons and a warning.

My fantasy ended abruptly. *Damn. It would've been fun.*

Dimm was initially confused by my apparent kindness. I slapped his shoulder hard in false bonhomie, making him wince in pain. His mouth opened in surprise, but I spoke first.

"My face looks this way because I was wounded during a fight against Spanish torpedo boats two months ago. That would've been while you were still enjoying life in Washington as a congressional liaison officer, after your little naval vacation tour of Europe last year and just before you whined to your political patrons to be given a ship command." I tightened my grip on his shoulder. "I'd really like to *engage* you further, Dimm, far more than you can imagine even in your worst nightmare, but I can't because Captain Chadwick wants to see me right now."

As I rose from my chair, the engineer gave me an amused wink. Dimm sputtered something, but I have no idea what he said. I was beyond hearing or caring by then. As soon as I attended to whatever Chadwick wanted, I intended to leave the flagship, whether it was a naval protocol faux pas or not.

Little did I know the evening was about to go from merely annoying to awful.

My head aching from the cigar smoke and meaningless racket, I followed Chadwick out into the passageway.

Capt. French Ensor Chadwick was not only Sampson's fleet flag captain, he was also *New York*'s commanding officer. We'd been friends since our days at the Office of Naval Intelligence back in the 1880s, when he did outstanding espionage work as a naval attaché in Europe. I trusted and respected the man. Many officers did.

Chadwick grinned at me. "Glad you didn't deck that pompous bore, Peter. Oh, don't look so surprised. I could see exactly what you were thinking. I was thinking the same thing."

"I wouldn't have really hurt him—well, not too much."

"Yes, you would have. And yes, he deserves it. But it'd be hard for us, for *me*, to ignore that sort of thing happening in the admiral's flag mess—at a formal victory dinner, no less. Besides, you don't need any other juicy rumors floating around about you. You've only got three more years until retirement. Try to make it, my friend."

His good nature calmed me down. So did the uncomfortable fact he was absolutely right about my career. "Good point," I admitted. "Thanks for getting me away from him."

"You're very welcome, but that's not why I called you out here." His features tightened. "The admiral wants to see you in his quarters right now. He has a special assignment for you ashore tomorrow."

"Ashore?" A flash of anger surged through me. *Special assignment? He's sending me back into that godforsaken jungle to handle a problem somebody else should've handled? I've done my part. There's no damn time for me to go ashore, anyway. I've got a ship to command.*

Reading my mind yet again, or perhaps the scowl on my face, Chadwick held up a hand and said, "I know you won't like it, but you are definitely the best man for it. The only man, in point of fact. The admiral will give you the details."

"But I've only been in command of *Dixon* a couple of days. I can't leave just as I'm taking over. And why the urgency? I saw the admiral this morning, and he didn't say a word about a mission ashore."

"He made his decision after he saw you this morning. Maybe your innovation in capturing that Spanish freighter reminded him of your abilities. Look, I understand your reaction, Peter, but it's only for one day. You'll be back on board *Dixon* by tomorrow night." A sly smile crossed his face as he added, "And by the way, there's another little reason I'm glad you didn't hit Dimm tonight. You'll be in charge of a division of ships for the invasion of Puerto Rico. Dimm's ship will be one of those under your command."

"What?!"

Chadwick shook his head. "I already know what you're going to say, and the answer is *no*. Sampson will not change his decision."

"It won't work. Dimm's senior within the rank to me. He'll complain to his pals in Congress for sure."

Chadwick shook his head. "Peter, he's senior only by six months, and Sampson has a lot more clout than Dimm, especially after this victory."

Glancing back into the flag cabin, he said, "Unfortunately, I've run out of time for gabbing with old friends like you. I've got to go back in there and hobnob with the elite some more, then politely kick them out, so go see the admiral without me." Chadwick paused, then added in a serious tone, "He's expecting you right now."

It wasn't a suggestion. Though my friend Chadwick was five years younger than me and had been a captain less than a year, his new position as flag captain was third highest in the fleet at Cuba and far senior to mine. The time for candid conversation had ended.

My response was an unenthusiastic, "Aye, aye, sir."

13

The "Conversation"

Room 247, State, War, and Navy Building, Washington, D.C. Thursday, 10 October 1901

M Y ADVERSARY IN THE CONFERENCE room rudely interrupted my narration to make a point. "So, the only reason for your hostility toward Captain Dimm was his candid statements about your disastrous past career and the opportunities you were generously given in the war against Spain to rehabilitate it?"

I looked steadily at Smith, every bit Reginald Dimm's equal in unmerited arrogance, and said, "Captain, that is a skewed description of the situation that I will not dignify with a response—especially in an informal *conversation* such as this. If you have a point, please make it."

"Yes," Smith sputtered. "I *damned* well *do* have a point. In your hatred, you decided to try to destroy Dimm's career, just like yours went into the bilge after your mutiny in sixty-nine!"

Rear Admiral Pentwaller raised a hand to silence Smith. "I'll have no more of that language in this room, Captain Smith." He turned to me. "Captain Wake, what was the result of the 1869 naval inquiry into your actions in relieving the captain of your ship from duty?"

"I was found to be justified in my actions, sir, because the captain was medically unfit to command."

"So it wasn't mutiny?"

"That is correct, sir. It was not mutiny."

Smith snarled, "Based on a clever legal obstruction, no doubt. The truth, Captain Wake, is that you have a history of attacking brother United States naval officers. On the twelfth of December in 1892, you attacked your own executive officer of the *Bennington*, Cdr. Norton Gardiner, at the Tampa Bay Hotel. Do you deny that too?"

Obviously, somebody had been busy dredging up the details of my past. Caldhouse's face clouded in concern. Pentwaller looked perturbed.

"Not at all," I replied. "But the facts are these. First, he was my *former* executive officer, having volunteered to transfer off our ship earlier that day. Second, I hurt him only to prevent him from doing something that would thwart our mission."

"Oh, really?" huffed Smith. "And just what mission was that?"

I smiled. "It's still secret, I'm afraid, per presidential orders. What I *can* say is that it had to do with a foreign assassination squad inside our country that was trying to kill a very well known foreign leader. They ended up failing in that. Consequently, a war was averted."

Smith shook his head, obviously disgusted at his inability to force me to incriminate myself. Caldhouse's face relaxed, and he said, "Well, I suppose we'll never know the details since it is still considered confidential. By the way, the scars on your face indicate that you've recently seen action. How many individual wounds have you sustained from various hostile actions in your career?"

What a ridiculous question, I thought. "I don't know, sir."

"Please estimate, Captain Wake."

Mentally adding up the list, I finally said, "About eighteen in all, sir."

"I see, and please name the locations where those wounds were sustained."

"Well, sir, back in the Civil War, I was wounded several times in Florida: at Peace River, the Big Bend, and in Charlotte Harbor. In the years after that I've been wounded at Panama, North Africa, Peru, the

Empire of Vietnam, Samoa, Haiti, and on several occasions inside Cuba before the war with Spain. I was also wounded in a coastal operation in Cuba at the beginning of the war with Spain. That's where I got the scars on my face."

Admiral Pentwaller scribbled on a sheet of paper inside the dossier, then looked up at me and asked. "Were many of those times while you were on clandestine intelligence missions?"

"From 1879 to 1892, most of them, sir."

"I seem to recall you've gotten some awards as well," Caldhouse said. "Please name those." Smith shifted uneasily in his chair.

Of course they weren't on my uniform that day. Medals are displayed only on dress uniforms on formal occasions. With each one I recited, memories of far-off places, people, and battles surged through my mind. "The Legion of Honor from France for a mission in Africa, the Order of the Sun from Peru, the Royal Order of Cambodia, the Order of Kalakaua from the Kingdom of Hawaii, the Sampson Medal for my service at Santiago, and the Navy and Marine Corps Spanish Campaign Medal for action in the Caribbean."

"I see," said Pentwaller, still writing. "What about ship or squadron commands?"

"Before *Dixon*, I commanded seven vessels over the years, sir— three during the Civil War and two after the war. Following my work in intelligence from 1882 to 1891 I commanded *Bennington* and then *Newark*. At the beginning of the Spanish-American War I commanded a composite squadron of five ships on operations on the northern coast of Cuba. After I recuperated from my wounds on that mission, I went back to Cuba with the Army, then commanded *Dixon* on her war cruise in the Caribbean."

"That's quite a professional history, Captain Wake," Pentwaller said. "So, Captain Dimm's pronouncement about you committing mutiny and destroying your career was a gross misstatement, was it not?"

"I thought so, sir."

"Sounds to me like Captain Dimm is fortunate he wasn't around when I started out," offered Rear Admiral Caldhouse, no longer sounding nervous. "We fought duels back then over lesser slanders than Dimm's."

"With respect, sir," sniffed Smith, who had remained silent during this latest round of questions. "Dueling has been illegal for some time now. We've moved beyond such things."

"Oh? You mean such things as an officer defending his *honor*?" asked Caldhouse, his eyes boring into the captain's. "Obviously, *some* men in our Navy have not moved beyond slandering a brother officer's honor."

Pentwaller straightened up from his note taking and said, "Gentlemen, it's after ten o'clock, more than three hours since we began. Let's take a break and resume in ten minutes."

Both admirals quickly rose, left the room, and disappeared down the passageway. I stayed in my chair, gazing over at the White House and thinking about what Dimm had done with his life since he left the Navy two years earlier. Smith went into an adjacent office and demanded to use the telephone. I couldn't hear his words, but when he reentered the conference room he appeared considerably more subdued. I stayed put, waiting for them all to return.

When we resumed, the atmosphere in the room seemed less tense. I was nowhere near relaxing, though. *Wait until I reach the controversial part. What will they think then?*

Rear Admiral Pentwaller opened with, "Let us return to your account, Captain Wake. When we adjourned, I believe you had been ordered on a mission ashore in Cuba. What happened?"

Scenes of that night filled my mind, and I took a breath before beginning again.

14

The Army

Field Headquarters, U.S. Army Fifth Corps, near Los Mangos, Oriente Province, Cuba

Wednesday Afternoon, 6 July 1898

CHADWICK HAD BEEN RIGHT. I didn't like Rear Admiral Sampson's assignment for me. Not one damn bit.

The admiral was preoccupied with messages to and from Washington when I entered, so his interview with me was one-sided and brief. Officially, I was to courier confidential messages from Rear Admiral Sampson to Maj. Gen. William Rufus Shafter, commander of all U.S. Army and Cuban forces ashore—about 35,000 men, all told— in the area of Santiago.

Unofficially, I was to determine the real military situation ashore. While the American naval victory had been complete, the American forces inside Cuba still had not vanquished the enemy at Santiago.

Five days earlier, the American Army had managed to capture the outer lines of enemy defenses outside Santiago, though just barely and at a great cost in killed and wounded. I knew the toll, for I'd been there with them. But two more fortified lines around the city were still in Spanish hands, and they were even stronger than those already taken. Still awaiting reinforcements—and facing the prospect of having his troops decimated in frontal attacks against the next sets of trenches, barbed wire, machine guns, artillery, and fortifications—Shafter had opted for a protracted siege of the city.

Beyond the Spanish army's defenses, other factors loomed menacingly. The United States had invaded at the wrong place in Cuba at the wrong time of the year: the jungles of eastern Cuba during the summer fever season. Malaria, dengue fever, yellow fever, typhoid, and dysentery had greatly weakened the regiments. In addition, the utter ineptitude of the supply chain had left the men only a few days away from starvation at any given time. Many of the rations that did reach them were rancid tinned meats. Worse than inedible, they were detrimental to health and morale. Regimental medical chests were hopelessly lost in supply depots or still on board ships. Only five ambulances had been landed.

Officers' concerns were mounting about the lack of ammunition, potable water, decent food, and medical supplies. The sole road to transport all these supplies from the beach at Siboney to the front line at Santiago was a single cart path that the incessant rains and heavy traffic had made into a river of mud.

Ultimately, I knew the question was simple: Would the Spanish inside Santiago surrender *before* the Americans died by the thousands from disease and were forced to withdraw—or would the Spanish stay in their hilltop defenses and outlive the Americans?

Sampson needed to know what would happen and when, for his fleet was Shafter's lifeline should the Army have to withdraw. The Navy was also responsible for transporting and protecting the upcoming Army invasion of Puerto Rico in addition to patrolling for lone Spanish raiders in the Caribbean and Atlantic.

The admiral did take the time to explain that he had chosen me because of my "recent experience and expertise inside Cuba." Until a few days earlier, when I'd received my new ship command, I'd been ashore as American liaison between the American and Cuban armies. My wife, Maria, had been a volunteer American Red Cross nurse in the field hospital at Siboney, and from her I had learned the real medical situation. I'd personally experienced the debilitating sickness sweeping the troops and seen the Spanish defenses at Santiago.

My connection with Cuba didn't start with this war. It dated from 1884, when I began naval espionage work on the island to gain information against the Spanish. By now I was considered the Navy's expert on Cuba, although many in the naval leadership derided me as an officer who'd "gone native" and a hopeless romantic, for I supported the Cuban patriots' long struggle for total independence from Spain—and any other nation. To the considerable consternation of some in the halls of power, I included *our* nation in that sentiment.

At dawn on the morning after the victory dinner I reluctantly departed my clean and orderly ship. Within an hour I found myself back ashore, trudging through thick, ropy mud. The winding narrow road from the beach at Siboney to Army headquarters in the hill country hadn't improved in the week since I last waded through it. Increasingly disgruntled at my fate, I finally arrived at the headquarters of the commanding general of the U.S. Army's Fifth Corps, Maj. Gen. William Rufus Shafter.

It wasn't destined to be a happy reunion. While I pitied *him* because he was the wrong man for that position, I knew Shafter absolutely despised me as a Navy intruder into the serious business of military campaigning ashore.

In a large tent inhabited by a dozen men clacking away at rapidly rusting typewriters and telegraph keys, I presented myself to the staff adjutant, a superannuated colonel who was scratching out a memo at his camp table. The colonel seemed a decent sort but was clearly overwhelmed by the enormity of his task. Still, he was an improvement over the obnoxious martinet I'd dealt with only a week ago. I wondered where that one had gone. Down with fever or dysentery, most likely.

The colonel gazed with open puzzlement at the muddy apparition before him. I could see the question forming in his mind. Why was a full captain in the Navy—his equivalent in rank—delivering messages? He didn't ask, but instead took me back outside and through a steady drizzle to the doorway of a crude Cuban farmhouse that was the general's personal quarters.

The house was a rarity in rural Oriente in having actual stone walls under its thatched roof. Not many such homes were left standing after three years of bitter scorched-earth war between the Cubans and Spanish. Its interior was still as sparsely furnished as I remembered— an army cot, bamboo side table, large folding map table, disheveled old swivel chair, field desk, and a crude cane chair for a guest. The air was dark and steamy inside the shadowy hut, and a cloud of bugs swarmed through the dim light of two oil lamps.

General Shafter was in shirtsleeves in the swivel chair, his massive bulk bent over the table as he intently examined a map of his area of operations. He appeared even sicker than when I'd last seen him. His thinning blond hair was soaked with sweat and plastered to his head, with a greasy strand falling down over his flushed brow. The yellowed eyes were more sunken, the shadows beneath them darker. Back in Tampa he'd weighed at least three hundred pounds, but his once well-tailored uniform looked almost baggy now. Sweat dripped from his chin as he frowned at the stained map.

After I was announced, I marched in and stood before him. Shafter glanced up irritably, the frown hardening.

"Wake, eh? Never thought I'd see *you* again. I finally got the reconnaissance report of the Spanish flank you were supposed to get to me the *same* night you disappeared. Because I didn't get it until three days later, it was far too late to be any use whatsoever. The Spanish had reinforced that area by then, and the opportunity to end all this mess was *lost.*"

Looking down at the map, I saw the Spanish lines in red pencil, the American lines in blue, and the Cuban forces in green. Multiple red lines thickly encircled the city, just inside thinner blue lines on the east and north, and smaller green lines to the northwest. There were two red lines in the area to which he referred, between the city and the Spanish coastal fortifications. There hadn't been any major enemy formations in the area when I'd conducted my reconnaissance. Had Shafter moved quickly, Santiago would now be in American hands.

It didn't matter that I'd *nearly* pulled off the impossible. The fact was that I hadn't.

"I couldn't get it to you on time, General. I was captured by the enemy. Twice."

He swatted away some gnats at his ear. "Yes, I heard about that. You haven't been much help to us, have you, Wake?"

I considered it a rhetorical question, but since he was waiting for a reply, I tried. "I did my best, General, and yes, sir, it wasn't good enough."

"That's an understatement. Thought I'd heard you'd gone back to the Navy to run a boat, so why are you here?"

I laid the dark blue naval courier envelope on the map—Sampson's official correspondence to the general. "The admiral asked me to personally deliver his confidential messages to you."

His face contorted into a sneer that reminded me very much of Captain Dimm's, my soon-to-be subordinate. "So, you're a courier, not a ship captain?"

"I'm both, General. I have been given command of the cruiser *Dixon*. But since I know the situation ashore, Admiral Sampson ordered me to come here and ask what the Navy can do to assist you. He also would like to understand your plans for the near future so the Navy can coordinate its operations with yours."

The chair groaned as Shafter sat back and glared up at me. "You want to know what the Navy can do to help? Get your warships into the bay and attack the city from behind!"

I'd explained all this to him before, but I remained calm as I explained it again. "That's not possible, General. The entrance channel is still mined. We can't sweep up the mines until the Spanish coastal fortresses covering them are taken. We've bombarded the fortresses, but they need to be actually captured by troops on land. The coastal campaign originally planned would have accomplished that. Since the plan was changed to an inland campaign, your troops are concentrated too far inland to capture the fortresses. The only way to get our fleet inside the bay is for you to move troops—an infantry brigade and battery of heavy artillery should do it—down to the coast to capture the fortresses. Otherwise it's a stalemate . . . sir."

I was well aware that it was Shafter who had changed the original campaign plan, without notifying the Navy. Naturally, he didn't like being reminded of the consequences of his decision. Especially by a fellow in Navy blue. His right hand clenched into a fist.

"You *dare* to lecture *me* on the disposition of my troops? The Navy doesn't tell the Army how to conduct a military campaign, Wake! And I don't have the luxury of extra troops to move around—all the regiments I've got are extended around Santiago's defenses, and those lines are too thin as it is. Over on the west side, I've got only those ragged Cubans you love so much, and their lines are completely porous. Spanish troops walked right through them and got in to reinforce the city's defenses a couple days ago. That added another five thousand enemy soldiers to Toral's army."

The general was right about the Cuban troops. They certainly were a ragged militia unsuited for trench warfare. Their impressive cavalry skills, which had captured well over half the island from the Spanish in the previous three years, were wasted in static European-style siege trenches and artillery duels.

After pausing for a wheezing breath, Shafter resumed. "No, we'll build up the siege methodically. Tell Admiral Sampson that General Miles is arriving soon with reinforcements. Once they land at Siboney and we get them up to the front, we'll use them to strengthen our lines and extend our troops all the way around the city to form a proper siege with proper American soldiers. Once it is in place and the city is strangled, the Spanish will surrender. After that, the Navy can do its job and carry the Army over to Puerto Rico, and we'll do this all over again."

I almost swore aloud when he said "siege." Drawing on my last reserves of patience, I tried to respond diplomatically. "All things being equal, sir, a siege would accomplish the mission admirably. But all things are *not* equal. Unlike the Spanish soldiers, your men are not acclimated to the weather and the tropical diseases here. They don't even have the proper uniforms for the tropics—they're wearing wool! Yellow fever has already begun to spread through your regiments. That and other diseases like dysentery and malaria are quickly degrading the fighting ability of your entire corps."

He grunted as if to dismiss my words. I ignored him and went on. "With all due respect, General Shafter, unlike your corps, who are mainly regulars, most of General Miles' reinforcements are untrained volunteers. It will take time to accustom them to the tropical conditions in Cuba and ready them to fight a well-equipped professional ʹenemy in prepared defenses. Time is something you don't have."

He was glaring at me, but I could tell my last comment registered with him.

I went on. "If the Spanish hold out another three weeks, then your force, including the reinforcements, will be decimated by disease, not bullets. And I assure you, sir, the Spanish *can* hold out. I've been inside their lines and the city."

Then I added something Sampson and I had discussed. "There is another way to employ General Miles' reinforcements, sir. It is bold but could dramatically alter the situation."

I'd gone too far. Shafter' face darkened dangerously. "I will not debate strategy with you, Wake. You delivered Sampson's correspondence and now you're wasting my time, so let me get back to work. Dismissed."

He picked up a report from his desk, swiveled around, and started reading it. With his back to me, further discussion was fruitless. Shafter had made his decision. Advice from the Navy was not wanted.

On my way out, I passed the colonel in the tent and wished him luck. He just stared blankly at me, his eyes watery. Then I smelled the vomit and saw the new stain on the front of his uniform. He was sick too.

I'd originally intended to immediately head back to the fleet boat landing at Siboney, report to Sampson, and get back to my ship as soon as possible. But instead, I decided instead to seize the moment and visit the siege lines around Santiago.

A dear friend was there. I knew he would speak candidly.

15

Waitin' for the Fevers

*First U.S. Volunteer Cavalry Regiment, San Juan Heights,
Oriente Province, Cuba*

Wednesday Evening, 6 July 1898

TWO AND A HALF MILES on foot got me across the battlefield I'd survived only a week before. The stench and grotesque detritus of war were still everywhere. After ascending Kettle Hill, I crossed the shallow valley where I'd buried two fallen Cuban army friends. Their graves were still there, the crudely fashioned crosses already gathering mold. I headed up the gentle slope of San Juan Heights to the siege lines. American soldiers were sprawled in and around the original Spanish trenches, which had been greatly expanded since the battle.

Walking along this line another half mile to the north brought me to my friend's volunteer cavalry regiment. To the west, where the Spanish waited, the twilight of a magnificent tropical sunset cast a yellowish tint on the clouds above me. There was no wind. Even the clouds seemed tired.

The whole place had a curious—no, ominous is a better word—quietness to it. There was no boisterous talk, no banjo music, no laughing, no sergeants cursing, not even the moaning of sick or wounded. Just an eerie quiet broken only by occasional slaps at mosquitos.

I asked a haggard-looking sergeant for his colonel. He peered at me for a moment, then his face brightened a bit. "Ooh, I remember *you*, sir! You was with us on this here hill when we took it. Now, warn't that a hell'uva day with all them Mauser rounds zippin' amongst us! Lord above, I'd take that any time over jus' sittin' here, waitin' for the damn fevers to kill us off."

I had no reply ready for that disheartening comment, and merely nodded when the sergeant said, "Follar me, sir," and set off through the pits and trenches to lead me to his commanding officer. He abruptly stopped in the gathering gloom and pointed. "Thar he be, sir."

The sergeant indicated a small cook fire set in a shallow depression apparently formed by an exploding shell, probably an American round fired from Pozo Hill to our rear. Behind the shell hole sat a drooping two-man officers' tent. A horse, which I recognized as my friend's mount, Little Texas, was tethered to a stake twenty feet down the eastern slope. An orderly was laying out some weedy-looking forage for the horse, who sniffed at it, then ignored it.

Col. Theodore Roosevelt, until three months ago assistant secretary of the Navy and my direct boss, sat cross-legged alone in front of the small cook fire, slowly spooning beans into a tin plate from a small pot. He saw my form approach from the shadows and began to rise slowly, almost hesitantly. I wondered if he was experiencing pain in his joints, a sign of tropical fevers. By the firelight I noted a sallow look to his skin, a lethargy in the eyes as he put on his spectacles and tried to make out the identity of this stranger emerging from the darkness.

The scene disturbed me. Theodore had been my dear friend since 1886. I had never seen him look the least bit unhealthy—until now. I recognized the symptoms, for I'd had them periodically ever since my 1879 mission in the jungles of Panama, and later in Indo-China in 1883.

Roosevelt had malaria.

As soon as Theodore recognized me, the famous grin instantly appeared, white enamel gleaming through the darkness. He stood straighter and his weariness vanished. He strode over to me and pumped my hand vigorously. "Well! I am pleasantly confounded!" he exclaimed. "Peter, how are you *here*, of all places? You never fail to amaze me. I've heard the most distressing rumors about you! I've a hundred questions. How is Rork? And your dear Maria? What have you been doing since we last saw each other?" He gave me a mock askance look, complete with raised eyebrow. "Getting in trouble or vanquishing the foe?"

When Theodore Roosevelt grins at you, it is impossible not to grin back, even in the bleakest of circumstances. "Mostly the former, I'm afraid, Theodore."

"You must be in the very deepest sort of trouble if the Navy sent you back here. Do sit down and tell me all about it!"

"It's a rather convoluted story."

"Then share it over this humble but tasty dinner. Tasty if you've been deprived of real food, that is. This particular treat is part of our spoils of war. Purloined from a dead Spaniard on a raid last night across the lines. Still, it's much better than the putrid garbage our own side gives us. Oh, how I miss Delmonico's in New York!"

We both sat down at the fire and I accepted the offer of a tin cup of black beans from the orderly. He also delivered a cup of coffee with a stick of sugarcane in it. Once we'd eaten and sipped some coffee, I told Theodore about my new assignment commanding *Dixon* (he approved); Rork's role in capturing the Spanish freighter (he slapped his knee in delight); and Maria, who had departed the war zone several days ago on a hospital ship bound for the States with sick and wounded soldiers. Roosevelt nodded thoughtfully, knowing of my worries over Maria's work in a field hospital full of diseased patients.

Then Theodore renewed his demand to hear what had happened to *me* since I'd last seen him the evening after the big battle ashore. I started with the three-man reconnaissance mission of the Spanish flank I had conducted for General Shafter and our capture by an enemy patrol and subsequent interrogation by the colonel commanding the massive Morro Castle—the very place I'd just suggested to

Shafter that he capture. Then I told Roosevelt about our transport into Santiago for interrogation at Spanish army headquarters, our over-powering of the guards, and our brief refuge inside a brothel Rork knew in the heart of the city.

Hearing that, Theodore rocked back with laughter. "Any port in a storm! Well done, Peter. I would expect nothing less from you and Rork."

I went on to tell him how Rork and I captured a small Spanish navy launch and attempted to make our way down Santiago Bay to the American fleet offshore, an effort that unfortunately ended with us treading water among stinging jellyfish all night. The next morning we were again captured by the Spanish, this time by the cruiser *Cristóbal Colón*, just as she and her cohorts were heading out of the bay to battle the American fleet. We had an involuntary ringside seat for that cataclysmic battle, albeit as the target of American high-explosive shells fired by my own son, the assistant gunnery officer of the battleship *Oregon*!

My tale ended with the agreeable details of my new command, which garnered another appreciative grin, for *Dixon* was one of the ships Roosevelt had decided to bring into the Navy before he resigned his post. My description of my current mission to meet with Shafter and assess the situation ashore for Sampson elicited a sage nod of Roosevelt's head. When I finished, a glance at my pocket watch showed I'd spoken for an hour, far longer than I'd intended.

"I can't stay much longer, Theodore. I have to get back to Siboney and out to my ship."

"Yes, of course. Thank you for telling me what happened. You've had quite an adventurous week since we last sat together on this hill, Peter."

"Yes, it hasn't been dull," I said with a weary sigh. "But before I go, what about you and your Rough Riders?"

Shaking his head woefully, he replied, "We've had none of that sort of action here since you left us. The occasional patrol or artillery round, a pro forma effort for both sides, really, but that's the extent of the excitement. By and large, the Spanish have stayed over there and we've stayed over here. I try to keep the men busy to keep their minds off our problems."

"How?"

"Mostly by improving the line, which is a sophisticated way to say digging trenches. Lots of trenches. Rather proud of them, actually. And, of course, everyone's major goal is getting some palatable food. The supply calamity hasn't improved nearly as much as these trenches."

I broached the topic Theodore and I had discussed before the battle, right after the Americans first landed three weeks earlier. "The sickness. How bad has it gotten in the last week?"

He exhaled deeply as his jaw tensed. "As bad as you warned it would get. About a quarter of my men are sick with tropical fevers, mostly malaria, with more every day. Yellow fever has started. I heard there was typhoid, but I haven't seen it in this regiment. *Everybody* has some form of dysentery, though. Some have terrible skin rashes, boils, infections. Doctor says it will get worse if we don't get decent food and water. He thinks some of the men might have scurvy, too."

"I've heard that General Wheeler and General Young are down with fever also."

"Yes, it's true. These dastardly tropical fevers are brutally egalitarian."

"The supply chaos is inexcusable, Theodore. Food and medicines should have been available by now. Are those reporter friends of yours still around here? They'll listen to you, and they have access to the long-distance cable. You've got to get the word back to the States."

Roosevelt was friendly with some of the most famous war correspondents, several of whom he'd invited to accompany his regiment. I'd heard that Theodore's literary entourage, and his resultant fame back home, were not appreciated by the Army's senior officers, especially Shafter, who feared the public would learn just how dire the situation in Cuba was.

"Alas, no, Peter. Most of the reporters have departed for more exciting locales. Some are loitering back at headquarters or at Siboney, though I did hear that Richard Harding Davis was around here someplace just yesterday. Look, you're entirely right about the chaos, but it isn't that Shafter isn't trying. He's sending requests to Washington. They say reinforcements and supplies of everything are on the way."

"What's next for you and your men?"

He almost growled, "We wait and dig more trenches, which is precisely not the way to employ cavalrymen. My boys signed up for real action, but most of the troopers don't even have their horses. We had to leave them behind at Tampa, as you recall."

I did, indeed. The chaos back in Tampa in early June had been a dismal omen of what would unfold in Cuba weeks later. I tried to sound a hopeful note for my friend. "Well, I've heard General Miles and his troops should be here soon."

Then I asked him the most important question—the one on which all other factors hinged. "How long do you think you can maintain an effective fighting force here?"

"Hmm . . ." He took off his spectacles and wiped them with his shirt. "I suppose this information will be repeated to Sampson?"

"Yes, but I'll keep the source anonymous."

He paused for a moment, then said, "Very well. It appears to me that we can last another month, at the most. However, it has become abundantly clear to me that by the middle of August, the situation will either be mitigated by better food and medicine and sanitation, or it will be a complete disaster with half our force laid low by disease."

He abruptly rose and went to his tent, returning with several envelopes. "Can you see that these letters get to my dear Edith? By the by, what's expected next of you and *Dixon*?"

"Right now, coastal blockade. But Sampson also told me I'll have a leading part in the Puerto Rico invasion. He thinks it'll be in a few weeks, but all of that depends on what happens here. Shafter will stay in Cuba, I think. My impression is that Miles will be in command of the invasion at Puerto Rico."

Theodore curtly nodded his approval. "Miles is a good man. Physically much stronger and better able to handle the tropics than Shafter."

Roosevelt surveyed the scene around us then said, "I just hope Miles executes his campaign better than this one. It has to be *fast paced* and cannot be allowed to degenerate into this sort of slow attrition."

"Puerto Rico is different than Cuba in many ways. It may be easier."

"Depends on the man in charge," Theodore said with a sigh. "That much I've learned." Then, in a determined tone, he announced, "I've kept you long enough. It's time for you to be off, Peter."

Mosquitos and flies droned around my face. "Please make a point of taking care of yourself, Theodore. Get some quinine from your doctor. You're no good to your men lying on a cot back at the hospital."

"Don't worry about me. I've been through worse. Winter in Dakota!"

We laughed as rain started to patter down around us. I could smell a heavy squall coming down from the mountains surrounding Santiago as we said our good-byes. Then I walked away from the trenches. Slogging down the hill into the wet darkness of the valley, I found the long road back to the beach at Siboney.

I couldn't bring myself to look back.

16

A Different Sort of General

Captain's Cabin, Transport Yale, *off Santiago, Cuba*
Monday, 11 July 1898

W HEN I REPORTED TO ADMIRAL SAMPSON late on the
night of July sixth, he merely nodded as if nothing I said
surprised him. Used to his usual stolid demeanor—something my own Maria accuses me of having in excess—I contained my
inner anger at being used for mere confirmation and very gratefully
returned to my ship. Belfort welcomed me with undisguised relief,
and indeed, it was good to be "home." Once in my cabin, I immediately had a hot bath and then collapsed in that very comfortable bed,
feeling damned decadent and enjoying every bit of it.

During the next four days we occasionally interrupted the monotony of the blockade by joining the other ships in shelling Spanish shore
fortifications near the entrance to Santiago Bay. It was useful target
practice, but it had little apparent effect. The Spanish guns returned
fire desultorily, causing no damage. The American siege went on.

Late in the morning of July eleventh, General Miles' convoy of reinforcements arrived off Santiago in three transports escorted by a gunboat. I was disappointed, having expected a larger force. Two hours later

I received a signal to join Admiral Sampson and Captain Chadwick on Miles' ship, the auxiliary cruiser–transport *Yale*, for a conference.

Like my ship, *Yale* was a converted passenger liner, though at 10,000 tons she was much bigger and faster, able to make twenty knots. On the other hand, she was much weaker in armament; her primary function was transporting troops, not engaging in battle. Why she wasn't more heavily armed and used for cruiser operations I never learned. It was yet another of the mysterious decisions made by the Navy in those hectic days.

Rear Admiral Sampson and Fleet Captain Chadwick arrived at *Yale* just as I did. When we all entered the captain's cabin, Maj. Gen. Nelson Appleton Miles was sitting at a table with two of his staff officers. As they all stood to greet us, I was immediately struck by how unlike Shafter this general was, in both form and manner.

Miles, only two months my junior in age and also from a small town in Massachusetts, had been the senior general of the U.S. Army since 1895. Rumor had it that he had tried to get a field command earlier in the conflict, but President McKinley and Secretary of War Russell Alger wanted him close by in Washington for his experience and judgment. Finally, after Shafter's Cuban campaign had slowed to an uncertain crawl, Miles had gotten the president's permission to go where the fighting was to be done.

Nelson Miles was very much the image of a veteran senior soldier— ramrod straight with a solid physique, steel gray hair, chiseled nose and chin, a sweeping mustache, humble yet serious eyes that missed nothing, and a measured tone that exuded quiet self-confidence. Though he had been awarded the Medal of Honor, he didn't wear it. He didn't have to. Everyone knew the story of his bravery, in spite of severe wounds, at Chancellorsville in 1863.

Besides our age and origin, Miles and I shared another characteristic, one somewhat problematic for an American commissioned officer after the Civil War. Neither of us had graduated from our service's academy. We both joined during the Civil War as volunteer officers and, unlike most volunteers, stayed in afterward. Three decades later, very few of our type remained in the armed forces. I was the only one still in the Navy. Such unorthodox beginnings are quietly disparaged behind one's back—and sometimes, as the reader has seen, to one's face—by the ordained ring-bearing "gentlemen" from both academies.

In the course of his long career, Miles had overcome such nonsense by producing results, ultimately reaching the Army's top position. The Navy's gilded elite is far more effective at obstructing advancement, however, and my career would never reach such heights.

Miles shook hands with each of us. Introductions were made all around as the seven of us sat at the table and coffee was served. The general graciously thanked Sampson for coming at such short notice, only hours after the fleet had concluded another bombardment of the coastal forts at the mouth of the bay. A coastal chart of southeastern Cuba showing inland mountains, roads, fortifications, and opposing military lines covered most of the table. Once the stewards withdrew, the general came immediately to the point.

"Admiral, I am here to accelerate the surrender of the Spanish inside Santiago. I know that General Shafter has the east and north sides of the city covered by American troops, though not in depth. The Cuban forces are stationed on the north and northwest sides but spread even more thinly. I understand there are no Cuban troops on the west and southwest sides of Santiago Bay."

"That is my understanding as well, General," answered Sampson. "When will your troops go ashore at Siboney?"

Miles shook his head. "I do not think it's wise to land east of the city, Admiral. Instead, I want to land my troops on the coast *west* of Santiago. That way we can complete the encirclement of the city and I can be in a position to support the Cubans in cutting off further Spanish reinforcements from Manzanillo. That will put additional pressure on the Spanish general—I believe his name is Toral—to surrender. Also, if we do have to attack, I am under the impression the defenses on the west side are less developed."

Now, that's interesting, I thought. *Miles has a remarkably good grasp of the situation—and doesn't want to get caught in Shafter's logistical mess over on the east side of Santiago. Landing the new troops on the west side is exactly what I was going to suggest to Shafter before he threw me out.*

Sampson gestured toward me. "General, I brought Captain Wake with me this morning because he conducted reconnaissance in that area, and other parts of Cuba, prior to our invasion. Captain, do you concur with that appraisal?"

I nodded. "Yes, sir. The Cubans could use the support, and the west side of the bay, inland of the coast, *is* less defended. There are, however, some strong batteries of modern heavy guns on the coast at Socapa, just west of the entrance to the Santiago Bay." I pointed to their position on the chart.

"Duly noted, Captain, thank you. I've heard of your work ashore and appreciate it," said Miles, regarding me closely before turning his attention back to Sampson. "Admiral, I am thinking of landing to the west of those batteries, taking them from the rear, then moving inland to join up with the main Cuban forces on that side of the bay." Miles let that sink in for a moment then said, "Therefore, I have two questions for you, Admiral. First, where precisely would you suggest we go ashore? And second, can you provide gunfire support for that landing and my subsequent advance to the east and north from the landing area?"

Sampson quickly replied, "As for gunfire support, yes. We can and will give you support for a landing and any other targets within our range, which would be up to three miles inland, since our ships will close only to within one mile of the shore. An effective signaling system will be necessary to guide shots on areas out of our view, of course. As for the landing place, Captain Wake has an idea. It's bold, but I believe it will work." He turned to me. "Captain, please brief the general."

I pointed on the map to a small cul-de-sac bay with a narrow entrance, several miles west of Santiago Bay's entrance. "This is Cabañas Bay, General. I have not personally reconnoitered it, but I did get reports of its suitability for landing from Cuban engineer officers back in mid-June. At the time, the Spanish had too many troops stationed in that area, so it was not chosen for General Shafter's landing. As of a week ago, I had confirmation from the Cubans that the Spanish have withdrawn their forces from Cabañas Bay and brought them back into the main eastern defenses of Santiago facing General Shafter."

As I continued, the officers leaned forward, intently studying the chart, which didn't show much detail about the little bay. "As you can see, the entrance is too small to get our ships inside. The channel is also only about ten feet deep at the shallowest point. But the transport ships could lay off and send their boats in to the small beach here, on the right-hand shoreline just inside the entrance. I'm told about twenty boats could be landed abreast on the sand.

"From that beach, paths lead inland to the east, behind the Spanish batteries. This area is hilly scrubland, not jungle, a further advantage. The jungle is farther inland, near the rivers. There is also a separate road of sorts that heads north from the beach about six miles toward the interior on the west side of Santiago Bay, where General García has many of his Cuban forces."

Miles tapped a finger on the table as he digested my information and scrutinized the chart. He put a finger farther west along the coast. "I've been told the Cubans have a base here, at Aserradero. What about landing there?"

"Yes, sir, the Cubans have secured that area. Before the invasion General García had his command post there. You *could* land on that beach, but it's open to the sea and usable only in calm weather. But that's not the main problem. Once landed, your men would have to climb a mule path up a thousand-foot mountain to get to the Cuban base, and after that march across country—there are no real roads— another twelve miles through the ruggedest mountain terrain in Cuba, just to get close to the western shore of Santiago Bay. I've personally done that route on foot and horseback, and it would be brutal, especially for new volunteers in the heat of July."

Miles cleared his throat with a rumbling sound but said nothing, so I went on. "Sir, I fully realize Cabañas Bay isn't optimal, or even near optimal, but it's the only landing place west of Santiago with road access north and east to the inner areas of Santiago Bay. On the positive side, the Socapa batteries have minimal gun traverse coverage of Cabañas Bay to their west—most of their guns are pointed southward, out to sea. You'd be able to get to their rear and attack, or just bottle them up there. They would be unable to attack you or escape."

Miles looked at Sampson. "When can we execute this Cabañas Bay plan?"

"The Navy is ready when you are, General," replied Sampson.

"Very good, then. I will consult with General Shafter as soon as possible and let you know, Admiral."

The meeting having concluded, I was about to depart when Miles quietly said to me, "Captain Wake, I hope you're right about that landing place. Everything depends on it."

Humiliating García

Cruiser Dixon, *off Santiago, Cuba*
Sunday, 17 July 1898

*E*NRAGED IS FAR TOO MILD a word to describe my reaction to what transpired on this day. What happened was a gross injustice to Major General Calixto García and his Cuban Mambi soldiers, an indelible stain upon America's honor, a refutation of our given word, and a monumental error of common sense.

It all began on the thirteenth of July, two days after the planning session in which Sampson and Miles had sought my advice. In those two days, negotiations for a truce between Toral and Shafter had progressed to the point of being not only feasible but probable. Miles went ashore and met Toral under a flag of truce, and it was clear the Spaniard wanted an honorable end to the fighting but needed the approval of his superiors in Havana and Madrid.

Miles had an ace up his sleeve, however, that might cement the deal. Although prior intelligence reports—including mine—had indicated Toral and his 15,000 men inside the Santiago defenses had enough food and water to hold out for some time, recently captured Spanish soldiers had let slip that most of their comrades had fewer than two hundred rounds of rifle ammunition apiece, and no replenishment was available. This was crucial.

At 9 a.m. on the thirteenth, as four thousand troops were landing at Cabañas Bay, Miles had that face-to-face meeting with Toral and told him that the Americans' primary goal in the global war against Spain was the immediate capture or destruction of Spanish forces in Santiago and eastern Cuba. He added that another 50,000 men were on their way to ensure just that result. Toral realized he would soon be overrun by at least 80,000 American soldiers. The implication was clear—agree to a "capitulation" now (the word *surrender* was never used, to preserve Spanish honor); and be repatriated to Spain with full military honors, or fight and be annihilated.

Toral turned to the British diplomatic consul in Santiago, who was helping to facilitate the negotiations, for advice. The Briton urged him to take the Americans' offer and avoid further useless bloodshed. Toral made a tentative agreement, certain his superiors would approve. The next day, the fourteenth, the official truce was concluded at an informal meeting of the generals near the adversaries' lines.

Significantly, at no point were the Cubans, who had struggled thirty years for their freedom from Spain and fought a large-scale war with incredible skill and courage for the last three years, consulted or even notified. That was Shafter's decision. As bad an insult as that was, even worse was to come.

On Sunday, 17 July, the U.S. Army force entered Santiago de Cuba and met the Spanish army in a formal capitulation ceremony at the central plaza. With solemn dignity, the Spanish flag was lowered and the American flag raised.

Shafter ordered that neither García nor any of his troops be invited to the ceremony or even allowed inside the captured city.

I found this out from Sampson at a conference on board the flagship that very morning. Sampson, who had a great deal of respect for García and very little for Shafter, was stunned. So was I, for I had been the American liaison officer with García for three extremely eventful weeks, from mid-June until 2 July, and knew him to be a consummate professional soldier.

Knowing of my long support for the Cuban cause, and appreciating my work ashore under arduous conditions, García had openly welcomed me to his camp and army, proclaiming me a brother in the cause of Cuban freedom. On behalf of Shafter and the American government I had assured him of our support, respect, and commitment to a free and democratic Cuba. I further advocated an allied campaign against the common Spanish enemy. With complete confidence in America's promises, García subsequently volunteered to subordinate himself and his army to Shafter's command. When I left the liaison assignment to return to sea, the Cuban general sent me a note thanking me and wishing me good luck.

As I was leaving my meeting with Sampson that morning of the seventeenth, one of the admiral's aides handed me an envelope addressed to me. Inside was a copy of a letter García had sent to Shafter that morning.

17 July 1898
Major General WR Shafter, American Army
Santiago de Cuba
Sir:
On 12 May, the government of the Republic of Cuba ordered me, as commander of the Cuban army in the east, to cooperate with the American army following the plans and obeying the orders of its commander. I have done my best, sir, to fulfill the wishes of my government, and I have been until now one of your most faithful subordinates, honoring myself in carrying out your orders as far as my powers have allowed me to do it.

The city of Santiago surrendered to the American army, and news of that important event was given to me by persons entirely foreign to your staff. I have not been honored with a single word from yourself informing me about the negotiations for peace or the terms of the capitulation by the Spaniards. The important ceremony of the surrender of the Spanish army and the taking possession of the city by yourself took place later on, and I only knew of both events by public reports.

I was neither honored, sir, with a kind word from you inviting me or any officer of my staff to represent the Cuban army on that memorable occasion.

Finally, I know that you have left in power in Santiago the same Spanish authorities that for three years I have fought as enemies of the independence of Cuba. I beg to say that these authorities have never been elected at Santiago by the residents of the city, but were appointed by royal decrees of the Queen of Spain.

I would agree, sir, that the army under your command should have taken possession of the city, the garrison, and the forts. I would give my warm cooperation to any measure you may have deemed best under American military law to hold the city for your army and to preserve public order until the time comes to fulfill the solemn pledge of the people of the United States to establish in Cuba a free and independent government. But when the question arises of appointing authorities in Santiago de Cuba under the special circumstances of our thirty years' strife against Spanish rule, I cannot say but with the deepest regret that such authorities are not elected by the Cuban people, but are the same ones selected by the Queen of Spain, and hence are ministers appointed to defend Spanish sovereignty against the Cubans.

A rumor too absurd to be believed, General, describes the reason of your measure and of the orders forbidding my army to enter Santiago as fear of massacres and revenge against the Spaniards. Allow me, sir, to protest against even the shadow of such an idea. We are not savages ignoring the rules of civilized warfare. We are a poor, ragged army, as ragged and poor as was the army of your forefathers in their noble war for independence, but like the heroes of Saratoga and Yorktown, we respect our cause too deeply to disgrace it with barbarism and cowardice.

In view of all these reasons, I sincerely regret being unable to fulfill any longer the orders of my government, and, therefore, I have tendered today to the commander in chief of the Cuban army, Maj

Gen Máximo Gómez, my resignation as commander of this section of our army.

Awaiting his resolution, I have retired with all my forces to Jiguaní.

I am respectfully yours,

Calixto García

There was no accompanying personal note from the man who once called me brother. The great Cuban warrior general, bloodied veteran of thirty years of combat, espionage, and political intrigue, and commander of one of the most remarkable military campaigns in history, let his acerbic letter to Shafter be his comment to me.

Shafter's humiliation of García was also, by extension, directed at me. The details outlined in the letter transformed my shock into shame as I grasped the enormity of what had intentionally been done. My initial doubts as to the motives and wisdom of those in Washington were now solidified into deep distrust.

Questions with ugly answers filled my mind: *Will anyone with political power in Washington speak up for the Cubans? How will the Cuban people view us, the people who promised them liberation and democracy but merely replaced one occupation army with another? Will the Cuban patriot army fight us now?*

I felt sick in my gut.

18

The "Conversation"

Room 247, State, War, and Navy Building, Washington, D.C.
Thursday, 10 October 1901

"So, Captain Wake, you disagreed with the official United States policy toward the Cuban militia at Santiago?" asked Smith.

"Are you asking for my candid personal opinion?"

"Of course. A simple *yes* or *no* will do."

"Yes," I replied. "But you are incorrect in calling them a militia. They were a regular army that had been in the field for three years and had fought and won battles against superior forces."

"And yet our own Army officers considered them then, and still do, a ragtag guerrilla band—correct?"

"They were and are wrong, just as you are."

Smith smiled, his tone insincerely sympathetic. "And this consensus among American officers about the Cubans has long angered you, hasn't it, Captain Wake?"

"Yes."

"And you think we should abandon our efforts to civilize the Cubans and should just leave the island—right?"

"Yes, Captain Smith. We gave them our word of honor that they would be free. After three years we are still there. Emblematic of being *civilized* is keeping your promises."

"Well, that interpretation makes our nation's leaders nothing more than liars. Is that what you are saying, Captain Wake?"

"In this instance, yes."

Pentwaller grimaced. Caldhouse sighed. Smith turned to Rear Admiral Pentwaller and announced gleefully, "I believe that Captain Wake has succinctly and irrevocably admitted his insubordination to the nation's senior leadership through disrespectful language. This conversation can move on to other issues now, sir."

There was a nervous pause in the "conversation," so I spoke up. "Admiral Pentwaller, Admiral Caldhouse, I was asked for my personal opinion and gave it candidly. When I ask my subordinates for their candid opinion, I expect just that. I listen to it carefully. I do not punish them for it. I ask them because I need to hear differing points of view in order to totally assess all aspects of situations. My own personal opinion has not in the past, and does not now, inhibit me from following legally proper orders or carrying out government policy."

"Yes, well, thank you for that clarification, Captain Wake," mumbled Caldhouse.

"Clarification?" Smith barked. "The man just admitted insubordination!"

Caldhouse looked disgusted. "Wake, have you ever stated your personal opinion of our Cuba policy in public or to civilians?"

"No, sir."

The admiral's frown was still there. "And in professional conversation among other officers?"

"When asked by a superior, yes, I have, sir, as I am honor-bound to do. But no superior has asked in several years. My assessment of the Cuba situation is well known in the Navy."

"Hmm . . ." Pentwaller said nothing more, only waving his hand to put an end to the subject.

Recalling my fury over the letter that day in 1898 also brought back mental images of another kind, although I did not share them with my audience.

19

Maria

Cruiser Dixon, *off Santiago, Cuba*
Sunday, 17 July 1898

THIS INFURIATING AND HEARTBREAKING DAY did have one
bright spot. A mailbag was delivered from the flagship that
afternoon. Along with official correspondence the bag contained a letter.

Catching a whiff of jasmine scent, I knew the sender even before
I read her name on the return address. Maria's handwriting is lovely,
with swirls and flourishes all in perfect alignment. My own is but a
busy scrawl. Suddenly, General García's letter and my hurt and anger
dissipated. I carefully opened the envelope and devoured the contents,
cherishing each word.

9 July 1898
My darling husband Peter,
Seneca made it to New York, and all who were on board her are
now in yellow fever quarantine. I have been installed at the officers' quarters in Fort Hamilton on the north shore of the Narrows along with the officers. Most of the enlisted men are at little
islands called Hoffman and Swinburne, a mile off the coast of

Staten Island. They are now in the care of the nurses and doctors here, and my meager medical abilities no longer are needed. The quarantine doctor, a nice man named Doty, assures us we will be released in two or three weeks if no signs of yellow fever or other communicable illnesses manifest among us. Like everyone, I have had dysentery, but I feel much better now. I've shown no signs of yellow fever. Time will tell.

I regret I could not remain in Cuba, for there was much to be done in the hospital at Siboney, and I had hoped that I could see you again. But my dysentery was affecting my ability to work, and I was becoming a burden on the others. When I was made aware of the glaring need for medical care for the sick and wounded soldiers on *Seneca* the issue was decided.

I forgot my own illness as soon as I arrived on board, for there were others far sicker than I. And as much as I hated to leave you behind, I received a miraculous gift as we steamed away from Siboney that gave me strength. A ship's officer told me that my husband was on a warship we were about to pass. I rushed out from the sick ward onto the crowded deck and saw you standing on your new ship! To know you are back at sea and away from the horrors of Santiago was the very best medicine for me.

Oh, Peter, I so desperately wanted to touch you, to feel your strong arms around me. But instead we steamed away from you, bound for New York to try to save these wretched souls. With each mile and each hour away from Cuba, my longing for you increased. You are the cause of my existence, and I live for the moment when we are together again. In the library at Fort Hamilton, I found a book of poems by an Englishman, Matthew Arnold. One of them expresses my sentiments exactly. It is entitled "Longing," and I send it from my heart to yours:

Come to me in my dreams, and then
By day I shall be well again!
For so the night will more than pay

The hopeless longing of the day.
    Come, as thou cam'st a thousand times,
    A messenger from radiant climes,
    And smile on thy new world, and be
    As kind to others as to me!
Or, as thou never cam'st in sooth,
Come now and let me dream it truth,
And part my hair, and kiss my brow,
And say, My love why sufferest thou?
    Come to me in my dreams, and then
    By day I shall be well again!
    For so the night will more than pay
    The hopeless longing of the day.

May we reunite sooner than we even dare dream and, once together again, stay entwined in mutual love for all our lives.
Your devoted and adoring wife,
Maria

I sat there for a long time, lost in dreams of days gone by and days yet to come. The odors of grease and metal, the petty officers' shouts, the banging of hammer and chisel on rusted iron, the incessant thumping of the engines and shafts, and the soul-sapping heat and humidity—none of that was real to me.

I was no longer on a warship. I was at our tranquil bungalow on Patricio Island. It was early springtime, and the cool night breeze was warmed by a magnificent sunrise bathing the bedroom in a golden haze. A mockingbird sang right outside our window. The scent of orange blossoms and gardenias wafted over us.

Waking past sunrise is decadent tardiness for a sailor, but I didn't care, for I was wonderfully retired from the Navy and far away from ocean storms and horrific wars and slimy politicians. It all felt delicious because Maria was beside me. My wife of more than five years always stills my worries, always rekindles my wonder. Our marriage was a life-saving gift for me at age fifty-four, arriving just as I'd given up hope for any happiness in my final years. I'd been resigned to dreary loneliness on the road to eternity. How wrong I was.

Maria's blue eyes twinkled as she yawned and sleepily suggested breakfast. I was about to agree, but the shiny black hair flowing around her silky skin and her wicked smile lured my caresses instead. Mutual caresses soon became a cuddling embrace.

When I suggested the first order of the day be something other than breakfast, she gave a delightfully naughty giggle, and I realized my suggestion had been her plan all along. My Maria knew what she was doing.

I felt so young again . . .

Thud!—I jolted awake.

A deep Irish brogue bellowed just outside the starboard port of my cabin. "Watch your friggin' load there! Ye bloody weak-kneed lummox, ye damn near took me foot off. Wipe that stupid grin off your face *right now!*"

Maria's image vanished.

This was not the first time I had caught myself daydreaming of Maria when I should have been focused on my ship and crew. It was beginning to worry me.

20

The "Transfer"

Cruiser Dixon, *off Santiago, Cuba*
Sunday, 17 July 1898

THERE WAS ONLY ONE VOICE like that. Seconds later, a heavy hand slowly pounded three times at my door and the Marine sentry announced my visitor's rank and name.

"Come in!" I muttered, angry at the loss of my daydream but also disturbed that I had been mentally so far away.

Chief Boatswain Sean Rork entered and stood at attention before me, beaming innocently. That didn't lessen my annoyance, because when Rork wears that expression it's a sure sign of guilt. He started speaking before I could say a word, another clue he was hiding something.

"Beggin' your pardon for that wee commotion outside your quarters, sir. Some o' them naval militiamen damn near nailed me with a bucket o' black paint dropped from aloft. Aye, I had to do a quick jig to avoid the friggin' thing."

"Surely it wasn't intentional?"

"Ooh, nay, sir. Those militia lads're a bit dimwitted, but there's not a mutinous bone in 'em." He waved his false left hand theatrically and grinned. "But me intrusion is for far better news, sir! The officer o' the watch said to report we've finished fixin' up the replacement for the steam cutter we lost to that Spaniardo captain. Got the new one sittin' all nice an' pretty up in the davits."

New steam cutter? While I had been suspicious before, now I was certain Rork was up to something. *Steam cutters are damned expensive and rare, especially in a war zone a thousand miles from a U.S. Navy yard. Something nefarious is going on.*

Rork, as chief boatswain of the ship, was responsible for all of *Dixon*'s boats, and naturally he would have looked for a replacement. Still, I looked him meaningfully in the eye. "What new steam cutter would that be, Rork?"

A stiff poker face replaced his innocent grin. "Sorry, sir. Thought you knew about it."

Thought you knew. That means the executive officer knew but didn't tell me. A rather important omission. "And where exactly did this new steam cutter come from?"

"*Bronx*, sir. Captain Dimm's ship. They kindly gave it to us just this very mornin'. Her boatswain said it was leakin' badly an' needed some work they didn't have the tools for, but he knew we did."

Of all the fleet, Rork picked Dimm's ship? Damn!

"They didn't have the tools to repair one of their own cutters? That sounds odd, Rork."

He nodded thoughtfully. "That's just what he said, sir. Thought it a bit odd me ownself, but the old sod is a longtime pal an' said he wanted it to go to a ship what would use the little darlin' for some real action. Said Captain Dimm never used it anyways, 'cause he likes to see the men sweat while pullin' oars in the ship's gig. Thinks it's more manly an' sailor-like. So *Bronx*'s chief boatswain said we could have it, sir."

As a gift? I doubted it. "Nothing's free in this Navy, and we both know it. So we got this steam cutter in exchange for *what*?"

"Oh, just some old stuff we had up in the boatswain's locker, sir. Cordage, fenders, a side ladder, an' some paint."

"They don't have their own supplies of those things?"

"Runnin' low, he said, sir." He paused at my obvious skepticism, then went on. "Me pal said they needed more fenders 'cause theirs've been crushed by dockin' so hard. Said the officers aren't that good at ship handlin' alongside a quay, sir."

The fact that a chief boatswain had shared such a derisory opinion of his captain and officers with another chief didn't surprise me. The Navy is run by chief petty officers, and they disdain incompetent officers because they frequently have to cover up for them. The fact it was Dimm's ship told me there was more to the story.

"Those items aren't equal to the value of a steam cutter. I smell a theft, Rork, and not even an artfully concealed theft, at that."

He held up both hands in protest. "Ooh, nay, sir, nay! 'Twas not a theft at all. This is all legal, fair an' square. *Bronx*'s paymaster signed the cutter over to us with a proper equipment transfer form an' all. Our supply an' equipment officer says everything's done all correct an' accordin' to naval regulations."

"I still smell a theft."

Rork almost pouted with false indignation. "Captain, you know I'd never steal such a big thing from another ship. Nay, 'tis all on the up-an'-up, an' there's nary a whiff o' worry for us on this, sir."

Then he had the audacity to grin.

How the hell did he get her supply officer to sign off on the transfer form?

"I want to see that paperwork immediately, Rork."

Rork's grin faded. "Aye, sir."

I swiveled around to the row of brass speaking tubes on the bulkhead behind me. Opening the lid on the one at the end, I shouted, "Bridge! This is the captain. Pass the word for the executive officer and the supply and equipment officer to see me in my cabin in ten minutes—with the documentation on the new steam cutter."

Rork was about to flee when I thought of one crucial detail.

"May I presume the steam cutter looks different now?"

He beamed. "Well 'a course, sir. Don't look nothin' like it used to. Nicely decked out inboard in some buff paint with a black stack, an' light blue topsides with a navy blue sheer line, an' *Dixon* lettered out in gold trim. Even got a fair-weather awnin' for the officers' thwarts in the stern sheets. 'Twill be a grand craft to be seen in, sir. An' by the by, it moves along at a far better clip than our old one, just the sort o' thing that might come in handy when we get to Puerto Rico."

He had a point there.

Rork had been trying to read Maria's letter upside-down on my desk, so I added, "Maria just arrived at New York and is in quarantine. She's feeling much better and shows no signs of yellow fever. With any luck, she'll be home at Alexandria in a couple of weeks."

He glanced up at the overhead beams and declared, "Well, thank the Lord for mercies large an' small!" He grinned at me. "Got to be gettin' back to me work, sir. These militia lads need constant watchin' over. Dismissed, sir?"

"Yes, you are. And you'd better be right about that steam cutter."

"Aye, sir, no worries. An' if I may be so bold before I go, any word on dear Useppa an' the arrival o' our baby? All well? I fancy bein' a grand-uncle!"

My daughter Useppa was expecting her first child in early November in Florida. Her husband, Mario Cano, a Cuban American lawyer, had become so close to me that I considered him a second son. He'd served in action with the Cuban army against the Spanish in a battle that saw both of us wounded.

Maria was very much looking forward to having a child in our lives. Her passion for the new baby was almost desperate, for she'd already lost so much in this war, including one of her sons, and clung to the hope an innocent new life promised. I did too.

"No, Maria didn't write anything about Useppa and the baby."

"Well, sir, the gun deck rumor is we'll all be home by Christmas, so we'll get to see the wee laddie then."

"Or wee *lass*, Rork. Could be a girl." I found myself smiling at memories of Useppa growing up, equal parts tomboy and adorable little princess. "Little girls are actually fun."

Rork smiled too. "Aye, that they are . . ." I could tell he was remembering little Useppa too. Then he straightened up. "Right, then, off I go, sir."

Belfort and Kilmarty arrived almost immediately, carrying with them all the proper paperwork for the transfer of the cutter from *Bronx*. Kilmarty remained silent, carefully watching me as Belfort apologized for the tardy report on the new cutter. He'd been wary about the deal, he explained, but the documents had shown the transfer to be completely legitimate. He laid them all out and we went over them. Nothing seemed missing. The transfer was officially legitimate.

After they left, a shaft of sunlight through the open port lit up my desk and Maria's letter in front of me. A sea breeze suddenly flowed into the cabin, cooling it ever so slightly. I looked outside. The weather was clearing up.

So was my mood.

21

The "Conversation"

Room 247, State, War, and Navy Building, Washington, D.C.
Thursday, 10 October 1901

"JUST TO MAKE THIS CLEAR, there was no theft because *Bronx's* supply and equipment officer had signed off on the transfer of the steam cutter. Is that correct?" asked Admiral Pentwaller.

"Correct, sir," I replied.

"Good," said the admiral with obvious relief. "That was one of the rumors floating around—that you'd stolen Captain Dimm's steam cutter. Now we can put that to rest."

Caldhouse smiled openly for the first time.

Smith kept his eyes on me, expressionless. Then he quietly asked, "Captain Wake, since the exchange of equipment and items was so unequal in value, did you never consider that the officer's signature on those forms might be a forgery?"

The admirals' faces went blank. So did my mind. Smith drummed his fingers on the table, waiting for my answer.

Although I was taken aback by Smith's insinuation, I nevertheless managed a firm response. "Certainly not. My men would not engage in such a scheme," I said, mentally recalling a few times when Rork had skated very close to the line of legality and my suspecting Kilmarty wasn't above a little larceny.

Smith merely raised his eyebrows and continued. "And if the signature *was* a forgery, and therefore a felonious theft, your officers and petty officers would be conspirators in that theft, correct?"

"Please let us know your thoughts on that, Captain Wake," added Pentwaller, who now looked grim.

"Admiral, I have no reason to believe that the signature was a forgery. And if it were, who might have been involved. This is all idle conjecture."

Captain Smith shook his head. "No, Captain Wake, it is not. I asked a valid question, and you did not provide a valid answer."

Pentwaller asked Smith, "How did you come to ask that question, Captain Smith?"

"Officers who were on *Bronx* at that time have been telling stories that allude to fraud and/or forgery being involved in the transfer of that cutter," he replied. "I have two statements en route here by train from New York. They should arrive this afternoon."

Pentwaller noted that information in the dossier, then said, "Well, *Bronx*'s supply and equipment officer, who signed the transfer form, should be able to either affirm or negate such a claim."

Smith shook his head. "No, sir. He died last year. Heart attack. Word is that he was ill while engaged in active duty on board *Bronx* during the war and was in no condition to closely watch over his subordinates at the time."

"Then whose statements are coming here?" asked Pentwaller.

"*Bronx*'s assistant supply officer and a petty officer. Both were naval militiamen during the war and still live in New York City."

"Then I want to see their statements. Meanwhile, Captain Wake, please continue with your account."

Still stunned by the forgery claim, I'm afraid my reply sounded befuddled. "Aye, sir. Where was I?"

Smith made no effort to hide his grin at my discomfiture.

There was an awkward lull, until Caldhouse kindly offered, "I believe the Santiago campaign was ending and the Puerto Rican campaign was about to begin."

22

Orders

Cruiser Dixon, *off Santiago, Cuba*
Wednesday, 20 July 1898

T HE GUN DECK RUMOR PROVED partially true. The Spanish did admit defeat—but only at Santiago. Havana and the rest of Cuba were still uncaptured, we had yet to invade Puerto Rico, and Manila in the Philippines had not surrendered. *Would* we actually be home by Christmas? It didn't seem so. There were still targets to hit, and I knew that *Dixon* was going to be part of the effort.

At 9 a.m. on the twentieth of July, three days after the formal Spanish surrender ceremony at the central plaza in Santiago de Cuba, the orders I'd been expecting finally arrived at my cabin. The large blue envelope was presented directly to me by one of Admiral Sampson's serious-faced staff aides—a clear indication of the document's importance, confidentiality, and urgency.

Sampson's typed orders were clear and concise.

8 a.m., Wednesday, 20 July 1898
New York, Flagship, North Atlantic Squadron
To: Captain P. Wake, USN, Cruiser *Dixon*
North Atlantic Squadron, Santiago de Cuba

From: Rear Admiral W. T. Sampson, USN

North Atlantic Squadron, Commanding

Reference: Naval Operations with Invasion of Puerto Rico

Classification: Strictly Confidential

Routing: Courier delivered—same day

Copies: North Atlantic Squadron file only

Captain Wake,

1. Effective immediately, *Dixon* is detached from Cuban block-ade operations with the North Atlantic Squadron and is assigned to the Transport Division of the naval component in the upcoming invasion and campaign at Puerto Rico. *Dixon* shall be made ready in all respects for sea or shore engage-ments with the enemy. Captain P. Wake will be senior naval officer in charge of the Transport Division and responsible for its command and operations.

2. The Transport Division shall consist of U.S. Army transports *Lampasas, Unionist, Stillwater,* and *Specialist.* Auxiliary cruiser *Yale* (with Maj. Gen. N. Miles, senior Army commander of the expedition, embarked), cruiser *Columbia,* cruiser *Bronx,* and U.S. Revenue Cutter *Windom* (with Brig. Gen. G. Henry embarked) will also be assigned to the Transport Division.

3. The Battle Division of the naval component will be under the command of Capt. F. Higginson, commanding the battleship *Massachusetts.* Captain Higginson is also the overall com-mander of all naval forces in the invasion campaign at Puerto Rico. The Battle Division will comprise the battleship *Indiana,* cruiser *Newark,* cruiser *Cincinnati,* cruiser *New Orleans,* gun-boat *Gloucester,* and gunboat *Wasp,* as well as any other naval vessel currently blockading Puerto Rico.

4. Captain Wake is hereby summoned to an operational brief-ing on board *Massachusetts* this day at two o'clock. All ships assigned to the invasion force will get under way from Santi-ago de Cuba no later than mid-morning of 21 July 1898 and will rendezvous with chartered colliers at Mole Saint Nicolas,

Haiti, the following morning, on 22 July 1898. After coaling all ships, both divisions will get under way for Puerto Rico.

5. Upon completion of service in Puerto Rico, cruiser *Dixon* shall return to Santiago de Cuba and revert to the direct command of the North Atlantic Squadron. Other ships in the Transport Division shall be assigned independently when they are no longer needed at Puerto Rico.

Capt. F. E. Chadwick, Flagship *New York*
Squadron Flag Captain for Rear Adm. W. T. Sampson, USN
North Atlantic Squadron, commanding

Belfort entered my cabin as I finished reading, and I showed him the orders. His bushy eyebrows arched. "Well, this could get mighty interesting, sir. The crew will be glad for the action. I notice they don't rate you as a commodore, but I think they should have. You'll have four transports and several warships in your division."

"It doesn't matter to me, John. This is just a convoy operation, and it'll only last a week or so. I just hope our invasion at Puerto Rico goes better than the mess here in Cuba."

Belfort and I immediately plunged into the details of taking on additional provisions, water, coal, and lubricating oil. We reviewed the status of *Dixon*'s routine repairs and maintenance, fuel types and amounts, boiler pressures and engine lubrication, magazine stowage by shell type, ready ammunition layout, damage repair equipment, sick bay list, probable type of gunnery action, boat stowage, and the many other factors that affect a ship's readiness for battle.

Afterward, we toured the ship. Excited glances from every corner showed an eagerness for action, for the word had quickly passed that the admiral's staff courier had arrived earlier and *something* was about to happen. In the view of the sailors, anything was better than the mind-numbing routine of coastal blockade and guard duty.

That afternoon, after a rain-soaked journey in my newly acquired steam cutter, I arrived in the captain's quarters of the battleship *Massachusetts* at the appointed time. Seated around the long table with me were all of the ship captains in the new naval group, including Capt.

Reginald Dimm of *Bronx*. General Miles and two of his subordinate generals were there as well. Miles nodded amiably to me. Each captain had been told of his assigned division and commander, so I knew Dimm was aware he was under me, but he ignored my presence and stayed at the other end of the table.

Coffee was served, and then all eyes turned to the large chart of Puerto Rico in the middle of the table. Officers pointed at various places on the island's coastline, discussing those locales' assets or disadvantages.

Then Captain Higginson, a solid, steady fellow with an enormous mustache, stood up and cleared his throat. I'd liked the man since our first meeting thirty-four years earlier on the Gulf coast of Florida during the Civil War. He was a vigorous young lieutenant then, and his subsequent career had been impressive. With a man like him in charge, this would be a well-run operation. The air in the cabin was thick with anticipation. Each officer leaned forward in his seat, eyes on Higginson, waiting to hear the details of his ship's part in this great adventure.

Except for one. Dimm stared out the open port to the sea beyond. He had yet to even look my way. I wondered what was behind his behavior—pre-combat nerves or anger that he would be my subordinate?

Higginson got right to the heart of the matter. "Gentlemen, you have read your orders and have been brought together this afternoon to go over details on the naval portion of the upcoming invasion of Spanish Puerto Rico. We will land General Miles and his troops on the northeastern coast of the island at Fajardo, forty miles by road from San Juan, at dawn on the morning of the twenty-fifth. The initial landing will consist of the 3,400 soldiers he has embarked in transports here in Cuba."

I thought the choice of Fajardo was a mistake. Why land an army division on a beach near a large concentration of enemy forces at the capital? There was direct rail transport from San Juan to Fajardo. The enemy could attack the landing within two hours—before the majority of our soldiers were even ashore. Even with naval gunfire support, it would be hard for them to break free of the beach and get inland, especially with the inexperienced volunteer state militia troops who formed much of Miles' command.

The southern coast of the island was far less defended, and the population less pro-Spanish, according to the intelligence I'd learned six months earlier, before war had been declared. Why not land there? But Higginson and Miles appeared confident, so I concluded Miles had obtained some new information about the disposition of Spanish forces on the island.

"A second element of 14,000 soldiers is heading to Puerto Rico on *Puritan, Leyden, Amphitrite,* and other transports from several of our southern ports. They will arrive at Fajardo soon after the first troops go ashore and immediately disembark to reinforce the land campaign."

Higginson glanced at the general, who was studying the chart. Miles abruptly looked up and nodded his concurrence, but in an absentminded way. I got the impression he wanted to add something, but instead he remained silent. I also noticed he was looking at the south coast.

Higginson went on. "The Navy will provide gunfire support of the landing and along the route of any military advance near the coast. The water is deep there, and we'll be able to get our larger ships to within a mile of the shoreline. As the Army's campaign closes in on San Juan, the Navy will bombard the city's fortresses. We've done that before, but it was more in the nature of a raid. This time we'll have more ships and be able to do real damage. Questions so far?"

No one else had a question, but I did. "What are the current estimates on expected enemy naval forces and their locations, sir?"

"Thank you, Captain Wake. Good question." Higginson allowed a slight smile to cross his face. "I was just about to explain that very thing. As of three weeks ago, the Spanish had the cruiser *Isabela II,* a torpedo boat–destroyer, and three or four gunboats in San Juan. *Isabela II* is fourteen years old, 4,000 tons, and carries four 4.7-inch guns, two torpedo tubes, and half a dozen 6-pounders. She is barque-rigged for sail and can do only twelve or thirteen knots under steam."

"The perfect target-practice ship," a young gunboat captain quipped. Several other officers chuckled.

Higginson didn't. "*Isabela* did withdraw from two engagements with our Navy at San Juan in June, but do *not* underestimate her torpedoes, gentlemen. Especially at night." The quipster turned red.

Higginson continued. "The torpedo boat–destroyer is the *Terror*. She fought pretty well in June but came away slightly damaged. We think she was repaired. Make no mistake, gentlemen, *Terror* is small, fast, potent, and very dangerous. She is British built, only two years old, can do twenty-eight knots, and carries half a dozen quick-firing guns and two torpedo tubes. At night, she could slip in through our protective screen and sink two of our transports with thousands of men on board. If she is still at San Juan, she could leave at sunset, make it to Fajardo, strike us, and be back home by midnight."

There weren't any wisecracks or smirks from the audience now. Dimm was finally paying attention, his small black eyes riveted on Higginson.

Commodore Higginson went on. "The gunboats at San Juan are *General Concha* and *Ponce de León*. *General Concha* is sixteen years old, medium-sized, and carries three 4.7-inch guns and three machine guns. She has a punch but can only do ten or eleven knots. *Ponce de León* is British built, two years old, and small, with a couple of 57-millimeter guns and a speed of twelve knots. There is also *Criolla*, an older small gunboat that is mostly moored to a dock in San Juan and not thought to be capable of making it to Fajardo. There have been rumors of another gunboat at San Juan, but I have no definite information."

A hand went up at the other end of the room. When he was recognized, the young naval militia officer asked, "Other than the torpedo boat–destroyer, do they have any actual torpedo boats in the area, sir?"

"We don't know," admitted Higginson. "If they do, they've been hidden well. And speaking of that, let me also point out that the Spanish may have dispersed their ships from San Juan already. They may be hiding among the Spanish Virgin Islands or in the coves along the coast, readying for a night attack against us. Also, there will be little moonlight on the twenty-fifth to help us see an attacker approaching. Our larger ships in the Battle Division will be staying well offshore at night to counter any large Spanish raiders that might be in the Atlantic heading that way. We have some unsubstantiated information that the Spanish might do just that."

Then Higginson added the most important part for *Dixon.* "Closer in to shore, *Dixon* and *Bronx* and the gunboats will protect the transports and supply ships from any enemy attack that might break through my division offshore. Captain Wake is the commander of the transports and their protective force, and one of our most experienced officers in combat against the Spanish. I'm absolutely sure he'll keep the transports safe, even from *Terror.*"

All heads swiveled toward me. I nodded but said nothing. Dimm looked down at the table and fidgeted with a pencil.

"In just a moment Lieutenant Carter will hand out operational details on ship-to-ship and ship-to-shore communications; characteristics of the landing area, coastal charts, and enemy land defenses; and naval general orders. Any last questions or suggestions?" Higginson paused, but no one said anything.

He turned to Miles. "General Miles, do you or your officers have anything to add, sir?"

Miles solemnly shook his head. "No, you have covered everything I can think of, Commodore. I thank everyone in advance for their efforts to make this operation successful."

The commodore spread his arms. "Very well, then. You have your orders, gentlemen. Good luck."

Carter handed the packets to the ship captains without comment. The subsequent departure of the officers was far different from our arrival. As we filed out onto the weather decks, no one spoke. Each man appeared gripped by the enormity of the task ahead. Some studied their orders. Others stared at the shimmering jade sea. Dimm exited quickly, before I had a chance to speak with him.

While making my way out, I thought about countering a night attack by a torpedo boat–destroyer like *Terror.* I had never done that. Indeed, no one in the U.S. Navy had ever done that. Questions filled my mind. *At what range could we spot* Terror? *Does she have Whitehead or Schwartzkopff torpedoes? How much time would we have to engage her before she launched them? How many hits would it take to stop her? What if* Terror *brings along small torpedo boats? Have the Spanish studied the devastating night torpedo attack by the Japanese on the Chinese navy at Weihaiwei three years ago? If so, we may be in trouble.*

Then there was the human factor. *Can I count on Dimm? How will he do in battle?*

I descended the accommodation ladder from the quarterdeck to the steam cutter under the broiling Caribbean sun. *Massachusetts'* watch boatswain twittered his pipe, and the officer of the deck and side-boys came to attention, saluting me in the ancient naval ritual. I found the routine comforting. Once I was seated in the stern sheets, the coxswain, a proud Maryland crab fisherman–turned–naval militiaman, steered the cutter away for *Dixon.*

In the near distance, a dozen warships wallowed in the Caribbean swells, their wartime gray paint making them look like giant sharks waiting for prey. Many were getting up steam as they waited for their captains to return. *Dixon* was out there among them, larger than many. Black smoke drifted from her funnel. The ensign swung lazily from the main gaff with the roll of the ship, the bright red stripes stark against a powder blue sky. I realized the invasion area at Fajardo would look just like this: ships as sitting targets, necessarily jammed together to make the landing more efficient.

That same grouping would also make a night torpedo attack against those ships more efficient. A vision flashed through my brain of thousands of dead men in the water at sunrise after the Spanish attack.

Though the tropical summer sun drenched me in sweat, in that instant my blood ran cold.

23

Into the Black Beyond

Cruiser Dixon, *in the Windward Passage between Cuba and Haiti*
Sunset, Thursday, 21 July 1898

THE INVASION FLEET got under way at 3 p.m.—over four hours later than planned—on Thursday afternoon, July twenty-first. Mechanical problems in several ships of both divisions were responsible for the delay. One ship in particular, *Bronx*, reported serious engineering difficulties. The ship's engineers were working on them but had no estimate of when she could be ready to weigh anchor. I dutifully passed this information along to the flagship, which acknowledged without comment. I envisioned Higginson pacing his bridge and fuming at the delay.

Finally, the culprit ships reported they were continuing to work on the problems but could get under way. Commodore Higginson signaled the fleet to weigh anchor. Each division was to steam at its best speed. And so, with *Massachusetts* and the Battle Division leading, the fleet headed east along the Cuban coast, past the Marine encampment at Guantánamo Bay, to the Windward Passage. Once there, we would steam across the passage to the rendezvous point at Mole Saint Nicolas, on the northwestern corner of Haiti, for final re-coaling and supplies.

Under sunny skies *Dixon*'s bow knifed into swells that had been rolling up from the southeast for the last several days. The swells indicated a distant storm in that direction, confirmed by a barely discernible line of dark clouds on the far horizon.

In addition to the mechanical problems and my Transport Division's resultant slower speed, there had been alterations to the naval formation. Three warships—*Yale*, *Windom*, and *Columbia*—had been deducted from my division and added to the Battle Division. I figured this last-minute change was to keep the Army generals embarked on those ships in closer contact with the overall naval commander. It was a decision I understood and that subsequently proved wise. Thus diminished in combative power, the Transport Division steamed to war, *Dixon* in the lead followed by the four transports and, trailing well behind, *Bronx*.

Near the eastern end of Cuba, our course changed from due east to east-southeast. We steamed along at eight knots, the frustrating speed dictated by the slowest vessel, *Bronx*, which reported she was *still* working on her boiler problems. Considering what Rork had told me about the ship and her crew's general lack of competence, I wasn't surprised. With growing worry, I calculated how this would affect us reaching the rendezvous point at Haiti on time. My initial hope that Dimm's people could fix the problem and get the cruiser back up to speed had turned into resentment. What should have been a simple and fast transit had turned into slogging crawl.

The swells grew larger as we crossed the Windward Passage, and the weather decks were periodically drenched by spray. Steadily pulling farther away ahead of us, *Massachusetts* and her cohorts became black specks trailing wisps of smoke blown to leeward by the wind. We were on our own.

At the end of the second dogwatch, or eight o'clock in the evening, I had just finished dinner in my cabin when Belfort knocked and entered. My executive officer was the only man in *Dixon* who could do that without summons or message. I had encouraged him to come by when he wished to discuss pertinent developments, or just to chat.

The bond between commanding officer and executive officer is crucial in a warship, where seconds count in a battle. Each of us needed to understand the other's strengths and limitations. Also, Belfort had to fully understand my intentions and plan for this mission before we went into action.

Belfort sat in the chair I offered and said, "Weather looks like it might pipe up a bit out of the southeast, sir. That cloud bank on the horizon is approaching much faster now. Only about five or six miles off. The top has gotten higher, too, probably from the effect of the mountains along the southern coast of Haiti."

"Pipe up? How much, do you think?" I asked, thinking about hurricanes, always a worry in July.

He read my mind. "Not bad—doesn't look like a hurricane to me. Not organized and steady enough. More overcast than squall line, so I think it'll be mainly rain. Wind's still only at fifteen, gusting to nineteen, and the swell is about six. But the barometer is at 30.15 and still falling."

"How fast did that fall happen?" I asked. Rapidity of barometric decline was important.

"It was at 30.20 an hour ago, sir."

I agreed with him on the probable forecast but wasn't about to chance it. "Signal our division: 'Secure for possible heavy weather from windward. Stay in line astern with a blue transom light focused to the ship astern.'"

Belfort acknowledged and was standing to leave when a messenger from the officer of the watch, Gerard, arrived at my door. After the Marine guard announced him, the young seaman, no more than sixteen, entered. With an astonished glance around my cabin—it was the first time he'd seen his captain's quarters, so vastly unlike his own—he blurted out the message.

"Beg pardon, sir! Lieutenant Gerard presents his respects and says a strange ship's been sighted just forward of our starboard beam, about six or seven miles off. He can't make her out exactly 'cause she's off in the rain and showin' no lights, but she's fast, and he thinks she's one of them Spanish liners."

Merchantmen were a common sight in the Windward Passage, but that last part got my attention. If the report was accurate, this was an entirely different matter from the Spanish cargo ship we'd caught off Portillo. This was dangerous.

From my intelligence work before the war, I knew that the Spanish government had appropriated several fast liners belonging to the Compañía Transatlántica Española in March. They were fitted out with guns—just as *Dixon* had been—and sent out to function as ocean raiders. One of them had been seen in the Mediterranean in mid-April, thought to be heading for Manila in the Pacific. But American reports from Manila Bay after our victory there on May first showed the raider wasn't there. She hadn't been seen by reliable sources anywhere since.

Other raiders were rumored to be heading for the Caribbean and the nearly defenseless East Coast of the United States, sparking panic in the great port cities in May and June. The government in Washington had been inundated with desperate pleas for Navy help from all the major, and many minor, ports on the Atlantic and Gulf coasts.

Commodore Schley, of recent Santiago naval battle fame, had taken his Flying Squadron out into the Atlantic to find the Spanish raiders and battle squadron. When he found nothing, he'd received new orders to join Sampson at Cuba.

But the fact Schley didn't find them didn't mean the raiders weren't out there. Many naval officers were still concerned. I was one of them, and now this sighting had me going through the various scenarios in my mind. *Is this mystery ship a raider? Are there others also close by? Are the transports their target, or is it the supply depot and ships at the beach at Siboney? Or the new naval depot at Guantánamo? Or our supply rendezvous at Mole Saint Nicolas in Haiti?*

If that obscured vessel was indeed a Spanish raider, the transports following astern of *Dixon* were at immediate risk. Higginson and his large warships were at least fifteen miles ahead of us—too far away to signal or be able to help us quickly. *Dixon* and *Bronx* were the transports' only defense until the battleships and cruisers could turn around and come to us—if they heard our gunfire or saw the flashes. By then it would be completely dark and difficult to tell friend from foe.

I dashed out the door, followed by Belfort and the seaman.

The bridge was packed with watch standers and the off-watch who had remained after the watch change. Standing on the starboard bridge wing, I glanced astern and was assured the transports were following along just as ordered. *Bronx* was the distant dark shape bringing up the rear.

On the western horizon behind us, the sun had just disappeared, leaving a mango orange glow beneath a purple sky. Puffy gold clouds backlit by the sinking sun floated serenely along to the northwest toward the blue-black mountain shadows of eastern Cuba. It was a tranquil sight. But no one else on board *Dixon* was looking at the panorama astern.

Their attention was on the sea and sky ahead of us to the east and south—on the gunmetal gray cliff of clouds stretching across the horizon above an opaque gray curtain of mist and rain that blended seamlessly with the sea. With plain eyes or binoculars, *Dixon*'s officers were peering into that growing gloom, trying to see the ship the look-out had spotted.

"Captain on the bridge!" called out the boatswain's mate of the watch rather tardily, for he too had been staring out at the rain heading our way. Instantly, conversation among the officers stopped. The off-watch half of them sidled to the port side of the bridge, the other half tried to look busy. The officer of the watch, Lieutenant Gerard, strode over to the starboard bridge wing where I stood staring into the growing night to the east. It was useless, I couldn't see a damn thing.

"Evening, Mr. Gerard," I said calmly. "What's our situation?"

"Evening, sir. *Dixon* is steady on course zero-nine-five with revolutions for eight knots. Current is setting us to the north a bit. Purial Mountain on the coast of Cuba is ten miles north on our port beam, and Punta Caleta is approximately twenty miles to the northeast on our port bow. We are about sixty-six miles from our destination in Haiti. *Bronx* is still repairing two of their boilers, which had pressure leaks and overheated valve seals, according to their last signal an hour ago.

"The Battle Division is up ahead, sir, hull-down on the horizon with only mast tops showing—until twenty minutes ago, anyway. Can't see even them now. Our transports are in line astern at thousand-foot intervals, with *Bronx* two miles astern of them."

He took a breath. I waited for the important part.

"Nine minutes ago, the foremast lookout saw an unidentified vessel just forward of the starboard beam at about seven miles, bearing seven-eight degrees relative. She's currently hidden in that rain over there, which is coming this way. I was able to get a brief look at her before the sun went down and she went into the rain. Captain, she's definitely not a cargo ship. She's a large liner of several thousand tons, almost as big as us, two-stacked and steaming without lights at about ten or twelve knots, bound from south to north through the passage."

"Black smoke or gray?"

"Couldn't tell exactly because of the mist and rain, sir, but it looked dark to me. Not sure, but probably bituminous."

That was another indicator she was Spanish. British ships used cleaner-burning anthracite, which produced gray smoke. But if she was British, and therefore neutral, why run without lights in a war zone, especially in limited visibility conditions?

"Who has seen her?" I asked.

"Only two of us, sir. Seaman Trombley, a young naval militia fellow with good eyes, was the lookout and saw her first. Then I saw her. I'm sure she's a Spanish liner. I've doubled the lookouts."

"Very good, Mr. Gerard. Please sound general quarters and get the men to action stations. Light off all boilers. Maintain course and speed for now. Also, send this signal to all transports and *Bronx*: 'Possible enemy ship sighted seven miles south-southeast, steaming north. Appears to be large liner, possibly converted into raider. Lost sight in the rain. All ships go to general quarters. Maintain course and speed but stand by to zigzag. *Dixon* will scout to the southeast. *Bronx* will stay astern of transports on original course.'"

Damn it all to hell, I cursed. If *Bronx* had been operating at full capacity I would have had her come forward to take the vanguard. But she wasn't. Due to her slow speed, I had to keep her in the rear.

As the orders were being echoed, I added to Belfort, "I know the flagship is out of sight, but signal *Massachusetts* anyway with the same alert about the possible raider. Maybe they'll be able to read it and take action."

I went back in the wheelhouse, noted the time, and then studied the chart. Around me, *Dixon* became a cacophony of noise as the Marine bugler sounded general quarters, boatswain's mates piped the call fore and aft, and petty officers shouted at their men to hurry to their stations. In seconds, hundreds of sailors were clambering up the starboard-side ladders and down those on the port side to their action stations around the ship. The number of men in the bridge doubled in four minutes. Reports of battle stations being manned and ready came into the bridge through the row of speaking tubes on the after bulkhead.

Above us on the signal deck, the chief signalman began flashing the signal lamp toward the division astern. In five minutes and forty-eight seconds, Belfort reported all stations manned and the ship cleared for action. Acknowledging signals from the ships astern were reported. None was seen from *Massachusetts* or any other ship of the Battle Division ahead of us.

Pointing to the chart table, tinted red by the glow of the night lanterns, I asked, "Have you worked out the closest point of approach to that vessel, Mr. Gerard?"

"Yes, sir. If the other vessel holds her estimated course and speed, and we hold ours, we will come within half a mile of her right here." He pointed a pencil at a small, faint circle he'd drawn on the chart. "She'll be either dead ahead or a point off our starboard bow, in approximately . . ." he checked the clock on the bulkhead, "twenty-six and a half minutes."

Belfort turned to me. "That's a big *if*, sir. We would've been silhouetted against the sunset sky before the rain covered them, so they must know we're here. They probably doubled back to the south."

"Entirely possible," I said. "But think about the other possibility. Where would they be headed if they continued to steam northbound, gentlemen?"

"To enter the Old Bahama Channel, sir," Gerard proposed. "And then run the blockade and get to safety at Havana or Matanzas."

"Or steam northwest up the Santaren Channel through the Bahamas to raid our coast," suggested Belfort. "Remember, we've got those supply and troopships coming down from Jacksonville and Charleston. That would be a disaster."

"No, it's someplace closer, I reckon, like our depot at Mole Saint Nicolas," interrupted Commander Pinkston, who'd just arrived looking unusually disheveled. "It's close and would be easy for them to bombard. Hit the coal pile and start a fire. Destroy the cable shack and supply warehouse. Then they'd head northeast between the Turks and Caicos Islands and the Dominican Republic. Once they're past the shallow Mouchoir Banks, they're free to roam the broad Atlantic." He continued earnestly, "Captain, that one simple strike in Haiti could knock out one of our fuel depots and communications stations, cause panic, and make us spread our forces out even thinner to search for the damned rogues."

Belfort wagged his head. "Plausible, but I don't think so. If they saw *us*, then they might've seen Higginson's big *Massachusetts* and *Indiana* and the cruisers ahead of us, clearly heading toward Mole Saint Nicolas. They won't chance tangling with *them*."

Pinkston had no counter to that. They all turned toward me.

"And if they've turned around to evade us, using the rain as concealment to head south, where then?" I asked.

"Attack the Army's supply ships at Santiago," suggested Gerard.

"Santiago and Siboney are too heavily guarded by Sampson," countered Belfort. "I'd wager they'll loiter here under the cover of the rain, then try to hit our transports. After that, they'll head north through the Windward Passage toward their original target, which just might be the Eastern Seaboard. Think of the panic *that* would cause!"

That was my assessment as well. We had to assume the worst.

"Thank you, gentlemen. Here is my plan of action. *Dixon* will immediately alter course to one-two-zero and increase speed to ten knots. We'll continue on that course for forty minutes. If we don't find that vessel, we'll rejoin the other ships and all head for Mole Saint Nicolas on varying courses and zigzagging to confuse the Spanish ship. Our first duty is to protect these transports, the second is to alert Commodore Higginson of a possible raider in the area."

As I finished speaking, the downpour reached us. The rain was so heavy that both our bow and our stern disappeared from view. In peacetime, such conditions in close proximity to other vessels call for every exterior light to be lit and the steam whistle sounded every thirty seconds to warn others nearby. Speed is reduced to provide more reaction time. Safety is paramount.

But we were at war. Nothing was safe. No one knew what lay ahead. Everything was accelerated in both speed and time. Concealment was vital for both American and Spaniard. Grimly, the men of *Dixon* steamed their ship into the rainy blackness ahead.

24

Smoke in the Rain

Cruiser Dixon, *in the Windward Passage between Cuba and Haiti*
Thursday Night, 21 July 1898

ORTY MINUTES LATER it was still raining. Not a blustery rainstorm, just a steady downpour from a thick cloud that covered the ocean like a blanket, the rain so dense its weight flattened the waves atop the long ocean swells. Our searchlight could penetrate the wall of rain a quarter mile at the very most. Astern of us, the transports and *Bronx* were lost to sight as they continued on their previous course.

When the enemy raider failed to appear, I gave the order to alter course to the north and rejoin the other ships. Gerard had figured out their probable position, and to his navigational credit, we saw their outlines on the port bow fifteen minutes later. Once back in the lead position of the division, I ordered the formation to begin evasive course changes, ten degrees to starboard for thirty minutes, then twenty-five degrees to port for twenty minutes, finally changing course forty degrees to starboard and staying on that heading for an hour. This longer zigzag course would get us to Mole Saint Nicolas near dawn. We would arrive well behind the heavy warships, but we'd make the rendezvous. Once there, an alert for the raider could be sent out to all stations in Florida and the Caribbean via the underwater telegraph cable.

It was while *Dixon* was turning onto one of these changing courses
that Rork appeared on the bridge. His battle station was on the foredeck near the forward 6-inch gun. He looked worried as he spoke first
to Gerard and then to Belfort, who gestured for Rork to follow him
over to me.

"Beggin' your pardon, Captain," Rork said to me in the formal manner,
as he is always careful to do in the presence of others, "but I'm thinkin'
that Spaniardo raider's somewhere near to windward, off our starboard
beam. I was standin' by the for'ard starboard 6-pounder just now an'
got a wee whiff o' funnel smoke. Didn't come from our own funnel, for
that's blowin' off to the port side. Besides, this smoke smelled like soft
black coal, not our own Navy anthracite. Can't smell it anymore, just
that one bit'uva whiff is all. An' since the wind's from the so'east an' gone
lighter, those buggers're likely no more'n a mile or two off our beam."

I didn't ask if he was sure. Rork wouldn't have left his battle station
if he wasn't certain. "Thank you, Rork. Carry on and let us know if you
smell it again."

Gerard and Belfort looked dubious but said nothing. They were
waiting to see what their captain thought of this unusual development.

"Rork could be wrong," I admitted, "but I doubt it. This fits with
what we have already seen tonight. And if he's right . . ."

Belfort nodded pensively. "Well, sir, if the raider continued her
original course and speed, she should've been off our bow. With this
wind, Rork would never have smelled her smoke then. So this means
they must have slowed down to let us go by so they could get a chance
of firing into the transports behind us."

"Yes, that's just what I was thinking," I said. "Any suggestions, gentlemen? There's not much time."

Belfort said, "Depends on that raider's armament, sir. Does she out-
gun us? Does she have torpedoes she can fire without giving away
her position?"

"We won't know that until it's too late," muttered Gerard.

As they spoke, a dangerous idea formed in my mind. It meant taking a huge chance, and there wasn't much time to carry it out. I shared

it with Belfort and Gerard as we looked down at the chart. Gerard drew a circle where he thought the raider was.

He looked up at me. "Might actually work, sir."

"At the very least," said Belfort, "it'll throw them off their intended plan of attack."

"Right," I said. "Get Guns down here and let's get it done."

Pinkston arrived from his gunnery control perch on the deck above the bridge, and I told him what I wanted. He never hesitated, giving me a quick, "Aye, aye, sir," before he climbed back up to his battle position. The rain was even heavier now, cutting visibility almost to nil. Belfort and I donned our foul-weather gear and went out on the starboard bridge wing.

I could hear the gunnery officer above us shouting into the voice tubes connecting to his gun mounts. Below me, all five of *Dixon's* secondary battery on the starboard side, the rapid-fire 6-pounder guns, traversed their barrels to points perpendicular to the ship. Even above the loud swish of the bow wave I heard the gunner's mates recite the loading and aiming procedure and the breech blocks slam home as the rounds were loaded.

Forgoing the speaking tube to the bridge, Pinkston called down to us, "All guns loaded, locked, aimed, and ready to fire, sir!"

In preparation for the side effects of the broadside, I closed my right eye and opened my mouth to equalize the pressure in my ears, then gave the order. "Fire!"

BOOM'OOM'OOM! Five muzzles roared simultaneously, and tongues of flame shot out from the side of the ship, starkly lighting up the night.

The ship heeled slightly with the recoil. The instantaneous concussion slammed into me as I gripped the bulwark. A dense cloud of caustic gun smoke covered the bridge. Some of the less experienced naval militiamen choked and coughed.

Dixon's blind volley sent five shells two miles out to an area calculated to cover a quarter mile. I figured they would at least deter, if not damage, the enemy raider—if she was still out there. With their muzzle velocity of 1,818 feet per second, we'd have to wait about five seconds until we knew if the shells hit anything.

It was a long five seconds. Then a solitary flare of light burst through the mist, followed by a muffled *boom*. The explosion illuminated the vessel's superstructure, showing we'd hit her afterdeck. The shell must have set off some ready ammunition, for an even larger secondary eruption rippled through the night.

I instantly recognized the ship, a regular visitor to Havana's harbor before war. Now that he got a good glimpse of her, so did Gerard. She was *La Marquesa*, a passenger liner built by a British yard for the Mediterranean route in 1891. Four years later, the Compañia Transatlántica Española bought her for the West Indies trade. As large as *Dixon*, the liner-turned-warship had been sitting there, hidden in the deluge, as we steamed by.

In the light from the explosion I could see that she had full steam up, smoke pouring from her funnels, and was turning slowly back to the east toward Haiti and a denser area of rain. A fire blazed up on her afterdeck, but the rain quickly doused it to a small flickering glow. Soon, her form was lost to us, and only that dim flickering light showed in the distance.

The explosion and fire had showed me her outline and identity, but not what kind of guns she carried, for she hadn't returned fire. Torpedoes were my big fear. She might have midship tubes.

We had to hit her again quickly, before she recovered from the surprise and counterattacked. "Commander Belfort, we're going to follow her turn to the east, but turn inside her to stay between her and our convoy. Right full rudder to course one-zero-zero initially, and stand by for more fast course changes after that. Increase speed to fifteen knots. All guns that bear on the target may fire at will as we turn."

Dixon's deck thrummed as we heeled over to port in the turn to starboard.

Just then the barely visible *Marquesa* shot back. It was only a light *pop*. I never saw a splash. The dim fire glow on her afterdeck flared again momentarily, then diminished a bit.

"It's a 122-millimeter Hontaria rapid-fire gun, sir," Pinkston called down to us. "Effective range of three miles, but she missed us by a quarter mile. Stand by for firing."

BOOM! Our forward 6-inch gun crashed out, followed by the forward 6-pounder gun to starboard. Our broadside guns couldn't bear on the target now because we were turning our bow toward the enemy ship.

"No hit on the bastard, damn it," Pinkston growled loudly to no one in particular. I tried not to smile.

"Mr. Pinkston, proper demeanor, if you please," admonished Belfort.

"Sorry, sir. No hit observed."

The enemy ship's bearing steadied—meaning *Marquesa* wasn't turning farther around to the south to circle back west and attack the convoy. Not yet, at least. She was fleeing to the east-southeast, into the great gulf formed between Haiti's two long pincer-like peninsulas. The Spanish ship would soon elude us, though, and then she would be free to attack when and where she chose.

Somehow, we had to stop her.

25

Ruse de Guerre

Cruiser Dixon, *in the Windward Passage between Cuba and Haiti*
Friday Night, 22 July 1898

"STEER DIRECTLY FOR HER," I ordered. To Belfort, I said, "Signal
the division: 'Enemy directly ahead of *Dixon* to the east. Maintain
your course and speed. *Dixon* is continuing attack.'"

"Aye, lookee there, them Spaniardos're slowing down! You'll nail
'em now fer sure!" a sailor below us on the main deck called out to his
mates on the forward gun.

Hearing that, I realized the glow was getting close much faster
than I'd anticipated. But why? *Maybe our first shot penetrated deeper
than I thought and we damaged her rudder or shaft? Will she try to run
ashore? No, that's too far away.*

The forward gun fired again, without visible effect. The range was
down to a mile, at most. Point blank. *Why no hit and explosion?*

"What the hell is going on here?" Belfort wondered aloud.

We were now closing rapidly—very rapidly—on that dim glow. My
mind raced with possibilities. *The other ship must be almost stationary.
Is this a torpedo trap? Will they turn and try to ram us?*

The 6-inch gun fired again, but there was still no satisfying explosion on the target. Epithets rose from officers and men on the bridge

and upper decks. Belfort chided them, then looked questioningly at me. I strained to see more through the binoculars, but I could see only a dim glow through the heavy rain and nothing of the form of that damned ship.

Just at that moment, what I was looking at became obvious to me. I had made a colossal mistake.

The enemy had used a very simple, and very old, *ruse de guerre*— one I'd employed myself many years earlier. Just as it had worked for me against Malay pirates in the South China Sea in 1883, it worked against me now. The Spanish raider captain had provided what I expected, nay, what I wanted, to see.

After our round had exploded on her stern deck and started a brief fire, *Marquesa* had dropped a raft of burning debris off her stern as a decoy. With the real fire on her deck now extinguished, and the American warship heading for the decoy, she'd slipped off into the rain. We'd been shooting at a small, drifting raft the entire time.

Behind us, my division was swallowed up by the rain and darkness. *But they should be close enough to read a signal.*

"Hard left rudder!" I ordered. "Steady on new course three-one-zero. Maintain current speed. Signal the division: 'Flames are a decoy raft. Enemy ship location unknown. All transports alter course by line ahead in column to due north. *Dixon* is returning to convoy. Do not give away your position by acknowledging this signal. Douse all remaining lights.'"

As we heeled over in the tight turn, I added to Belfort, "We should be close enough now. Shine the searchlight on those flames for a moment, then sweep the eastern horizon from north to south."

The shaft of light vaguely showed the outline of a raft, maybe twenty-five feet in length, bobbing on the swells. It appeared to be made of burning furniture piled atop two small ship's boats lashed together. By now the rain had almost extinguished the fire. The searchlight sweep of the horizon showed nothing of the enemy cruiser.

"Damned clever trick," said Belfort. "That Spanish captain knows his business. I never would've guessed it. How'd you know, sir?"

"Memories," I muttered back, furious with myself and anxious about the consequences of my error in judgment. Belfort then asked the question dominating my mind.

"Where do you think the raider is now, sir?"

"Not sure, but she's got to be one of four places. The captain might have gone back to his original northerly course, put on speed, and is northeast of us, close to the Haitian coast, readying to turn west and attack the convoy from ahead. Or he continued east toward Haiti, intending to hide somewhere along that coast. Or he's south of us, running away into the Caribbean. Or he went south and then circled around to the southwest of us to attack the transports from behind. If he does that, then *Bronx* will have a chance at him—*if* they can spot him in this soup. In any case, we need to get between the raider and our troopships."

I thought through the geometry of the possibilities and made a decision. "Signal all ships in division: 'Continue in steaming column at same speed and course. *Dixon* will rejoin and take position ahead to protect transports from attack ahead and to starboard. *Bronx* will protect astern and to port. Do not give away position by acknowledging this signal.'"

Belfort walked into the wheelhouse and gave the orders, then returned to stand beside me out on the bridge wing. As *Dixon* began her turn, we both stared ahead, seeing and hearing nothing but that incessant rain. Word from the stern lookout arrived at the bridge. Just after our signal to the others, he'd seen the vague outline of a large ship for two seconds in the mist astern of us. He couldn't identify the ship or her heading.

After acknowledging the lookout's report, neither of us spoke. I sensed Belfort's empathy for the weight of my decision. He broke our silence, saying more to himself than to me, "The transports are hidden by the rain, too. That raider'll have a hard time ever finding them."

As it turned out, so did we. It took us fifty-seven incredibly tense minutes and two zigzag legs to the west and north. Every man on the upper decks strained to find them. Then one indistinct silhouette morphed into solidity on our port bow. Soon, another materialized, and another. They were in a line ahead, just as they should be. But the count was one short. There were only the four transports. *Bronx* was nowhere in sight.

I brought *Dixon* up alongside the aftermost transport and used the speaking trumpet to ask her captain if he knew *Bronx*'s position, which should have been just astern of them. He was a grizzled old merchant seaman with a foghorn of a voice.

"Hell if I know, Captain Wake! *Bronx* was right behind us, but then she turned back to the northwest after your signal. We lost sight of her in the rain and never saw her again. We've been out here unprotected since! Do *you* know where she went?"

Northwest? I inwardly uttered a foul oath. *Why would Dimm go northwest, away from the convoy? He'd been ordered to go north so the division could reunite and head for Haiti. Did* Bronx *misunderstand my signal? And where exactly was Dimm now?*

In any event, I had to stay with the transports. I couldn't go off looking for the missing cruiser. The officers and men on the bridge were exchanging worried glances. An entire warship under my operational control had disappeared.

I didn't answer the transport captain, mainly because I had no good answer. Loud enough for all around me to hear, I said to Belfort, "Signal the transport to continue her course and stay astern of the others. *Bronx* can't be that far away. Might have had more boiler trouble. She'll show up soon."

My lack of conviction was obvious, but everyone dutifully nodded. For the rest of the night, we watched for *Bronx*. Every dark speck on the horizon turned out to be another squall.

Dimm and his ship never appeared.

26

Sunrise

Cruiser Dixon, *in the Windward Passage off Mole Saint Nicolas, Haiti*
Friday Morning, 22 July 1898

A S THE EASTERN SKY LIGHTENED just before six in the
morning, Belfort and I were still on the bridge. *Dixon's* crew
was still at their battle stations. The rain had ended an hour
earlier, swept off toward Cuba and the Bahamas by a rising wind. The
only cloud cover was the perennial thin shroud of charcoal smoke
over Haiti on our bow. Behind *Dixon,* like ducklings following their
mother, steamed the line of transports.

The Spanish raider and *Bronx* were nowhere to be seen. I doubted
they'd clashed—we would have heard the gunfire. To all appearances,
our enemy had slipped away, and our colleague had fallen behind
with increasing mechanical troubles.

I was drained of mental and physical strength but couldn't leave the
bridge—not with the enemy out there, perhaps just over the horizon,
and one of my ships missing. Too much was happening; too much
might still happen. Decisions would have to be made. I stood there
leaning against the railing and trying to concentrate as dawn arrived
and horizons appeared.

Gulping the mug of coffee that appeared in front of me, I felt it surge into my brain, increasing my acuity. But my body still ached to lie down, if only for ten minutes; my arms and legs felt weighted with lead, slowing my every movement.

You're just too damned old for this, announced my coffee-enhanced intellect. *Maria is right. Admit it and retire early. You should be in bed with her right now, not dealing with fools like Dimm.*

As I stood there draped over the bridge wing bulwark—something no ensign is ever allowed to do—overcome by worry and exhaustion, my mind returned to that delicious dream of Maria lying next to me in bed at our bungalow at Patricio Island. That scene became real while *Dixon* faded from my consciousness. The throbbing engines, whining generators and fans, rushing wind and waves, and greasy metallic lubricant smells receded, replaced by singing birds and palm leaves rustling in the breeze. Maria's head rested on the pillow beside me. She smiled at me as her elegant fingers softly caressed the scars on my face. The morning land breeze wafted jasmine and gardenia into the room. It was so peaceful in that bed—no problems, no superiors' egos, no subordinates' failures, no enemies . . .

My eyes burst open when the mizzenmast lookout shouted down, "Bridge there! *Bronx* bow on, broad on our port quarter at the horizon, about seven or eight miles off and steaming this way, sir!"

Stop daydreaming! I can't allow this to happen again. Warship command requires constant attention and instantaneous responses to situations. Was I losing that ability?

I hurried across to the port bridge wing and stared astern of us. Nothing. But wait. Yes, there was a mass emerging from the darker background of western horizon. I couldn't tell if she was *Bronx*, but a lieutenant near me confirmed it with disdain in his tone. I focused my binoculars on the ship and was able to make out more details. She showed no obvious major damage.

The foremast lookout began reporting other ships far ahead of us. Against the background of Haiti's brooding brown-clad mountains, the silhouettes of *Massachusetts* and her Battle Division were closing on Mole Saint Nicolas. Off to the northwest, on our port beam, the after lookout reported a fleet of ten transports and supply freighters, escorted by two small gunboats, emerging from the Old Bahama Channel—the additional invasion forces coming from Tampa, Jacksonville, and Charleston. The rendezvous was coming together, just as planned.

"Does anyone see the raider?" someone asked. No one answered. It wasn't necessary—the horizons were clear. Just when *Dixon* and the fleet could have properly dealt with her, *Marquesa* was nowhere in sight.

Massachusetts was too far away to signal with flags, but I reckoned that since the sky behind *Dixon* was still somewhat dark when viewed from the flagship, they would be able to see our searchlight.

As if reading my mind, Belfort asked, "Orders, sir?"

"Yes, send this signal to *Massachusetts* by searchlight, if you would, Commander. 'Enemy raider, probably liner-cruiser *Marquesa*, seen steaming northerly at latitude 19° 14' N and longitude 74° 28' W at 9:13 p.m. last night. *Dixon* attacked and hit her but lost her in heavy rain. Raider unseen since then.'"

Twelve minutes later, a bright light flicked on and off several times on board *Massachusetts*.

"Signal from *Massachusetts*, sir," called down the duty signalman from his station above us. "Signal from *Dixon* acknowledged. Upon arrival at rendezvous, Captain Wake report *Massachusetts*."

I turned to Belfort. "Acknowledge the flag's signal, then signal the division: 'Alter course to zero-five-five degrees.' Reduce our speed, then signal to *Bronx*: 'Come alongside within hailing distance.' Also, you may secure the ship from general quarters and resume regular watches. I'll be in my cabin until *Bronx* gets here."

Bronx acknowledged the order, and I was heartened to see her speed up as she headed for us. I got in a precious twenty-two-minute nap in my bunk before Belfort came into my cabin and nudged my shoulder. "*Bronx* is just astern and coming alongside to port, sir."

Studying her approach from our bridge, I saw it was done well, with a minimum of corrections. I also saw no apparent signs of battle damage or reason for her failure to follow orders. Then, as her bridge came even with ours, I noticed something else. Dimm wasn't in sight. *Bronx*'s executive officer was handling the ship.

He stood on her starboard bridge wing and saluted me, then raised a speaking trumpet. "*Bronx* reporting as ordered, sir!"

Through my own trumpet I inquired, "Where is Captain Dimm?"

"Sick in his cabin, sir."

"What kind of sickness?"

"Ah . . . I don't really know, sir."

"What does your doctor say?"

There was a long pause. Then he said, "Captain Dimm has not allowed the doctor or anyone else in his cabin, sir."

It was a stunning statement. Belfort gasped. Down on the main deck, Rork glanced up at me with narrowed eyes. In the wheelhouse, the petty officers carefully avoided any reaction, but several lieutenants openly watched for their captain's response.

A wave of rage went through me at the very thought of Dimm doing such a thing, especially in wartime with the enemy close about. I wanted to go on board his ship and personally confront him right there and then, but the sea was still rough and I was short of time. The confrontation would have to wait until we reached the anchorage.

I raised my trumpet again. "I will come on board *Bronx* when we reach Mole Saint Nicolas. You will now follow us to the rendezvous, taking position astern of the column. What speed can you make?"

"Normal speed now, sir. Repairs are completed."

"I want a complete readiness report from you when I come on board at the rendezvous."

"Aye, aye, sir."

The two ships parted, with *Bronx* dropping astern of us.

Dixon's ship's bell clanged eight times, the duty boatswain's whistle shrilled, and the change of watch was called out. On the bridge, officers and men reported in and others departed, quietly spreading the word in whispers about the strange communication from *Bronx*. Everywhere I looked, furtive glances slid away from mine, and I knew the entire ship would be abuzz with speculation within minutes.

It wouldn't do to add to the gossip by letting my seething fury show, so I kept my next words as neutral as possible. "Commander Belfort, please resume our course and speed to the rendezvous point at Mole Saint Nicolas. The moment we are anchored, I'll go to *Bronx* first, then head for the flagship. Have the steam cutter ready for instant service the moment the anchor is holding. I will now take a turn around the decks before having my breakfast."

"Aye, aye, sir," he replied before turning to the officer of the deck with a comment about idlers and lollygaggers loitering about the wheelhouse.

The off-watch disappeared, the boatswain piped the crew to breakfast, and I hoped Belfort would soon find enough work for everyone to keep them too busy to engage in gossip. That was a vain hope, and I knew it. On a warship, the crew is never too busy to gossip.

27

A Silent Ship

U.S. Navy Fleet Anchorage, Mole Saint Nicolas, Haiti

Friday Morning, 22 July 1898

MOLE SAINT NICOLAS is a small, funnel-shaped bay that narrows from two miles wide at its entrance to a quarter mile near the innermost shoreline. It is surrounded by bare, rocky hills long since denuded of their trees by the native charcoal burners. The pungent haze that results from this practice across Haiti shrouds "the Black Republic" like a gaseous malaise. Mole Saint Nicolas is a depressing place in both appearance and ambience.

But it was convenient and safe enough in 1898 for American warships to have colliers come alongside and load coal while Haitian boatmen brought out tropical fruits and cured meat. For Higginson, just as important as the fuel and supplies was the cable station on shore. That crude hut linked the fleet with the transoceanic telegraph line from the Caribbean to the United States.

Massachusetts, Indiana, and the other ships of the Battle Division had already anchored and begun coaling from a flotilla of small colliers when *Dixon* led the Transport Division into the outer bay. Under the lee of the land, the water was calm, with only a slight undulating swell coming around the point. A wig-wag message from the flagship directed *Dixon* and her charges to anchor ourselves farther inside the bay near the decrepit-looking village.

The bay was crowded. Since there was little room to maneuver, I anchored *Dixon* fore and aft with her bow pointed out to sea. I signaled my subordinate captains to do likewise, and also to maintain steam in at least two boilers for a rapid departure if that should prove necessary. The transports, chartered to the Army but mastered and crewed by civilians, did a reasonably creditable job of it.

After that was accomplished, all eyes on *Dixon's* weather decks watched *Bronx* come in. I couldn't see who was conning her, but as the chain rattled out her hawsehole and she backed down on the anchor, a string of strident epithets in a familiar nasal voice blared from her bridge. Clearly, Dimm had resumed command.

Ten minutes later, accompanied by Rork, I went on board *Bronx*. After scaling the Jacob's ladder, I came face to face with the ship's executive officer on the quarterdeck. I noticed him scrutinizing the steam cutter as we came alongside and waited for a comment or accusation. He said nothing about the boat, however, only explaining in a careful monotone that Captain Dimm awaited me up on the bridge. Notably, he offered no further clarification regarding our dialogue at sunrise or the situation on board. Since others were within hearing, I didn't press him.

As I was escorted by the executive officer up the ladders to the bridge, Rork descended into the ship's interior to visit the chief petty officers' mess. To return a borrowed manual, he said straight-faced to the quarterdeck watch. That, of course, was not his true assignment.

Capt. Reginald Dimm was standing by the chart table when I arrived at the wheelhouse door. The executive officer announced me and promptly disappeared. I found that odd, but then his behavior all along had been unusual. I also noted the wheelhouse was uncommonly vacant. An ensign and several men were out on the bridge wing trying unsuccessfully to seem occupied and not to be eavesdropping through the open bridge doors.

For his part, Dimm just stood there in his whites, watching me with those dark little eyes as he wiped a rivulet of sweat from his cheek.

He didn't look sick at all to me—everybody was sweating in the heat. In fact, Dimm didn't even look tired. More than anything, he looked perturbed, as if my visit was an inconvenience.

He bypassed the usual civilities and snapped, "What is the purpose of this unexpected visit, Wake? I am very much occupied with the ship's business this morning."

"I'm glad to see you've recovered your health, Captain Dimm. I told your executive officer at dawn that I would visit your ship to receive a report on your readiness, so my presence cannot really be unexpected. Let's go to your cabin and discuss our operations. I don't have much time before I see the commodore."

He puffed up a bit and demanded, "And why can't we just discuss it right here, on my bridge?"

I kept my reply in a level tone. "Because I said so, Captain Dimm."

He let out an exasperated sigh, muttering something like "damned impertinence." Marching out the door, he said, "Follow me." At his cabin, he flung open his door, plopped down on the chair at his desk, and swiveled around to face me.

"All right, since you've been put temporarily in charge of this division of ships, you're operationally senior to me. What do you want?"

I closed the door and remained standing, looking down on him. "Captain Dimm, what is the condition of your boilers and machinery?"

He waved a hand dismissively. "They're working now. Yesterday, we had to take two of our six boilers off-line to fix leaks in the tubes and the shell. We also had to put in new seals on the outflow valves after they overheated. But it's only a temporary measure and bound to fail eventually. This tub was in terrible shape when I got her in New York. I told the Navy yard that at the time."

He paused. I said nothing.

He resumed, "And now I'm telling *you* that my chief engineer says the boilers need a complete refit at the Philadelphia Navy Yard—that's the closest place that can handle the job. But I reported all this to you when we left Santiago."

No, he hadn't. His patently thin alibi did not agree at all with my recollection of events and, in fact, was a bald-faced lie. "That's not correct," I said calmly. "Just before the fleet got under way you sent a messenger with a verbal report that you had some boiler leaks and a bad valve. All ships have that problem periodically. You reported nothing about major malfunctions or needing to go north for major repairs."

"But *I* will say that I *did* tell you, Wake," he said arrogantly, "and that *you* wouldn't let me leave this area to do the necessary maintenance. So that means *Bronx*'s inability to keep up with other ships is *your* fault, not mine."

"That would be an intentional lie, Captain Dimm," I informed him quietly.

"*No*, it is my recollection of the matter, Wake. And I don't think Higginson or Sampson will like hearing that it happened with a ship under their overall command. By the way, neither will the Secretary of the Navy in Washington or the press in New York. And considering your record for mutiny and insubordination, I've no doubt that a lot of powerful people will believe *me* rather than *you*."

He preened in appreciation of his own cleverness, but that faded when I switched topics. "This morning at sunrise your executive officer reported to me you were sick in your cabin. Are you sick or not, Captain Dimm?"

His manner became even more defiant. "Yes, I certainly *was* sick. I wasn't feeling well yesterday afternoon and retired to my cabin to rest. I got up an hour ago and feel much better this morning. What business is that of yours?"

"An hour ago? You were in bed for more than fifteen hours? Why wouldn't you allow your doctor to attend to you?"

"Because he's a quack and an idler, one of those young naval militia volunteers who have descended upon the Navy like a plague. I needed some rest, that's all. I'm fine now. In any event, as I said, it's none of your business. This is my ship and I'll sleep when I want to."

"So you stayed in your cabin the entire time your ship transited a combat zone?"

"I *told* you I was unwell. It's this damned tropical heat."

"Did you go to your bridge when you heard *Dixon* engage the enemy last night?"

"Engage the enemy? Don't be ridiculous. You fired some rounds in the dark and a rainstorm and probably don't even know what you hit. Don't make it sound like you singlehandedly fought Trafalgar last night."

"Did you or did you not go to your bridge when you heard the gunfire? If you don't answer, I'll ask your officers."

At that point, his smug arrogance gave way to a tantrum, complete with drooling spittle and pounding fist. "No, I didn't go to the damned bridge! My executive officer is fully competent to handle *basic* ship maneuvers. I rested so that I would be ready should something actually *important* come up."

"Why did your ship leave her station astern of the transports?"

"Boiler troubles, as I've just told you. And I don't like your tone and insinuation, Wake. I've about had it with your holier-than-thou attitude."

I'd had enough, too. "Dimm, you're incompetent as a commander of a warship."

He nearly jumped out of his chair. "Really? Who the hell are *you* to say that? You're *nothing*, Wake, just a jumped-up Civil War volunteer the Navy kept on to do the skullduggery no true gentleman would do. A quaint museum piece left over from thirty years ago whom no one wants around anymore. Mark my words, your days in the Navy are dwindling fast. Do yourself and everyone else a favor. Stop pestering people and retire."

Dimm's face had turned crimson, and his stylish pompadour had become a sweat-soaked mess. When his mouth began to open again, I felt the same urge I had at the dinner—a quick jab into his fat belly would end his ability to talk for a while. But he suddenly closed his mouth and sat there glaring at me.

"That was quite a performance you put on just now, Dimm," I said. "Unfortunately, I don't have the time to finish this little dialogue because Commodore Higginson is expecting me. In the meantime, coal your ship and be ready for further action. The collier will be coming alongside in an hour. I will deal with you later."

With that, I walked out of Dimm's cabin. As I descended to the main deck, I noted the ship was still unusually quiet. Cautious looks followed my progress, but no one spoke. *Bronx* was a silent ship. That boded ill.

I passed the executive officer at the quarterdeck. He gave me an apologetic glance and gestured to the quarterdeck ladder, but also said nothing. I debated delaying my report to Higginson to interview the executive officer and the engineer to get a readiness report. In the end, I decided to forgo speaking with the senior officers of *Bronx*, knowing they had their own careers to protect and doubting that any would be candid about the man who ruled their lives. No, I would hear from Rork what was really happening on board Reginald Dimm's ship.

The boatswain trilled his pipe and the side-boys saluted as I went down the side, but hesitantly, as if they were afraid to be too loud or demonstrative. Rork was waiting for me down in the steam cutter with a grim look on his face. Something was wrong. Badly wrong.

28

The View from the Lower Deck

U.S. Navy Fleet Anchorage, Mole Saint Nicolas, Haiti
Friday Morning, 22 July 1898

AS THE CUTTER HEADED toward *Massachusetts*, I went forward and sat next to Rork at the amidships thwart, just aft of the puffing and clanking engine. I learned long ago that the lower deck frequently knows far more about what is going on in a ship than the officers do. And the petty officers know more than anyone. I needed to know the real condition of *Bronx*. So, with the engine noise covering our discussion, I asked Rork what his senior petty officer pals had told him.

Rork eyed *Bronx* receding astern of us before turning to look at me. "Nothin' good, sir. 'Tis an unhappy ship, indeed. The exec's runnin' the whole shebang by himself, for the captain don't have much sea experience an' the old salts know it. An' besides that, there's nary a day goes by that the captain ain't sayin' he's sick from some bloody damn thing or another."

"You mean the captain's imagining it? Like a hypochondriac?"

"Aye, sir, that's what the lads think, though they don't use that fancy a word. They say it's nerves."

"Nerves" was the polite way to say fear. I had been wondering about that very thing.

"What about the boilers and engines? How bad are they?"

"Routine maintenance for some o' the tubes an' valve seals. The lads said they're repairable on board. The chief engineer an' the executive officer wanted to repair 'em last week, but Captain Dimm said nay, that he was goin' t' get Admiral Sampson's permission to take the ship north to get her repaired in the Navy yard. But then *Bronx* got assigned to this Puerto Rican thing under you, an' he lost his chance to leave for the States 'cause he knew you wouldn't approve it."

Rork leaned in closer, glaring at the coxswain to get him to look away.

"By the by, sir, Captain Dimm thinks you arranged for him to be subordinate to you on this Puerto Rican thing because of the argument with him that night at the admiral's dinner."

"The chiefs told you that?"

"Aye, they did."

"How the hell did they even know about that?"

"Seems the senior wardroom steward heard the exec tellin' the gunnery officer that Captain Dimm told *him* you was actin' threatenin' toward him at the dinner. Afore the end o' watch, it was all 'round *Bronx* that their captain hates you an' is out to make you look bad in front o' the brass hats up north. Chief yeoman himself typed a letter Captain Dimm wrote to Admiral Sampson about you."

"A letter about me? What did it say?"

Rork shrugged. "He wouldn't say a word o' what was in it, beyond it was bad. It was sent to *Massachusetts* this mornin' right after droppin' the hook an' afore we arrived at *Bronx*. Chief yeoman says it'll get to the admiral back at Cuba in three days—after Commodore Higginson sees it."

I shook my head in disgust. "Hell, I didn't want him under my command—or anywhere near me. Did they say what happened last night after *Bronx* got our signal?"

"You'll not like this part either, sir, not one wee bit. Seems when our signal was read, the executive officer went straightaway to the captain, but the door was locked an' he wasn't allowed inside the cabin. They commenced to yellin' at each other through the closed cabin door. Captain finally ordered him to steam slow 'cause of the engine repairs an' steer off to the nor'west. Said he didn't believe it was really a Spaniardo ship we was firin' at, an' he didn't want to get court-martialed for followin' your orders if that ship turned out to be an innocent neutral. The exec had no choice but to follow his captain's orders.

"The lads heard the whole thing from down the passageway an' thought it was bizarre as hell, but what could they do or say? Captain Dimm don't trust a soul on board. Thinks they're all out to get him. He's already hauled a bunch o' the crew up on charges. Got two seamen in the brig on bread an' water now for disrespectin' a superior officer. They smiled at Captain Dimm, an' he took it as them bein' smart aleck. The chiefs think he's completely daft."

"Would the chiefs testify in a court-martial?"

Rork gave me a look of *what, are you crazy?* "No, sir. Nary a chance."

So Dimm was more than incompetent; he was paranoid—and perhaps a drunk as well. Now that I thought about it, he'd refilled his wineglass numerous times while trying to impress his superiors at the admiral's dinner table. "Any signs of Dimm drinking a lot in his cabin, or that he was drunk last night?"

Rork wagged his head. "First thing I thought too, sir. I asked the lads, but they've seen no sign o' him drinkin' or usin' laudanum. The bloody bugger's barmy enough without 'em."

A few minutes later, I discovered the strange behavior of Captain Dimm was not my worst worry. My life was about to get very complicated, very fast.

29

Alterations and Deceptions

Flagship Massachusetts, *Mole Saint Nicolas, Haiti*
Friday Morning, 22 July 1898

I WAS QUICKLY SHOWN into Higginson's cabin, which even at midmorning was already stifling. General Miles and Commodore Higginson were sitting at the chart table intently studying a chart of the south coast of Puerto Rico. No one else was present, which I thought peculiar. I'd assumed several of the other captains would be there.

"Ah, Peter! Come on over here and join us," said Higginson as he gestured to a chair at the table. "First, let's hear about that raider you signaled us about. Then you can explain why your ships fell so far astern of us yesterday."

"She's a Spanish liner-turned-raider, sir. Our lookout and navigator only got a fleeting look at her before she disappeared in the rain last night, but I got a better look when we hit her. She's probably *La Marquesa*. I knew her before the war. We managed to hit her stern with a lucky shot that set off a secondary explosion, probably ready ammunition near her after-gun mount. That's the good news. The bad news is that we lost her."

Miles tactfully busied himself by studying a report while Higginson listened to me explain my failure. "After we hit her stern and saw flames, the raider doused the fire and launched a flaming raft as a decoy. I erroneously focused on that while the raider escaped in the heavy rain, course unknown. No sign of her since then. Could be hiding in southern Haitian waters, or backtracked south into the Caribbean, or slipped through into the Old Bahama Channel and the north coast of Cuba."

"I think most likely south and back into the Caribbean," Higginson said after a moment of thought. "We or one of the ships coming down from the States would've spotted her if she'd gone northwest to the Old Bahama Channel or northeast around Haiti and back toward San Juan. Maybe she'll attack our fleet auxiliary ships at Siboney."

"Perhaps, sir, but they're heavily guarded by Admiral Sampson's main body of warships. She could exit the Caribbean near the Virgin Islands and hit the Eastern Seaboard. Her captain has a lot of options."

"Yes, that he does." Higginson drummed his fingers on the table, then stopped. "And now, what about that delay in keeping up with my division. What happened?"

I kept the answer short. My admission of tactical failure was bad enough. I wasn't going to embarrass the Navy, Higginson, or myself in front of General Miles with a report on Dimm's behavior. "Boiler and pressure valve problems on *Bronx*. They are temporarily repaired now, and she is functional. The division's speed will be at least twelve knots. And when you have a moment, sir, I'd like to talk to you about a personnel issue."

Higginson's face tightened when I mentioned *Bronx*, but he simply replied, "All right, we will do that later. Right now, I need to tell you that your assignment has been altered."

My own face tightened, which made the commodore smile. "Don't worry, I think you'll appreciate your new mission. You'll be on independent assignment—and everybody in the Navy knows you like that sort of thing just fine. General, why don't you let Captain Wake in on the new overall plan, then I'll give him the details."

"Certainly, Commodore," said Miles, putting his papers down. "This is partly a result of your earlier advice to me, Captain Wake. Interestingly, it corroborated the information from some of my people who have reconnoitered Puerto Rico. So, after much thought, I've changed the plan of invasion. The landing will not be at Fajardo. It will be at Guánica on the south coast."

Miles noted my reaction. "Yes, I know it's a big change, but there's a very good reason for it. I've discovered that the original plan somehow got out to the press up in Washington, and the idiots printed it. Now the whole world knows about Fajardo. Evidently, there are even press boats running around that coast waiting for us to arrive!"

The general's tone was calm, but his eyes were angry. Then the shadow of a smile appeared. "So I'm going to let all of them continue to think the Fajardo landing will take place as originally conceived. We're not letting knowledge of the real landing place slip out to anyone beyond the few who absolutely need to know. You are one of those few. The war and Navy secretaries and the president up in Washington, Admiral Sampson at Cuba, and the press mob everywhere will find out *after* we've landed at Guánica. We are going to execute a grand deception, Captain Wake, and make a rapid landing of my forces at Guánica before any effective defense can be mounted. A fait accompli."

General Miles' sudden change in strategy was a valid decision with which I agreed, but the deception was something else entirely! I was taken completely aback. The audacity was impressive, but the potential consequences were enormous. Deliberately deceive the service secretaries and the *president*? If the invasion went badly—like the recent one in Cuba had—Miles and Higginson would be court-martialed for insubordination, or worse. Then I realized Miles and Higginson wouldn't be the only scapegoats at the court-martial. *Good Lord, these two are dragging me into this.*

"What are my orders, sir?" I warily asked Higginson, thinking about my retirement pension in three years and Maria's dreams for our future.

"First, Peter, what is your fuel state?"

"Our bunkers are three-quarters full, sir. I was going to coal this morning with the other ships. *Bronx* is about to start as we speak. Then *Dixon* will go after her."

He shook his head. "No, your ship will have priority on coaling. I'll have the collier signaled to switch from *Bronx* to *Dixon*. I want your bunkers topped off as soon as possible. Let's see, you'll need only a quarter of your bunker capacity. That should take about three hours, correct?"

I pictured all hands toiling nonstop in this heat. "Yes, sir. It'll be difficult, but we can do it in three hours," I replied.

"Good," he said, then called for a staff officer and directed him to make the signal. Turning back to me, he said, "After coaling, *Dixon* will get under way immediately at best speed for Guánica. We've been told that the locals will not resist a U.S. landing, and the Spanish have no large army or militia formations in the area."

"If you get under way by," he paused to consult his pocket watch, "high noon, what would you estimate your time of arrival at Guánica to be?"

I quickly did the math for a continuous 18-knot transit of approximately 480 miles, the last 80 of which would be against the trade wind and current in the Mona Passage. "At full speed in good weather, and going by way of the north Hispaniola coast, then down through the Mona Passage, *Dixon* can be there in thirty hours, sir. Tomorrow evening at six o'clock."

"Very good. Once at Guánica you will connect with the anti-Spanish locals ashore. General Miles has the name of a contact for you. You will ascertain the strength of the anti-Spanish sentiment and confirm that the Spanish army has no major forces in the area, and also that Guánica Bay is actually conducive to landing troops there.

"You will *not* tell the locals *when* we are coming, of course. If anything, lead them to think that this is only a diversionary probe still several weeks away."

"Aye, aye, sir."

General Miles took over. "Once ashore, my troops will go east twenty miles along the coastal road to capture Ponce and its harbor. We need the docks there to efficiently offload the follow-on reinforcements and supplies. Once in possession of Ponce, the Army can then send fully supplied columns across the southern half of the island to secure it, and then eventually head north through the mountains for the capital at San Juan."

Miles curtly added, "This invasion army will *not* be supplied in slipshod fashion across beaches," a pointed remark about General Shafter's campaign in Cuba. The invasion army in Cuba had been ashore a month and was only now using the dock facilities in Santiago to efficiently bring supplies ashore. For most of that month the beach at Siboney and that miserable trail inland had been the only supply route—a logistics disaster. The Puerto Rican invasion would have none of those supply liabilities. The new plan sounded much smarter than the Fajardo beach landing, which would have echoed Siboney.

"Yes, sir, I understand that completely. How long do I have at Guánica to assess the situation before the landing force arrives?"

"Not long at all, Peter," said Higginson. "General Miles and his staff are transferring to *Massachusetts* this morning. The squadron will get under way before dawn tomorrow morning, the twenty-third, and rendezvous with you five miles offshore of Guánica at midnight of the twenty-fourth. That gives you between 6 p.m. tomorrow and midnight the next night to assess the situation and ensure a safe landing.

"When we arrive, you will report your findings, and the general will make his final decision on landing at Guánica. If it's *yes*, the troops will go ashore at dawn on the twenty-fifth, before the Spanish have time to react to our presence."

"Aye, aye, sir. And what of the ships in my Transport Division, sir?"

"As you depart this anchorage at noon, you will signal your ships that you are on independent assignment and that each captain will immediately come to the flagship for new orders."

"Aye, aye, sir. Since I don't have much time to get things ready on *Dixon*, may I have that moment with you now, to go over the personnel issue?"

Miles got the hint and stood. "I've got quite a lot of things to accomplish as well, gentlemen. I'll see you in a little while, Commodore. Good luck, Captain Wake. Much depends on your assignment."

After Miles departed, Higginson wearily said, "All right, Peter. It's Dimm, isn't it?"

30

The Burden of Command

Flagship Massachusetts, *Mole Saint Nicolas, Haiti*
Friday Morning, 22 July 1898

"Yes, sir. It *is* about Captain Dimm. I've lost confidence in his ability to command his ship."

Higginson leaned back in his chair and took a long breath. "That's quite an accusation, Peter. Tell me why."

I kept my explanation concise and factual and limited to my personal observations. I did not include the information Rork had received from his counterparts in *Bronx*. I knew Higginson had already received Dimm's letter of complaint about me, but I said nothing about that either. As I spoke, Commodore Higginson intensely studied me. When I finished, he took a moment and stared down at the chart, then looked back up at me.

"This is bad timing, Peter. I need every ship I have. But I also can't ignore this. Are you willing to put your allegations in writing, with a request for action on them?"

"Yes, sir, I am. I will send you a report before my ship gets under way recommending Captain Dimm's immediate relief from command and transfer to a staff position outside the war zone."

"Will *Bronx*'s executive officer support your claim?"

"Sir, I've briefly spoken with him about his captain's behavior in order to ascertain the situation, but not about his captain's competency or any future decisions regarding it. Judging by his behavior and what he said, no, I do not think the executive officer will go out on a limb and support my view. He'll remain neutral. That's to be expected. He's still relatively young, and you and I both know that sort of thing might end his career."

"Hmm, I seem to recall a similar situation in your distant past, when you made a difficult decision, then successfully defended it. That ended reasonably well."

His description of my court-martial was rosier than my memory of it. "My career survived, yes, sir, but rumor and innuendo have followed me ever since. Some people still believe what I did back in sixty-nine was mutiny. Dimm is one of them."

"Yes, well, back to the case at hand. Since Captain Dimm only recently arrived in this theater of operations, I have no independent understanding or evidence of his incompetence, or of *Bronx*'s state of operational readiness. So any corrections of the problem will be based completely on your report. I presume you know that Dimm has influential supporters in Congress and the administration, and they'll come after you for instigating this."

They would come after him, too. But Higginson, a decisive and respected officer, didn't mention it. "Yes, sir, I do. Dimm pointed that out himself. That's one of the burdens of command, Commodore."

"Can *Bronx*'s executive officer take temporary command?"

I recalled the crisp ship handling when he'd had the bridge, then remembered the man's reticent manner just two hours earlier. "He is apparently competent enough to work the ship, sir, but a new commanding officer would bring fresh energy to the ship and crew. There are some senior staff officers with Admiral Sampson who could take command and do a good job."

Higginson nodded somberly. It would have been simpler and faster to raise the executive officer into command. What I suggested involved more people and far more time.

"Very well, then. Get your ship coaled, get the report sent to me, and then get under way for Guánica by noon. Once I read your report, I will make the decision."

I noted he never mentioned Dimm's letter about me. I wanted to ask what was in it, but didn't, and merely said, "Yes, sir."

The commodore rose and reached out a hand. "Thank you for bringing the Dimm matter to my attention. And good luck at Puerto Rico, Peter. I'll see you there soon."

On my way out of his cabin, Higginson called out to me, "Oh, and Peter . . ."

I reentered. "Yes, sir?"

"You should know that General Miles specifically asked for you on this mission. He remembered your advice at Cuba and is impressed with you. If this Guáncia operation goes well, it's your chance to change your reputation with some of the old guard up at the Navy Department. And it wouldn't hurt to have a victory under your belt when Dimm starts his revenge. I think you know what I mean."

"I do indeed, sir. We'll get the job done."

By the time I returned to *Dixon*, Higginson's orders were already being carried out. The collier was alongside with her booms swung over the coal chutes on our main deck. Lines of men were lugging giant sacks of coal from the cargo nets and emptying them down the coal chutes into the bunkers below. The entire main deck was coated with coal dust, and everyone, officer and enlisted alike, looked almost African.

Belfort met me on the main deck looking perplexed. I could tell he was wondering the reason for the sudden swirl of action and attention to *Dixon*.

"I'll fill you in on everything, John, but first I have an important report to complete for the commodore. Come to my quarters in an hour."

Once at my desk, I called for my clerk's typewriter to be brought to me. Normally, the clerk would take dictation and type out the document. But this situation had to be kept confidential, so I pecked away on the Remington's keys myself.

Commodore F. J. Higginson, USN
U.S. Battleship *Massachusetts*, Mole Saint Nicolas, Haiti
Reference: Capt. R. Dimm, USN, Cruiser *Bronx*
22 July 1898
Commodore Higginson,
Sir,

I regret that it is my duty to report that Capt. Reginald Dimm, USN, commanding officer of the cruiser *Bronx*, a warship under my command in the Transport Division of the Puerto Rican Invasion Squadron, which is under your squadron command, is unfit to retain his command. I make this assessment by reason of the following information:

1. On the afternoon of 21 July 1898, *Bronx* was assigned by your order to assist *Dixon* in convoying four troop transports through a war zone off the island of Cuba toward the island of Puerto Rico, via the USN supply anchorage at Mole Saint Nicolas, Haiti. This entire division of six ships was under my command on board *Dixon*. Though all the ships were fast enough to make fourteen knots, the convoy was reduced to steaming at only eight knots because *Bronx* reported ongoing boiler maintenance problems.

2. On the afternoon of 21 July 1898, while engaged in the aforementioned convoy duty, Captain Dimm went into his cabin feeling "unwell." He did not allow either his executive officer or his ship's doctor inside the cabin. Captain Dimm stayed alone in his cabin for more than fifteen hours, refusing assistance and refusing to exercise command of his ship.

3. Late in the night of 21 July 1898, *Dixon* was engaged in a naval battle with an enemy ocean raider–cruiser. During this naval action, Captain Dimm did not go to and remain on the bridge of *Bronx*, though his own ship and the convoy were in peril. Instead, he stayed in his cabin and left control of his ship to his executive officer.

4. After the battle, in the dark early morning hours of 22 July 1898, with the enemy raider still in the area, Captain Dimm, still locked in his cabin, ordered *Bronx* away from her assigned convoy guard station to a position far astern of the convoy. The ship thus was not in the proper position with the convoy when the sun rose later that morning. This was a direct violation of my signaled orders to *Bronx* to maintain her position guarding the convoy. The explanation later given was "boiler troubles."

5. On the morning of 22 July 1898, once the convoy had arrived at the squadron anchorage at Haiti, I personally visited *Bronx* and found Captain Dimm in apparently good health on the bridge. I asked him to explain his failure to command his ship during a naval action and follow his superior's maneuvering orders. Captain Dimm was surly and insubordinate, failing to provide any answers other than that he had confidence in his executive officer's ability to run the ship; his boilers were defective and needed a major refit outside the war zone at Philadelphia; he didn't believe *Dixon*'s fight was an actual naval action; and he had been feeling unwell earlier but was now in good condition and in command.

Based on these facts, it is my opinion that Captain Dimm has been derelict in his duty to properly maintain his ship, has failed to follow orders in combat, has been insubordinate to his superior officer, and is clearly unable to continue in command of *Bronx*. I have lost confidence in Captain Dimm's ability to command *Bronx* and recommend that an officer of suitable rank and experience be immediately assigned to relieve him. I also recommend that Captain Dimm be reassigned to administrative staff duties ashore in an area outside the war zone.

Respectfully submitted,

Capt. P. Wake, USN

Cruiser *Dixon*

Senior Officer, Transport Division

Puerto Rico Invasion Squadron

The reader will note that, as in my verbal report to Commodore Higginson, I included none of the information Rork obtained from *Bronx*'s senior petty officers. Not having any confidence that anyone on *Bronx* would testify, I included only information of which I had personal knowledge.

Chief Rork personally delivered the sealed envelope to Commodore Higginson and stood by waiting for a reply while the commodore read the report. He was dismissed without a response. Before leaving *Massachusetts*, however, Rork stopped for a chat with her chief yeoman and learned that about half an hour before he presented my report to the commodore, Captain Dimm had received a summons to report to the flagship at 1 p.m. for a meeting with Higginson.

As we steamed past *Bronx* at noon, our signal flags snapping in the wind, I saw my signal being reported to Dimm on the bridge wing. He stood there staring at me, no doubt plotting his revenge. As we rounded the rock-bound point of Cap du Mole and felt the first swells roll under us, I turned away from *Bronx* and Reginald Dimm and dismissed them from my mind.

I had much bigger things to worry about.

31

The "Conversation"

Room 247, State, War, and Navy Building, Washington, D.C.
Thursday, 10 October 1901

S MITH COULD BARELY CONTAIN his self-righteous indignation. "So, after being prevented from physically attacking Captain Dimm at the admiral's victory dinner, you decided to destroy his reputation and career by slandering him in your report."

"Is that a question or a statement, Captain Smith?" I calmly inquired, which agitated him even more.

"A question!" he blurted out. "And you'd damned well better answer it!"

"Very well, then. You are wrong on both accounts, Captain Smith. First, I was not *prevented* from attacking Captain Dimm at the admiral's dinner. I *decided* not to. Second, my report on Captain Dimm's lack of ability to command contained no slander—only what I had personally observed. The proper term is *libel*, by the way. Slander is verbal. Libel is written."

"It was innuendo and opinion!"

"No, it was completely factual," I countered. "I included no opinions from anyone else. I can assure you it would've been far worse if I had. And at the conclusion of my report, I likewise included only my

155

own professional assessment and recommendations. Indeed, I think I was remarkably kind in recommending only a transfer and not a court-martial for dereliction or cowardice."

Smith's nostrils flared at those words, and Caldhouse twitched his hands with a worried look in his eyes—the informal "conversation" was getting out of control.

"We need to get back on the continuing narrative of Captain Wake," Pentwaller grumbled. "I want to know what happened next. We will return to the issue of the report on Captain Dimm later."

"Yes, sir," I acknowledged as Smith glowered at me.

"Now, where were we, Captain Wake?" asked Pentwaller before nodding his head in recollection. "Oh, yes, you were about to perform your mission at that village in Puerto Rico."

"Yes, sir. The clandestine preinvasion reconnaissance mission at Guánica."

Smith muttered under his breath, "And to *intentionally deceive* your president and commander in chief."

I had to admit—inwardly only, of course—that Captain Smith was right about that. I ignored him, turning my attention solely toward the admirals. "As I was about to say . . ."

32

The Enchanted Isle

Guánica Bay, Puerto Rico
Saturday Evening, 23 July 1898

ALMOST FIVE MILES ASTERN of us, *Dixon* lay wallowing in the Caribbean swells, awaiting our return in four hours. If we didn't make it back by five o'clock in the morning, Belfort was to take the ship well over the horizon to the south and return for us the following night.

We were fortunate to have low clouds obscuring the quarter moon in the eastern sky, allowing us to proceed in darkness as the steam cutter neared the bay. The night air was calm, but the sea wasn't. I could hear the surf breaking on the dark, rocky shores on both sides of the channel ahead. I was thankful because it would mask the sound of us chugging toward the narrow entrance to the bay, which I estimated to be two hundred yards ahead of us.

The square shape of a structure on a cliff came into view dead ahead—the Guánica lighthouse at the mouth of the bay, unlit for the duration of the war. I figured Spanish lookouts would be posted there. I turned to the large form behind me. "It's time."

Rork nodded, then whispered to the engineer beside him and the seamen forward, "Stop the engine. Stand by your oars, lads."

The engineer slowly bled off the boiler steam as the sailors forward gently set their muffled oar looms down into the locks. The cutter slowed rapidly once the propeller stopped, and I realized we had an ebb tide to deal with.

Rork hissed, "Right, lads, give way together. Nice an' easy an' steady. An' keep it bloody *quiet*."

The cutter crept forward toward the gap I could now see between the cliffs. The opening widened as we got closer until I could see it was the eight-hundred-foot-wide passage I'd memorized on the chart. I looked up at the lighthouse on the cliff to the right, expecting the inevitable shout of alarm or challenge, or a gunshot.

Maybe they've sent the alert quietly, I worried, *so as not to let us know they see us, and draw us farther into a trap. That's what I'd do. If they open fire, we're sitting ducks in this boat.*

The boat was heavy, the ebb was stronger than I'd first realized, and the men were pulling hard. The sound of the surf crashing on either side of us blotted out the swish of the oars, but I couldn't imagine that even in the darkness the lookouts wouldn't see a twenty-seven-foot cutter passing beneath them into the bay.

We finally came abreast of the hilltop lighthouse and then slowly passed it, the ebb tide even stronger here where it funneled through the passage. The men strained even harder, the oars bending with every stroke.

It took another forty-two minutes to fight that ebb one mile to the open bay and the thick mangrove jungle west of the beach of Guánica. As we neared the beach, I made out fishing skiffs drawn up on the sand. I knew the actual village lay a quarter mile north of the beach.

There was a crucial component to our plan. General Miles had confided that his spy in prewar Puerto Rico, a U.S. Army captain named Whitney, had heard about a bakery owner in the village, Pablo Mateo Cordero, who was disaffected with the Spanish regime. Cordero was an older man with influence in the area. Whitney had never personally met Cordero but was confident the information was reliable. My job was to find Cordero, and from him, to ascertain if the political and military situation in the area was favorable for an American landing.

We hid the cutter in the red mangrove shallows. The boat crew stayed in the cutter as Rork and I went over the bow to slosh through the shallows to shore. After a brief search we found an animal path meandering east through the mangroves, which were full of hungry mosquitoes and no-see-ums. The path took us through the mangrove forest to the beach where the boats were drawn up.

Near the boats we found four crude huts and a frame shack with a pole in front from which drooped a ragged Spanish flag. So far, we'd seen no one. Not even a dog had challenged our presence. We started north on the cart road.

The village seemed to be at a crossroads where a cow path coming from the west intersected with the cart road, which continued north into the hills. There were no lights showing, no movement among the shacks and huts, and no sounds other than the occasional snore emanating from a hut. The place was much smaller than I had expected, perhaps two hundred inhabitants at most.

Rork and I stayed in the shadows, my plan being to examine the storefronts until I saw Cordero's name painted on the glass front window of a *panadería*—a bakery. Many owners lived above their shops, and I hoped Señor Cordero did too.

Naturally, while Rork and I hoped for the best, we were prepared for the worst. Besides the Spencer 12-gauge pump-action shotgun in my right hand, I had my Merwin-Hulbert .44-caliber, six-shot revolver with the very useful "skull crusher" grip in a holster inside my belt. Rork carried his beloved pair of Model 1861 Navy Colt .36-caliber revolvers tucked away in his belt along with a cutlass, and his 1887 Winchester 12-gauge lever-action shotgun was in his good right hand.

We were ready for anything, but there seemed no need for such an arsenal. The entire village was peaceful; even the ubiquitous Puerto Rican dogs were asleep. It seemed impossible there was a war going on.

My initial plan to find the bakery went by the board when I discovered there was no glass in the windows of the few shops, only louvered shutters, which were closed. But there were some rudimentary signboards. We edged along the main street, and near the end of the line of stores finally found the bakery. There was no sign, but the residual smell of yeast gave it away. A simple apartment was perched above. In the alleyway beside the bakery, a crude stairway rose to the dwelling's door.

A gap in the clouds allowed the quarter moon to show through, and I consulted my watch. It was a little before three o'clock in the morning. I wondered what time Cordero began his baking for the day. We were already behind my self-imposed schedule. The interview with Cordero would have to be brief because I had no intention of missing our rendezvous with the ship and remain ashore—or drift around at sea—until the next night. I crept up the stairs, testing each step for creaks. Rork followed, his head swiveling to spot any adversaries.

At that moment, our good luck ended and Fate evened the odds.

Just as I was about to knock on the door, the clouds thinned and the moonlight revealed our presence to a large black dog stretched out just down the alley. His huge head lazily turned toward us, but he made no protest.

Then the stairs creaked under Rork's foot. It was enough to awaken the beast completely. He leaped to his feet emitting deep growls. The growling turned into barking, which broke the still night. The dog lumbered to the bottom of the steps, where it stopped and stared up at us.

A neighbor yelled for the dog to shut up. It did stop barking, but the snarling got worse. It began climbing slowly up the steps, bared teeth stark white in the moonlight.

Inside the room above us, a man cursed in Spanish and stumbled into something. I saw through a window's thin curtains a lamp being lit. The man clomped heavily toward the door, cursing the dog the whole time. I knocked on the door. The man now cursed whoever was bothering him in the middle of the night.

The dog got halfway up the steps and stopped, ready to attack. Rork, an avowed dog lover, sighed and asked me, "Kill him?"

He had his cutlass out. Something in me rebelled against logic and I said, "Not yet."

The door lurched open. A thin, gray-haired, stubble-chinned man clad in a nightshirt appeared in the doorway. He stopped in mid-epithet when he saw us. The moonlight was glinting off Rork's blade. Rork quickly returned it to his belt and tried to smile benignly. The man stepped back behind the door, looking like he was going to slam it shut and scream for help. I put my foot against the door and held out my hands in a gentle gesture of friendly greeting.

"Señor Cordero?" I asked as politely as the circumstances would admit. By now, more dogs around the neighborhood were barking in angry competition. Several other voices were swearing at them to stop. A hundred feet away, light suddenly filled the alley as a man walked out of his shack into the open. A nearby window glowed yellow. The whole damn village was waking up.

"*Si*," he said warily, intently studying our uniforms. "*¿Norteamericanos?*"

A rock flew through the air toward the dog, thrown by the man in the alley, who was now advancing in our direction. *How can he not see us on the stairs? What will he do when he does?* I sped up my whispered introduction.

"*Si, señor, de la armada de los Estados Unidos.*"

Cordero peeked out from behind the door and replied in excellent English. "The American Navy? Has the invasion started?" He reached for my hand. "Welcome to Puerto Rico—the Enchanted Isle!"

At a heated shout from the alley Cordero dragged me through the doorway and frantically motioned for Rork to follow. As our impromptu host closed the door and bolted it, the man outside shouted again, demanding to know exactly who we were.

"Shush. Stay quiet," Cordero warned us as he blew out the oil lamp. "That fool is a Spanish loyalist. Fortunately, he is still drunk at this time of night. Tomorrow I will tell him he was sleepwalking again and waking up the neighbors." He laughed at his ingeniousness. Then he let out the same kind of sigh Rork had moments before. "However, my new American friends, I suppose eventually we will have to kill him."

That comment and Cordero's instantaneous decision to bring us inside told me a lot about this man. "Señor Cordero, there isn't much time." I introduced myself and Rork, then said, "Let's get to work."

"Do not worry, Captain Wake. I am ready," he announced. "We have waited a long time for you."

The lamp stayed out as Cordero answered my questions, giving me an overall picture of the Guánica area that I committed to memory as he spoke. The fellow was remarkably thorough. He reported on Spanish police and military forces, pro-Spanish loyalists in the Puerto Rican population, pro-American people who wanted to join our country, and those others who wanted a totally independent country of their own. According to Cordero, the loyalists were a minority, as were those seeking total independence. Pro-Americans were the majority and included prominent citizens.

When he mentioned that he'd been a harbor pilot years ago and volunteered to be the pilot for our ships, I said, "Thank you for the offer of assistance. When can you be ready?"

There was no hesitation. "I told you. We have been waiting a long time. As soon as I am dressed properly, I am ready to do my duty."

I decided to alter my plan and bring a guest to my meeting with Miles and Higginson. "Then come with us right now, Señor Cordero."

33

Explaining Guánica

Flagship Massachusetts, *off the South Coast of Puerto Rico*
Sunday Midnight, 24 July 1898

THE NEXT NIGHT IT WAS also dark and cloudy when Higginson's ships arrived at the rendezvous position well south of the coast, right on time at midnight. Cordero stood beside me on *Dixon's* bridge watching them emerge from the black Caribbean night. He was almost overwhelmed by the sight.

"This is the beginning of our liberation," he said in solemn awe. "We will finally be free!"

Cordero's passion was understandable. According to Whitney's information, he had been a vocal proponent for American annexation for twenty-five years and had been harassed and threatened by Spanish loyalists for it. But I'd already seen enthusiasm in this war turn into arrogance, then disaster. I couldn't shake the vivid memories of the failures in Cuba and their toll in American lives.

"There is still a lot to do," I reminded him. "Danger comes at every turn in this kind of operation, and not always from the enemy. We have to stay clear-eyed about this."

He swept his hand across the horizon, where a dozen large black shapes were already in sight. His words came out in hushed awe. "But

Captain, your navy is powerful. The Spanish will certainly run when they see these ships."

I was about to tell him that the Spanish didn't run from us at Cuba and made us bleed for every yard gained, but Belfort stepped over to us. "Sir, lamp signal from the flagship: 'Captain Wake report to Commodore. Steam cutter is alongside and ready to take you.'"

"Very well, Commander," I acknowledged. "Follow me, Señor Cordero. We're going over to meet the commodore and the general to brief them on the situation ashore. Remember, *they* will make the decision whether to land here or not."

"Yes, yes, of course, sir," replied Cordero quickly. That's what he *said*, but I could tell his mind was fixed on visions of victory and liberation. How could it not be, with the battleship and cruisers and transports he could see all around us?

As we came up to the steel cliff of the flagship's hull, my Puerto Rican companion nervously brushed at his threadbare suit. After quickly rendered arrival honors by the quarterdeck watch, the junior officer of the watch led us below. Señor Cordero had been impressed by *Dixon*, but the enormous *Massachusetts* had him gaping in wonder. The massive guns, rumbling engines, immaculate Marine guard, clanging bells, hundreds of men busily transiting endless ladders, hatchways, and passageways all combined to astonish him. The old fellow was, for the first time since we'd met, speechless.

At the doorway of Commodore Higginson's private quarters I told Cordero to wait out in the passageway with the Marine sentry. A flag lieutenant ushered me inside. Three chairs were arranged around a small table displaying the chart of the coast. An oil lamp overhead swung slowly on its chains while an electric light on the bedside bulkhead cast its glare. Miles and Higginson rose from their chairs and shook my hand. They appeared tired and tense.

The commodore wasted no time. "Did you find the contact? Is our element of surprise compromised?"

"I did, sir, and your information was correct. Pablo Cordero is the village baker and a staunch supporter of Puerto Rico becoming

American territory. He gave me a full briefing on the situation. And no, sir, we are not compromised. According to Cordero, everyone in this area still thinks the invasion will be at Fajardo."

"Good," Higginson said with evident relief.

"I brought Cordero out to *Dixon* with me so he couldn't, even inadvertently, give away our operation," I continued. "He is also a former harbor pilot for Guánica and has volunteered his services. He's waiting outside in the passageway, if needed. His English is quite good; he learned it while dealing with Americans as a cargo broker in Ponce. He does, however, tend to ramble when talking."

The commodore shook his head. "We've no time for rambling, Peter, so leave him with the staff for now. Just tell us what exactly you've learned of the situation ashore."

"And begin with the type and number of enemy forces," interjected Miles.

"Yes, sir. There are no significant Spanish regular forces in Guánica itself, sir, only a platoon of loyalist militia. The town is about a quarter mile north of the bay at the end of a cart path leading up from the beach. It has maybe 150 to 200 people and is surrounded by sugarcane fields. The beach itself had fishing boats drawn up the slope and a few huts. One of them is a customs house—just a shack, really—with a Spanish flag on a pole. There's a small boat dock in front of the customs shack, but it's in shallow water and will need to be lengthened out into deeper water to handle all the men and matériel we have to bring ashore. It will also need to be widened because it's only three planks wide."

"This doesn't sound promising," muttered Miles.

"I agree, sir. The main beach needs to be secured, but there's another place better for disembarking troops and materiel." I pointed to the northeast corner of the bay on the chart. "To the east of that main beach, a small, shallow stream comes down from the hills and empties into the bay. And farther over to the east of that stream and curving around to the south is another beach running north and south on the east side of the bay with a steeper slope. It also has a couple of fishermen's huts and some boats, but the dock is slightly larger and juts out into deeper water. That dock would be easier to adapt for your needs. I recommend that location as the primary disembarkation and supply offloading place."

I anticipated his next question and answered it in advance. "From that beach, a cart road follows the eastern bank of the stream. A landing force can ford the stream to get west into Guánica or follow the cart road north to where it meets the main east-west road. Moving east along that road will take you to Yauco, and eventually, Ponce."

"Is this second beach suitable for ships' boats to land troops directly on the sand?" asked Miles.

"Yes, sir. It's wide enough for about a dozen boats to beach abreast at a time. Boats with cargo can use the dock. Tidal range is a little less than two feet, so that won't be a problem. There is some surge in the bay from the southeast winds right now, but not much."

Higginson put his finger on the chart. "Depth of water in the bay? What size ships can get in there?"

"We sounded the entrance and the eastern bay. Twenty-five feet is the minimum in the middle of the entrance and the eastern bay. There is shoal water on the bay's northern side and western end. It's four to five feet deep off the northern main beach, and ten feet near the eastern landing beach. The big transports will have to loiter close offshore and disembark their troops into boats from there, but smaller troopships and gunboats can maneuver inside the bay and get within two hundred yards of the northern beach, and much closer to the eastern beach."

He nodded his acknowledgment and I continued. "Commodore, I suggest sending *Gloucester* in as direct gunfire support for the landing. She draws only twelve feet and can get relatively close to shore. Her guns can reach all probable targets once she's inside. Captain Wainwright is just the man for it."

"What about Spanish lookouts and artillery batteries?" the commodore asked.

"There are no artillery batteries reported, sir. The lighthouse on the cliffs to the right side of the bay's entrance is their lookout point. The weather for dawn looks to be clearing, and they're likely to spot our ships at daylight. Cordero says the lookouts communicate via relay messengers, who run the two miles from the lighthouse along the cliffs on the eastern side of the bay to the main beach and then up to the town. From there, the alarm will be carried by fast rider to Yauco, about seven miles inland and to the east, and the news will be sent by telegraph to Ponce and San Juan."

Miles bent forward over the chart. "I understand this place called Yauco is where there are more Spanish troops."

"Yes, sir. There is an undersized local militia battalion stationed at Yauco, with only a few men on duty at any time at their barracks while the others are at home. I estimate the barracks should get word within half an hour, at the very quickest, of the lighthouse lookout first sighting our ships. Once the militia force is called out, armed, and formed up—which I estimate will take an hour, at least—it will take them another two hours to march to Guánica. So, I figure we have about three hours to land, secure both beaches, capture the town, set up defenses, get the dock strengthened, and get our troops on the road for Yauco."

"You say the dock at the eastern beach needs strengthening. How much work would that be?" asked Higginson.

"Three or four hours of basic work by military engineers should do it. As for lumber, we're in luck. Cordero reports there is a house being built near that beach, with a stack of planks and beams next to it."

Miles curtly accepted the good fortune. "Fine. I've got a company of engineers and a pontoon dock with me, so that can get accomplished rapidly. What is the condition of the main road from Guánica to Yauco, and from there to Ponce?"

"This is the dry windward coast of Puerto Rico, sir, so the summer rains aren't as prevalent as elsewhere. According to Cordero, the road to Ponce, via Yauco and Guayanilla, is in good condition and can sustain a column of troops and wagons."

"And what of the population? What does this man say we can expect from them?"

"He told me that most Puerto Ricans in the southern half of the island are ambivalent about the war, and he can't be certain which side they'll support. Many of the merchants want the island to be American, and Cordero gave me a list of eight of them in the Guánica area. Some Puerto Ricans, particularly in the cities, want the island to be completely independent, while the Catholic Church and some of the large landowners want it to stay under Spain. The local militia leaders are, of course, Spanish loyalists."

"So, we don't really know if they will fight us, do we?"

"According to Mr. Cordero, there are no Spanish regulars at Guánica, and the local militia won't resist. Elsewhere inland, you're correct, sir—we don't know for sure. There might be considerable resistance. But remember, the most effective of the Puerto Rican militia units were called up and sent to fight against the rebels over in Cuba last year. I faced them in fights ashore at Siboney and Guásimas, and I can report that they were pretty solid. The militia left in Puerto Rico now, however, is generally not of that quality. Cordero thinks they might run, but I think he's being overly optimistic for battalion- and larger-sized units. Their national and personal honor is a stake, and that's a serious thing for the Spanish."

Miles looked up from the chart. "I see. So, if I do decide to invade here at dawn, do you have any suggestions on how exactly I should conduct operations ashore in this part of Puerto Rico, Captain Wake?"

I didn't expect that question.

34

The Stick and the Carrot

Flagship Massachusetts, *off the South Coast of Puerto Rico*

Sunday, Midnight, 24 July 1898

HIGGINSON SHOT ME A wary glance then shrugged as if to say, *go ahead and tell him*. I knew Miles was a much different general than Shafter, so I decided to be candid.

"This invasion must be fast and overwhelming, sir. Not methodical and plodding. Your troops have been cooped up on crowded transports for days, some of them for weeks. Many are seasick and not at peak physical condition. They are not used to boat work or landing on hostile beaches. Because of this, even a small enemy force could inflict casualties out of proportion to their number."

Miles nodded his agreement and I went on.

"The Army's landings in Cuba at Daiquiri and Siboney were unopposed. The soldiers simply waded ashore and walked inland because the Cuban army had already cleared those areas of enemy forces. We won't have that here. And, of course, there are the inevitable drowning and equipment mishaps like those we saw when our soldiers landed in Cuba. In addition, unlike at Cuba, the men for your initial landing are inexperienced volunteers, not regulars."

"And your recommendation to solve that?" Miles asked flatly.

I thought I detected a tinge of resentment in this comment. He probably wouldn't like my suggestion, but I figured it didn't matter at that point.

"General, I recommend you use a naval landing force to seize the beaches and the village. We constantly train our sailors and Marines to accomplish just these sorts of things. They are well armed, experienced in boat work, and in good physical shape. Once they've established the beachhead perimeter, land your engineers, strengthen and enlarge the eastern dock with the pontoon, then land the troops and push inland *quickly*."

Miles didn't look as angry as I'd expected. "I can see the merits of that," he said to Higginson. Then he turned his attention back to me. "Please continue, Captain."

"It is vital that the Spanish do not have time to set up defenses. Respond to any real enemy resistance with naval gunfire and wipe them out. *Gloucester*'s guns can accurately reach two miles inland. That is the stick." I paused to let him consider that. "But General Miles, it is just as vital to remember the carrot. That will be far more important to the American invasion in the long run."

His eyes fixed on mine. "And what exactly would the carrot be?"

"Convince the Puerto Rican people you *respect them* and want to gain their support. It must be more than just through written and spoken words. It must be through actions. That didn't happen in Cuba."

I didn't go further into Shafter's failures at Santiago or his humiliation of the Cubans. It would have been counterproductive. Miles knew full well what had happened there, but he and Shafter were "Old Army" colleagues. I was Navy, an outsider, and had already pushed the issue far enough.

The general studied me for an instant, then said, "You're right, Captain Wake. That *didn't* happen in Cuba. The campaign for Puerto Rico will be very different."

"I'm sure it will be successful, sir. You've already achieved strategic surprise—nobody here is expecting you." Then I asked them both, "Do you want to talk with Cordero?"

The commodore gestured in the negative. Miles said, "Not at this time, Captain Wake. But I do have a request. Can *you* land with Mr. Cordero when the sailors go ashore? I'd feel better if you were both there right at the beginning."

Higginson quickly nodded his assent to me, so I said, "Yes, sir. Both Cordero and I will go ashore with the landing party to solve any problems that may come up. I'll leave *Dixon* offshore under my executive officer and go in on *Gloucester*."

"I concur. Good luck, Peter."

Turning to Higginson, the general smiled for the first time. "All right, Commodore, in four hours your sailors and my soldiers will invade Puerto Rico."

"Aye, aye, sir," the commodore declared. "Don't worry, we'll get the beaches and village secured. Your landing will go well. Then it'll be on to Ponce, by land and sea."

"Yes, indeed it will." The general stood. "Well, I've much still to do, gentlemen, so I'll bid you good night, or what's left of it."

Once Miles left, Higginson stopped me from following the general out the door.

"Peter, hold up a moment. Before getting under way from Mole Saint Nicolas I got a reply to my cable request to Rear Admiral Sampson for the relief of Captain Dimm. It was denied. The explanation was not enough suitable replacement officers available. *Bronx* will arrive here tomorrow afternoon for further orders."

I can't say it was totally unexpected. Sampson was right. He was short of senior officers able to take command of a cruiser, and also short of competent staff officers. Still, I couldn't help wonder what other factors had played into the decision—political factors. And what of the letter Dimm wrote Higginson about me? The commodore still hadn't acknowledged it. I thought about bringing it up and again decided not to.

"Yes, sir," I replied. "I understand. I've a lot to do to get ready for the landing, sir, so by your leave, Cordero and I will head over to *Dixon* now and then over to *Gloucester*."

35

Invasion

Guánica Bay, Puerto Rico
Monday Morning, 25 July 1898

BACK ON *DIXON*, I told Cordero to get some rest and decided I had to do the same. After an hour of fitful sleep in my cabin, I joined Cordero and Rork in transferring over to *Gloucester*. I left Belfort in charge of *Dixon* with orders to stand offshore and bombard any coastal target designated by the flagship. I doubted there would be any.

On *Gloucester*'s main deck, surrounded by busy sailors in organized commotion, I surveyed the sky to see if my weather prediction was proving correct. It was. The overcast had dissipated into clear skies. The pale white half-moon was slowly descending to the west, stars glittered orange and silver above, and a faint tinge of gray was spreading along the eastern horizon. The celestial scene was beautiful and tranquil.

"Excuse me, sir," said a sailor as he brushed against me. I lowered my gaze to a different sight entirely. *Gloucester* was the tip of a mighty spear heading into battle. In the predawn twilight, the dark shapes of the squadron stretched out behind us. The preparations by two thousand men on a dozen ships had led to this moment. A chill went through me, for all those men were heading for this place at this time because of my recommendation and an Army general's trust in it.

The deck rumbled as *Gloucester's* engines were put into gear. Orders were called out and a party of men rushed past me carrying ready rounds for the forward deck gun. Rork had already joined the landing force on the main deck. Cordero and I went up to the bridge and joined the other officers and men, all of us with stern, determined faces.

At 5:20, Lt. Cdr. Richard Wainwright calmly gave the order and the operation began. The gallant little gunboat—until six months earlier she'd been J. P. Morgan's private yacht, *Corsair*—accelerated to her full speed of seventeen knots and headed due north toward Guánica Bay.

Soon the dim outline of Punta Brea, the farthest point of the Pardas Peninsula, passed by half a mile away on the port side. Close aboard to starboard was the unseen peril of Lajas Reef. Ahead of us we could see the silhouette of the Puerto Rico mainland. To the east, the line of the horizon took form. Then, gradually, the narrow gap in the shadowy cliffs became visible, followed by the white tower of the lighthouse.

Wainwright stood on the bridge wing as we entered the gap, magnificent mustache twitching with each order given, his grim eyes constantly sweeping back and forth across the cliffs. I knew he was assessing the ways something could go wrong and anticipating what he would do in each case.

Below on the main deck, the sailors crouched at their gun mounts. The landing party, each man burdened with weapons and gear, stood swaying in a line, their lieutenant in front of them, waiting for the order to board the boats, one on either side of the ship.

I saw outlined against the sky on the dark cliff high above us to starboard two men running toward the town, but no one else. During the passage through the narrows and into the bay we would be a 240-foot-long sitting duck for any artillery battery on the cliffs able to depress its guns far enough to reach us. There would be no way to return fire, for our guns couldn't elevate that high.

The enemy's silence made those ninety seconds seem much longer to the pounding metronome of my heart. As always in this sort of situation, questions flooded my mind: *Is this a trap? Did I miss something? Did the Spanish lay mines since my reconnaissance? Was Cordero wrong about there being no artillery emplacements? Was Cordero wrong about everything?*

Just before we emerged into the bay itself, Wainwright reduced speed drastically then gave his helm orders. *Gloucester* heeled over in a slight turn to port, which took her to the center of the bay. Then she heeled again in a tight turn to starboard, her velocity fading rapidly with the shaft disengaged so the ship could approach the main beach slowly.

We planned to capture the main beach south of the village first, since it would be the likely route of a Spanish attack. After securing the main beach we would seize the deeper eastern beach and its larger dock to land the troops.

The sun peeked through valleys in the rocky eastern hills, then rose higher, sending shafts of amber light across the bay to illuminate the western shore. The main beach and its rickety dock were still in the shadows, but an ensign spotted the dock five hundred feet dead ahead. Seconds later, the rising sun flooded the area in light. The timing was eerie, as if stage lamps had been turned up for the performance.

Gloucester turned hard to port, and Wainwright reversed the shaft until she stopped, maneuvering until she was broadside to the beach. Her forward gun was trained on the distant village and her after gun aimed at the customs shack on the beach, where that forlorn-looking Spanish flag still drooped from the bamboo pole. The whole place looked ridiculously unimportant.

The officer of the watch reported our location by bearings on landmarks, and our depth at eighteen feet. I thought it quite a remarkable achievement: even though it was his first time in the bay, we were precisely where Wainwright had earlier told me he wanted to be when looking at the chart. But he never showed a hint of satisfaction. Too much still needed to be done, and too many things still could go wrong.

"You may board the landing force and send them ashore," he said to his executive officer, never taking his eyes from the shore.

It was time for us to go, so I led Cordero down to the port side of the main deck to meet Rork at the slightly smaller second boat, which was being loaded with ammunition and supplies.

"Fine day for it, sir!" he said jauntily. The two revolvers and cutlass jammed in his waist belt, faded blue bandanna around his neck, and lever-action shotgun in his good hand gave him a piratical air. A lopsided grin and errant strands of gray hair waving across his face completed the image.

This was an amazing transformation from his sickly demeanor just a few days earlier. That version of Rork, an old man whose body was racked by malaria and arthritis, had changed completely; he now appeared ten years younger and perfectly fit. He was clearly enjoying himself. I wondered if I had been mistaken about his health. Then it occurred to me that Rork might have found a tot of rum someplace; chief petty officers' "goat lockers" are infamous for their hidden stashes. In any event, there was nothing to do about it now.

Rork gestured toward the boat hanging out on the davits and lowered enough for the gunwales to be level with the main deck. Its crew was perched among crates and boxes. "The lads're ready to go, sir. Don't want to be late for this grand little show, do we?"

There was a cheer over on the starboard side as the landing force's launch was lowered. They were soon under way for the dock. On our side of the ship, we got some offers of "good luck" as we clambered on board, Rork in the bow and me in the stern; the heavily laden boat was swayed down the side and landed in the water with a resounding *plop*. Once away from the ship, the crew began pulling hard at the oars in an effort to catch up with their faster fellows in the launch.

As we neared the rickety dock at the main beach where the fishing boats were drawn up, I looked back and saw the small transports entering the bay behind us. *Lampasas* was in the lead, with General Henry and his soldiers on board. On shore I saw men moving along the cliffs to our right, along the path from the lighthouse to the village. Several figures by the fishing boats on the beach turned and began running off to the north toward the village. They didn't stop to take down the ragged flag on the pole at the customs hut.

The launch reached the landing first. Half the sailors leaped out and formed a semicircle on the beach with their rifles held at the ready. The other half jumped into the knee-deep water and began unloading a Colt machine gun, its tripod, and boxes of ammunition, which they carried to a small hillock in the sand by the hut. The lieutenant in charge marched up to the flagpole, yanked down the Spanish flag, and hauled up a small American ensign.

When our boat grounded at the beach a moment later, Rork, Cordero, and I slipped over the side and waded ashore. Rork and I advanced warily beyond the sandy beach and paused by the hut. The sailors were intently scanning the area, but no enemy was in sight. Somebody joked that we must've landed at the wrong place. The sailors' tension eased a bit. They had been crouched down, rifles at the ready. Now several stood and gazed quizzically at their petty officers, who admonished them in colorful language to stay alert.

And thus did the United States of America officially invade Puerto Rico. It had been an effort of perhaps ten minutes, and not a single shot had been fired by either side. There was no resistance. Not even a protest. For the sailors, the entire event became something of a lark, like the annual fleet landing-force training exercise.

Cordero spread his arms wide in triumph and beamed at me. "You see, Captain Wake. I told you—there will be no problems. Our people have been waiting for you. Even the few pro-Spanish in this area would not dare to oppose such military might!"

The sailors around us grinned at his theatrics, but I couldn't help thinking that it was too good to be true, that Cordero's euphoria and the sailors' complacency were about to end.

I was right.

36

Honor Satisfied

Guánica Bay, Puerto Rico
Monday Morning, 25 July 1898

L IEUTENANT HUSE AND Lieutenant Wood, the officers in charge of the landing force, weren't complacent at all. With one eye nervously watching the full captain who stood near them, they executed everything by the book, arranging their thirty men in a large perimeter centered on the machine gun set up near the hut. Pickets were sent out. Ammunition, supplies, and water beakers were brought up to the line. Petty officers were ordered to keep their men quiet and vigilant.

There was a lot of activity in the bay by this time. Another boatload of sailors was approaching the eastern beach and that crucial dock. The smaller transports had begun disembarking their soldiers into the boats. Just off the beach, *Gloucester* was covered with men at lookout and gun positions searching for the enemy. I saw the sun glint off Wainwright's binoculars as he studied us.

The sun was getting higher fast. It was already hot on the beach, and the faint morning land breeze was fading. A cloud of biting bugs found us, adding to our discomfort.

As he slapped the tiny pests away, Rork's enthusiasm faded and he gave vent to a long blue streak of epithets. Cordero, watching Rork battle the bugs and curse the island, made a light-hearted comment in Spanish about Rork's manhood. Rork straightened and glared at the Puerto Rican. The Puerto Rican, who was not much older than Rork, glared back. I sighed at the idiocy of it all and moved that way to intervene, for we still needed Cordero's goodwill with the locals in the area.

At that precise moment the first shot rang out.

All our heads swiveled toward the path that led north to the village. Four hundred feet away, a dozen men in the light blue uniforms of Spanish soldiers had suddenly appeared, spread across the cart road. I realized they must have crawled to that position then stood up. One man stood apart, holding a saber in one hand and a pistol in the other. He raised the saber and pointed it toward us. The line of militia soldiers knelt and raised their Mauser rifles. He made another flourish with his saber and the militiamen fired a volley at us.

None of us was hit.

"Oh, no!" cried out Cordero as he stamped a foot in anger. "That damned fool Méndez is trying to salvage his honor. The idiot will get somebody killed."

I remembered the name from Cordero's briefing the night before. Lieutenant Enrique Méndez López was the officer in charge of the local detachment of the 4th Volante of Yauco's militia battalion. According to Cordero, Méndez had a grand total of eleven men under him in Guánica.

I was furious. "Damn it all, Cordero! You assured me just last night that Méndez had no heart for fighting and would never attack us! You said he and his men would flee to Yauco when they saw us come ashore."

His haughty air evaporated, and he seemed to shrink a few inches. "I am sorry, Captain," he mumbled. "Truly, I did not believe he would fight."

I'd been a fool. Cordero had wanted to please me, and I had wanted to believe him. On that flimsy basis I had assured General Miles that there were no Spanish regulars at Guánica and that the local militia wouldn't resist.

Another volley blasted out. Again no one was hit. Cordero repeated that he was sorry. The petty officers told the sailors, all of whom were aiming at the Puerto Ricans, to hold their fire until the order.

Rork groaned. More than any other American on that beach, he knew I hadn't wanted this to happen. I'd wanted an uncontested landing with no Puerto Rican blood spilled. If we wanted the islanders to help us push the Spanish regulars back, killing them wouldn't help.

Damn it all! I had to think quickly and make decisions. Had I been wrong to trust Cordero? Was the Yauco militia battalion already on the way? Were they already in the village waiting to spring a trap on us? There could be only one decision here. Our follow-on forces had to get ashore, formed up, and on the road to Yauco right away. Lieutenant Méndez and his men were in the wrong place and would have to pay the price.

I turned to the senior of the two naval lieutenants ashore. "I suggest you use the machine gun on them, Lieutenant. Also, wig-wag *Gloucester* to drop a couple of rounds on them."

"Aye, sir," he calmly replied, nodding to a petty officer who stood up and faced the ship, rapidly whipping the red and white flags around in the message to open fire.

The Colt machine gun clanked out twenty rounds at the militiamen. They instantly dropped to the ground, out of view. When the gun stopped firing, they jumped up and began running up the path toward the village. Several were limping. Méndez turned and fired his pistol at us, a useless gesture at that range, then followed his men.

Behind us, *Gloucester*'s after gun quickly fired several rounds that burst among the departing Puerto Ricans. I heard a distant scream. Several pops sounded as militiamen stopped and fired back at us. Once again, none of our sailors was hit. The retreat resumed, but this time Méndez was limping too.

"Looks like that's it, sir. They're running off," observed the lieutenant, with more amazement than certainty.

"It does appear so," I replied. "But beware; that could be a false retreat to draw us into a trap in the village." I didn't add that it was a ruse I'd used successfully against the Spanish in Cuba in late April. A flicker of a smile crossed Rork's face—clearly he remembered that day. "I would advance, Lieutenant, but carefully, not at a run."

"Why don't we just level the place with the ship's guns, sir?" the lieutenant suggested.

"Normally, we would do that very thing and be done with it. But we need the locals' help—we're invading a large island with a small force, Lieutenant. We certainly do not want the islanders angry at losing their homes or family members and then looking for revenge against our rear supply areas as the army goes inland."

He briefly thought that over and said, "Yes, sir. I see your point."

The sailors moved their line forward another thirty yards, each man studying the terrain ahead. Any signs of complacency or skylarking had completely disappeared. Nobody wanted to be the one to get an unlucky stray bullet fired by a scared enemy militiaman.

After peering intently through his binoculars, the lieutenant sent two sailors to scout the road all the way to the village, warning them to walk on either side of the road and move cautiously. Prudent decision. He was handling it all very well. I was beginning to respect the lieutenant.

Over on the right flank, some American volunteer soldiers from Illinois were beginning to land, their boats going right up to the dock as the plan had envisioned. I could hear their sergeants issuing a continuous stream of basic reminders to them. It was a scene very different from the regular troops I'd seen in Cuba, who knew what to do and needed only to be told the immediate objective. Within seconds, half the volunteers were spreading out and moving up the slope to the low hill nearby. The other half was heading our way to connect the two beachheads.

Rork returned beside me carrying a battered old seabag he'd retrieved from the growing pile of supplies and equipment on the beach. Inside were various personal supplies, weapons, and extra ammunition. He handed me my shotgun, then slung the bag over his left shoulder and readied his own shotgun in his right hand. Rork was all deadly business now: constantly moving eyes, steady voice, lanky frame slightly tensed, and shotgun leveled and ready to fire.

He gestured out to the bay. "Some o' the soldiers' boats're heading to this beach now, sir. An' it looks like some engineers've arrived to build up the dock over at the other beach."

I nodded my acknowledgment and turned to the lieutenant. "It appears active resistance has ended here at the beach, at least. My companions and I are going to pass forward of your lines and head on up into the village. I want to make sure the village surrenders without an attack. Maintain your main line of defense here and pass the word along to the Army to meet us up at the village as soon as possible."

He looked perplexed for a moment—senior officers are not supposed to venture out into enemy territory—but then automatically rendered an, "Aye, aye, sir."

I turned to our dejected guide. "Cordero, you will walk ahead of us to the village. We'll be right behind you with our shotguns. I hope there is still a chance everything goes peaceably."

His eyes showed that he caught my not-so-subtle meaning, and he silently started up the road. We followed two paces behind. Cordero's gait was more a reluctant plod than a walk, and I told him to speed up.

We caught up with two astonished sailors who were cautiously darting forward from bush to bush alongside the road on their scouting mission. Rork called out to them, "Fall in astern, lads, an' stay ready for action in case there's treachery ahead."

They glanced at each other, then choired, "Aye, Chief," and started walking up the road behind us.

"Thought we could use the reinforcements, sir—an' they have rifles," Rork explained. "Might be handy for reachin' out farther than a shotgun."

"Good idea, Rork."

At the edge of the village, several men were standing under a mango tree watching all this unfold. They weren't in uniforms and didn't appear to have weapons, but they weren't looking too friendly either. I counted seven of them. No one else was in sight at the village.

As we approached closer, Rork and I leveled our shotguns at them, just in case. Behind us, the sailors raised their rifles.

Cordero suddenly stopped and turned to me. Grasping my arm, he said, "Wait! I know those men, Captain. Do not shoot them!"

"We won't unless they give us cause to, Cordero," I replied, jerking my arm free. "If these are the friends you told me about, you'd best make sure they don't do anything I might think is threatening."

"Yes, Captain, these *are* my friends. Do not worry. They will welcome you," Cordero said as he waved at the men. They hesitantly waved back, openly amazed that their compatriot was with the *yanquis*.

I still wasn't convinced of their good intentions. Cordero's previous assurance that there were influential members of the community who would welcome the Americans meant nothing now. We continued approaching, our shotguns still leveled.

Cordero called out to them in Spanish, asking where the militia soldiers were. The men pointed beyond the village to the north, one man saying they were heading toward Yauco and that several were wounded. Now back among his brethren, I noticed Cordero had recovered his confidence, and he shot me an I-told-you-so look. I ignored it and continued watching for signs of ambush.

When we got to within forty feet of them I realized the men were no threat to anybody, American or Spanish. They were only frightened locals, mostly older men dressed in their Sunday best to greet the invaders. They weren't sure what they should do, or what we would do. Cordero had been right all along—in this, anyway.

I rather self-consciously lowered my shotgun and smiled. Rork followed suit but continued to glare at them. The sailors shifted their rifles to the port arms position.

The apparent leader, better dressed than the others, stepped out of the shade. He came forward toward me with an outstretched hand and hopeful smile, then slowly said in awkward English, "Welcome to Puerto Rico."

Cordero performed the official introductions. "Captain Wake, these are the gentlemen I told you about. This is Agustín Barrenechea, and here are Vicente Ferrer, Juan María Morciglio, Simón Mejil, Salvador Muñoz, Cornelio Serrano, and Pascual Elena. They are all friends of the United States."

The next few minutes were consumed by a rapid-fire exchange between Cordero and his fellow islanders, with much agitated gesticulating toward the northeast, shrugging, and finger-pointing in the air for emphasis. Afterward, Cordero reported a summary of the discussion, which had been too fast for me to follow.

"Captain Wake, everyone in the village has fled into the hills. Lieutenant Méndez has retreated up the road toward Yauco with his men. Half of them are wounded. Robustiano Rivera, the keeper of the lighthouse, has also gone to Yauco."

His summary ended with theatrical volume and flourish. "These gentlemen give you their word that the village of Guánica is empty, defenseless, and innocent. They hereby put it and themselves under your personal protection, Captain Wake, and that of the great United States of America."

The Puerto Ricans applauded and bowed toward me. I nodded respectfully at them. "Thank you, gentleman," I responded. "It is an honor to have you as new friends, of both myself and my country. The United States Army will be arriving here shortly, and you should surrender to them. They will treat you with dignity and compassion."

I paused before asking my next question. "Now, Señor Cordero, are you and your friends here absolutely *sure* that Méndez and all his militia have gone from the village?"

Cordero shrugged slightly and cast me a rueful smile. "Of course, Captain Wake. There is no reason for them to stay. Méndez has faced the gunfire of the *norteamericano* colossus and shed his blood for Spain, so his reputation is assured and his honor is satisfied. For the Spanish loyalists of Puerto Rico, Lieutenant Enrique Méndez López will forever be the glorious hero of Guánica."

He shook his head in wonder. "The boy king of Spain might even reward the fool with a title and money when this is over, if his Austrian mother the regent allows him."

"Well, good for Méndez," I replied. "But he damned near got all his men killed and the village leveled, and for nothing."

To those who read this narrative years later, I will admit that at that moment I thought Méndez had been quite brave to face American gunfire, especially *Gloucester*'s shells. I hoped the Spanish would indeed recognize his beau geste, foolish and futile as it was. In my defense, I will say I turned fifty-nine that summer, and I suppose one gets a bit more sentimental with age.

37

In All Their Glory

Guánica Village, Puerto Rico
Monday Morning, 25 July 1898

ORDERO SAID NOTHING IN reply, so I continued, "All right, back to the issue at hand. Ask your friends what they know about the Spanish militia and regular units this morning."

Cordero translated my question to his friends, and once again a lively debate erupted. He finally turned back to me. "The authorities at Yauco have been told of your arrival, and the warning has gone out by telegraph to Ponce, and from there to San Juan. The Spanish regular infantry regiment at Ponce has not left the city, but the militia regiment at Yauco has been alerted and is forming under their commander, Lieutenant Colonel Francisco Puig."

"How large is the Yauco militia? When will they arrive here?"

"Colonel Puig has about 250 foot soldiers, without cannons or machine guns. They should be here within two hours. I have met Puig. He is a real soldier, Captain Wake. A veteran of combat. I would consider him very dangerous."

"Thank you, Cordero. Please have your friends wait here. Our Army troops should be along shortly."

Consulting my pocket watch, I discovered it to be almost ten o'clock. The morning had gone quickly. A glance back at the beaches showed Army engineers already busy strengthening the docks, especially the larger eastern one. Several hundred blue-coated American soldiers were already ashore and forming up by companies. The bay was crowded with the gunboat, several small transports, dozens of ships' boats, and some of the beached boats that had been confiscated for troop transports. The Spanish would be too late to stop us from landing and consolidating our position at Guánico, but they could still ambush the American column on the road through the hills to Yauco.

I turned around to see Cordero hesitating a moment, then he quietly said to me, "Captain Wake, my friends and I have placed ourselves, and our families, in great peril by openly greeting you and your fellow Americans. I am certain people in the hills are watching and have seen this. If the Spanish recapture this place, we will be shot and our families will lose their homes and farms."

Behind him, the other village men looked at me solemnly. Cordero looked down at his feet as he said, "I know you do not trust me, Captain Wake, because of my mistake about Méndez. But your Army *must* protect our families and this village from retribution by the Spanish or the loyalists. Please tell me your soldiers will not just pass through and go to Ponce without leaving us some protection." It was as close to begging as Cordero could bring himself.

"Señor Cordero, my earlier distrust of you has been relieved by your good work here and now. I thank you for that. My own work at Guánica is almost done and I will be leaving, but the United States Army is here to help the people of Puerto Rico. They will not abandon you. I have already spoken to General Miles about that very thing."

At that, Cordero and the others literally breathed sighs of relief. Then Cordero led my entourage, trailed by the village welcoming committee, through the town to show us it was deserted. I congratulated them all and received beaming smiles and handshakes in return. The awkward and wary stage had passed, and everybody was now looking forward to the future.

Rork nudged me and glanced back down the road we'd just walked up. "An' speak o' the devil, here comes Uncle Sam's blessed Army, sir. Just in time to get the glory."

I turned around. The U.S. Army was indeed arriving. And rather gloriously at that. Marching four abreast up the path was a volunteer regiment from my home state, the Sixth Massachusetts Infantry. The already sweating volunteers were led by a colonel in full regalia sitting astride a white horse. Just behind the colonel, the Commonwealth's white flag with blue shield emblem was being undulated in the still air by the regimental bearer. I noted with interest that one of regiment's companies at the back of the column was composed of black soldiers.

A group of mounted senior officers was trotting up beside the regiment. As they passed the column and grew closer to us, I saw a general's star insignia glinting in the sunlight on the shoulder straps of the lead officer. Brig. Gen. George Garretson, commander of the 2nd Brigade, and currently the senior officer ashore at Guánica, slowed his horse to a walk when he spotted me.

"Ah, yes, Captain Wake. We met at a meeting on the transport ship." The general sounded somewhat ruffled. He clearly wasn't used to finding senior naval officers on land, out in *front* of his soldiers. "Since you are here, I presume all is well in hand and there are no hostiles in the area."

"Correct, General," I replied pleasantly, realizing Garretson had not been told that *his* superior had sent me here. "There was a slight skirmish when a pro-Spanish militia detachment attacked our naval landing force, but the enemy was repulsed and has withdrawn from the area. I've met with a delegation from the village. They are pro-American, and the place has surrendered and is open to you. My men and I have also walked around just to make sure the town is empty of people. The delegation is waiting for you, and their leader is Señor Cordero. Your brigade should have no problems here, sir."

"So where is the enemy now?" he asked, peering at the hills inland of the village.

"The enemy militia unit was last seen in those hills over there, heading north along the road to Yauco." I pointed to the northeast. "The Spanish in Ponce and San Juan have been alerted, and Colonel Puig and his main militia battalion in Yauco are forming up to march here along that same road."

Garretson focused his binoculars on the road, then said, "Yes, I see some movement over there. Well, once my brigade is consolidated we'll head that way to meet them. By the way, I am leaving a company here to guard our supply base, so I suppose your sailors can return to their boats."

"Thank you, sir. Since it looks like we're no longer needed, we'll do that."

The Massachusetts regiment marched by and Garretson turned his horse toward the village, then abruptly stopped. "Oh, I almost forgot, Captain. My staff said there was a Navy messenger looking for you over at that far dock, where our Illinois regiment is coming ashore. Something about an urgent message from your commodore."

As the general and his staff galloped off to the village, Rork and I headed over to the far dock. After we'd gone a hundred yards, I spotted a fellow sprinting our way at full speed. Rork grumbled something about bad news traveling fast.

The runner was a young ensign, which meant the message was important, for usually the messenger would be a sailor. He arrived completely out of breath, soaked in sweat, and gasped for air for a few seconds before blurting out, "Are you Captain Wake, sir?"

I smiled at the question. How many naval captains were ashore at Guánica? Rork scowled at the young man's lack of decorum in failing to render me a salute.

"That I am, Ensign. Are you the messenger I hear is looking for me?"

Recovering his wits, the fellow stood at attention and carefully said, "Yes, sir. Ensign Porter, sir, assistant signal officer of *Massachusetts*. I have a message for you from Commodore Higginson himself, sir." He extracted a sweat-dampened blue envelope from his inside tunic pocket and held it out to me. Opening it, I found a handwritten note inside.

10 a.m., 25 July 1898

Captain P. Wake

Ashore at Guánica, Puerto Rico

Upon receipt of this message, immediately discontinue your duties ashore and return to flagship for orders. Also, I have signaled DIXON to prepare for sea.

Commodore Higginson

The ensign piped up, "Sir, I was told to take you to the commodore in our steam cutter. It's at the dock waiting for us."

"Then let us go, Ensign," I replied.

As we followed the ensign to the dock, Rork, who'd read the message over my shoulder, whispered to me darkly, "I'm thinkin' 'tis the attack at Ponce an' the commodore wants us to go in first an' calm the locals, like we did here." He shook his head and growled, "But that'll be damned dicey thing to pull off at Ponce, what with a full regular regiment o' Spaniardos to deal with."

The Ponce attack, planned for one or two days after the capture of Guánica, was to be an overland march from Guánica combined with a naval landing at the harbor, a complex operation that had the potential to go badly. But wouldn't Higginson have told me earlier about playing a crucial role in that operation? *Dixon* was scheduled to stay offshore to help with bombardment if needed during the Ponce landing. No, this must be something else. As we reached the dock, I suggested, "You know, it just might be that that raider's been seen again."

Rork, who had been noticeably running out of energy throughout the morning, perked up. The frown disappeared. "Ooh, that'd be good news. I'm ready t' get away from this hellhole. Me old bones're tired as hell o' these damned jungles! Just hope that wily bugger's gone someplace nice. Like Barbados! It'd be just grand to visit there again."

I humored him with, "That it would, Rork."

"Been what, six years since me last port call there?" He grinned at the memory. "They've positively wondrous hospitality—an' that Barbados rum. Aye, they love us Yankee sailors at Barbados!"

Rork was beaming as he envisioned that "wondrous hospitality." I didn't have the heart to tell him the last place a Spanish raider would go was a pro-American British colony. I suspected someplace south, someplace considerably less "grand" than Barbados.

The dock and beach were crowded with soldiers disembarking from ships' boats, which were lined up waiting to come in. The other dock was jammed with men also. Thousands of soldiers were arriving at Guánica. Once ashore, they formed up quickly and marched inland toward Yauco.

So far, it had gone much better than the invasion at Cuba.

38

A Calculated Risk

Flagship Massachusetts, *off the South Coast of Puerto Rico*
Monday, 25 July 1898

"PETER, WE'VE GOT A new development, and you've got
a new assignment," announced Commodore Higginson the
moment I entered his cabin. He motioned me to a chair in
front of his desk. "That raider you encountered back in the Windward Passage was seen yesterday down at Aruba. You were correct,
she's *La Marquesa*."

"Aruba? That's a bit of a surprise. She must've raced directly there.
Impressive speed."

Higginson handed me a large courier envelope, its seal already
broken, and I pulled out the papers within. The commodore continued, "Here's the background. Washington got a cable alert from the
U.S. consul down in the Dutch colonial capital at Curaçao. Naval
headquarters immediately forwarded the report by cable to Admiral
Sampson at Santiago, along with orders from the Secretary to detach
cruisers to search for and destroy the raider. The admiral cabled our
naval depot at Mole Saint Nicolas, but we'd already departed. Since
we've no cable connection from there to here, the depot sent a fast
dispatch boat to get the admiral's orders to us. It arrived just as you

were going ashore. Inside that courier envelope are the consul's cabled intelligence report and also your orders from Admiral Sampson."

Obviously, Higginson must have included the senior officer at the supply depot in the new plan so he knew where to reach the commodore in an emergency. Good decision. I wondered if word had gotten back to Sampson, and thus to Washington, that the invasion force had landed at a different place, but I didn't ask. Higginson's tired face precluded it.

The documents Higginson alluded to were telegraph tapes pasted onto several pages of paper. The first was the consul's report, which I was surprised to see written in plain text. That meant everyone on the Caribbean cable network, including the Spanish, knew the information it contained.

XXX—7-24-98—7:47AM—TO SECSTATE-WASH—X—SPAN RAIDER MARQUESA COALING ARUBA—X—STERN DAMAGE—X—6-IN GUN ON BOW & STERN—X—2 TORP TUBES—X—6 GUNS EACH SIDE—X—DUTCH ORDER HER DEPART TUES AT NOON—X—UNK DEST—X—USCONSUL SMITH—XXX

Well, that validated my concern the night of our encounter in the Windward Passage—*Marquesa* did indeed have torpedo tubes. It would have been helpful to know if they were bow or midships tubes and what type the broadside guns were, but diplomatic reports seldom had that kind of detail. They were always abbreviated due to the exorbitant cost of word space in international telegrams. Navy cable communications included more details because we had a bigger budget to pay for the longer descriptions, as well as encoding.

I looked up at the commodore. "*Marquesa* must've used up all her fuel in the sprint to Aruba. And her captain is being far stealthier about his coaling than Admiral Cervera's fleet was back in May. They openly coaled at the main Dutch port at Curaçao before steaming for Santiago de Cuba."

Higginson nodded. "Yes, Cervera certainly did, and the Dutch heard plenty about it from Washington at the time. This time around, I'll bet the Dutch didn't even know ahead of time that *Marquesa* was coming to coal at Aruba—it's a pretty out-of-the-way place. The big question is where is she going from there?"

I pondered aloud. "It won't be Santiago or here at Puerto Rico. *Marquesa* can't match a regular cruiser, much less a battleship. No, it'll be someplace undefended and target rich."

"Lots of American cargo vessels in a harbor," Higginson suggested. "One quick strike to cause widespread panic."

I knew of only one place that answered that description.

"Got to be Panama, Commodore. The harbor at Aspinwall is undefended since the French abandoned their canal project, and most of those freighters waiting for overland cargo transshipment are American owned."

He nodded thoughtfully. "I concur, Peter. The Colombians own the place, but they've got no real naval presence. American cargo bound for Asia has to go across that little railroad to the Pacific side. The Aspinwall bottleneck on the Caribbean side is the perfect target for a Spanish raider. Insurance rates will skyrocket, the shippers will panic, the press will shriek, and the politicians will thunder and look for scapegoats in the Navy."

I went over to the Caribbean chart on the bulkhead and spread out my fingers to use as dividers to measure distance. "Let's see, Aspinwall is about six hundred miles west and then southwest of Aruba. *Marquesa* can steam approximately eighteen knots sustained. She'll also have the prevailing winds and current helping her while heading west. If she is getting under way at Aruba tomorrow at noon, she could be at Aspinwall in about thirty-three hours. That makes it nine o'clock Wednesday night."

I returned to the chair. "We don't have any naval vessels down in that area, do we, sir?"

"Not yet, but we will soon." Higginson pointed to the remaining two pages in front of me on the desk. They weren't telegraph tapes pasted onto paper but Navy messages that had been deciphered and typed out in plain language. "Those are your orders from Sampson, Peter. I'm afraid you won't like them."

He was right.

XXX—7-24-98—8:51PM—SHIP MOVEMENT ORDERS FOR AUX CRUISER DIXON—FROM RADM SAMPSON-NOR-ATLSQDN—X—TO DIXON-CAPT P WAKE—COPY TO COMMO HIGGINSON & AUX CRUISER BRONX-CAPT R DIMM—X—DIXON & BRONX ARE HEREBY DETACHED FROM COMMO HIGGINSON—X—BOTH WILL IMME-DIATELY SEARCH CARIBBEAN FOR SPAN RAIDER MARQUESA LAST SEEN AT ARUBA EARLIER THIS DATE—X—RAIDER DESTINATION UNK—X—US COAST POSSIBLE TARGET—X—FIND ENGAGE & DESTROY RAIDER—X—BRONX WILL SEARCH AREA FROM LONGI-TUDE 75 DEGREES TO THE WEST & NORTH TO CUBA—X—DIXON WILL SEARCH AREA FROM LONGITUDE 75 DEGREES TO THE EAST & NORTH TO ANTIGUA—X—NO OTHER SHIPS AVAILABLE AT THIS TIME—X—CAPT WAKE IS SENIOR OFFICER IN COMMAND FOR THIS OPERATION WITH AUTHORITY TO DIRECT DIXON AND BRONX—X—CAPT WAKE WILL MAINTAIN CABLE COMMS WITH THIS COMMAND AT EACH PORT VISITED FOR LATEST INTEL & ORDERS—X—ALL CONSULS IN AREA ALERTED & ORDERED TO ASSIST YOUR EFFORTS—X—ACKN RCPT & ADV DEPARTURE TIME—XXX

The seventy-fifth degree of longitude was a line going north from Barranquilla, Colombia, to Guantánamo Bay, Cuba. *Dimm is under my command? And Panama is in his area?* I couldn't believe it. "The admiral actually wants *Dimm* to search the Panama area, where the damned raider is probably headed! Why don't we send *Bronx* to the east and I'll take Panama? And where is *Bronx*, by the way? Isn't she supposed to be here at Gúanica by now?"

The commodore's tone hardened, and I knew I was on thin ice. "Yes, per my original orders, *Bronx* was headed here after coaling in Haiti, but obviously things have changed. In addition to the printed-out cable report and orders from the admiral, I also received a typed report from Dimm in the mail. Turns out he got Admiral Sampson's orders just before getting under way for here, so he headed directly to the southwest Caribbean instead. And no, he didn't include a precise destination. As for *Bronx*'s boiler trouble, Dimm wrote that temporary repairs had been made and he would fulfill his mission from the admiral."

"But Dimm's a—" I stopped in mid-sentence when the commodore gave me a look that meant *don't say anything you'll regret*. I quickly calmed down and intoned a respectful, "Yes, sir."

Higginson's expression softened a bit. "Peter, you know Admiral Sampson doesn't have any other ships to choose from. *Bronx* and *Dixon* are it—every other ship is needed to protect the invasion forces at Cuba and Puerto Rico. So if *Marquesa* does go west, Dimm and *Bronx* will have to take her on. If she goes east, you'll get another shot at her. Per the admiral, you are in charge of this operation. Beyond the basic parameters laid out in the orders, do you have an idea where you'll patrol? And by the way, what is your fuel state? I've got no colliers here now. They won't arrive for several days."

Fuel—the perennial overriding issue for ship captains. During the days of sail, at the beginning of my career, the wind was free. In the Caribbean, winds were fairly predictable and dependable. But those days were long over. Now, ships were addicted to burnable black rocks and tethered to those places that had huge piles of them.

"I need a fair amount of coal, sir. Our full-speed run here used up half our bunkers. As for our patrolling area, I'll stay along the Colombian coast. I have a hunch *Marquesa*'ll be down there, where she can hide among the coastal islands and bays as she goes west toward Panama."

His face tightened again. "Hmm. That leaves most of the eastern Caribbean open. She could get out into the Atlantic."

"Yes, sir, that's a possibility. But the Leewards and Windwards form a good picket line to the east, so if *Marquesa* tries to escape the

Caribbean that way, the consuls are likely to hear of it. They can cable the alert to Washington, and the Navy can send ships out from the U.S. East Coast to find her."

"Very well, I concur. Depending on consuls isn't the best scenario, but we've no real choice. As for your coal, you'll have to go back to Haiti."

I shook my head. "I think not, sir. It's about the same distance from here to Curaçao as back to Mole Saint Nicolas, so I'd like to head directly to Curaçao and get coal there. *Dixon* can make it, although there won't be any extra in case of emergency."

"I don't like that," Higginson said quickly. "You need to have a reserve in case of storm, battle, or breakdown. It would be far more prudent for you to return to Mole Saint Nicolas and coal there before heading south."

I didn't mention that as of a few minutes earlier I was no longer under his command. Instead, I brought up the urgency of the situation. "There's no time, sir. That would add three or four days, at the very least. *Marquesa* will be on the move tomorrow, and maybe before then. I want to get *Dixon* into the area where *Marquesa* was last seen as soon as possible. It's a calculated risk, I fully admit, but this is exactly the moment to take it."

I forged on. "This will work, Commodore. But I need a cable sent to the consul at Curaçao to *quietly* set up coaling for *Dixon* as soon as we arrive there, without the Spanish hearing about it ahead of time, if possible. Can you get a cable to that effect immediately sent to him via our station in Haiti, sir?"

Higginson didn't look convinced, but he acquiesced with a sigh. "All right, Peter, I'll agree. I'll have the dispatch boat run back to Mole Saint Nicolas right away and have the cable sent to Curaçao, but the timing will be tight. I'm not sure it will reach the consul ahead of your arrival."

"Yes, but there's a chance. Thank you, sir. Will there be anything else?"

Evidently my expression betrayed my impatience, for Higginson chuckled. "No, Peter, nothing I can think of right now. You'd better get going. I'm immersed in this Ponce operation. Still hoping we can get in and capture that harbor and the main ship docks without much trouble."

"Sorry I won't be here to help, Commodore. I wish you the best of luck with the Puerto Rican operations. I think General Miles' plan is a good one and it'll all turn out well."

By then, the momentary tension between us had disappeared. Higginson stood and reached out a hand. "Thanks, Peter. Good luck and good hunting."

"Thank you, sir," I said as I shook the commodore's hand, my mind already consumed with the two dominant questions facing me: Where exactly was the Spanish raider, and where was Capt. Reginald Dimm?

39

The "Conversation"

Room 247, State, War, and Navy Building, Washington, D.C.
Thursday, 10 October 1901

CAPTAIN SMITH, WHO HAD been sullenly silent while I described the events at Guánica, chose this moment to speak up. In doing so he erred, for his ulterior motive finally oozed out into plain sight.

"It is manifestly apparent, Captain Wake, that at the very outset of this new mission to find the raider you were openly jealous that Admiral Sampson had ordered Captain Dimm to search the western Caribbean. It was that jealousy that led you to violate your orders to stay in the eastern Caribbean, leave your patrol area by hundreds of miles, instigate international discord with two different countries, fail to keep in contact with Admiral Sampson, and subsequently malign Captain Dimm's reputation, wasn't it? Please be candid and just admit it."

I'd discerned almost immediately on entering the conference room that morning that my summons and the ensuing "conversation" stank of politics. That a coordinated effort to smear my reputation was under way was beyond doubt. During the entire time I "conversed" with these officers, the dominant question in my mind was the extent of the cabal against me.

Caldhouse appeared to be somewhat supportive of my narrative. Though Pentwaller openly disdained Smith's behavior, he remained carefully inscrutable concerning his opinion of me and my actions in the war. Smith didn't even try to maintain an impartial air. Clearly, Dimm and Smith were part of the conspiracy. *But who else? And what the hell is their goal?*

I was due to retire very soon—I had only two and a half months left in the Navy. I currently held a staff job with no authority over anyone, not even most of my own staff. *So why are they trying to disgrace me? Is it to discredit negative information about Dimm? Probably. Almost certainly. As an added bit of revenge, are they trying to thwart my pension?* After Smith's incessant sniping, my conclusion was *yes* to both questions.

As for others involved, I could not believe the Secretary of the Navy was a party to the scheme. If anything, I got the feeling he wanted this nonsense to go away. The U.S. Navy didn't want a public scandal to tarnish the glory of the fleet's victory in the war. Infighting among senior naval officers at Washington was a long-standing and notorious tradition, surpassing in depth even the U.S. Army's low standards of internecine behavior. I supposed the Secretary had decided that this informal and private discussion session was the best way to placate those who wanted to destroy my reputation.

So, who else has a grudge against me? It must be someone from that mission during the summer of 1898. That meant *Dixon*. One of my own men. The list of officers and crew paraded through my mind. *Yes,* I reluctantly acknowledged, *there are a couple of possibilities.*

Pentwaller cleared his throat. "Captain Wake, can you please answer the question?"

My mind snapped back to the present. "Oh . . . sorry, Admiral." I turned toward my foe, for such he clearly was. "The answer to your question, Captain Smith, is a simple one. Jealous of Dimm? Certainly not. I would have to respect him to be jealous. Upon receiving the new orders, I initially found it hard to believe that anyone with the sea and combat experience of Rear Admiral Sampson would entrust a man like Reginald Dimm with a crucial function in wartime. And I also knew that on this mission *Dixon* would end up having to compensate for Dimm's deficiencies and inevitable failures. Thus, my reaction to the news was negative."

Smith looked bored with my answer and waved his hand dismissively. That did it for me. With rage mounting inside me by the second, the high-pressure relief valve for my self-restraint tripped open and I began to vent my true opinions—candidly, as requested.

"As for my orders from the admiral, I *never* violated any of them, which you will see when I get to the next part of the account. Any attempt to construe my actions otherwise, as you have done, is a gross manipulation of the facts to fit a nefarious lie. That lie is part of the patently false portrayal of Reginald Dimm's character now being carefully constructed so the political bosses in New York City will appoint him to fill the state's vacant congressional seat. And *you*, Captain Smith, have demonstrated your willingness to spread perverse slanders to achieve my professional humiliation as part of that effort, because I am one of the few officers who know what *really* happened with Dimm in the Caribbean in 1898. You are frightened it will come out and Dimm's political career will be ruined. That makes you just as shallow and petty and devious as Dimm or any other bilge rat."

The admirals exchanged shocked glances. Pentwaller was about to speak when Smith puffed up in his chair. His contemptuous nonchalance had morphed into cold anger. His face was beet red, and his right index finger jabbed toward my face from a foot away. "Wake, I have already shown that *you* have consistently violated various rules of conduct among officers, and naval regulations as well. And I will shortly have evidence proving that you ignored specific orders from Admiral Sampson. In wartime!"

I heartily wanted to take that chubby pink finger and bend it backward until it snapped in two, but I forced myself to issue a mere verbal response. "You have shown nothing but your own political sycophancy, Smith. Like a schoolboy gossip you've spread lies and innuendo as Dimm's pet toady. You are trying to set me up today so

Dimm can call for my dismissal from the service just as soon as he takes his seat in Congress. What's your payoff, Smith? Appointment as customs collector of New York?"

"*That's enough from both of you!*" thundered Pentwaller. "Admiral Caldhouse and I are here to discuss naval operations during the war, *not* to listen to bickering between two men who should know better. You will both behave with the decorum of senior officers while in my presence or *my wrath* will descend upon you! Is that perfectly clear to each of you?"

The admiral waited, glaring at us.

"Yes, sir," I said, with true remorse, for regrettably he was right. "I apologize for my unprofessional lapse in self-control toward Captain Smith."

My antagonist's response wasn't as genuine. That knowing sneer reappeared as he looked at me, then obsequiously replied to the admiral, "Oh, yes, sir. Perfectly clear."

Pentwaller looked still too worked up to speak, so Caldhouse took over. "We've gone past the usual time for luncheon, so let us adjourn now for an hour to have something to eat. When we return, Captain Wake can continue with the narrative of the mission to find the Spanish raider."

"Damned good idea, Admiral," growled Pentwaller.

Where the others went I don't know. I returned to my office and ate a sandwich sent up from the canteen. When we all returned to the conference room an hour later, the air was still tense. The "conversation" ruse was over. Without waiting for permission, I went right into my account of what happened at Curaçao.

40

Captain "Perhaps"

Cruiser Dixon, *Willemstad, Royal Dutch Colony of Curaçao*
Wednesday, 27 July 1898

WE ARRIVED AT CURAÇAO just past three in the afternoon—siesta time, a cultural import from nearby Venezuela. The Dutch captain of the port, a long-retired naval officer with a weary, florid face, came on board with the harbor pilot. This was an unusual courtesy; normally a ship captain went to the port captain's office ashore. No doubt this gesture of respect was extended because *Dixon* was an American warship in a current state of belligerency with another European power in the Caribbean, and the Dutch were in an uncomfortable position of neutrality.

I could see the port captain wanted to gab, but I had other priorities. Wasting no time with the expected naval civilities, I quickly asked for any information he had about *Marquesa*, where I might find the U.S. consul, and when we could begin filling our coal bunkers.

His face drooped more with each succeeding question. "Ach ... I regret to say, Captain Wake, that my answers will be unsatisfactory to you. As to your first question, I received a report this very morning that the Spanish raider has departed Aruba, where she had been trying to refuel secretly from a chartered collier under the lee of Basiroeti, a remote swampy part of that island's north-western coastline.

"Of course, when word reached Curaçao of the raider's arrival, your consul requested action from me, so I gladly sent orders for *La Marquesa* to depart our peaceful colony. The Spanish ship left this morning, even earlier than we expected. That is very good, because in these islands we are peaceful merchants, Captain. We want no war here."

I ignored the "peaceful" reference—the Dutch loved war among neighbors if it increased their profits—and asked the question I knew he expected. "Where was she heading?"

"She was last seen heading west, perhaps toward Punta Gallinas in Colombia. Or perhaps she fled when she heard *you* were in the area?" He said the last with a tinge of jest. When I didn't reply, he went on. "As to your country's consul, who is an honorable man and my good friend, he took a boat to Aruba two days ago to see the raider for himself. I do not know when he will return. Perhaps today. Unfortunately, his office assistant will be of no help to you, for the man has been ill in bed for a week. Indeed, he may be ill for some time. He is new to our islands."

"Is there no one else in the consul's office?" I asked. "A clerk?"

He shrugged. "This is only a small and forgotten colony, Captain, far away from the important islands of the Caribbean and our mother country in Europe. The United States has but a small office here. There has been no one there since the consul left for Aruba. Perhaps when you next cable Washington, you can suggest adding another man to the consulate office?"

This meant that no one had gotten Higginson's cable asking the consular office to arrange for quick coaling on *Dixon's* arrival. My frustration mounting, I said, "I need coal, and quickly. When can I start?"

Another regretful shake of the head. "Ah, yes, coal. We usually have five thousand to eight thousand tons available right alongside the wharf. And, of course, out of our long friendship with the United

States, I *would have* immediately ordered the wharf to be cleared for you to have priority, but your timing has been very unfortunate. We were already down to two thousand tons when the French West Indies Squadron arrived last week. They refueled here on their way from Panama to French Guiana. They seemed to be in a hurry and demanded all our coal. All of it. Ach . . . the French . . . they can be so difficult. We had to sell it to them."

He leaned over and lowered his tone conspiratorially. "I believe the Frenchmen's haste had to do with that Dreyfus prisoner at Île du Diable. There is much trouble over that man. Perhaps even a civil war in France?"

I ignored the Dutchman's prattle. I didn't care about Dreyfus or France, or the port captain standing before me. He wasn't important anymore. I'd come all the way here, against Admiral Higginson's sage advice, and found no raider, no coal, and no consul. And the damn raider was last seen heading west, the direction of Panama. The important thing was finding fuel.

Belfort, seeing my grim expression and clenched fists, stepped up and invited the port captain to accompany the gunnery officer down to the wardroom for lunch, an expected courtesy. Once they had left the bridge, Belfort quietly said, "I just rechecked the ONI *Ports* book, sir. Closest port with coal is Colón."

Damnation! Colón, the Spanish name for Aspinwall, was on the north coast of Panama. "We can't make it that far. We need coal much closer than Panama."

"We could telegraph for a charter collier to come here," he suggested.

"No, that would take a week or more, far too long."

I walked to the chart table, lifted the Curaçao chart, and began studying the chart beneath it of the Venezuelan and Colombian coastline to our south and southwest. I rummaged through my memory for information about the ports of that coast. A recent piece of intelligence about Colombia came to mind, sparking an idea. A very dangerous idea.

Just then, the signals officer arrived on the bridge and said, "Our boat just returned from shore. They found a telegram waiting for us. I just decoded it for you, sir. It's from *Bronx*." He somberly handed me the communiqué sheet.

I read it twice, then slammed my fist on the chart table.

"What is it, sir?" asked Belfort. "Is *Bronx* already at Panama?"

"No. This was sent yesterday. Dimm put in at Kingston for boiler repairs and coal. No mention of how long it will take." I didn't add my opinion of the situation or Dimm.

Belfort simply said, "Oh, hell . . ."

"Yes, indeed." I took a deep breath. "All right, obviously we are alone on this mission and need to take the initiative right now. So here's what I need you to do straightaway. First, I want you to get steam back up on the boilers. Then send a cable to *Bronx* at Jamaica to steam as soon as possible for Panama. Send one to Rear Admiral Sampson at Cuba that there is no coal at Curaçao and *Dixon* is heading west to look for some at a small port. Also, get that old Dutchman out of the wardroom and off the ship as soon as you can, then heave the cable short and get the hook ready for weighing. I want to be under way in no more than thirty minutes. The course will be due west at ten knots. Understand all that?"

"Yes, sir. And you said west at ten knots? We'll never make Colón with the fuel we have on board."

"Which is why we're going to a place called Riohacha on the Colombian coast."

"Never heard of that port, sir. It's not listed in our ONI reference book." He bent over the chart and found Riohacha. "Looks pretty small. Doesn't appear to have dockage for ships. You been there, Captain?"

"Twenty-five years ago, right after some Americans opened a coal mine in the mountains inland. Once the coal is brought down to Riohacha, they lighter it out to ships anchored off the beach. It then goes to other ports in Central America, mostly Honduras and Costa Rica. It's a very small operation. You're right, there's not much at Riohacha, but we'll get our coal there, one way or another."

"And you don't want me to put the part about Riohacha in the cable?"

"Correct. The political situation in Colombia is rather delicate right now, and there's no sense in alarming the admiral. He's got enough to worry about."

Belfort looked doubtful, but he merely looked down at the chart and traced the coastline with his finger. "It's about two hundred miles from here to Riohacha. With our fuel consumption at ten knots and a fair wind and current helping us, we should be there by tomorrow at noon."

"I concur."

Belfort raised an eyebrow. "But, of course, when we refuel at foreign ports, we need that country's official authorization. So once we get to Riochaca, we'll need authorization from the Colombian government to obtain coal. And you know even better than I do, Captain, that the Colombian government doesn't much like Washington because of the canal mess, and I think they might not look kindly on an American warship getting coal on their mainland coast."

"True. But that's only if they know. There are several things in our favor, John. One, the central Colombian government is in chaos after the last election, and everyone in the region thinks a civil war is coming. Two, Bogotá is a long way from Riohacha, so it will take awhile for them to find out. Three, Colombia has no navy to prevent us from getting the coal, and many people on that coast have no love for the central government, so they might help us. And four, for the right amount of money the local mayor—whoever he is—will play along, and technically he is a government representative. We only need sixty tons to get the three hundred miles from Riohacha to Colón. That'll be a four-hour loading job if everything goes well, and then we'll have a twenty-hour run at fifteen knots to Colón."

Belfort let out a long breath. "This all seems pretty dicey, Captain. Odds are heavy against us pulling this off without repercussions. And if it goes bad, the brass up in D.C. will have your head on a platter."

I noticed he didn't add that his own head would be sitting right alongside it. "Yes, I admit it is dicey. But there's no other option, John. We have to find that raider."

Belfort set his jaw. "Aye, sir. I'll get started right now."

Twenty-nine minutes later *Dixon*'s chain was clanking up through the hawsehole.

41

As Fate Would Have It

Cruiser Dixon, *Riohacha, North Coast of Colombia*
Thursday, 28 July 1898

Riohacha was just as I remembered it—a dingy, forgotten little port—and perfect for our purpose. Down on the main deck, curious sailors did their own appraisal of the place as we approached. Though I couldn't hear their whispered assessment, the wagging heads told me they'd decided Riohacha offered no apparent incentives to entice them ashore. *Yet another benefit*, I decided.

Within minutes, the anchor was let go and *Dixon's* steam cutter was taking me into a shallow creek that emerged from the wide, flat beach in front of the town. We tied up at a small dock just inside the creek's first bend behind the beach. A crowd had already gathered to scrutinize the *norteamericanos*. Everyone in Colombia knew the gringos wanted the country's province of Panama so they could finish the abandoned French canal. But why were the *yanquis* at Riohacha? The buzzing, pointing crowd parted to allow a tall man, apparently the mayor, to approach me.

Don Heraldo was a handsome, trim fellow in his early thirties with intelligent eyes and a mane of jet black hair. A magnificent mustache flowed across his mahogany brown face. He was easily the best dressed of the lot in his red tie, gray vest and jacket, and battered old bowler hat. I got the impression from his bearing and the crowd's deference that he had some education and money. I wondered if he had a financial interest in the coal mine inland.

After we'd exchanged names, Don Heraldo asked abruptly why our warship was anchored off his town—an unusual departure from the norm in Hispanic culture. It would typically take an hour of polite blather to get around to that question.

I appreciated his brusqueness and surmised he was demonstrating to the crowd his command of the situation. On the other hand, I knew that my reply needed to incorporate at least a little blather. It wouldn't do to disrespect a Latin American official in public. I used my best Spanish, which was admittedly slow and with less than perfect grammar, complete with a half bow and flourish. Naturally, in the finest tradition of international diplomacy, I started out with a blatant lie.

"Your Excellency, the friendship of our two great nations is long and heartfelt. It is always a pleasure and honor to visit the Republic of Colombia, land of the legendary hero Simón Bolívar. Nothing would give me more pleasure than to celebrate that friendship with a special dinner on board my ship for you and the business leaders of Riohacha, but alas, I regret to say we do not have enough time for such a delightful diversion."

The crowd tittered with delight. They were getting quite a show. Don Heraldo clearly saw through my fancy words but rewarded my effort at diplomacy with a half-smile and level gaze that told me to continue.

I made another little bow, with an appropriately sad expression and brief shrug. "No, we are here only long enough to purchase some coal for the ship. From a very pleasant visit here many years ago, I remember that there is a small coal mine in the hills, not far inland. We will, of course, pay in American gold dollars. Would you know the price per ton, or should I ask someone else? Perhaps someone from the mine company. I remember they were Americans."

There was a collective gasp from the crowd when I mentioned gold dollars. A sly grin crossed Don Heraldo's face. The crowd leaned closer.

"Yes, Captain Wake. As fate would have it, I am *exactly* the person you need to talk with about the coal. There is no reason for you to go all the way to the mine. I can handle everything."

"And what about the Americans? Don't I need to deal with them?"

"No, no, Captain. They are gone now that the Colombian government has ruled that the coal company belongs to our nation. But do not worry. I know everyone involved and can take care of this entire transaction for you. How much coal do you need for your ship?"

"Sixty tons. And I need it now."

He thought for a minute and turned for a quick conversation with an older man in the crowd. Don Heraldo curtly nodded and turned back to me. "That is a lot at such short notice. There is a pile of coal nearby in the town—more or less about twenty tons, I believe. We must divert the rest from its current journey to a previously contracted buyer. It will require a few hours to get that coal here."

"What is your price per ton?"

"Fifty dollars for each ton," Don Heraldo said with a remarkably straight face. The crowd ruined his poker façade, however, by gasping again. They'd never heard of anyone paying such money.

I almost laughed when I heard the price, but I returned a level gaze of my own. "Twenty dollars a ton is more than triple the price in Curaçao, and double what you might get from the government buyers in Bogotá. But because I want to help you and this town, of which I have such fond memories, I will pay you twenty-two dollars in cash for each ton. This is an excellent arrangement for you and Riohacha, and time and the meager state of my funds will not allow me to bargain on the price any further. I will give you half right now and the other half when the coal is completely loaded—but *only* if it is done within four hours. If it is not all loaded within four hours, I will not pay the second half of the money. Time is of the essence for me."

The crowd studied Don Heraldo while he did some quick mental calculations, absentmindedly pulling on his mustache the entire time. I could tell he felt the pressure from them to make the deal.

Finally, he said, "Twenty-two dollars in gold for each ton of coal. That is $1,320 in total. Half now is $660." He held out a hand with a smile.

I raised my right hand to emphasize my next words and said, "Pure, hard coal only—*no rocks*. We will be checking the coal sacks."

The smile ended and the hand was withdrawn. The air grew deathly still as the people watched for their leader's reaction. Don Heraldo and I locked eyes for several seconds.

"Of course, Captain," he said at last. "You need not have said that." Touching his chest, he declared, "We Colombians are honest people. You will have only the finest coal."

His face neutral, the right hand went out again, waiting for mine. I waited for five seconds, then offered mine in a strong grip. We shook hands to consummate the deal. The crowd cheered.

I nodded to Lieutenant Gerard, standing beside me. He waved to the boat crew. The coxswain, escorted by four armed, stern-faced Marines, lugged a small but obviously heavy box over to me and stood holding it.

I opened it, counted out thirty-three gold twenty-dollar coins, and put put them in the mayor's hand. "Here is your down payment, Don Heraldo. I look forward to personally presenting you with the balance in four hours."

The village instantly became an anthill of activity. Over the next four hours the men of Riohacha packed every fishing boat, lighter barge, and dinghy with massive sacks of coal, rowing them out to *Dixon*, where they were swayed up and over the gunwales and then emptied down the coal chutes into our bunkers. Our engineers periodically made a great display of checking the bags for rock filler, but found none. There was no deception or delay. I was pleasantly surprised.

In the end, Don Heraldo came out to *Dixon* for his payment, afterward confiding with a certain glee that the buyer whose coal had been diverted to us was the national government, for use by their army steamers on the Magdalena River, 150 miles to the south. Those steamers were patrolling against the antigovernment rebels who were beginning to make their presence felt in the region. The smell of revolution was in the air, he said with a touch of relish.

Further questions revealed that Don Heraldo himself was a supporter of the rebel movement in the region, so depriving the government's army of the coal was thus no problem for him. In fact, he had his eyes set on higher office, something far more important and remunerative than mayor of a small town, once the impending revolution was won. I suggested secretary of the treasury, where the possibilities of personal gain would be endless. His eyes sparkled at the thought, but he said nothing.

As Don Heraldo was departing, he offhandedly mentioned that government officials in Bogotá would doubtless make an official complaint to the American ambassador about my "theft" of Colombian military stores. But I should not be concerned, he said, because I had acted on the side of liberty and against tyranny.

Having offered this rosy epilogue, he descended down into the coal barge waiting alongside. As it steamed toward shore, Don Heraldo couldn't resist one last comment, calling out to me in pretty good English, "So it appears we are comrades on the same side, Captain Wake. ¡*Viva la revolución!*"

I chuckled at his cynical wit and waved a sincere good-bye. True, Don Heraldo was just another in the long line of thieves I've met around the world, but I did grudgingly appreciate his sense of humor. He would need it if his revolution failed. Minutes later, *Dixon* was under way, bound southwest to the distant Colombian province of Panama, and I put the events at Riohacha out of my mind.

42

The "Conversation"

Room 247, State, War, and Navy Building, Washington, D.C.
Thursday, 10 October 1901

"**S**O THE RUMORS ARE TRUE," pronounced Captain Smith gleefully. "By your own admission you *did* steal a foreign power's military stores without that government's permission."

"Completely false, Captain Smith. I did not *steal* military property. I paid a Colombian official fair and square for the coal. *He* stole it from his own national government. Besides, and I shouldn't have to remind you of this, we were engaged in a war, and that enemy raider had to be found quickly. The complaint from Bogotá was a minor side effect of my action."

Smith harrumphed at that. "The Colombian government still uses your action as an excuse to deny us rights in Panama, Captain Wake."

"Oh, belay that drivel, Smith. The Colombian national government will sell us rights as soon as we agree to their ridiculous price. It has absolutely nothing to do with theft of national military stores. They know we want the old French canal. The politicos in Bogotá want the most money they can get for it. And if and when we pay, I guarantee that damned little of the money will end up in the Colombian national treasury."

Smith was on the edge of his chair by this point. "But you do admit you got Colombian military coal at Riohacha!"

Pentwaller intervened in a tired voice, "I see no direct intentional theft in that situation at Riohacha, so we will leave it behind. I want to hear what happened next. I believe you next arrived at Panama, Captain Wake?"

Caldhouse looked at me encouragingly, "Where you believed *Marquesa* was headed."

"Exactly, Admiral," I replied. "But what we found there wasn't what we expected."

43

Gonna Be Big Trouble, Sure as Hell!

Cruiser Dixon, *Aspinwall (Colón), Department of Panama, Republic of Colombia*

Friday, 29 July 1898

FTER AN EVENTLESS TRANSIT from Riohacha along the low, coral reef–encrusted coast of Panama, we approached Colón. With the crew at general quarters, guns manned and loaded, and lookouts searching for targets, *Dixon* rounded Galeta Island and steamed for the outer channel buoy of Limón Bay. Three pilot boats bobbed at the channel entrance waiting for new ship arrivals, and one of them came alongside. I could see the inner bay crammed with anchored ships waiting their turn to offload cargos at the Colón docks off our port bow.

Five miles ahead lay the Mindi River entrance to the once-vaunted French canal across the Isthmus of Panama. Over the last decade it had declined from a wonder of the world into an abandoned dream mired in workers' deaths, technical failures, and financial fraud. A French shell company, Nouvelle du Canal de Panama, had been formed a few years earlier to sell the equipment and assets for $109 million. So far, nobody was buying. Some of that equipment was in view. The rusting dredges and barges run into the mangroves at the river mouth made for a depressing sight.

Not a single warship was visible in the bay or at the docks.

The harbor pilot arrived up on the bridge, an ancient relic stinking of sweat and fish, with a thick Maine accent and a cantankerous attitude. He introduced himself in a mumble, cursorily acknowledged my own introduction, and went to stand beside the helmsman. I saw him noting our battle readiness and intense examination of the surroundings, but he said nothing about it. Instead, he began ordering course headings and speeds in a tetchy tone and rum-soaked foul breath. My officers were barely able to contain their distaste.

I ventured closer and asked him, "Pilot, has there been any sign or word of Spanish ships here lately, either merchant or naval? Especially a liner or a collier?"

He looked at me like I was an idiot. "Why the hell would *they* come here? Those bastards don't even come here when we *ain't* shootin' at 'em. Hasn't been any trade here for Spain since the local banditos kicked 'em out for Colombian independence back in the 1820s!"

"Do you know if our consul, Mr. Wright, is in Colón right now?"

"Nah, he's over on the other side for some sort of meeting. I think he's working on getting one of our gringo compatriots out of jail there. Only got a clerk in the consular office right now, and he's useless as a barnacle."

"Other side" meant Panama City, on the other side of the isthmus, on the Pacific coast. The pilot jabbed an arm toward the southwest, the shallow part of the bay. "Head over there and anchor. Course southwest. Reduce speed to revolutions for five knots."

I had no intention of anchoring there, or anywhere. We were still desperately short of coal. The last load of coal had only been a stopgap measure to get *Dixon* here. We needed full bunkers to search for *Marquesa*. "Thank you, Pilot, but no. We'll not do that."

To Belfort, I said, "Continue on this course, but stand by for course changes and reduce our speed to five knots."

The pilot rounded on me. "Why the hell ain't you headed where I just told you to go?"

"Because we're not anchoring, Pilot. We need to top off our coal bunkers right away from the coaling pier. I'm invoking American naval priority for coal and provisions. The company who has the coal sales concession here is American, and subject to my invocation."

The pilot wasn't impressed by my local knowledge and legal abilities. "Oh! Invoking American naval priority, are we? Well the high and mighty've arrived now, ain't they? But no can do, Captain Wake. The Colombian provincial governor shut down that coaling pier *yesterday*, so you ain't gettin' in there."

"Why did the governor shut it down?"

"'Cause the gringo owner didn't pay the governor's new special tax of ten cents a ton on coal sales. Ha! Just guess where that money's bound to go! That's why the consul is over on the other side, trying to get his fellow American, the fella who owns that pier, out of the jail. And things're about to get even more fun around here. You see, Captain, in a couple of days the Panama Railroad's gonna run outta' coal. When *that* happens, it's gonna cost *everybody* money and shut down every friggin' thing on both sides 'a the isthmus. A gringo owns that railroad too, by the way, and he's got one *hell'uva* lot more clout than you or your fancy . . . *in-vo-ca-tion* . . . do! But the governor's not paying one little bit of attention to that. He's holding out for that money. Yep, he's playing for keeps on this one."

This surly bastard has a point, I thought. *Even in the middle of a war, Dixon wouldn't be as important as that damned railroad.*

Time was the dominant factor. I asked, "When will the consul be back?"

He looked at me with disdain. "It's *Panama,* Captain. Tomorrow? A week from tomorrow? Ain't no U.S. government business while he's gone. *Nada.* And with the American coal pier shut down, there ain't no other option for you or anyone else, 'cause that greedy bastard of a governor's had the coal business in Colón cornered for years. Hell, not even Uncle Sam's Navy's gonna get coal right now—either alongside the pier or by barge out in the bay. Governor's a hard-ass when he gets his back up."

I looked through my binoculars at the five main piers jutting out from the forlorn Colón waterfront. Pier One, the northernmost, was the port's coal pier. It and Pier Two were owned by the Panamá Railroad, which had its Colón office beside the coal pier. The coal company's office was in the far end of that building. Both looked closed.

Unlike the other piers, Pier One was empty—no ships or even people—but I did see a large crane with one of those newfangled bulk mineral–handling conveyors. That was a welcome and pleasant surprise. It wasn't there on my last visit, in ninety-five. Beyond the pier was a hill of coal—probably several thousand tons of the stuff. The hill was adjacent to the town's main street of commerce, Front Street, and the railroad tracks that ran parallel to it. That railroad, which ran all the way to Panama City on the Pacific coast, was the most important feature of Colón. The trains I could see on the sidings were stationary.

"Pilot, do the Colombians have a guard detail at the coaling pier?"

"Don't need one. Governor just posted a big official order on the door and put the word out that anyone who violates it'll get shot. Folks know he ain't bluffin'. He'd love to have just cause to nail some gringos."

The pilot leaned back against the chart table and folded his arms across his chest, casting me a self-satisfied look. "So, you gonna anchor in the bay over there by Limón Point or not?"

The sight of that crane and coal, and the absence of a guard detail, settled the decision I'd been cogitating since learning the governor had shut down the coal pier.

"No, we're not, Pilot. And you may stand aside, in the corner over there. You will still get your fee, but your services are no longer needed, and I don't want you in the way."

That got the pilot's attention. He shambled over to the corner and stood there, speechless.

To the executive officer, I said, "Commander Belfort, first, call out the landing party. Second, have the quartermaster steer for that pier marked Number One. Third, continue at this speed until five hundred yards out, then stop engine and drift in to the pier starboard side–to. Understood so far?"

"Yes, sir," he said, and began issuing the orders.

When he'd finished, I continued, "I want the landing party to land immediately upon coming alongside the pier. They are to form a perimeter around the entire pier and that coal pile. Any local who physically obstructs our action will be brought here to me. Anyone who shoots at our men will be killed. So far?"

"Understood, sir."

"Good. Once the pier, coal yard, and defensive perimeter are secured, we will muster all remaining hands on board—officers and men alike—to load the coal ourselves, keeping half the gun crews at their stations. Our engineers will have to operate the existing equipment on the pier."

This time he acknowledged with gusto, "Aye, aye, sir!"

Eight and a half minutes later, Belfort reported the landing party manned and ready on the main deck. Line handlers fore and aft were ready as well, and the engineers were coming up from their mechanical dungeon to go ashore.

The pilot, who'd observed all this with silent astonishment, recovered his caustic manner and shook his shaggy head. "You're a damned fool, Mr. Navy Man, 'cause you're starting something *real* bad now. Just wait 'til the governor hears about this over on the other side. These spics hate all us gringos, but they won't be shooting *your* ass. Oh, no, they'll wait 'til this warship's gone and then make life holy hell for the rest of us gringos who're stuck down here trying to keep this Gawd-forsaken place running."

When he ran out of breath, he moaned, "Oh, this's gonna be big trouble, sure as hell!"

Six minutes later we were alongside the pier. The deck crew, led by Rork on the foredeck, lassoed the pier bollards with bights of light messenger line, then hauled the attached main lines around the bollards and back to the ship. The mooring lines were tautened by the fore and aft secondary capstans, and the ship sidled up to the pier. The moment Rork shouted that *Dixon* was securely moored, Lieutenant Gerard led the boarding party of forty sailors and Marines down the lowered gangway onto the pier, where they fanned out to capture their assigned objectives. Meanwhile, *Dixon*'s gun crews made a show of traversing their barrels around to demonstrate our ability to hit targets anywhere in sight.

Minutes later, Gerard had captured the office building and coal hill. He quickly set up a thin perimeter defensive line around the seized area and stationed lookouts on top of the building.

I turned to Belfort. "Very well done, John. Now, let's get that crane and its elevator-conveyor apparatus running, and those coal cars under way. We need to begin loading the stuff as soon as possible."

"Aye, aye, sir," said Belfort. "The chief engineer and his assistants just went ashore, and we're sending more men over now to help load the coal. We'll get it loaded fast with this modern machinery, once they figure how to run it."

The pilot chose that moment to spit out his opinion from the after corner. "Ha! That there's theft from brother Americans, pure and simple. Your career's over when Washington hears about this, Mister!"

By this point I was mightily tired of the old goat. The fool hadn't even demonstrated good harbor pilot skills. "All right Pilot, you are no longer needed on board this ship and will leave immediately. The duty boatswain's mate will assist your departure."

After that lump of misery was escorted out, Ensign Barnett arrived on the bridge. He'd been chomping at the bit for the last three weeks, trying to get involved in the landing parties, boarding parties, or special details to which other officers had been assigned. At last he was going to get his chance for some action.

"Mr. Barnett, you will encode my cable messages to Admiral Sampson at Santiago and to Captain Dimm at Kingston, Jamaica. Send them from the post office in the town hall. You will also see if there are cables waiting there for us. Take two armed sailors with you. Go three blocks south along Front Street, then left on Sixth Street; the town hall is at the corner of Bolivar and Sixth. The post office people will probably not be helpful, but it is crucial you make *sure* these messages are sent, even if you have to sit at the sending key yourself." I handed him a piece of notepaper with the two messages printed out in pencil. The first was to Sampson.

XXX—RADM SAMPSON-NORATLANSQDRN-SANTIAGO-CUBA—X—AFTER NO COAL AT CURCAO DIXON STOPPED AT NEAREST COAL PORT AT RIOHACHA-COLOMBIA—X—GOT SMALL AMT COAL—X—NOW AT NEXT CLOSEST COAL PORT AT COLON-PANAMA TO COMPLETELY REFUEL—X—RAIDER NOT HERE—X—BRONX IN KINGSTON AS OF 3 DAYS AGO—X—DIXON WILL HEAD NORTH FROM HERE TOWARD JAMAICA TO SEARCH FOR RAIDER—X—WILL CABLE NEXT SITREP FROM KINGSTON—XXX

The next was to Dimm.

XXX—CAPT DIMM-CRUISER BRONX-KINGSTON-JAMAICA—X—ADVISE YOUR SHIP STATUS AND SEARCH PLANS IMMEDIATELY—X—DIXON REFUELING IN COLON-PANAMA—X—RAIDER NOT HERE—X—UNK WHERE—X—AFTER COAL DIXON WILL HEAD NORTH ON SEARCH—XXX

Barnett's face lit up. "Aye, aye, sir! I'll get this done straightaway!"

Our communications having been attended to, I descended to the pier to see for myself what exactly we had captured. The entire dock area was covered in a thin layer of black dust, and smoke from ships at the other piers drifted through the air. Colón was as dirty and stench-ridden as I remembered.

I needed to know if *Marquesa* had been here, and I certainly was not going to rely on the pilot's word. The pertinent information would be found in one of two places. The port captain's office was the obvious place, because they kept all kinds of records of the goings-on in the port. But since the port office was part the Colombian government, I doubted I would get any assistance there. That left the coal company's office, because if the raider refueled at Colón, there was only one place to get it done. I headed for the office building beside the pier.

The company's front door was locked. Fortunately, it wasn't a very good lock, and I had no difficulty jimmying it open with my pocketknife. In the outer office I found a schedule board on the wall depicting a list of ships booked for coaling over the past week and for the next few days. I went down the list. It all appeared routine. Four hundred tons here, two hundred there. None were Spanish registered. Embarrassed by my felonious method of entry, I decided to leave.

Then one of the names caught my eye.

44

A Caribbean Lady with
a German Accent

Cruiser Dixon, *Aspinwall (Colón), Department of Panama,*
Republic of Colombia
Friday, 29 July 1898

I'D SEEN THAT SHIP BEFORE at various ports in the Caribbean over the preceding six or seven years. SS *Karibische Dame* was a German-owned collier contracted to the Imperial German Navy to refuel their West Indies station ship, SMS *Greier*, when she was far from major ports.

The schedule board showed the collier had come alongside the pier and restocked her coal holds only two days ago. I found that odd, because I knew *Greier* was currently at Cuba evacuating German nationals from the war zone and taking them to the German émigré community at Vera Cruz, Mexico. The warship would have many options for refueling at large ports in that area of the Caribbean and the Gulf of Mexico, so why was her contracted collier filling up with *two thousand tons* of coal way down here?

Increasingly bothered by the posting about the *Karibische Dame*, I stared at the board, reviewing everything I knew about German operations in the Caribbean. *This is more than merely odd, it's uncharacteristically inefficient on the part of the Germans. There must be more to this. Paperwork! Look for the paperwork. Coal transactions are always documented.*

I began looking through filing cabinets in that outer room, trying to locate the invoice file with *Karibische Dame*'s cargo-loading contract. I found the contracts for the others listed on the board, but not a thing about the German ship. I went through two other rooms and checked every desk and filing cabinet. Still nothing. In the back of the place there was a locked door to the one remaining room. The boss's office.

I've already captured an entire pier and coal pile, and burgled this company's office—so in for a penny, in for a pound, I reasoned. I used my pocketknife to pry the lock's bolt out from the doorframe, forced open the door, and sat down at the owner's desk. The drawers were locked, but the knife made short work of them.

In the bottom drawer, among files about office staff, deals with the Colombian government, and the boss' personal financial affairs, I smiled when I found a file labeled "Caribbean Lady"—the translation of *Karibische Dame*.

I spread the file on the desk and began reading. It was, like all the others, in English, and the invoice inside contained intriguing information. No wonder the boss kept it hidden. The collier had paid the company ten dollars a ton, almost double the norm for coal at Colón, and it was loaded in two days of round-the-clock effort. A special fee of $2,000 had been added for all that extra labor, and the entire $22,000 bill was paid for by the imperial German government through a bank draft with the Hamburg-Sudamerikanische Dampfschifffahrts-Gesellschaft, the Hamburg South American Steamship Company. That company was also familiar to me. It controlled a lot of the shipping to and from Latin America and Europe, and consequently had substantial influence with the region's governments through payments of taxes and fees, some of which were even legal.

Obviously, the Germans paid top dollar because they were in a hurry. But why the urgency? A suspicion formed in my mind, engendered by my previous work in the Office of Naval Intelligence, where I had gone up against the Germans in the Pacific and in Latin America. A handwritten note scrawled on the bottom corner of the page confirmed my suspicion: "Must be done loading by Wednesday at noon so ship can depart for Providencia."

Providencia? There was nothing at Isla Providencia. No, *usually* there was nothing . . . but these were not usual times.

In that very instant, all the myriad bits and pieces from the past week coalesced into a clear picture in my mind. None of this was odd or inefficient. In fact, the whole damned thing was actually quite logical and very damned efficient. *Hell, it's an incredibly brilliant plan of deception.*

With newfound hindsight I could see that the evidence had been there all along. There was only one country in the world closely allied with Spain's interests in the Caribbean: Germany. The Spanish army used German-supplied rifles and artillery to great effect against American soldiers fighting in Cuba. I'd seen that firsthand only four weeks ago. German immigrants and commercial enterprises were all over the Caribbean and Latin America, and were rapidly gaining political and commercial power. I'd fallen afoul of them for years. The German government had been using these émigrés to expand the country's shipping, rail, and agricultural empires in the hemisphere, including the Hamburg South American Steamship Company. They were a very real arm of Kaiser Wilhelm II in Berlin.

Germany had long coveted a naval base near the canal that the French—their traditional enemies—were building but had never managed to get one, though they'd come close at Curaçao a decade earlier. Over the past ten years the Germans had also shown an increasingly open antipathy toward the longtime U.S. commercial dominance of the area. Germany most certainly wanted Spain to win the war. Such a defeat would diminish U.S. influence in the Americas and open the way for German expansion. I had a very good idea where they would insist on getting a naval base lease as recompense for their help: Guantánamo Bay, which our Marines and sailors, alongside Cuban patriots, had just captured from the Spanish in June after desperate fighting.

So, as part of that help, the Germans were going to coal a Spanish raider at the remote island of Providencia, well offshore of Nicaragua's notorious Miskito Coast in the southern Caribbean. Both Colombia and Nicaragua claimed the island, along with some adjacent ones, but it was Colombia that exercised a nominal civil government there. The island's remote but central location in the Caribbean made it an excellent choice. Cuba, Puerto Rico, and the predominantly American shipping in the Yucatan Channel were all well within three or four days' steaming range.

It was evident that *Marquesa* had not gotten much coal from the other collier at Aruba; thus the reason for her sudden departure. Providencia must have been the planned refueling rendezvous all along. *Then why stop at Aruba? Simple—it was an intentional deception to draw U.S. warships in the wrong direction.*

And the raider's ultimate target after Providencia? I tried to think like the Spanish, desperate to hold on to the shreds of their empire. They still held Cuba and Puerto Rico but had no hope of resupply or reinforcement to those islands against the mounting capabilities of the U.S. Navy, which was closely blockading them.

The Spanish had only this raider, and maybe one more. Their targets needed to be audacious and significant enough to cause panic— panic sufficient to pressure the United States to the negotiating table, where Spain could salvage something of its West Indies colonies. The Cubans despised Spanish rule—they would never agree to continue it. But maybe Madrid thought Spain could hold on to Puerto Rico.

I pondered that requirement for suitable targets—audacious and significant. It was that same fear of Spanish raiders attacking the undefended American ports that had sent Commodore Schley and his Flying Squadron around the Atlantic on a fruitless search for the Spanish fleet in May. Our fleet thought that that threat was over once the Spanish fleet was located and destroyed at Santiago. *But that wasn't so,* I realized. *A single raider would reignite it.*

Marquesa would hit America's ports along the Gulf of Mexico and the lower Atlantic coast.

It would be a lightning raid—Tampa, Key West, Savannah, Charleston, maybe Wilmington—taking perhaps six or seven days at full speed. Then she would disappear out into the Atlantic, rendezvous with a collier at the outer Bahamas, the Azores, or Canaries, and try to make her way home to Spain. *She'll meet with the German collier in the remote islands of the Bahamas. No one would stop a neutral German collier in international waters,* I decided after assessing the alternatives.

The outer Bahamian islands were remote, but close enough to reach from Charleston. Transfer the thousand tons remaining on *Karibische Dame* under the lee of Acklins Island or Mayaguana Island. It would take days for word to get to Nassau without a transoceanic cable to the outside world. By the time the Royal Navy arrived to defend Britain's colony, or the U.S. Navy arrived to attack their enemy, the raider and her German collier would be long gone.

With growing clarity, I realized this wasn't the original plan for *Marquesa.* That had been scheduled to unfold a week earlier but was thwarted when *Dixon* engaged her in the Windward Passage. Now the raider was executing an alternate plan. Madrid and Berlin must have been scrambling to make it happen.

To boot, they're using American-owned coal to fuel their ship to go after American targets! Damn, the Spanish captain is superb! I've got to meet this fellow someday.

I did some reckoning and deduced that *Karibische Dame* would've arrived at Providencia the previous afternoon. I knew exactly where she would be anchored. I'd been there—the last time in 1892. Transferring large amounts of coal from ship to ship while they're rafted together requires calm water and a lot of time. Santa Catalina Bay on the northwest coast of Providencia was ideal for the purpose—sheltered from the easterly trade winds and with water deep enough to accommodate both ships' drafts. I guessed they would transfer a minimum of eight hundred tons of coal, and probably more. That would take three or four days of exhausting work in the tropical summer sun.

It is far easier and quicker to load coal alongside a pier, especially with substantial mechanical assistance, as we were about to do at Colón. I was planning on stuffing *Dixon's* bunkers with a thousand tons. How long would it take us? The German collier had loaded twice that amount at the dock quite quickly.

While accomplishing that, I also had daunting political obstacles to overcome at Colón. To a large degree our success, and maybe even survival, would depend on my ability to keep the Colombian governor of Panama either mollified or cowed.

I also had to warn Sampson at once with another telegram. Would he and the leadership in Washington believe my assessment and prediction?

45

Mechanical Monsters

Cruiser Dixon, *Aspinwall (Colón), Department of Panama, Republic of Colombia*

Friday, 29 July 1898

A s I walked back to *Dixon*, the crane–coal conveyor, steam and smoke puffing from its stack, was rumbling into position alongside her. That smoke was spreading over the town, a clear signal to everyone what we were doing.

The strange new contraption was strikingly big, towering over even *Dixon*'s high sides. Though I'd heard that one of Edison's engineers had created the machines, I'd never personally seen one in operation. A monument to complex mechanical engineering, with all kinds of clanking, whirling, and shrieking parts, it was symbolic of a new generation of American inventions. *Dixon*'s engineers swarmed over it like children with a new toy, exclaiming its virtues to each other. I'm no engineer; I just hoped the damned thing would work.

A small yard locomotive manned by *Dixon*'s engine room artificers towed up the first coal car from the coal pile. Then a secondary boom lowered a cable, which was attached to one side of the car and hauled up. The car tipped over, spilling the coal onto the crane's six-foot-wide leather-and-rubber conveyor belt, which rose on a forty-degree angle, clanking over ratchet wheels along the way, to a position ten feet above the ship's main deck. Once there, the coal went over the belt's end and plunged down through a stout canvas sleeve into the chutes leading below to the coal bunkers.

By the time the cloud of dust dissipated, another coal car had arrived under the crane. I stood there mesmerized by the process. I estimated that each car carried about four tons of coal, and a car was tipped onto the conveyor every five minutes. The entire operation was nothing short of a marvel. Just a few days ago we'd loaded sixty tons by hand in four hours and were damned proud of the achievement. This machine would do that in an hour and a quarter. At that rate, we could load the thousand tons in only twenty hours.

The process was faster, but also much messier. Every time the coal plunged down into the canvas sleeve, a plume of black coal dust rose and dispersed over the ship, the dock, and the town. Already, my ship's topsides, which had been cleaned above and below of Riohacha's coal dust, had become filthy with a sticky mixture of coal and mechanical grease. It was a sight to break an old sailor's heart. The mess couldn't be avoided, however; it was just another of the depressing aspects of modern naval service.

My heart swelled with pride that my men had figured out how to master the crane and conveyor, machinery I doubted they had ever seen before. Accordingly, I altered my course to head over to the crane and congratulate the chief engineer, Lieutenant Commander Sheats.

He was up in the wheelhouse (if that's what you call it) of the monster along with several of his men. Down near where I was standing was his assistant engineer, Lieutenant Campbell, a dour and disliked fellow who nevertheless had a natural affinity for mechanical beasts. I'd not had a chance to get to know him yet and resolved to do so once we got under way for Providencia.

I was about to hold out my hand and say, "Well done, Mr. Campbell," when there was a loud thud and clang aloft. Everyone instinctively looked up, but far too late. A three-foot-long cylinder of iron had already plummeted into Campbell's head and penetrated down into his torso, turning it into unrecognizable mush, only four feet away from me.

Half a dozen men saw it happen, but no one moved, including me, veteran of a dozen bloody battles. We were all stunned. Unlike a battle injury, this was completely unexpected, instantaneous, and irreversible.

The mechanical monster's steam engine never missed a beat. Above us, the secondary boom, now minus a crucial component, swayed away from its prior position. The conveyor and the canvas sleeve swung away from over the deck chutes, spewing the load of coal all over *Dixon's* main deck and the dock.

Sheats thundered over the sound of the engine from his perch, "Dammit, stop your friggin' dillydathering and get that damned boom under control *right the hell now!*"

Of course, he hadn't seen the cause of the mechanical failure, or its deadly consequence. Somebody yelled to stop everything, and another shouted for the chief engineer to get down to the pier right away. Steam rushed out of a relief valve, and the rumble diminished as the crane ceased moving. Sheats emerged and saw Campbell's gory corpse, swore viciously, and began descending the ladder.

I sadly admit that during these first few moments I just stood there, still stunned, as sailors gathered around me and the body of the lieutenant. After staring at the misshapen lump that he had become, everyone swung their gaze toward me.

Sheats spoke first, in a monotone. "The boom's central linkage bolt failed under strain, Captain. Shattered and fell on Ian. Probably from excessive rust and improper maintenance by the locals."

In that instant I finally regained my wits. "Can it be repaired, Commander?"

"Yes, sir. We'll jury-rig a new boom linkage right away and watch it closely."

I nodded and said, "Make it happen, then. We've no time to waste. Have some men take Mr. Campbell's body away to the ship. We'll bury him at sea, where he belongs."

To the crowd of hardened old sailors and horrified naval militia-men surrounding me, I declared, "A sad accident, men. Mr. Campbell is *Dixon's* first mortal casualty in this war. He may not be our last. And now, we owe it to Mr. Campbell to finish what we started here. We must have this coal if we are to find the enemy raider that is threatening our Navy and our home coasts. A lot of people are relying on us right now, so let's get this coal on our ship."

With that, I walked away, bound to my cabin to write the expected letter to Campbell's family back in New York City. As I trudged through the afternoon heat, I tried to recall something positive about the man. He was a wizard with machines. Other than that I couldn't think of a thing. What could I possibly write that would give them any comfort?

Little did I know then that Campbell's condolence letter would not be the last one resulting from *Dixon's* visit to Panama.

46

Politics and Crime

Cruiser Dixon, *Aspinwall (Colón), Department of Panama, Republic of Colombia*

Friday, 29 July 1898

"WELL, THIS IS INTERESTING," muttered Belfort to Guns Pinkston as I entered the bridge. The executive officer was standing in the portside door to the wing and had binoculars to his eyes aimed at the main street of Colón. The bayside street was long known among sailors for its bloody bars and seedy brothels, so anything was possible.

Just at that moment, the petty officer of the watch belatedly noticed my arrival and announced my presence. Belfort shot the petty officer a reproving look, then turned to me, clearly embarrassed. "Sorry, Captain. I didn't see you come on board or I would've met you on the quarterdeck."

Indeed, he *should* have been embarrassed. It was a serious breach of the ship's security. The quarterdeck crew failed to keep a proper lookout and were also caught unawares by my return, then failed to promptly notify the bridge. But I didn't bring any of that up. I was far more interested in what Belfort had been watching.

"What do you see, Commander?"

"A gathering over there, sir," he said. "Coming this way."

I took up a pair of binoculars and followed the line of Belfort's gaze until I saw the object of his attention. "Oh, yes, I see them."

A motley column of men—perhaps fifty of them—was approaching the coaling pier. They wore assorted degrees of uniform attire ranging all the way from matching coats and pants to plain rags. Many were carrying long guns; some had machetes. One was carrying a banner. Not the Colombian flag, but something black and red.

"I've no idea what they want, sir," said Belfort.

I knew. "They're rebels. That flag is the same damned flag Pedro Prestan's rabble carried back in 1885. Our Navy had to intervene to save lives on all sides back then. I don't know why they're coming this way, but it's another complication we don't need. All right, pass the word to our perimeter guards that those people are to be kept *outside* the perimeter. Their leader may be brought here if he wishes to speak to me."

"Foremast lookout to bridge! Another group coming this way on the main road from the rail yard to the south. About a mile off. Looks like soldiers. Maybe a hundred or more of 'em."

I focused my glasses on the group. Yes, the shiny *Pickelhaube* helmets and fixed bayonets showed them to be Colombian soldiers. They were marching three abreast up the road toward the docks, a young officer in the lead. The local garrison, I supposed, more accustomed to police duties than battle.

"Orders, sir?" asked Belfort quietly.

"Yes, I want an officer sent to the soldiers with a message from me. Pass the word for Lieutenant Wundarn. Bring him to my quarters."

At my desk I composed a note in my grammatically deficient Spanish, using a dictionary for the difficult words and putting the whole thing on the ship's official stationary. I also wrote it out in English as a record of my action and intent.

29 July 1898
Colón, Panama, Republic of Colombia
Dear Sir,
To the commander of the troops of the famous Army of the Great Republic of Colombia who are stationed at Colón, I extend my

utmost respects and good will on behalf of myself, my ship, and my nation.

Please be assured that my ship is visiting Colón solely for the purpose of refilling our coal bunkers. To that purpose we have requisitioned the American-owned coal company's supplies and equipment, as per our national privilege. We will, of course, be paying the company for the coal. We will also be honored to pay the governor of Panama's special new tax directly to the governor's office, through your person, with a further fee included as remuneration for the additional security costs the Colombian army has incurred as a result of our presence.

It is my intention to depart Colón as soon as possible, probably tomorrow, leaving everything at the company and in the town in the same condition as when we arrived.

It is also my desire to have the honor and pleasure of your company at a special dinner on board my ship this evening to recognize the long friendship between our two countries. Please do me the great favor of accepting my humble invitation by immediately replying upon receiving this note.

With pleasure, I am your most obedient servant, etc.

Capt. Peter Wake, USN

U.S. Cruiser *Dixon*, commanding

Postscript: For your information, there is a group of bandits demonstrating openly with a rebel flag in the park at the corner of Front Street and 4th Street. They are not my concern, but as we are brothers in military fraternity, I thought you should know.

I read it aloud in English to Belfort and Wundarn when they arrived. The executive officer chuckled. "Nicely done, sir. Diverting their attention from us, along with an attractive inducement that will ensure their amity."

"That is precisely the intent, Commander. I hope it works."

Wundarn, who had not shown any initiative in the three weeks I'd been in *Dixon*, stood there with a scrunched-up, puzzled face.

I could almost see the wheels turning very slowly in his head. He wasn't the right man for this job, but the Colombians would be more impressed by an officer, and he was the only officer I could spare to be a messenger.

"Mr. Wundarn, I read this to you so you'll know our peaceful intent and can demonstrate that intent through your demeanor. We do *not*, I repeat, do *not* want any confrontation with the Colombian officials. I know you don't speak Spanish, but just show quiet American confidence, politeness, and deference to the Colombians. Now is the time to be *charming*, Mr. Wundarn, and bring me the officer's reply promptly."

"Aye, aye, sir. Charming."

I doubted Wundarn had the ability to be charming but hoped he might rise somewhat to the occasion. As soon as he left my cabin, Belfort gave me a progress report on everything else.

"Campbell's body is in the cooler, sir. Sheats has the boom jury-rigged and the coaling restarted. Gerard reports that the rebels are staying in the park, outside our perimeter, but they're getting quite drunk and raucous. Evidently they think we'll protect them from the Colombian soldiers while they proclaim a new republic. Gerard told them *no*, we weren't going to be involved in any of that. Ensign Barnett hasn't returned yet from sending the cable, and neither have Paymaster Kilmarty and Paymaster Kennedy, whom I sent ashore to get fresh provisions at the market. I'm expecting all of them back soon."

"The market is out on the edge of town, at least eight or ten blocks away. Were they armed?"

"Yes, sir. And the cooks they took with them were armed also."

"Why did Kilmarty go ashore? He's in charge of supplies, not provisions."

"He suggested it, Captain, because Kennedy's young and can't haggle like he can."

Well, that's true, I thought. *But where exactly is their superior, Paymaster Lieutenant Shalby?* That social scion of Baltimore, who gloried in his self-perceived naval militia prestige, had seldom exercised leadership in my time on board. "Shalby didn't go? Why not?"

I could tell Belfort sensed my unease. He was forming an answer when a knock suddenly sounded on my door. "Seaman Perry, sir! Messenger from the officer of the watch, Lieutenant Commander Pinkston, who presents his respects and requests your presence on the bridge right away, sir!"

When we got there, Ensign Barnett was standing at attention. No one else was inside the bridge. Pinkston didn't waste time.

"Mr. Barnett just got back, sir. There were no cables waiting for us or any U.S. naval vessel, and your telegrams were sent with no problems. But there is a new problem. He reports that Paymaster Kilmarty and Paymaster Kennedy are both under arrest by the local police, along with their entire party."

Belfort's jaw dropped. Mine clenched. "For what?" I asked Barnett. "And how do you know this?"

Barnett said, "Sir, Mr. Kilmarty has been arrested for the rape of a little girl—they say he attacked her at the market. All the others were arrested for accessory to rape. Right after I got the telegrams sent off, I saw our officers and men being taken into the jail at the city hall. When I asked the chief of police what was happening, he got very angry and yelled at me in Spanish, sir. For a second I thought they were going to try to arrest me and *my* men just for being Americans. Finally, I figured out it was about a girl supposedly attacked by Mr. Kilmarty."

The crime was horrendous, but Kilmarty's guilt or innocence wasn't the issue here. He was an American naval officer and, therefore untouchable in foreign ports. That national status always had been, and always *must* be, protected—with no exceptions. Even for someone like Kilmarty, whom I neither liked nor trusted.

I wasn't surprised by the allegation against Kilmarty. It was in keeping with everything I knew about the man—his salacious stories, his bragging, and his general sense of entitlement. As I recounted to my readers earlier in this memoir, my internal alarms went off as soon as I met him. But that didn't matter either. It was wartime, and this charge was an obstacle to finding and destroying the enemy raider. Kilmarty *would* face justice, but not in a Colombian court.

Turning to Belfort, I said, "I want you to put our Marine officer in charge of the perimeter. Yes, I know Mr. Ostermann is only a new second lieutenant, but he'll have to step up and handle this. Then you will brief Lieutenant Gerard and Chaplain Reeher on the situation and bring them to my quarters in ten minutes. We don't have much time, and we're going to solve this damned mess right now."

Once Belfort acknowledged the order, I said to the signal officer, "Mr. Barnett, you are going back to the telegraph office. Encrypt these messages and get them sent to Admiral Sampson at Santiago de Cuba and to Captain Dimm in *Bronx* at Kingston, Jamaica."

I handed a sheet of paper with the handwritten messages to Belfort, who glanced at it, then looked up at me questioningly before passing it along to Barnett. The messages were simple.

To Sampson—Have new information indicating *Marquesa* headed Isla Providencia to meet German collier *Karibische Dame* and refuel. Afterward, raider might head north through Yucatan Channel and raid U.S. Gulf ports. *Dixon* will head to Providencia upon completing coaling here at Colón tomorrow. Am sending cable to *Bronx* at Kingston to head to Providencia immediately. —P. Wake

To Dimm—Have information raider *Marquesa* headed Isla Providencia to refuel from German collier *Karibische Dame* soon. Get *Bronx* steaming immediately for Isla Providencia to engage raider. *Dixon* coaling now in Colón and will depart immediately on completion tomorrow. —P. Wake

"New information, sir?" asked Belfort. "Anything I need to know?"

"I'll explain it all to you later, John, but first I've got to deal with this Kilmarty disaster."

I departed the bridge in a foul mood, already resolved to defend a man I despised.

47

The Unimaginable

Cruiser Dixon, *Aspinwall (Colón), Department of Panama,*
Republic of Colombia
Friday, 29 July 1898

I WASTED NO TIME WHEN Lieutenant Gerard and Chaplain Reeher presented themselves before me, both men looking equal parts surprised, worried, and determined.

"You've been told what happened ashore. This is going to be resolved quickly, so listen carefully because I'm telling you how *we* are going to do it."

I tried to submerge my fury at Kilmarty for putting us in this position as I briefed them on the plan and their roles in it. It was simple—and risky. No one ventured a question or suggestion, though Reeher looked like he really wanted to. After I'd finished I led them all out of my cabin. Belfort went up to the bridge while Gerard and Reeher followed me down the gangway to the pier.

We walked quickly across the tracks and Front Street, passing the rabble in the park, half of whom were already snoring off their drunken quasi-rebellion while the others argued over grand strategy. As we turned left on Sixth Street toward the city hall, we spotted the Colombian army detachment marching up Front Street, plainly bound for the revolutionaries. *Maybe my note worked.*

There were five disheveled policemen lounging in front of the city hall, apparently on guard duty. We marched right through them and up the steps. They bristled indignantly, but none raised a hand to stop us. Ignoring the protestations of functionaries in the anteroom, I strode into the chief's office, catching that worthy by surprise. I knew the type: a well-fed gangster with a shrewd sense of how to make a buck. His feet up on the desk and hands relaxed behind his head, he was regaling a fawning lackey with details of how he was going to spend the money he would charge the *norteamericano* Navy for bail on the prisoners when I arrived. The number was a nice round figure: a thousand dollars.

Spanish is a valuable language for American naval officers to know. Those operating in this hemisphere need to understand what adversaries are saying about them. Although there are times when I prefer not to reveal my linguistic ability, this was not one of them. In his own lingo I demanded of the chief, "Where is the girl, and where is her father?"

Completely taken aback by my rude entrance, he dropped his feet to the floor and his hands to the desk. "Ah . . . the father is in the other room right now, sir."

There weren't that many rooms in the place. I didn't ask which one. Probably the one we'd just passed. "Good, I will speak with him right now."

I walked out of the office and into the room beside it. At a small table sat a dark-skinned man in his mid-thirties with plaintive, grief-stricken eyes. He was alone in the room, and I guessed the chief had just finished his interview with him. I sat down in the chair across from him.

"I am Captain Peter Wake, of the United States warship *Dixon*. Paymaster Kilmarty is under my command. This is Lieutenant Gerard, and this is our chaplain, James Reeher, a man of God."

I softened my voice and held out a hand. He looked at it but did not offer his own. I lowered mine and said, "May I talk with you, sir? I want to know what happened. But first, how is your daughter?"

The chief showed up at the door and tried to enter. Gerard closed the door against him, saying in Spanish, "It is the defense counsel's privilege to interview the witness, Chief. Privately."

"Maria is at home, crying," said her father, who never did introduce himself. "She is only fourteen, sir. And she is frightened of men in uniforms."

I understood that sentiment very well. He was a peasant laborer and his home was a thatched hut, if he was lucky. Peasants all around the world dreaded any interaction with officialdom, for it almost always meant the loss of their money or possessions—or the infliction of pain if they had no money or possessions to give. That dread was even worse with foreigners in uniform.

"Maria is my wife's name," I said gently. "Does your daughter Maria need any medical attention? I have a doctor on board my ship. I can have him come to your home."

The door shook as the chief forced it open a crack. Gerard hissed at him, "Stay out. Next time I will shoot you."

The door closed. I heard a buzz of excited voices outside. This was taking longer than I wanted, but I had to tread carefully.

The father, his eyes darting between the door and me, softly said, "She is not cut or bruised. But she is hurt . . . where he attacked her. Her mother is with her now."

"Sir, do you know what happened? Can you tell me?"

Suddenly, tears coursed down his cheeks. "Yes, sir. Maria told her mother and me. She was helping her mother sell our mangoes at the market. Your officer, the fat one with the red face, wanted more mangoes, so Maria went to our cart behind the market to get them. He followed her and attacked her. She tried to scream for help, but he held her mouth closed. Afterward he left her there. Her mother found her on the ground. Another seller in the market told the police." He hesitated, then said, "My Maria is still a child, and now she is no longer a virgin."

His words sickened me. I didn't want to hear any more details. The door rattled. The chief was trying to enter again. Gerard drew his revolver. I stopped him. "No, I've heard enough. Let him in."

The chief blundered in, quickly puffed up like a turkey cock, and said, "This is an outrage! You *yanquis* think you can do anything? One of our poor girls is assaulted and—"

"Stop!" I shouted at him. Then, in a calmer tone, I announced, "I find that there is sufficient cause to believe a crime was committed by Paymaster Kilmarty. The bail will be one hundred dollars for all the Americans, paid directly to you, Chief. All my men will be released this instant. Also, two hundred dollars will be paid to the girl's father by my chaplain. Be warned that I will later check to make sure unscrupulous government officials have not robbed them of that money. My chaplain will now go to the family's home with the father, meet the mother and daughter, and console them as well as he can. He will also take a statement of what happened from the girl and her mother."

The chief, expecting an argument, not agreement, sputtered something unintelligible. Ignoring this pompous gangster in a police uniform, I turned to the distraught father.

"Sir, I give you my word of honor that Paymaster Kilmarty will be subjected to American naval discipline. It is very strict. I also apologize to Maria, to you, to your wife, and to your entire family on behalf of the people and government of the United States." As he looked uneasily at me, I reached out and grasped his hand. "Sir, please know Americans do not condone this kind of behavior. There will be justice for this terrible crime."

The father nodded his head slowly, still watching me warily. "Thank you, sir."

"Will you now please take Chaplain Reeher and Lieutenant Gerard to your home?"

The father's answer was barely audible, "Yes. It is not far."

I stood and faced the chief. "Here is your bail money for my men."

He reached for it, but I closed my fist around the five gold twenties in my hand. "Bring me Kilmarty and the others immediately. Then you will get the money. And do not try to obstruct us on the way back to our ship. That would make me angry at *you*."

Though he merely shrugged to save face and said nothing, the thug's eyes revealed he fully understood my threat. Moments later, he got his money as my officers and crew emerged from the city hall and started back to the ship.

Kilmarty was uncharacteristically quiet as we walked back to the ship, but also somewhat defiant now that he was out of the jail. None of the others walked near him. None spoke about what had happened. The journey passed in the silence of shame, intensified by the towns-people stopping to stare at us with palpable loathing, for the word had already spread. My wrath mounting with each step, I steeled myself not to give in to my instinct as the father of a daughter and a career naval officer. This had to be done according to the book. The Navy wouldn't want the public to learn that an officer had done such a thing, but I wasn't going to allow the senior leadership to thwart justice because I hadn't followed regulations.

Once up on *Dixon*'s main deck, in a tone loud enough that the nearby crew could hear me over the clanking of the coal loader, I informed Kilmarty that he was under close arrest for the crime of rape of a child and confined to his cabin. He would remain there pending our return to the fleet and a general court-martial. I added that if he left his cabin, whatever the reason, he would be instantly confined in the brig. He looked disbelieving when he realized his rescue from a Colombian jail was not part of a cover-up on our part, and his surliness turned to fear. His fate was to be prosecuted and imprisoned for a long time. His family would be humiliated. In reply to my announcement, he trembled out a feeble, "Yes, sir."

An hour later, as I was writing up the official account of my ini-tial decisions and actions regarding Kilmarty, Chaplain Reeher and Lieutenant Gerard appeared at my quarters and made their report. The chaplain had spoken with Maria, with her mother present, and received the same description of events. Reeher wrote out a state-ment, which both girl and mother, being illiterate, signed with an X. Both men were visibly affected as they described what came next. The family gratefully accepted the money, then laid out some weak tea and stale guava cakes for the "honored visitors." It was the only food in the hut.

Reeher ended his report by saying, "I did my best to console them, but this is an unimaginable horror for that girl, sir. The community will shun her, no man will want to marry her, and God forbid she is pregnant." He paused hesitantly. "Will Kilmarty *really* be prosecuted?"

"You saw that I gave her father my word of honor that he would be prosecuted, Chaplain. Therefore, he *will* be prosecuted, even if I have to personally pay for transporting the victim and witnesses to the court-martial, wherever it is held."

48

Revolution, Coal, and a Friendly Warning

Cruiser Dixon, *Aspinwall (Colón), Department of Panama, Republic of Colombia*

Friday, 29 July 1898

WHEN I RETURNED TO THE BRIDGE, the coaling was continuing and a new development was unfolding, with an interesting twist. The confrontation between the Colombian army and the insurgents—which I had done my best to instigate so both sides would be kept busy enough to leave *us* alone—turned out to be quite a show. We watched it all from *Dixon's* bridge, our guns manned at half strength but ready to fire if needed.

Intriguingly, the militia soldiers didn't appear to want to attack the inebriated rebels, who for their part merely giggled and issued ridiculous insults when the army contingent approached. Instead of immediately assaulting the insolent rabble, the soldiers marched up to the park and proceeded to do close-order drills, and not in the most imposing military manner, either. This presumably was meant to scare the rebels into submission or retreat. After a solid ten minutes of this comical performance a surrender was arranged, complete with a solemn ceremony in which the rebels turned over their guns and the leader of the revolution presented his rusty old machete to the *commandante* of the soldiers.

At dinner in the wardroom that evening, the Colombian *commandante* explained that the miscreants were given parole to go home to their families. The Colombian spoke surprisingly good English, which, he explained, he had learned when he was stationed at the embassy in Washington.

"You must understand my men are only local conscript militia doing their required two weeks of annual duty. Most of them are related to those men in the park. The only reason the rebels even assembled was because you seized the coal pier. They thought to take advantage of your presence—and your presumed support—to pursue their rebellion against the government. That, of course, the government cannot allow."

My officers nodded in congenial agreement, for the *commandante* was a charming fellow. He was originally from Cartagena, he told us, and had been assigned to Panama City on a routine tour of duty. But he got on the wrong side of a general and was reassigned to command the militia at Colón as unofficial punishment. I commiserated, saying it happens in all militaries. Then I asked why the rebels didn't actually fight the army in the park.

"Oh, that is quite simple, Captain. When you declined to get involved, they decided to get drunk instead," he said with that telling sigh of resignation that says so much in the countries to our south. "They are not dangerous or bad men. There was no reason for bloodshed. On Monday, my men will go home from their duty and everyone will gather at *la taberna* and laugh over this affair."

The wardroom had a good chuckle over that. All in all, my officers and I had a delightful dinner with the officer, and that lighthearted occasion was just what *Dixon*'s wardroom needed to help relieve the dreadful afternoon.

Of course, this entire time the rumbling and clanking of the crane and coal conveyor never ceased or slowed. The continued pace impressed the *commandante*, who expressed admiration for the stamina and mechanical abilities of the *norteamericanos*. But I got the impression he wanted to say something else.

As I walked him to the quarterdeck after dinner, he finally asked me the question I knew had to be brewing in his mind. The jovial smile had disappeared. "When will you finish with your coaling, Captain Wake?"

Knowing the Colombian governor on the other side of the isthmus would be cabled my reply within the hour, I answered carefully. "Tomorrow. I'm not sure precisely when."

He nodded thoughtfully, then leaned closer so his words could not be heard by others. "I hope it is by noon, well before the two o'clock train from Panama City, Captain Wake. For that train will have a battalion of three hundred *regular* soldiers, veterans of the fight against the rebels at Buenaventura last year. The governor has no sense of humor, Captain, and your presence here embarrasses him."

As I was digesting that extraordinary warning he shook my hand. "Thank you for the wonderful dinner and friendship you have offered. I wish for you to have your coal loaded safely by *noon*," he emphasized, "then a rapid departure, a bon voyage, and a short war. Good luck, sir."

After that, the remarkable gentleman left *Dixon* and descended to the pier. As I watched him walk away into the night, I stood thinking about the situation. As if to punctuate our dilemma, a deluge of rain suddenly cascaded down. The noise of the rain pounding on our steel decks and superstructure was deafening. You haven't seen rain until you've been in Panama in July and August. It arrives without fail each evening and falls with an oppressive weight.

The elements themselves seemed to be conspiring against us. *The coal dust will turn to soup in this,* I muttered to myself as I looked out into the black night. *And that will get into everything the dust missed. Plus, the work of the coal-loading detail will be that much harder.*

I ducked under the quarterdeck's overhead as Belfort came up looking agitated. *Now what?*

"Captain, Mr. Barnett just got back from the post office. Admiral Sampson's reply to your message came back within minutes. Pretty quick turnaround. They must be taking this seriously."

By the light of the quarterdeck lamp, I read Barnett's decrypted copy of the cable, which he had typed up in the proper form for the signal files.

> From: RADM W. Sampson, NorAtlantSqdn, Cmdg, Santiago, Cuba
> 3:10 p.m., 29 July 1898
> To: Captain P. Wake, Cruiser *Dixon*, Colón, Panamá, Colombia
> Priority Cable Comms-Urgent-Coded
> RECVD YOUR CABLE #7-29-98-01—X—BRONX STILL REPAIRING AT KINGSTON AND ORDERED TO GO TO PROVIDENCIA TOMORROW—X—NO OTHER SHIPS AVAILABLE TO INTERCEPT RAIDER—X—ADVS WHEN DIXON DEPARTS COLON—X—GOOD LUCK—XXX

Belfort was right. It was an extremely quick turnaround. I was relieved that Sampson was taking my report very seriously. But was Dimm?

"Any reply from Dimm?"

"No, sir. Mr. Barnett stayed awhile longer in case one came in, but nothing arrived." Belfort's face brightened. "But Barnett did find out some fresh news from Puerto Rico, sir. He brought us the local Colón newspaper for today with a cabled news report from a journalist with General Miles' army dated just yesterday. Turns out the Spanish surrendered Ponce without a shot! Miles now possesses the entire harbor and docks and is unloading his supplies for the cross-island campaign, which is already under way."

It was stunningly good news. "Well I'll be damned. Miles actually pulled it off."

I thought of Theodore back in Cuba, that damned supply road from the beach at Siboney, and thousands of men waiting to die of sickness. Right then the rain abruptly let up, no longer covering the sound of the loading conveyor engine, whose rumbling brought me back to the moment.

"What is the coal situation?" I asked.

"Three hundred and fifty-five tons so far, Captain. The men have been doing watch on watch, so they've gotten *some* time off, but I'm worried about Sheats. He took Campbell's death pretty hard, sir, and hasn't taken any rest since then."

Belfort sounded tired, too. I consulted my pocket watch. Eleven o'clock. Sheats had been at it for seven hours. At fifty tons an hour, it would take another thirteen hours to load the remaining coal. That meant noon tomorrow. *How the hell did the* commandante *know?*

"Pass the word from me to Commander Sheats that he will immediately take two hours off and rest *in bed* in his quarters. His chief petty officer will take over during that time. I do not want Sheats disturbed at all while he's resting. And while I'm at it, I want *you* to take the same time off. *Dixon* will not be served well by having her senior officers nearly stupefied with exhaustion and making bad and tardy decisions. Understood?"

"Yes, sir."

"Very well. I am not tired right now, too much on my mind, so I will stay on watch for the time you and Sheats are below. You can relieve me in two hours. John, I want either you or me on the bridge the entire time we're in this hellhole."

"Aye, aye, sir."

"Good, because we're getting under way at noon and heading directly to Providencia Island. Now get some sleep."

49

Alone

Cruiser Dixon, *Providencia Island*

Monday, 1 August 1898

HAVING DEPARTED COLÓN without further complications, crimes, bribes—and, most crucially, before that battalion of regular infantry arrived—we steamed past San Andrés Island the second morning out. That evening at sunset we arrived at Providencia. It was a very tense approach. There are reefs all around the island, particularly to the south, east, and north. Our route was from the south-southwest. As I expected, *Bronx* was nowhere to be seen.

My plan was simple. Approach Santa Catalina Harbor with the rays of the setting sun behind us lighting up the ships inside the harbor, and also blinding enemy gunners trying to hit us. We would open fire the instant we spotted *Marquesa* anchored inside. Our gunners would try not to hit the German collier, or anything else afloat or ashore, but there were no guarantees. Gunnery on a ship is a tricky business. The best gunners in our fleet had a rate of 55 percent accuracy at four miles, and *Dixon* wasn't equipped with the best guns and fire control.

Should we fail, the consequences would be dire. We *had* to cripple the Spanish raider before she could emerge from the tiny anchorage. She was too big, too fast, and too powerful to take chances with.

The more diplomatically astute among my readers might fairly object to my tactic, for the island was claimed by Colombia and was technically neutral. But I judged that the havoc *Marquesa* might wreak if she got loose made the gamble worth it. Besides, I'd already caused a commotion at the Colombian ports of Riohacha and Colón and, no doubt, would have to deal with the repercussions from the armchair warriors in Washington about that, so what was one more Colombian commotion on the list?

I fully expected the word of our arrival to pass quickly down the island, and that someone on the south end of the island would get word to the Spanish ship before we reached the anchorage. But we were as ready as we could be. My men were at their battle stations aloft and alow, all guns were loaded and locked and searching for targets. The lookouts were doubled, and *Dixon* was charging forward at her full speed. We were steaming faster than most horses could gallop, so perhaps we could still surprise them.

I stood on the starboard bridge wing intently peering through my binoculars as we passed a mile off the southern point and steamed along the western shoreline bound for Santa Catalina Harbor. At his fire-control perch above me, Pinkston was itching to fire his guns. Below me, the forward 6-inch gun was already traversed to the expected bearing of the enemy once the harbor came into view.

On our port beam, the sun was less than two fingers above the horizon. We had twelve to fifteen minutes of sunlight left. We'd see the anchorage in two minutes.

"Reduce revolutions to ten knots," I ordered. "Right standard rudder to course zero-one-zero. Set the battle flag."

Dixon almost seemed to exhale as the thumping of her engines diminished, a steam line bled off, and her propeller slowed. She swung gently over to the new course, her bow pointing at Santa Catalina Island, just now coming into view. Our twelve-by-eighteen-foot battle flag snapped in the wind as it soared up the halyard and streamed aft.

We were seconds away from seeing our target. Gerard reported in a matter-of-fact voice from the chart table that we would pass within a hundred yards of the reefs off the village of San Felipe. Every man on the bridge held his breath. The silence was only external, though, for inside my head blood pounded in my ears.

The anchorage came into view. It was empty.

We were too late.

To Belfort, I said, "Left standard rudder to course three-five-zero. Maintain speed. Keep a sharp eye for ships on the horizons and also for reefs close by. We'll steam to the north to make sure *Marquesa* isn't lurking out there somewhere, then we'll return to the anchorage and get some intelligence about her."

The tension evaporated, faces eased, breathing resumed, and *Dixon* buzzed with whispered opinions. We steamed north along those treacherous reefs for an hour, sighting nothing, then circled back to the west and used the range lights to carefully creep into the anchorage two and a half hours later.

Within five minutes of our backing down on the hook, a Colombian official came alongside in a launch and was conveyed up to my quarters, where I had a bottle of Matusalem rum waiting. I do not share this famous Cuban nectar with others lightly, but this opportunity to gain valuable intelligence called for such a sacrifice. Naval regulations had banned nonmedicinal liquor since 1893, of course, but this rum wasn't for pleasure. No, it was a valuable tool for loosening foreign tongues.

I prepared myself for the inevitable posturing and pontificating, knowing it was going to be a long night. Belfort came in, looked worriedly at the bottle, and took a chair. I introduced myself and Belfort to the Colombian gentleman, who was attired in a uniform of sorts that had seen better, and cleaner, days.

Reflecting the island's multicultural history, his English was a curious Caribbean creole patois with a delightful, almost Irish, lilt. "Captain Wake, I am Don Alberto Vargas García de Zaragoza, alcalde of the Municipality of San Andrés and Providencia, within the Department of the Archipelago of San Andrés, Providencia, and Santa Catalina, a treasured part of the Great Republic of Colombia. As such, I very

much welcome this visit to our humble but proud islands by a warship of the famous navy of our esteemed friends, the United States of
North America."

He said that mouthful without pausing once for breath and with
one eye on the bottle the entire time.

Excellent. We're about to become very good friends. "And it is indeed
an honor and pleasure for us to visit your beautiful island, Don
Alberto. May I offer you some of this excellent Cuban rum?"

"What a delightful suggestion, Captain Wake! Thank you very much."

I poured a decent amount into my best glass, trying not to cringe
at such an expenditure of my cherished rum. I put it in his hand with
a polite flair, then poured a lesser amount into my glass and Belfort's.
The executive officer briefly frowned again but did not decline.

I raised my glass. "To our dear friends, the people of the Great
Republic of Colombia!"

And so it went, toast followed toast, followed by descriptions of
beloved family, tales of past battles won and of long ago loves lost.
Initially, Don Alberto was hesitant to share details of *Marquesa's* visit.
The fellow had an impressive ability to hold his liquor and his tongue.
That lasted for three nearly full glasses and almost an hour. On the
fourth glass our friendship blossomed. He giddily told the entire story
to his newest best friend.

It seems *Marquesa* arrived before the German collier, but her crew
stayed on board and had very limited interactions ashore. As he had
done with me, Don Alberto came out to the ship and met her commanding officer, Capitán de Navío José Grinda y Ugarte. I pressed Don
Alberto for his impressions of my adversary. He described Grinda as
my age, trim in build and clean-shaven, with gray hair and sad eyes. Not
timid eyes, he further explained, but eyes that had seen too much life,
and perhaps too much death along the way. He said Grinda's demeanor
was thoughtful and quiet, but resolute, as if he knew his navy was losing
the war but he still had an important duty to carry out.

I digested that information, adding it to what I already knew from
the Spanish raider's actions and deceptions. *Grinda is an experienced*

man fighting without illusions. He is able to think like his enemy—me— predicting my next move and creating a scenario in which I alter my move to be beneficial to him. That makes him a very dangerous foe.

Two days after *Marquesa* had arrived in the anchorage, the *Karibische Dame* steamed in from Colón and rafted alongside the raider. For the next couple of days the Germans and Spanish labored around the clock to transfer coal to the raider's bunkers. With a sly grin, Don Alberto informed us that both ships had departed Providencia that very morning after dawn, the German heading east and the Spanish raider, her bunkers now full, bound north.

Almost reading my mind, Belfort, heretofore silently observing as he took tiny sips, inquired if any American warships had been seen in the area. The answer was *no*. Belfort quietly groaned.

Ten minutes later, Don Alberto was being gently assisted into his launch while Belfort and I had a talk on the stern.

"Damned shame there's no transoceanic cable here," Belfort muttered. "We could've used it to warn Sampson that the raider's heading north, just like you thought she would. So, what do we do now, sir?"

"Head for Swan Island," I said. "It's right on the raider's course to the Yucatan Channel. The islanders might have seen her go by. That would confirm her course and give an idea of her speed."

"There's a chance Grinda could also steam northeast and try to sneak back into Cuba at the Isle of Pines."

"That would be the safest thing to do, but a man like Grinda won't take that course. Too many shoals and reefs in that area that would limit his movements. He'd be boxed in and could be easily blockaded from offshore. No, I think Grinda is heading north into the Gulf of Mexico. He wants to stay free and keep his options for attack open."

Belfort nodded. "When do you want to get under way for Swan Island?"

I looked out at the unlit channel through the reefs and into a black void. Coming in, we had used the shore lights as a range to gauge our approach. The squall line now moving in obliterated those. Steaming out in the dark would be a dangerous game of roulette with the odds heavily stacked against us. The rain reached *Dixon* and we walked forward to the superstructure.

Wait 'til dawn, I told myself. *That's the wiser course, and you're exhausted.* I gave myself a mental shake. *I can't. There's no time to dawdle.* "We leave now—going out slowly on the reverse course to our entry."

Belfort was carefully neutral in his acknowledgment. "Aye, sir."

50

Lunacy

Cruiser Dixon, *Great Swan Island, off Honduras*
Thursday, 4 August 1898

W<small>E ARRIVED AT DAWN ON</small> Thursday, two windy, wet days after that nerve-wracking departure from Providencia. There is no real harbor at Great Swan, only a few open anchorages on the west and north sides of the island that are somewhat sheltered from the trade winds. There were none at Little Swan Island, just to the east. I chose the western end of the bigger island, letting go the hook in eight fathoms.

Once the ship was secured I ordered certain arrangements, for I already knew who to talk with and how to prepare for his arrival. Thirty minutes later, King Alonso stepped from his longboat onto our lowered gangway and stopped to take in the splendor laid out before him. Then he ascended the ladder, clearly savoring every moment.

I must say my men did it up in fine style. The moment our visitor's head reached the elevation of the quarterdeck, Belfort shouted out the ceremonial commands, our Marine detail stamped their boots and slapped their rifles to present arms, the boatswains sounded a triple pipe call, the side-boys snapped to, the gunner's mate fired off twenty-one blank rounds, and all hands who had previously manned the rails doffed their covers. President McKinley himself wouldn't have received a better salute.

I am sure everyone on *Dixon* that morning wondered what the hell had become of their relatively sane captain and precisely who the derelict approaching our quarterdeck was. I couldn't blame them. Our visitor did have the appearance of a New York City vagrant who had robbed a theatrical costumery attic. Where else could one find red pantaloons, a blue tunic, and a plumed bicorn hat? He even had a sword—one of those flimsy long, thin types that are useless in a real fight.

Alonso Adams was a former merchant ship captain who acquired the Swan Islands in 1893. He formed his own country in 1894, proclaiming himself king, and was well known to enjoy the pomp and ceremony that went with his title. I'd met him in October 1896, just before the end of my command tour of duty in *Newark*. We had stopped at Swan for a day to check the situation on the island, for there were rumors of odd things going on there. Forewarned about his affinity for royal attention, I treated him like the king he claimed to be, all the while carefully examining the place and its inhabitants. In the end, I found no crimes, just eccentric people, Adams chief among them.

In Alonso I gained a professional acquaintance situated in the midst of a very important trade route in the Caribbean. Revolutionaries, merchants, politicos, mercenaries, pirates, and warships all steamed by the Swan Islands. Many stopped for a visit.

In the ensuing two years, King Alonso had written me every six months at my post in Washington with progress reports on his miniature kingdom, including the occasional tidbit of regional gossip from visiting ship captains and scoundrels. I was his best, probably his only, contact within the American government. He needed me far more than I needed him.

As of early 1898, his subject population consisted of five Americans (mostly his family), fifteen Honduran farmers, three Caymanian fishermen, and a wayward Italian. His dream of attracting investors—hopefully a rich American company—and starting copra production was fading. I knew he would look upon my visit as a source of legitimacy, a flicker of hope for that dream.

King Alonso grinned from ear to ear as he stepped from the gangway to the quarterdeck. He knew naval tradition and appreciated the show for him. Raising his hat over his head and waving it, he yelled, "Hurrah for the U.S. Navy!" Then he grasped my hand in a viselike grip. "Wonderous to see you again, Captain Wake! Thank you for the excellent welcome. And to what do I owe this unexpected pleasure?"

"War brings us back together, King Alonso. Come into my quarters and we'll discuss it."

In my cabin I offered him neither rum nor food. The show was over and pretenses gone. He sat down in my guest chair, a serious expression on his face. "What do you need, Peter?"

I leaned forward on my desk. "Solid intelligence. Alonso, did you see another ship, a liner a little bigger than *Dixon*, steam by toward the north within the past day or so?"

His eyes widened. "Yes, as a matter of fact I did, at sunrise two mornings ago. A two-stack passenger steamer converted into a cruiser. I could see her gun mounts. She showed no colors, but I figured she was American. Making about fourteen, fifteen knots. Came from the south, like you."

"Heading north, toward the Yucatan Passage?"

"Yes, when she went by us she was steaming north. But curious, that. I figured she was heading to the Gulf to go around and join the Navy blockade at Havana. But yesterday afternoon, a Honduran fishing smack stopped here for water, and the skipper said he had almost been run over by a big passenger steamer in the middle of the previous night. In the last four months since the war started, I've seen only one steamer of that description—the one that passed our island the day before."

The near collision didn't surprise me. Fishing smacks often neglected to show lights. I was prepared to dismiss it when Alonso added, "But Peter, here's the odd thing about that near collision. It didn't happen north of here—it happened about thirty miles *east* of Swan Island,

and the steamer was headed just south of east. And now I'm getting the impression from you that she's not American. Is she Spanish?"

Alonso was much sharper than his public buffoonery would indicate. And I knew that in spite of his role as the monarch of the Swan Islands, he still thought of himself as an American at heart. "Correct. She's a Spanish raider. Is that fishing skipper still here? I want to talk with him."

"No, he left for the mainland last night. So, you thought the raider was going up into the Gulf of Mexico to raid our ports?"

"Yes." I allowed myself a frustrated exhale. "It seemed logical, given the evidence."

He gave a sympathetic chuckle, then said, "Well, let's see what this new evidence shows." Turning the chart on the table toward him, he jabbed a finger. "The smack encountered her east of here a little over twenty-eight hours ago. That means the raider must've gone north just far enough to be seen by ships in the Yucatan Channel area and thus initiate an alarm. That would serve to decoy our Navy's ships to that area. But then she circled around to the south to this area under cover of darkness and subsequently headed off to the east-southeast. Smart deception, well played by her captain. However, every gain has a price. That raider's detour north means she has lost some ground to you, my friend. You're only a day behind her now."

Obviously, Alonso had done some dodgy deceptions of his own during his merchant marine past. Probably smuggling here in the Caribbean. His evaluation was uncannily similar to my own. "Thank you for the help, Alonso. I'll be getting under way now. Can I quickly share some of our pantry provisions with you?"

He showed a pathetic little smile, knowing he wasn't needed anymore. "Thank you, Peter. Decent food is always welcome. I've enjoyed your visit immensely, but I won't delay you any further. You must go and stop that raider before it can do harm. I may be a king nowadays on this little island, but I'm still an *American*, first and foremost!"

Alonso departed eight minutes later, *sans* the *gran salute*, lugging a basket of tinned food from my personal larder. I say "my," but actually it had been kindly donated to me by my predecessor. After Alonso and I waved good-bye to each other, I returned to the bridge. I was about to order steam to be brought up and the anchor weighed but was stopped by an anguished scream on the deck below.

We dashed out to the starboard wing and looked down to the main deck just as there was a splash in the water alongside. A man had plunged headfirst into the clear tropical water and still going down, propelled by his legs kicking furiously. He was attired in a dress white officer's uniform. The gold braid on the cuffs of his sleeves reflected the sunlight as he went downward. I groaned inside.

It was Kilmarty.

His descent slowed. Then his body contorted and doubled over, legs still kicking and arms now flailing. He appeared to be halfway down to the sandy bottom fifty feet below us. Spinning around, he looked up at the crew lining the rail. No, he looked directly at *me*. A mass of bubbles erupted from his face. Then he sank farther down, feet first— still looking up at me.

A young sailor dove in from the main deck and got down pretty far, but not nearly far enough. The body was too deep by then. The sailor gave up and rose back to the surface, gasping for air. Below him, I saw Kilmarty land on the bottom in a sandy cloud and roll over facedown.

Dixon didn't have any boats in the water, but the gig was lowered quickly and picked up the sailor. The coxswain lowered a grapnel line and began the difficult business of trying to hook and haul the body up from fifty feet below the surface.

"Good God," Belfort murmured, his face reflecting his shock, "I swear it looked like Kilmarty was laughing at us when that last air came out of him."

"It was an optical illusion, John," I said, hoping to spare him the nightmares that I knew would certainly come. But I didn't really believe what I told him, for I'd seen that look before on a drowning man, back in 1886 in New York Harbor. The nightmares had come to me.

The master-at-arms arrived and explained what had happened. When a meal was being delivered to Kilmarty's quarters, he head-butted the petty officer guarding his room and ran down the passageway. Then he went up the nearby ladder to the main deck and made his way forward to the quarterdeck. He surprised the detail that was securing the gangway, gave a blood-curdling scream, and dove overboard.

The master-at-arms was a Maryland naval militiaman and a police inspector in civilian life. Before reporting to us on the bridge, he had re-created each step of Kilmarty's actions in the ship himself and found it had taken less than ninety-eight seconds to get from the cabin to the quarterdeck. He ended his report and stood there stoically awaiting my wrath.

But I wasn't angry, merely surprised that Kilmarty had chosen to end his life this way; and it does me no credit to admit to my readers that a small part of me was relieved as well to have the matter settled. Instead, I dismissed the master-at-arms and then quietly addressed my executive officer. "Commander Belfort, I want your full summary report, accompanied by sworn statements from all witnesses, on my desk by sunset. As soon as the body is recovered, we will steam out of here on a course due east, with revolutions for fifteen knots."

"Aye, aye, sir. And as for the body, what do we do with it?"

"Keep it until tomorrow morning. He had not been tried and convicted yet, so his body will get a decent but quiet Christian burial by Chaplain Reeher, *without* naval honors."

On my way below, I heard the chief gunner's mate tell one of his cohorts, "It ain't even eight bells yet, but I can tell ya one thing, this here is the most damned bizarre day of my life. Tin-pot kings and our own officers jumping overboard. Friggin' lunacy all around!"

I wearily agreed.

51

The "Conversation"

Room 247, State, War, and Navy Building, Washington, D.C.
Thursday, 10 October 1901

SMITH INTERRUPTED YET AGAIN. This time he jumped to his feet and paced as he spoke, his voice getting louder and louder. Caldhouse and Pentwaller looked disgusted but said nothing. "So, let me get all this straight, Wake. Your trail of international debacles, embarrassments to the United States Navy, not to mention numerous violations of naval regulations, continued unabated up to this bizarre meeting with a delusional eccentric who calls himself King Alonso on some useless island in the middle of nowhere. And that certifiable fool's assessment of the situation is how you finally deduced your folly in ever going into the western Caribbean—when you damn well should have stayed in the eastern Caribbean, where the raider was headed and *where you were ordered by Rear Admiral Sampson to go to in the first place!*"

Smith's attempt to browbeat me was laughable, and I almost did just that. But I caught Pentwaller's frozen expression and refrained. "If that was a question, Captain Smith," I replied, "the answer is a simple *no*. Alonso Adams is not the one who changed my mind and strategic plan. I adjusted my assessment of the situation as events unfolded and new intelligence emerged."

To the admirals, I explained, "Captain José Grinda proved himself brilliant at *guerre de course*. He was every bit the equal of Raphael Semmes, an adversary *some* of us here fought in the 1860s and still remember with respect. Fortunately, I discovered Grinda's last deception in time to avoid it. And that was entirely due to the information gained from the aforementioned Alonso Adams at Swan Island."

I swung my gaze to Smith. "That is what's supposed to happen when you command in wartime, Captain Smith. You make the best decision and take action based upon what you know at the time—not what others learn later in comfortable hindsight, far away from the theater of war."

Caldhouse nodded at that, maybe remembering back to three decades earlier when the U.S. Navy had chased Semmes around the world. Pentwaller's face remained stony. I thought I saw a glimmer of agreement—though whether for Smith or for me was not apparent.

Smith wasn't fazed at all by my reply. Instead, he merely shifted his tactics, and his aim, to a much lower level. "And now tell us why exactly *did* you drive Paymaster Michael Kilmarty to suicide? Why did you take the word of some dusky, flea-bitten little whore over one of your own? Why did you then charge him with *rape*—of a *native*, for God's sake? Why not wait to make any charges until you returned to the fleet, where more dispassionate decisions could be made? And once you placed him under arrest, why did you choose to further *humiliate* Mr. Kilmarty—an *officer* with years of service in the Maryland Naval Militia—by confining him to quarters? Please tell us your reasoning, Captain Wake, because I, many other officers in the Navy, and Mr. Kilmarty's widow and family in Baltimore want to know what the hell you were thinking."

Well, here it is. Dimm's ultimate weapon against me—NAVY CAPTAIN HUMILIATES OFFICER INTO SUICIDE will be the headline in tomorrow's Baltimore Sun. Dimm's people have probably paid the Kilmarty family to support all this. My superiors will abandon me; I will be brought before a court-martial, and my retirement denied; and Dimm, that ignorant lout, will become a congressman. Well, that may happen, but not without a fight, you bastards.

"You ask what I was thinking? I was thinking of the sworn testimony of the victim and the statements from the witnesses—American and Panamanian witnesses—after the fact. There was overwhelming evidence that Kilmarty had committed a serious violent crime against a *child*. Far from tormenting or humiliating him, I treated Kilmarty with remarkable restraint. His subsequent suicide was obviously a product of his guilty conscience and his cowardly unwillingness to face the charges, his family, and his hometown."

Smith started to interrupt again, but I cut him off. "No, be quiet and listen! My report, which you have *clearly* not read, was personally handed to my immediate superior, Rear Admiral Sampson, when *Dixon* returned to Cuba in late August 1898, as per naval regulations. In the three years and two months since then, there has been no disapproval, request for further information or revision, or additional comment on the report by anyone in my chain of command."

I stood up to bring my gaze level to his. "That means, Captain Smith, that you are nothing but a—"

Pentwaller held up his hand. "*Don't say it*, Captain Wake. Captain Smith is voicing his concerns, as he is entitled to do. Some of those concerns *have* reached higher levels in the Navy, though none has been reduced to formal writing or accusation. That is precisely why we are informally *conversing* here today. Admiral Caldhouse and I are trying to parse rumor from fact. And I will not excuse any further breach of expected conduct by either of you." He looked from me to Smith. "Is that understood?"

I lowered myself back into the chair. "Yes, sir. I understand."

Smith stayed standing and merely nodded. Pentwaller studied his pocket watch and uttered a low growl. Smith quickly said, "Yes, sir."

"Good. Then sit *down*, Captain Smith. Your point about Paymaster Kilmarty has been made and responded to by Captain Wake, who will now continue."

Caldhouse offered helpfully, "I believe you were about to head east from Swan Island and search for the raider. I'm quite curious about how that developed."

With a tired sigh, Pentwaller added, "It appears your recitation is nearing its chronological end, Captain Wake. I hope so, for Secretary Long is expecting me when this conversation is done, and it has already gone long past the time allotted."

52

The Gamble

Cruiser Dixon, *Latitude 15° 32' N, Longitude 78° 11' W,*
Central Caribbean Sea
Sunday, 7 August 1898

TAKING DECISIVE ACTION ON Alonso's secondhand information from the Honduran fisherman was a huge gamble.
Everyone on board *Dixon* seemed to understand that, and the
lookouts anxiously examined any smudge or cloud or large wave on
the horizon. On the second day steaming east from Swan Island, they
spotted a large ship in the distance on the port bow that was slowly
heading southbound. Battle stations were manned and the extra boilers
lit off. *Dixon* picked up speed, her bow aimed right at the other ship.

Then we realized it wasn't the enemy raider. It was *Bronx*.

Only Belfort and I knew what Dimm's orders had been from Admiral Sampson and where his ship was *supposed* to be at that point: much
farther west, searching for the raider on the route from Providencia
Island to the Yucatan Passage. Her present position and course, 150
miles south of Jamaica, indicated *Bronx* had left Kingston only the
day before—a week late—and was heading toward Panama and away
from her ordered operations area.

We kept our course and sent a signal by light for *Bronx* to close within hailing distance. Belfort didn't say a word as he watched Dimm's ship get closer. He didn't have to; his clenched jaw and cold eyes said it all. I probably had the same appearance as I stood there envisioning yet another confrontation with Dimm in half an hour.

As I waited, though, it came to me that we had suddenly been given a valuable opportunity. I smacked the railing and laughed out loud. Belfort looked at me in disbelief, and so nervously that I wondered if he thought I was losing my mind.

To ease his concern, I explained, sotto voce, "See here, John. Captain Dimm's consistent failure to execute his orders, which you know has infuriated me in the past, has actually worked out well for us this time. Think about it. This is an opportunity."

Belfort still hadn't grasped it, so I explained. "We've had no communications with the admiral or the outside world since Panama. That means nobody knows what we learned at Swan Island. They still think *Marquesa* is heading to Yucatan. But because Dimm has showed up here, where he shouldn't be, we can send him to warn the U.S. consuls in the eastern Caribbean, Sampson in Cuba, and Higginson in Puerto Rico, as well as our naval assets in the Atlantic and the Mediterranean, of the raider's course and possible destinations. We've got to continue the chase, and *Bronx* is our only way to spread the warning."

He got it then. "The cable station at Kingston."

"Exactly! At full speed, *Bronx* will be back in Kingston tomorrow by noon. Through the telegraph cable system in the Caribbean, everyone from Washington to Trinidad to Costa Rica can get our warning by tomorrow evening."

His face relaxed a bit. "And the best thing is that *Marquesa* doesn't yet know we know. Where *do* you think she's heading, sir?"

"I think she's making a break for it, either to get home to Spain or to raid our East Coast or transatlantic trade route. We've got too many warships in the Greater Antilles for her to escape that way. My guess is she'll stop briefly at Venezuela for a last-minute coaling before transiting through the more remote southern Lesser Antilles at night. After that she'll be out in the Atlantic and free."

Belfort nodded. "It's a long way to Spain—she'll need that extra coal to make it the whole way. But why Venezuela?"

"Grinda knows it's one of the few places still friendly to the Spanish, so nobody will be looking for him there."

I called out for Ensign Barnett and went inside to the chart table, where I quickly wrote out a message on a signal sheet. When Barnett appeared, I told him, "Encode this message and send it by signal lamp: 'Wake to Dimm. Head back Kingston immediately full speed. Upon arrival, quickly send following warning cable below to both Sampson and Navy Dept at Washington. After sending message, head to Le Guaira, Venezuela, to assist in intercepting the raider. *Dixon* will check Puerto Cabello, Venezuela, first, then meet you at La Guaira.' Get an acknowledgment that Captain Dimm has received it."

XXX—SPANISH RAIDER MARQUESA LAST SEEN 30 MILES EAST OF SWAN ISLAND SEVERAL NIGHTS AGO—X— RAIDER WAS BOUND EAST-SOUTHEAST—X—RAIDER PROBABLY NOW IN CENTRAL CARIBBEAN—X—PROBABLY BOUND FOR ATLANTIC VIA FINAL PORT IN VENEZUELA FOR COAL & PROVISIONS—X—DIXON IS 1 DAY BEHIND RAIDER & WILL CHECK PUERTO CABELLO & LA GUAIRA IN VENEZUELA—X—BRONX WILL FOLLOW ONCE CABLE SENT AT KINGSTON—X—RECOMMEND YOU ALERT ALL U.S. CONSULS IN EAST CARIBBEAN AND ALL USN SHIPS & STATIONS IN CARIBBEAN-ATLANTIC-MEDITERRANEAN—X—RECOMMEND USN SEND ANY AVAILABLE SHIPS TO WINDWARD ISLANDS TO INTERCEPT RAIDER—X—FURTHER RECOMMEND ALL U.S. CONSULS IN LESSER ANTILLES CHARTER BOATS TO SERVE AS NIGHT LOOKOUTS BETWEEN THE ISLANDS AND THUS WARN IF RAIDER TRIES TO

PASS THROUGH—X—DIXON SHOULD REACH PUERTO
CABELLO IN 4 DAYS AT MOST—X—WILL ADVISE BY
CABLE ON ARRIVAL—XXX

For the first time since coming under my command, Dimm showed remarkable enthusiasm for following an order. In minutes, *Bronx*'s signal lamp winked an acknowledgment of the message and she heeled over in a tight turn to the north. Soon she was steaming north at a speed I'd never seen her make before.

Belfort cast me a sardonic smile and observed, "It would appear her boilers are finally repaired, sir."

"It certainly does appear so, doesn't it? But the important thing is that we are closing in on that raider. It won't be long now 'til we find her and finally stop the threat."

Belfort nodded grimly. "We're ready, sir."

53

Arrival

Cruiser Dixon, *Puerto Cabello, Venezuela*
Thursday, 11 August 1898

I<small>T WAS ANOTHER DRIZZLY NIGHT</small> with reduced visibility, and I was profoundly grateful for the strong Dutch lighthouses at Curaçao and Bonaire. They were our first land fix since Swan Island, 862 miles earlier, and confirmed we were on the right course for our objective. This in spite of slogging against strong trade winds and seas that reduced our speed over the bottom to only ten knots while increasing our fuel consumption. The Dutch islands, however, are still 70 miles north of the nearest Venezuelan coast at Punta Zamuro, and fully 110 miles northwest of Puerto Cabello.

From Punta Zamuro down to a tiny place called Venepal, the Venezuelan coast trends north and south, forming a dangerous lee shore against which the trade winds and seas crash. At Venepal, the coast curves around to the east toward Puerto Cabello, seven miles away, where the coast returns to its usual east–west line. This large corner of the Caribbean is known as the Golfo de Triste—the Gulf of Sadness—because of the many shipwrecks there. I hoped that name wasn't prophetic for us.

Steaming those final miles at eight knots along a Venezuelan coast where the lighthouses notoriously didn't function had been tense for Gerard, Belfort, and me. No, the word "tense" is an understatement. It was mentally excruciating and exhausting, reminding me once more that I was no longer a young man. *Maria's right. It's time for me to retire.*

In the end, we made it without ripping our guts out on one of the many offshore reefs, colliding with one of the hundreds of unlit fishing boats, or blundering into torpedoes fired by an unseen enemy raider, which was my greatest fear. When we determined by dead reckoning plots that we were offshore of our destination, I ordered *Dixon* on an eastward course and reduced her engine speed to slow ahead. Everyone on the bridge breathed a sigh of relief.

My plan was straightforward. Loiter in the darkness off Puerto Cabello until just before the sun rose in four hours, then poke in a little closer to survey the harbor for the raider while still remaining in international waters. According to the Law of the Sea, if *Dixon* actually entered the harbor and *Marquesa* was there already, the first one to depart would get a twenty-four-hour head start before her adversary could depart to chase her. By the time the second ship left, the first would be in international waters, and no battle would be fought in innocent neutral territorial waters. Here, unlike in Colombian waters earlier, I decided the legal way was the best way.

The reader might fairly ask at this point why I suddenly became so respectful of the law. Why not go in, spur the raider to depart, then flaunt international law and quickly follow her? Or just go in and attack her right there? The answer was simple. Unlike Colombia, Venezuela had a navy, and Puerto Cabello was a naval station for that navy. The proud Venezuelans would certainly fight *Dixon* to honor their sovereignty, and I would have to completely destroy them in addition to the raider, suffering major damage or destruction in the process. The repercussions of that battle would be instant and far-reaching.

Staying in international waters in such weather at night was a tricky business, but several things indicated our position off that dreaded lee shore. The lead line told us we were in 292 feet of water and the bottom composition was of sand and shell. The sound of surf rumbled on a nearby reef islet to the west. A vague loom of light reached us from a building in the port. And the dim comings and goings of fishing smacks sailing through the misty darkness all assisted us in plotting our position as about four miles off the harbor at Puerto Cabello.

We steamed slowly in a circle, a darkened ship in a dark night, each man on board knowing that if our enemy really was in the port, the fishermen would have told her of our presence by now. Would she come out in the dark? There was no difficult winding channel at Puerto Cabello that would take time to transit—it was a short, broad, and straight run. The raider could weigh anchor and be on us in less than five minutes. The first we would know of *Marquesa*'s presence would be her torpedoes disemboweling *Dixon* in a mass of flame and concussion. And even then we wouldn't be able to see her in that murk. We'd finally spot her when she used her guns to finish us off as she ran by our sinking ship. That is precisely what I would've done if I were Capitán de Navío José Grinda.

For the rest of the night, that scenario played out in my mind as I leaned against the bridge wing bulwark and tried to think of anything I'd overlooked. Around me, the men of *Dixon* stayed at their battle stations, stared shoreward, and silently waited.

54

Prize Money

Cruiser Dixon, *Puerto Cabello, Venezuela*

Friday, 12 August 1898

T HE RAIN HAD ENDED, but the wind was still blowing as dawn lightened the eastern horizon. At last, the sunrise lit up the small harbor in shafts of diffused amber light. Every binocular and telescope in the ship was focused on the anchorage.

And suddenly, there she was.

Anchored in the middle of the small harbor, *Marquesa* had only a wisp of smoke drifting from her funnels—not enough steam up to get under way. It was the first time we'd actually seen her in detail. At long last, our 2,487-mile journey—from the Windward Passage to Guánica in Puerto Rico to Curaçao to Colón to Swan Island and, ultimately, the coast of Venezuela—was done. The searching was over. Cheers erupted along *Dixon's* decks.

International law regarding belligerents entering and departing neutral harbors does not apply to ship's boats, so I immediately sent Ensign Barnett in the steam cutter to find the cable office in the town and send an encoded message to Admiral Sampson and to the Secretary in Washington.

XXX—SPANISH RAIDER MARQUESA ANCHORED IN
HARBOR AT PUERTO CABELLO-VENEZUELA—X—
DIXON REMAINING OFFSHORE IN INTERNATIONAL
WATERS & WATCHING FOR RAIDER DEPARTURE—X—NO
INTERACTION YET WITH VENEZUELAN GOVERNMENT
BUT EXPECTING HOSTILITY—X—WILL NOT HAVE TIME
TO CABLE WHEN RAIDER DEPARTS—PLEASE SEND
BRONX & REINFORCEMENTS—XXX

When he returned to the ship, Barnett reported that no cables had
been waiting for us. Venezuelan authorities had stopped him on his
way back and declared they were not happy to have two foreign belligerents here, pointedly warning *Dixon* about entering the harbor to
engage the raider and adding that a Venezuelan gunboat was heading
to Puerto Cabello to enforce the nation's territorial integrity.

Barnett also informed me there was no U.S. consulate—the nearest
was at La Guaira, sixty miles to the east—so the usual requirement to
check in with the consul didn't apply. That was a pleasant bit of news,
for consuls can be a huge hindrance in situations such as this. There
also was no Spanish consulate, Barnett told me, so Grinda and I were
equally free on that point.

Bolívar arrived in the port the next day. I knew of the Venezuelan
gunboat from my previous sea duty in the Caribbean. She was only six
years old, and her two shafts could push her to nineteen knots, faster
than *Dixon*. Her 2,600-horsepower engines were so efficient that she
could steam for 3,400 miles at 10 knots. Outrunning or outdistancing
Bolívar was thus not in the cards for *Dixon*. I noted she kept steam
up all the time, ready for departure at a moment's notice. With her
large-caliber Hontaria main gun, several Nordenfelt secondary guns,
additional rapid-fire guns, and two large torpedo tubes, the Venezuelan gunboat would be a very tough opponent. I had no intention of
making her one.

Over the next two days I sent Barnett in by steam cutter twice a day
to check for cable messages to us and listen for pertinent information.

Other than the initial reply from Sampson tersely stating no reinforcements were available and *Dixon* was to continue to watch the port, nothing arrived. *Bronx* wasn't mentioned. According to my communicated plan, *Bronx* should be arriving at La Guaira soon, where the consul should inform Dimm of the latest information, which included orders to reinforce us. Once he received those orders, *Bronx* could reach us in about five hours at full speed. Until that happened, though, *Dixon* was on her own.

During his jaunts ashore, Barnett, who possessed only rudimentary Spanish and was politely escorted by constables everywhere, was still able to gather fragments of news about the raider and her captain. Grinda was gathering both fresh and dry provisions and loading a small amount of coal—he didn't need much to top off the raider's bunkers—and was allowing his men a final liberty ashore before getting under way. Of particular note, *Marquesa's* bottom was being scraped by divers, and her boiler flue tubes were being cleaned. It all sounded to me like preparations for a fast exit and a long voyage.

During this time, Grinda didn't want for liberty ashore himself. Secure in the knowledge his ship was safe in the harbor, he attended high-society dinners each evening as the honored guest. The main conversational topic among the locals, Barnett reported, both the well-to-do and common folk, was the pending sea battle. The current bet among the barstool experts in the waterfront taverns was that it would happen two hours before sunrise some morning soon, and the Spaniard would pummel the *yanqui* and then head out into the Atlantic.

That timing was my prediction too. With that in mind, as *Dixon's* officers and crew went over their weapons and engines several times a day, Belfort, Pinkston, Gerard, and I went over tactics. We discussed every contingency we could conjure up, including how to fight the ship if we were hit by torpedoes or if both Belfort and I were killed.

During these two days, most of the crew—and, I suspect, many of the officers—were thinking and talking about a far more pleasant topic: prize money. Varying opinions were rendered as to what *Marquesa's* value would be once adjudicated in the U.S. admiralty court at Key West. Regulations were consulted on the distribution rates of prize money among the officers and crew. Our previous experience with the Spanish freighter and her gold heightened the sense that we were bound to have better luck this time—the romantics on board declaring it would be poetic justice, the religious proclaiming it would be none other than God's will!

All this was based on the rather farfetched notion that we could actually *capture* the Spanish raider, a near impossibility. But such dreaming didn't hurt anyone, and I said nothing to dampen the men's spirits. Even the usually taciturn Belfort smiled at the conversations in the wardroom.

It had been thirty-three years since my last prize money. In fact, Rork and I were the only ones on board who had ever gotten prize money. Memories returned, and I will admit that after two days of listening to these discussions on how each would spend his money, I succumbed to a bit of it myself. I knew exactly what I would spend it on. The very first day of my retirement, Maria and I would embark on a relaxing voyage to Europe as first-class passengers on a Cunard liner. Waited on hand and foot, and with no responsibilities. Blissful decadence, indeed.

I went to sleep Friday night dreaming about it.

55

Battle Stations

Cruiser Dixon, *Puerto Cabello, Venezuela*

Saturday, 13 August 1898

CAPTAIN GRINDA CHOSE HIS moment well: 3:42 a.m. on a rainy night. A light northerly wind kept his funnel smoke from alerting us as we slowly steamed east at five knots about five and a half miles offshore. *Dixon*'s stern lookout saw a short, fuzzy line of pale gray in the misty dark. Fortunately, the seventeen-year-old lad was self-confident enough to report it. That pale line turned out to be *Marquesa*'s bow wave.

Grinda's perfect timing also meant the raider departed precisely when we were heading away from her at the end of our leg to the east. This was our farthest point away from the port, six miles. We were just starting to circle around to starboard and begin the reciprocal course to the west when the raider was spotted.

I say we "spotted" *Marquesa*, but we couldn't even make out her shape, just her bow wave. Our forward main gun quickly began traversing to aim at the raider as we turned. Now that we were approaching her, it was our only gun that could bear on the target.

"Bridge, there! I can see the hull and structure of the ship now. She's large, two funnels, long deck housing. It's the raider, all right! Steaming fast toward the northeast."

Belfort sent a midshipman up the mast to get a more detailed report. I called inside the bridge. "Mr. Gerard, have you been able to calculate the target's exact position, course, and speed?"

Gerard had anticipated what I would ask. He'd just been at the pelorus trying to gauge the relative bearing and range of the raider. Now back at the chart table, he reported, "Target is estimated at about two and three-quarter miles offshore, sir, steaming northeast and gaining speed very quickly. I estimate she is at about seventeen knots now. From *Dixon*, the target bears west-southwest, range is just over four miles."

Estimates! I heartily wished *Dixon* had one of Lt. Bradley Fiske's new naval stadimeters. Then we'd know *precisely* the raider's relative bearing and range, and from that her position, course, and speed. Fiske's new device had been in the fleet for barely three years, and only battleships and armored cruisers had them.

The midshipman shouted down to us, "Bridge, there! That Venezuelan gunboat is under way at the harbor mouth, following the raider's course."

"Don't worry about them. They're just observing to make sure we allow the raider to get to international waters before we attack," I asserted to calm everyone's jittery nerves, then asked the navigator, "Mr. Gerard, what converging offset course will enable our portside guns to bear?"

"Course three-four-five should enable the forward portside guns to bear, sir."

"Very well. Commander Belfort, bring the ship to course three-four-five. Make revolutions for eighteen knots. Hold fire until I give the order."

Right then I noticed that *Marquesa*'s bearing had changed. Gerard presented an update. "Captain, the target's present chart position is approximately three miles off the coast. She has turned to port and is now steaming due west at eighteen knots. Target's range is now three and a half miles, sir."

West? Grinda's staying close to that dangerous lee shore? "Come left standard rudder to course two-seven-five," I ordered. "We will stay slightly to seaward of the raider."

After passing the order along, Belfort marveled, "Grinda's staying right on the territorial line. He turned west so we can only use our bow gun. Any stray rounds from us might impact in Venezuelan territory."

"Yes, but he'll have to turn to starboard soon because of the trend of the coast northward. Plus, once he's turned northerly, that's a lee shore with offshore reefs. Grinda's playing a dangerous game. He must turn very soon, and both he and I know it."

"Ah, just maybe he's got some help, sir," Belfort said, pointing at the Venezuelan gunboat. *Bolívar* was changing direction too, following the raider and staying in between the two belligerents as we all charged westbound along the territorial limit. We couldn't fire at *Marquesa* without hitting the Venezuelan ship.

Someone in the dark bridge uttered a long and vulgar oath, which Gerard quickly silenced. Then, bent over the pelorus, he updated his position report.

"The bend in the coast at Venepal where it trends northerly is approximately seven miles ahead of us, which makes it three and a half miles ahead of the target. Target is beginning to turn to starboard, Captain."

"Very well," I acknowledged. "Right standard rudder to course three-four-five. Mr. Gerard, advise the target's speed and course when she gets settled on it."

Bolívar began turning too. But because she began her turn after both *Marquesa* and *Dixon*, the Venezuelan gunboat was slightly behind both of us as all three ships steamed north.

Showing phenomenal rapidity in his calculations, Gerard announced his findings less than two minutes later. "Bearings indicate the target has now completed her turn and settled on a course of due north, sir, right along the Venezuelan territorial limits. Her speed has remained steady at eighteen knots. Target is just forward of our port beam at a range of three miles. *Bolívar*'s range is two miles off our port quarter, sir. She appears to be slowing."

"Closure rate on the target?" I asked.

"Captain, our closing rate shows we will converge with the target in one hour and eleven minutes. However, if the target maintains her present course and speed, in one hour she will pass three miles off-shore of Cayo Sombrero, which is half a mile off Mayoquin Point. From that area northward, the coast trends away to the northwest and the target will have more sea room to maneuver to leeward."

This was one of the scenarios Belfort and I had anticipated—a parallel chase with the range narrowing as time went on. If *Marquesa* had midship torpedo tubes, she could fire a spread of them into us at under two miles.

"Target range is staying steady at just under three miles, sir," reported Gerard. "Target's chart position is still northbound along the three-mile limit. *Bolívar's* range has increased to almost three miles from our port quarter. She's steaming along the territorial limit also and two miles astern of the target."

"All portside guns and fore and aft main guns are laid on the target," repeated Belfort from Pinkston's voice tube report, then added, "Question from Pinkston, sir. Is *Bolívar* now also a designated target?"

I was about to reply in the negative when Belfort said, "What the hell's that?! Are the Venezuelans opening fire?"

The lookout shouted from aloft, "*Bolívar* is firing, sir."

A small flash from the Venezuelan gunboat flickered through the haze, followed by several more. Then there was a continuous stream of flashes. There was no sound, so the gun must be one of their smaller ones. That didn't make sense. *Why are they shooting, and who are they shooting at? Why use their smaller guns?*

This was one scenario Belfort and I hadn't anticipated. There were no splashes near us, so the Venezuelans must shooting at the raider. Still, I couldn't take any chances.

"Have the after main gun and numbers four and five portside secondary guns lay on *Bolívar*, but do not fire. Stand by to open fire with the forward main gun and numbers one to three secondary guns on *Marquesa*. Stand by for rapid helm orders."

Why isn't Grinda firing back at the gunboat? Or at us?

Gerard continued his droning update. "Target course is continuing steady. Range is now two and a half miles. The coast trends away a bit sir, so the target chart position now appears to be slightly beyond the three-mile coastal limit, sir. I put it at three and a quarter miles east of the Venezuelan coast."

We were running out of time. It was now or never. "Mark it so in the log, Mr. Gerard. Gunnery officer, have the guns that are laid on the enemy raider stand by to fire."

Belfort repeated the command. Mouths opened to equalize the pressure in anticipation of the guns' concussions.

This was it. "Guns that are laid on the target raider, *fire!*"

BOOM! A twenty-foot-long tongue of flame erupted from the forward main gun just ahead of us. Simultaneously, our portside smaller guns opened up. The combined blast wave swept through the bridge.

A glaring light flashed from *Marquesa*'s foredeck. A hundred yards off our starboard side, a fountain of white foam erupted against the blackness. The round had passed within feet of the bridge as it crossed over *Dixon.*

Belfort passed along the gunnery results. "Commander Pinkston reports two near misses within fifty yards of the target. Range is good."

"Guns laid on the raider may fire at will," I ordered. "Keep watch on the water for torpedoes. Stand by for rapid turns. What is the gunboat doing?"

"Not sure," said Belfort as more flickering flashes of light came from the gunboat. I realized several were long flickers. Then I saw the pattern.

"No—wait!" yelled Barnett, madly grabbing the signal book from the shelf. "That's a lamp signal! The Venezuelan gunboat isn't shooting, she's *signaling!*"

The signalman beside Barnett reported, "I think the gunboat was flashing something in Spanish to the raider, sir. Now they're flashing to us in plain English. Here it is."

He handed me the logbook. In block letters was a simple message.

XXX—STOP SHOOTING—X—WAR ENDED YESTERDAY —X—ARMISTICE IN EFFECT—X—PER CABLE FROM USA THIS MORNING—XXX

I couldn't believe it. Belfort looked at the logbook, then at me. "The war's over?"

Suddenly, three of our secondary guns on the port side let go a staccato salvo. *BAM! BAM! BAM!* The forward main gun let loose. *BOOM!*

Simultaneously, *Marquesa*'s foredeck lit up again, a second later the muffled boom arrived just as the round hit the water just astern of us. I heard shrapnel hitting the ship.

"Near miss close alongside target's midship!" called out Pinkston from above. "We've got her bracketed now. Firing for effect!"

All of this took mere seconds. I came to my senses and grabbed Belfort's arm.

"*No! Cease firing!*" I shouted loud enough for Pinkston to hear on the deck above us. Belfort raced to the voice tube and repeated it to the gunnery officer.

To Barnett, I ordered, "Reply to the gunboat: 'Message understood.' Send plain message to *Marquesa*: 'War is over. We have stopped shooting.' Then turn the searchlight on and aim it vertical." That was an international signal to cease firing. To Belfort, I ordered, "Come to course zero-one-zero and reduce revolutions to ten knots. Maintain all gun lays on the main target and the gunboat, and stand by."

We waited in silence, our eyes locked on *Marquesa*, now only two and a half miles away in the mist and clearly reducing her speed. *Bolívar* came up close astern of the raider, and the two exchanged signals. A moment later, *Marquesa* slowed even more, matching our speed and maintaining a course parallel to ours. Her searchlight suddenly lit up and went vertical.

I began to breathe again.

56

The "Conversation"

Room 247, State, War, and Navy Building, Washington, D.C.
Thursday, 10 October 1901

THE SUN WAS LOW IN the west when I finished. The conference room was getting darker, for the lamps hadn't been lit. Outside the window, long shadows alternated with splotches of yellow light in the presidential park. The mourning drapes covering the White House, visible through the window, added to the general air of darkness in the conference room.

I'd lost track of the time and only now realized that most of the offices in the headquarters were probably closed and locked. Certainly the senior staff had departed. I wondered if Secretary Long, not known for devoting lengthy hours at the office, was still waiting for Pentwaller.

The admirals had listened intently. When I ended, Caldhouse sighed pensively. Pentwaller, who had been eyeing me sternly the whole while, glanced at his pocket watch. To my surprise, Smith had quietly paid attention to my narration of the confrontation with the raider. Then his manner changed back to its norm. With his small black eyes narrowed, Smith was about to say something when Caldhouse spoke up. "Captain Wake, please briefly summarize what happened next and your career since August of 1898."

"Aye, sir. First, let me report that fortunately neither *Dixon* nor *Marquesa* had any casualties from the near misses. After Captain Grinda signaled his surrender, I put a guard crew on board *Marquesa* under Commander Belfort and escorted her back to the fleet at Santiago de Cuba. The Spanish crew gave our people no problems at all during that transit, and I had the pleasure of meeting Captain Grinda, a superb tactician and a true gentleman. Once at the fleet anchorage, per orders from Washington, *Marquesa* was allowed to remain in Spanish hands and was later used to transport Spanish soldiers home to Spain."

Caldhouse chuckled. "So, no prize money for this ship, either?"

I smiled ruefully. "No, afraid not, sir."

"Did *Bronx* ever arrive at Puerto Cabello?" asked Pentwaller.

"No, sir. When she arrived at La Guaira later that day, she received cabled orders that she was now detached from my command and was to return to the fleet."

"What was *Dixon*'s next assignment?" Pentwaller asked curtly.

"*Dixon* was used to transport a thousand American soldiers from Santiago de Cuba to the Camp Wikoff quarantine center at Montauk on Long Island. By that point, Chief Rork's recurring malaria had flared up again, this time rather badly. He was taken ashore to the hospital at Montauk. My malaria also recurred, and I was hospitalized in the quarantine camp for a month. Commander Belfort was given command of *Dixon*, which he richly deserved. I'm glad to report he made captain last year."

Caldhouse asked, "And your career since then? You've been ashore, correct?"

"Yes, sir. On leave from October 1898 until January 1899, when I was assigned to the Bureau of Ordnance. I stayed there as an inspector of the East Coast yards until November 1900, when Admiral Dewey gave me my current assignment as an adjunct member of the General Board of the Navy. It's my final assignment, sir. I'm due to retire out in seven weeks, on the first of December."

"Which projects have you worked on there?" asked Pentwaller.

I had to be very careful in answering. My adjunct position with the board coincided with counterintelligence work against the Imperial Germany Navy's spying efforts inside our country, which had culminated in operations plans to attack the United States. These officers weren't privy to any of that. I nonchalantly replied, "Aside from some work on U.S. naval operations in South America, assessing naval yard efficiency, and establishing a naval station at Culebra Island, my main project has been naval contingency plans against European aggression in the Western Hemisphere, particularly the Caribbean." Then, I added, "In fact, I thought *that* was the purpose of my summons to this meeting."

The last came out with a tinge of sarcasm. I couldn't help it. Pentwaller's eyes flared briefly. *Oh, hell, that was a stupid thing to say.* Before he could speak, Caldhouse changed the subject. "And how many years of naval service do you have, Captain Wake?"

"Thirty-eight and a half, sir, beginning in May 1863 at Key West with the East Gulf Blockading Squadron."

"Ah, yes, Admiral Bailey," said Caldhouse with a nostalgic smile. "Good man. He did a very good job of it down there." Caldhouse turned to his colleague. "Well, Admiral Pentwaller, I can't think of any other questions at all. Are we done?"

Pentwaller closed the dossier and resumed his Sphinx-like pose. "Yes, I believe we are. Thank you, Captain Wake, for candidly recounting your wartime operations on *Dixon.*"

Is this finally over? I wondered, resisting the urge to look at my pocket watch. *I just want to go home. Maybe I can still get the late train.*

But, no, it wasn't over. Smith, hitherto silently watching the admirals, slapped his hand on the table. "That was quite a stirring sea story and recitation of a naval career, wasn't it, gentlemen?" he said to the admirals. "And after listening to all this self-aggrandizement for these many hours, I fully understand the hour has grown late. So please allow me to briefly summarize the various long-standing complaints about Captain Wake's behavior that led to this conversation today and have now been confirmed by his own testimony, er, ah . . . *words.*"

With that smirk I had grown to loathe, he looked at Pentwaller. "Permission to do so, sir?"

The admiral growled something and waved his hand to go ahead.

Smith took a deep breath and began speaking rapidly from his notes. "Thank you, sir. I will be concise in delineating Captain Wake's many violations and general disdain of naval regulations."

Smith stood up and started pacing again. His voice rose and fell like a preacher's, hands gesturing theatrically. I got the impression he'd been rehearsing for this moment.

"The first charge is the attempted attack on a brother officer, Capt. Reginald Dimm, while at Rear Admiral Sampson's formal victory dinner on board the flagship. I have heard that Wake has committed similar maniacal attacks on brother officers in the past, one in particular against a subordinate at the Tampa Bay Hotel in 1892.

"The second charge is insubordination, with three separate subcounts: disparaging official U.S. policy regarding the so-called Cuban army, disparaging official U.S. policy regarding our occupation of Cuba, and calling our national leaders liars in their dealings with the so-called Cuban leaders!

"The third charge is theft or diversion of government property in the form of *Bronx's* steam cutter.

"The fourth charge is dereliction of duty in failing to use due diligence in ascertaining whether there was fraud involved in that acquisition, and by whom.

"The fifth charge is conduct unbecoming a naval officer of the United States by the use of both slander and libel against Capt. Reginald Dimm in verbal and written reports.

"The sixth charge is failure to follow a flag officer's orders, *in wartime*, by ignoring Rear Admiral Sampson's orders to remain in the eastern Caribbean where, by the way, the enemy raider actually did show up.

"The seventh charge is leaving one's post or position without orders, *in wartime*, as evidenced in the fact *Dixon* was at the opposite end of the Caribbean from her assigned patrol area.

"The eighth charge is theft of a friendly foreign government's military supplies in diverting the coal at Riohacha, Colombia.

"The ninth charge is theft of an entire privately owned coal yard, company office, and wharf at Colón in Panama.

"And the tenth and final charge is conduct unbecoming an officer in the abject harassment and humiliation of a commissioned officer in the United States Navy, Paymaster Michael Kilmarty, which drove that officer to his horrific death and devasted his grieving family and community.

"And I respectfully demand that the record state my official recommendation that these charges be formally made in a court-martial against Capt. Peter Wake. I am now done, sir." Smith sat down, puffed up with victory.

Pentwaller gazed at Smith for several seconds, then said, "*There is no record*, Captain Smith. As I have repeatedly stated to you, this was a conversation, not a legal proceeding. If you want to make a legal complaint against Captain Wake, go file it with the Naval Judge Advocate's office down the passageway in Room 278. And speaking of records, wasn't there some important document from New York that you said would prove your allegations? You said hours ago that it would be here this afternoon. Where is it?"

Smith hesitated, then said, "Ah . . . I checked during our last break, Admiral. Unfortunately, it seems to have been delayed, sir." He gave a nervous chuckle. "It seems there was some sort of problem up in New York with getting the sworn statement. Clerical mistake, you know." Smith ended on an upbeat note. "But I am certain it will arrive tomorrow, please rest assured on that, Admiral."

Pentwaller looked at Smith with undisguised disdain. "I will rest quite assured tonight, but it will have nothing to do with you, Smith. And now, gentlemen, it is time to—"

A knock loudly sounded the regulation three times on the door. Pentwaller's face darkened and he barked out, "What the hell is it? Enter!"

Clearly used to enduring curmudgeonly senior officers, the messenger entered and stood stoically at attention, a small envelope in his left hand. It was white, not the usual navy blue. "Secretary Long presents his compliments, sir, and says to inform you he's going home. He requests you telephone him there when you are finished here. There is also a confidential written message for a member of your meeting."

"From who?" grumbled the admiral.

The messenger stepped forward, leaned over, and whispered in Pentwaller's ear, handing him the envelope. Pentwaller's eyes widened briefly. Nodding his acknowledgment to the messenger, who then quickly left the room, the admiral spoke to his old friend Caldhouse. "As far as I'm concerned, we're done with this." Caldhouse nodded his agreement. To the gathering, he said, "Gentlemen, you are dismissed."

He stood, as did we all. Ignoring the rest of us, and normal decorum, Smith immediately marched out of the room. Caldhouse trudged out behind him, clearly exhausted. As Pentwaller turned to leave, he pressed the envelope into my hand. "Seems you have one more summons, Captain Wake."

With that said, he walked out too. I was left alone in that room where I had bared all my decisions and actions in the summer of 1898. My attitude was as dark as the room. After hearing Smith's final summation of my crimes, I realized Maria's and my dreams of retirement were dashed. I would never draw a pension. Dimm and his cronies had far more power and influence than I did, and their trap had been well laid and sprung.

The charges would be filed the next day right down the passageway in the judge advocate's office. The court-martial would be held in a week. A week after that, I would be dismissed from the Navy. My lifetime of commitment to the naval service and the nation would end in disrepute and penury.

I rose from the table and plodded out of the room. By the electric lamp in the passageway, I glanced down at the envelope to see what further trouble I had to deal with. My heart stopped. Across the center was my rank and name, scrolled in fancy calligraphy. The upper left corner was embossed with the sender's formidable address:

The Executive Mansion
of the
President of the United States of America
1600 Pennsylvania Avenue
Washington, District of Columbia

With trembling fingers I hurriedly tore it open. Inside was a handwritten note to me. Holding it up to the lamp, I read the small rambling cursive with growing anxiety.

10 October 1901, 5:12 p.m.
Would you kindly step over here to my office as soon as you are done at the Navy Department? I have something of the utmost importance I would like to discuss with you in private. It won't take long.
TR

The note had been written only an hour ago. What could the president want to discuss with me that was so urgent? The obvious answer was the litany of accusations against me, which he must have heard about. With my heart pounding, I realized I wasn't even going to make it to a court-martial. The new president would ask me to resign quietly and thereby spare his administration the embarrassing public spectacle of my prosecution.

I hadn't seen Roosevelt since his assumption of the presidency following President McKinley's assassination. His summons addressed me as "Captain Wake," not Peter. It was an ominous sign.

Eleven minutes later I was standing at the west side door of the presidential mansion showing my summons to an elderly black doorman. He beckoned me inside, softly saying something I didn't hear, for my mind was occupied with figuring out how to tell all this to Maria. As I entered, the somber mourning drapes around the doorway fueled my increasingly melancholy mood about the death of my career.

The irony was not lost on me.

57

Why Am I Here?

The White House, Washington, D.C.
Thursday Evening, 10 October 1901

I WAS SHOWN INTO THE private dining room on the first floor, where the president was eating dinner with two friends: the famous writers William Allen White and Joseph Bucklin Bishop. The raucous Roosevelt family was eating separately in the family quarters upstairs, which they'd moved into a few days earlier. When I entered the dining room, the three men were in the midst of a serious discussion. I began to make my apologies and back out.

"No, no, Peter," said Theodore as he stood. "The subject I need to discuss with you tonight is of absolutely crucial importance but quite private in nature. Come with me to my office. Gentlemen, please excuse me," he said to his dinner companions. "I shall return shortly."

Without waiting for their reply, he strode at his usual fast pace out of the room, up the nearby stairs to the second floor, down the hallway, and into his private office. Even though Roosevelt was twenty years my junior in age, as I trailed behind him I felt like a wayward schoolboy about to be disciplined by the headmaster. Our longtime friendship would count for nothing here. Roosevelt closed the door, then gestured for me to sit down in the guest chair.

The president sat down at his desk, exhaled sternly, and looked me in the eye. "Peter, I know you've had a long day and just want to go home. Don't worry, you will soon."

I dutifully said, "Thank you, sir," then waited for him to come to the awful point, my heart pounding.

It came quickly. "Peter, I have two things to go over with you. First, I know you are eligible for retirement soon—in December, I believe."

Well, this is it. I willed myself to take what was coming like a man. "Yes, Mr. President. I turned sixty-two in June and am eligible to retire at any time, but I must retire no later than the end of the year. The date will be December first. Maria and I have been planning this for the last two years."

"Ah, the lovely and charming Maria! I haven't seen her for far too long. I hear Sean is doing well. Home on leave from the Philippines conflict, I believe. And your daughter's child—how is the new baby? Maria must have spoiled him completely by now. I can't wait until I'm a grandfather, but it'll be awhile, I suppose."

This wasn't unfolding as I'd anticipated since opening that envelope. *Well, he's an old friend and is just trying to make this less traumatic.* With genuine appreciation, I said, "Thank you for asking, sir. Young Peter is fine. He's almost three now and quite a handful. And yes, Maria loves spoiling him, much to Useppa's chagrin, I think."

Theodore's famous ear-to-ear grin spread across his face. "Grandparents' privilege!"

I suddenly felt tired of the banter. I just wanted to face the bad news and get the whole thing over with. "Why am I here, Mr. President? Is it the accusations against me?"

58

Only for a Year . . .

The White House, Washington, D.C.
Thursday Evening, 10 October 1901

THE GRIN DISAPPEARED. "What? That spurious gossip? Lies, spread by mere pretenders who haven't done a hundredth of what you have accomplished for our Navy and our country? No, of course, not. Your conversation with Pentwaller and Caldhouse today took care of all that as far as I am concerned. They are satisfied, and so am I."

So Pentwaller is satisfied with my explanation of what happened? He certainly didn't act that way. Just to make sure, I said, "I thought it was the prelude to my dismissal, sir. You mean I can still retire?"

"Of course! You never did anything requiring disciplinary action, Peter. Now, back to the point. You're here now because I want to talk to you about something quite different."

As I visibly breathed a sigh of relief, Roosevelt leaned forward. "Peter, please don't retire. I need you. The nation needs you. Right here, working with me."

I was stunned. "But retirement is mandatory at my age, sir. Besides, you have a naval aide already."

"Yes, yes, I just assigned Commander Cowles, my brother-in-law, that duty. But it's mostly social protocol and of little import. I need *you* in a capacity that's truly vital. I want you to be my special assistant, working only for me, on *important* matters—as we did in the old days! But now you will have far more power to get things done. And yes, before you ask, that old rascal Rork can join you. How is he, by the way? Enjoying his new life of leisure?"

After recovering from the bout of malaria after the war, Rork had gone into a long-overdue age-mandatory retirement. It had not been a success. The Navy had been his home since he was a teenager. He spent most of his time brooding in his small apartment near the Latrobe Gate of the Washington Navy Yard, staring out the window at the place he longed to be. Rork would leap at this chance to get back in action.

"He's bored already, Mr. President."

A sly smile spread across Roosevelt's face, and I knew he was already aware of Rork's dissatisfaction. "That's because Sean Rork is a man of *action*—just like you, Peter. It is time for you both to sink your teeth into real challenges, not fritter away your lives in mindless bureaucratic frivolity at the Navy Department or slow death by lethargy in retirement."

"Mr. President, thank you for the honor. It means more than I can say. But I can't. You know full well that I don't agree with some of the nation's new imperialistic policies. As the conversation today brought out, senior naval leaders are aware of that. Some have accused me of being one of the anti-imperialists. And maybe I am one."

"Yes, yes, of course you are, Peter—just like your friend Mark Twain. That is *precisely* why I need you! Look, I've got enough fawning yes-men. I need men who will tell me the *facts*, and their opinion, without fear or favor." He wagged his head and laughed. "And you, my old friend, have never been accused of being a sycophant."

Roosevelt's shallow flattery wasn't working. I shook my head. "We gave our nation's *word* to Cuba, Mr. President, along with the other places we captured from the Spanish. 'We are your liberators, not subjugators.' That's what we told them, and they believed us. They don't anymore."

He bowed slightly in acknowledgment of my point. "I fully agree about Cuba, Peter. I want us out of there in no more than another year. I need you to be part of the effort to make Cuba a viable independent country. Think of it, you'll be able to help make your friend José Martí's lifelong dream come true."

Flattery to my professional pride having failed, Theodore was blatantly appealing to my heart. Martí had died six years before, killed fighting the Spanish to gain independence for his people. He had repeatedly voiced his fears that the United States would exert commercial and political dominance over the island when independence from Spain was finally achieved. The U.S. occupation had gone on for three years now, and many Cubans were resentful, ridiculing our high-sounding rhetoric of 1898 and echoing Martí's warnings.

"Mr. President, it's more than Cuba. My son just came back from more than a year of combat in the Philippines, fighting the very people who fought the Spanish to get their independence. We were told they would be overjoyed to join us as a distant American possession. They're not overjoyed; they're enraged. The war there will go on for years."

Roosevelt's face hardened as his eyes went into that cold stare his opponents knew so well, but he damn well needed to hear what I had to say, whether he wanted to or not. "As you personally know, sir, we were very lucky in Cuba that the Spanish surrendered before fever casualties depleted our army. The Filipinos won't be so obliging. Unlike the Spanish colonizers in Cuba, the Filipinos are fighting for their homeland. So where and when does this stop? We've lost more than a thousand men already. How many more soldiers and sailors will we lose? And what if the people of Guam or Puerto Rico or Hawaii or Samoa rise up? Do we start killing them too?"

I'd crossed the line with that one. He stood, set his jaw, and answered in a rapid-fire lecture. "None of these people can govern themselves, and you know it. Japan and Germany both have their eyes on the Philippines and are just waiting for us to stumble. And furthermore, you know the Kaiser wants naval bases at Guam and Puerto Rico. I will *not* allow any of that!"

I calmed my rhetoric but held my ground. "Sir, I favor independence for all these colonies, along with continuing close commercial ties. We can lease bases for our Navy. That way we can still influence their governments. It would be a commercial empire, not a military one, and much cheaper in treasure and blood for us. And it will be much easier to sell to our citizenry."

He allowed a rare and brief shrug of acceptance of my view. "Valid point, Peter, but the *reality* does not support that concept right now, and we cannot abandon our present responsibilities. These places are weak without our governance and protection, and will quickly fall prey to the Japanese and European empires. Independence in the future by a plebiscite, yes. But for right now, American tutelage in democracy and commerce and military defense is the answer, and will continue to be the policy of our government."

There was some legitimacy in what he said. "I understand that, sir."

Roosevelt's brow creased in worry. "And speaking of the Japanese, I am concerned about this confrontation brewing between them and the Russians in China and Korea. I may well need your informed views on that issue in the near future."

I fully agreed with him on that concern. It was well known that Roosevelt didn't like Tsar Nicolas II or the feudal regime that had ruled Russia for centuries. That he was now worried about Japan's naval and military ambitions was significant, however, because he was a great admirer of Japan's remarkable modernization and martial spirit. So much so, in fact, that he became an expert in judo and jujitsu, and the Japanese ambassador was a close friend.

The Russians, like most Europeans and many Americans, were grossly underestimating the Japanese. I'd heard several Russians in Washington seriously refer to the Japanese navy as "trained monkeys." If Japan won a war against Russia, which I thought quite likely, their next target would undoubtedly be the Philippines. Our Navy—my son and my friends—would be in the thick of that conflict.

"I concur, sir. The probable outcome of a Russian-Japanese war could be a problem for us in the near future."

"Indeed, Peter. Of course, beyond foreign affairs, there is another reason why I need you here with me."

"Sir?"

The presidential index finger stabbed the air. "World events and scientific developments demand our Navy be of the highest quality. We must *modernize* it. We are now ranked third, behind Great Britain and France. Germany, Russia, and Japan are considered our equals. That is *not* good enough. We need to be, and I intend us to be, ranked *first* in the world."

That sort of navy will be very expensive, I thought, *and will take awhile to build, equip, man, and train. The domestic political effort will be enormous. And the Brits won't like being number two.*

The president warmed to the subject, his favorite for decades. "Think of what you and I could achieve in this regard, Peter! Wireless telegraphy, steam turbines, oil replacing coal, new optical gun sights, aeronautical machines, submarines, improved training for both enlisted and commissioned men, fast torpedo boats and destroyers, in-depth naval intelligence operations, and, of course, implementing Captain Mahan's strategy of naval dominance on a global scale. *Now* is the time—and *we* are the two men who can make it happen! No one will dare attack our country, or our hemisphere, with such a Navy!"

I thought him absolutely right on the scientific naval subjects but was tired of hearing about Mahan, whom I considered overrated. I'd always thought Capt. Alfred Mahan a lackluster seaman at best. He had gotten lucky fame for his book of commonsense ideas on strategy. Roosevelt, however, loved the fellow and promulgated his theories and books to everyone who would listen. That was only natural—Mahan's ideas on strategy supported Roosevelt's ambition for far-flung colonies.

"I'm not sure about becoming larger than the Royal Navy, but I fully agree on modernizing our Navy, sir. Scientific innovations are increasing at an ever-quickening pace, and we must stay ahead of potential adversaries." I added flatly, "Especially now that we have all these new possessions to defend."

He ignored my lukewarm addendum and nearly shouted, "Precisely, Peter!"

Clearly, my views on colonial politics hadn't swayed Roosevelt, so I switched tactics to a far more personal appeal. "Mr. President, Maria will never consent to me abandoning retirement. She's been planning—"

"Oh, worry not on her part, Peter. She'll come around on this. In fact, Edith is over at your home in Alexandria right now explaining my views to Maria, and also warning her that you'll be a bit late tonight. Your dear lady is a very perceptive person, and I am sure she will completely understand how very much your president and your nation, not to mention the people of Cuba, need your help. You won't be in jungles and battles anymore, old chap. This position will be far more sophisticated than that."

Edith is talking about this with Maria? How dare Theodore assume he can do that! Far from comprehending my rising ire, his face lit up with the very idea of me working for him again. "Naturally, if I send you somewhere as a special presidential envoy, Maria will be able to accompany you. Oh my goodness, the two of you will be a truly formidable partnership for diplomacy!"

Theodore wasn't used to anyone, much less a longtime friend, saying *no* to him, and his assumption that he could co-opt my retirement increasingly angered me the more I thought about it. I was thinking of a polite way to firmly and finally quash the entire notion without losing our long friendship when he spoke up again. He said it in an offhand way, as if it was a minor detail he'd just remembered.

"Oh, and your promotion is scheduled for early in the evening of next Wednesday, the sixteenth. It will be right here in the White House at six o'clock. I'm having a special private dinner afterward with you and Maria as my honored guests."

Truly, reader, I have never been so surprised. "Promotion! What promotion?"

59

Bamboozled

The White House, Washington, D.C.
Thursday Evening, 10 October 1901

THE PRESIDENT'S EYES TWINKLED mischievously at his success in stunning me. "The promotion you have long deserved and will need for this position, of course! My special assistant *has* to be a rear admiral if he is to get answers for me and get things done for our Navy and this country. Congress is confirming your flag promotion tomorrow—*if* you say *yes* tonight. Of course, I know you are not the sort of man to say *no* and shirk your duty to your country, especially when her commander in chief personally asks you to serve."

Congressional confirmation tomorrow? I strongly doubted that. I'd never been politically connected and had no friends in Congress. Besides, I'd been a captain since 1893 and understood how the Navy worked. There weren't any non–academy graduate flag officers left in the Navy, and the senior Annapolis ring-knockers didn't want any upstarts polluting their ranks. I'd always known my present rank would be my last.

This was classic Roosevelt—enthusiastically dangling the carrots of justice for Cuba, professional challenge, and achievement along with an appeal to my sense of honor and duty. I had to admit, he'd pulled it off masterfully, and it was damned tempting. But was it worth ending Maria's dream of our tranquil retirement? I couldn't do that to her.

"Mr. President, really, I can't—"

"Oh, for goodness' sake, you're not doing anything that will hurt or anger Maria. You are merely continuing to serve your country for a while longer. Really, Peter, we both know you aren't the kind of man to sit and patiently wait to die, even with the beautiful Maria at your side. Not yet. You still have valuable work to do in modernizing the Navy. In addition, you know the world, and you know me. We function well together. Now see here, Peter, this is only for a year. Then you can go home and grow vegetables, stare at the grass, and waste away if you want."

I weakened. "Only a year?"

Roosevelt, the champion debater, knew he was beginning to overcome my defenses.

"Yes, and what a *bully* year it will be! Just think of it, Peter. All those pompous officers who looked down on you for decades won't be condescending anymore; they'll be saluting you."

I confess to being just petty enough to smile at the image of that.

The president got that sly look again. "Oh, and speaking of that, there's a second thing I wanted to go over with you tonight. It has to do with a certain scoundrel named Reginald Dimm. He's been waiting in the public anteroom to see me for more than two hours. As I believe you know, he is set to be sworn in tomorrow as the interim representative for the vacant congressional seat from New York City. I've been told he already has his committee assignments. One of them might interest you—the House Naval Affairs Committee."

I stared at the president in shock. *Dimm is here, now? Why?* My notions of a bright future deflated. Dimm and his cohorts had already set his trap for me, and once sworn in he would snap it shut. With my reputation ruined, the president's grand plan for me was impossible.

I hadn't seen Dimm since that summer of 1898. He'd left the Navy in 1900 to ally himself commercially and politically with Republican Party boss Tom Platt, the Machiavellian senator who ran the political machinery of New York City. I'd heard that Dimm had slithered into the lifestyle easily and was making a lot of money brokering real estate properties in Manhattan and Brooklyn. He'd even gained acceptance among the social elite who strutted into Delmonico's several nights a week. I knew Platt and Roosevelt were longtime political acquaintances but definitely not personal friends. Roosevelt hated even the appearance of corruption. Platt reeked of it.

Before I could think of what to say, Roosevelt spoke into the telephone on his desk. "You can show Dimm into my office now."

As Dimm swept grandly into the office, I saw that his good times had given him an expensive suit, some glittering gold jewelry, and an even more pronounced air of self-importance. His new life had also added to his girth, which had grown to the point of obesity. Success had eroded some of his hair, however, and the remainder was flamboyantly swept up on one side and combed over his head to the other side.

Time had also increased his proclivity for fawning over superiors. All smiles and enthusiasm, he reached out a hand for the president standing in front of him. "Mr. *President!* How very *kind* of you to see me—"

Then Dimm noticed me sitting there and nearly choked.

The president didn't shake Dimm's proffered hand, smile, invite him to sit, or engage in small talk. Roosevelt's eyes were decidedly cold as he stepped right up in Dimm's face, his words coming out fast and intense.

"So, Dimm, I hear you've been telling people you came down here from New York to give me a blunt message from Big Boss Platt. Well, you've wasted your time. I spoke with Tom Platt on the telephone three hours ago." Roosevelt looked over at me and beamed. "Excellent long-distance wire connection, too. Platt could hear and *fully appreciate* every single word I said to him. Remarkable what science has accomplished these days, isn't it, Peter?"

I nodded and the president turned his attention back to the increasingly distressed man before him. "Don't you agree with Captain Wake, Dimm?"

Dimm couldn't take his eyes off me as he sputtered, "Ah, yes, sir."

Roosevelt continued. "Oh, yes, it was a very *candid* conversation with Tom Platt. In fact, he learned some things about you and your past that he didn't know before. Things that the newspapers will learn tomorrow should I wish it, since I happen to be dining this evening with two very well known writers. Platt also learned what *isn't* going to happen in your future. Do you know what that is?"

I could hardly hear Dimm's reply. "Ah . . . no, sir."

"Tomorrow, Dimm, you are *not* getting sworn in by the Speaker of the House as the newly appointed congressman from New York. Oh, no. You are going to get on the morning train and go back to New York City and report to Boss Platt. I understand he has found a suitable position for a man of your character—in a tenement neighborhood of the Borough of the Bronx, I believe. I rather like the irony of that. *Bronx* was the name of your last ship, wasn't it?"

"Yes, sir." Dimm looked like he was about to cry.

"I hope you speak Italian, Dimm. It will help you know what they're saying about you in your new slum. You may leave now. You are no longer needed in Washington."

A stone-faced usher appeared and led the plainly shaken Dimm from the room. Once the door closed, Theodore's grin returned. "My, that was fun!"

He paused then said, "Oh, yes, one more thing. Just so you know, your arduous day was at my instigation. I asked Secretary Long to assign Rear Admiral Pentwaller to get to the bottom of the rumors about you. I knew he would do a thorough job of it. Even invited one of Dimm's pals to join the discussion, just to see what all they were cooking up against you. I didn't want any nasty surprises to muddy my plans for you.

"This afternoon, Pentwaller informed me by telephone of the entire sordid attempt to sully your reputation and stop your retirement, and he assured me that he found nothing of substance in those rumors. You might also be interested to know that Capt. Percival Smith is going to get some time at sea—the Bering Sea to be precise—so he can channel his energies into something more productive and honorable. In fact,

I believe his orders are being delivered right about now. He leaves by transcontinental train tomorrow morning for Puget Sound Navy Yard to begin his coastal survey supervision assignment in Alaska. Should get there in time for the start of the Arctic winter!"

He walked to the door and held it open. "Peter, it's time for you to go home to your lovely Maria. You are hereby officially on leave until next Wednesday at six o'clock sharp. Be ready to enjoy your accolades, for they are long overdue, my friend. And now, duty calls me to return to my dinner and the political discussion of agricultural tariffs and taxes. Dull stuff, I can assure you, but necessary."

Still dazed by this turn of events, I left the White House, escorted by the same usher, who this time was smiling. It wasn't until I was halfway to the train station that I realized the new president of the United States had just bamboozled me into not retiring.

I dreaded going home and facing Maria.

60

Silver Stars

The Blue Room of the White House, Washington, D.C.
Wednesday Evening, 16 October 1901

NAVAL OFFICERS IN FULL DRESS uniform filled the elegant room. Each face brought a dozen memories of shared peril and laughter. As always happens with sailors, old acquaintances told sea stories of battles and storms, port calls and ships, clinking their glasses in camaraderie at the end of each tale. In addition to the mirth of nostalgic yarns, the atmosphere in the room was filled with pleasant anticipation of what was about to happen.

I am proud to report that the crowd included Adm. George Dewey, the Navy's senior and most famous officer, who had been my rescuer in the South China Sea almost thirty years before; Rear Adm. John G. Walker, the chief proponent of ONI during my long years there, and new president of the Isthmian Canal Commission; Capt. French Ensor Chadwick, new president of the Naval War College; Rear Adm. F. J. Higginson, the new commander of the North Atlantic Squadron; Rear Adm. William T. Sampson, preparing for his retirement; Capt. John Belfort, on leave awaiting orders after ending three years in command of *Dixon*; Lt. Cdr. Robert Gerard, just assigned as executive officer of a gunboat fitting out at the Washington Navy Yard and heading for the

Philippines; and Lt. Ross Barnett, who was getting ready to ship out for the Asiatic Squadron.

I stood in front of the marble fireplace, flanked by my family. The huge mirror above the mantel amplified the lights of the giant chandelier above as if a ship's searchlight were shining on us. All eyes in the room kept glancing our way, and it was easy to see why.

My Maria was impossibly beautiful. All eyes had followed her as she moved gracefully across the room in a shimmering light blue silk gown that accentuated her still impressive figure. Her Madagascar dark sapphire pendant and earrings—two-hundred-year-old family heirlooms from her Spanish past—mirrored her indigo eyes. Unlike the other Navy wives there, who seemed dowdy by comparison, Maria wore her long black hair swept up in the new French chignon style, secured by diamond-trimmed barrettes. No woman there—or indeed anywhere—could hold a candle to her.

I took a moment to soak up the grandeur of the scene. How far Maria and I had come from the hellish war in Cuba! My mind flashed back to the heartbreaking vision of her in a bloodstained Red Cross nurse's smock in the jungle, her body frail from dysentery but her spirit radiating love and strength. Tears filled my eyes, and I had the irresistible urge to hold her. I gave in and took her into my arms— right there in the crowded room. To the murmured approval of the naval elite in that historic room we slowly kissed, lost in ourselves.

Someone looking at us then would never imagine the vociferous arguments we'd had the previous week about the promotion and assignment that went with it. But all was said and done now, and thankfully over. Maria swallowed her disappointment and misgivings and stood by me. That meant everything.

Rork, once again in uniform, and the only noncommissioned officer in the room, stood just to my left. After Maria and I kissed, he clapped his good right hand on my shoulder. "Well done, sir, and executed in proper naval fashion!"

That got a big laugh in the room and a chorus of agreement. Rork went back to swapping outrageous sea stories with Admiral Walker, and I noticed that his Irish brogue was growing thicker. That was usually an indication of serious rum consumption, but I didn't care. It was good to see him happy again. At that moment, surrounded by his adopted family, who loved him dearly, and the veterans in Navy blue, who respected him greatly, Chief Boatswain's Mate Sean Aloysius Rork was back in his prime, and gloriously enjoying it all.

Newly promoted Lt. Cdr. Sean Wake, USNA class of 1890, returned only two weeks from patrol boat duty in the vicious fighting on the other side of the world, looked every inch the experienced naval officer as he stood next to Rork, his namesake. After eleven years as an officer with service all over the world, my son's reputation was a good one. In spite of my accumulated enemies, his future was secure. He was due to join the European Squadron next month and had recently told Maria and me about a special young lady in his life, implying she might soon become more than a close friend. I noted with pride how he handled all the brass in the room with composure. I knew then there was no need to worry about him anymore.

My daughter Useppa and her husband, Mario Cano, were there from Tampa for this momentous occasion. Young Peter, their toddler son and my namesake, wasn't present, of course, but I knew I would see him soon. He was a lively tyke who already loved being in and around water. He also proved to be exactly what Maria needed to bring peace back into her heart. Having endured so much loss and tragedy in her own life, she poured love into his.

A Marine in the hallway suddenly snapped to attention. The string quartet along the far wall went silent as Commander Cowles entered and announced, "Ladies and gentlemen, the President of the United States, and Mrs. Roosevelt."

Theodore and Edith glided in, parting the crowd as they headed for Maria and me. The two ladies embraced as Roosevelt heartily pumped my hand, beaming his pleasure at the occasion.

"What a perfectly *magnificent* evening—just look at all this Navy blue and gold gathered here to see one of our very finest receive the tribute and reward of a grateful nation!"

A round of polite applause followed. Theodore cut it abruptly short with a curt wave of his hand. "Admiral Dewey, distinguished guests, ladies and gentlemen, I propose we not dawdle with more speeches but instead steam at full speed ahead to the matter at hand. Therefore, I order that Capt. Peter Wake, United States Navy, please step forward."

Maria reached up and kissed me on the cheek, touching the newly issued Sampson Medal on my chest. I stepped up to the president with Maria on my right and Rork on my left.

Roosevelt cleared his throat and solemnly declared, "Captain Peter Wake, by the authority invested in me by the Constitution of our United States of America, and with the approval of the Congress of the United States, I hereby promote you to the rank of rear admiral in the United States Navy. Congratulations, Admiral."

Commander Cowles stepped up beside the president and held out a tray holding two pairs of silver stars sitting on a square of blue velvet. Roosevelt removed the eagle rank insignias of a captain from my collar. Then Maria, with tears in her eyes, and Rork, who looked a bit misty-eyed himself, each took a pair of silver stars from the tray and pinned them on a side of my tunic collar. Admiral Dewey shook my hand, and the audience applauded and cheered.

While the president basked in the revelry, Maria took his hand in hers, smiled sweetly at him, then whispered with a hard edge only he and I could hear.

"This isn't going to be for only one year, is it, Theodore?"

Her comment caught me by surprise. Maria and I had discussed that possibility, but without reaching agreement on what to do if and when it arose. I knew it worried her.

Roosevelt took her pointed question in stride. Continuing to flash his grin at everyone in the room, he leaned over and quietly replied, "Perhaps, my dear, but only if he wants to stay a bit longer and help me with a few things."

Then, before Maria or I could respond, the president turned to the crowded room and gestured to me. "Ladies and gentlemen, I am mighty glad we have a man like Rear Admiral Peter Wake helping our country at the beginning of this new century—*America's century!*"

Everyone, including Maria, cheered.

Acknowledgments

My thanks go to some very important people around the world who, in ways large and small, helped make this book happen. First and foremost, I am grateful to my brilliant and lovely wife, Nancy Ann Glickman. In addition to being my morale and welfare officer when "the book biz" gets frustrating and exhausting, she is also my business manager, publicist and media liaison, lecture/book tour facilitator, and historical astronomy and ornithology researcher. Her invaluable influence is evident throughout this book.

Heartfelt thanks go to those in Cuba who have helped me research my trilogy of novels about the Spanish-American War (known in Cuba far more accurately as the Spanish-Cuban-American War): Roberto Giraudy (Ministerio de Cultura de la República de Cuba), Ela López Ugarte (Centro de Estudios Martianos), Dr. Justin White (professor of Spanish linguistics in Florida and coordinator of my reader tours in Cuba), Victor Julián Avila Ametller (Director of the Historical Museum of the Grand Masonic Lodge of Cuba), and George Fernandez (guide and transport facilitator). Together we have climbed the hills, walked the jungles, pondered the dilemmas, and been amazed at the outcomes of 1898. They are far more than professional colleagues; they have become dear and trusted friends.

Through the kind introduction of my aforementioned friends I was fortunate to meet with some renowned historians at Santiago de Cuba: Dr. Miguel Ronald Moncada (legendary historian who spent days with me in various offices and also out in the field), Dr. Omar López Rodriguez (Oficina del Conservador de la Ciudad de Santiago), Dr. Olga Portoundo and Juan Manuel Reyes (Oficina del Historiador de la Ciudad de Santiago), Juan Antonio Tejera Palzado (President of the Asociación de Cine, Radio y TV), and Dr. Carmen

Montalvo Suárez (Director of the Centro Estudios Antonio Maceo Grajales). And let me not forget Antonio "Tony" Tejeiro Montesino, who drove my team for days up steep mountains, along muddy jungle roads, and through narrow city streets in his beautifully maintained 1952 Chevrolet sedan. All these talented people helped me not only with historical facts but also with the unique cultural flavor of the area and people of Oriente, Cuba.

My appreciation also goes to my late father, Robert Charles Macomber, my Uncle Raul Laffitte, and dear friends Mario Cano and Chaz Mena, each of whom provided unique views on the culture and history of Spain, Cuba, and Puerto Rico.

At the "Enchanted Isle" of Puerto Rico, Anna Martin and my friends at Casa Por Fin on the beach at Rincón were wonderful hosts. It was there, seventeen years ago, that I decided to someday tell this story of the American invasion.

On the subject of ship handling, my profound respect and thanks go to some real masters I've observed performing that difficult art, which can go dreadfully wrong in a heartbeat: Capt. Paul Welling, USCG (USCGC *Eagle*); Capt. Chuck Nygaard, USN (USS *Spruance*, USS *Vicksburg*); Commodore Ronald Warwick, RNR (RMS *Queen Mary 2*); and Captain Ullrich Nuber, German Merchant Marine (MV *Hamburgo*). They made it look easy. It isn't.

And finally, I present my great appreciation to the thousands of Wakians around the world. They have buoyed me with their enthusiasm, helped me on some very arcane research, and challenged me with intriguing ideas for new projects. I am profoundly blessed to have the very best readers an author could desire, and I love spending time with them. Two of them, Mel and Judy Balk, even let me live at their wonderful hideaway home on Upper Captiva Island to finish the manuscript of this book. Thank you all!

Onward and upward, my friends, toward those distant horizons . . .
Robert N. Macomber
The Boat House
St. James, Pine Island, Florida

Sources and Notes by Chapter

Chapter 1. The "Conversation"

Wake is on the staff of the General Board of the Navy, a policy study group formed in 1900.

The Sampson-Schley controversy was over which senior officer should get credit for the great naval victory at Santiago: Commo. Winfield Scott Schley, the tactical commander in the fight, or Rear Adm. William T. Sampson, the fleet commander. The argument raged for years, with disparaging comments from both sides. Wake is on Sampson's side.

Six bells in the forenoon watch is 11 a.m.

The naval battle of Santiago had been fought the day before, on 3 July, and the land battle of Santiago had been fought on 1 July. Wake was in the middle of both these American victories. See *Honoring the Enemy* for details.

Chapter 2. The Ship

Dixon's armament may seem paltry today, but at the time it was standard for hastily converted passenger steamers. The 6-inch guns were manufactured at the U.S. Naval Gun Factory in Washington, D.C.

States began forming naval militias in 1890, with Massachusetts being the first (though New York sometimes disputes this). Since 1890, thirty-one states have had naval militias, and naval militiamen have been activated during times of war or crisis. The most recent activation was for a 2014 blizzard in Buffalo, New York. Currently, only six states have naval militias: Alaska, California, New York, Ohio, South Carolina, and Texas.

The Mark 3 6-inch gun was designed in the 1880s, and 109 were built for the U.S. Navy. It fired a 105-pound shell with an approximately 9,000-yard effective range. The Navy used it until the 1920s.

The Driggs-Schroeder rapid-fire 6-pounder was a modification of the gun designed by the Hotchkiss Company in the 1880s. The Navy used the gun from 1890 to 1910, and the Coast Guard used it until 1946. It fired a 9.7-pound shell two miles at a rate of twenty-five rounds per minute.

Chapter 3. The Men

"Black gang" is the old naval slang for crewmen who worked in the coal bunkers, boiler rooms, or engine rooms, because the coal dust and lubricating oils they worked around penetrated their skin and stained it black. It does not refer specifically to African Americans.

Chapter 4. Rork

A "Liverpudlian" is a person from the port city of Liverpool, England. For more about Wake's and Rork's perilous mission in the Empire of Vietnam and Kingdom of Cambodia, read *The Honored Dead*.

The senior petty officers' quarters were called the "goat locker" because the ship's stock—fresh meat, eggs, and milk during voyages lasting months or even years—were kept nearby for safekeeping. It also ensured the senior petty officers got the best food. The term is still used today.

Chapter 6. A Ghost in the Night

Ordóñez 5.9-inch guns, designed by Colonel Salvador Ordóñez and built at Spain's Royal Ordnance Works at Trubia, were used from the 1880s to 1937. They were considered inferior in shell weight and range to U.S., German, and British guns, but were cheaper to make.

Chapter 8. Confusion

The forecastle, often contracted to "fo'c's'le" in sailors' lingo, is the compartment at the forward end of the main deck (or the deck below it). In the 1500s to the 1700s there was a fighting superstructure there, hence the origin of the name, which is still used. In those days, the fighting superstructure at the rear end of the ship was called the "stern castle," but that term is no longer in use.

Chapter 9. The Captured Freighter

"French leave," which means to run away from adversity, is a classic example of British and American sailor humor. It was first used during the Napoleonic Wars (1790s–1815) and is still heard from old salts today.

A "sea lawyer" is someone who complains by spouting rules and regulations. It is considered a serious insult.

Chapter 12. From Annoying to Awful

To read more about the professional and moral dilemma Wake faced in 1869, read *A Dishonorable Few*.

Rear Adm. William T. Sampson (1840–1902) was a quiet, respected naval officer with a fairly routine career who led the inquiry into the destruction of battleship *Maine* at Havana in February 1898. He subsequently was made a temporary rear admiral and given command of the Caribbean fleet that fought the most significant naval battle in U.S. history to that time. He died four years after the war.

Capt. (later Rear Adm.) French Ensor Chadwick (1844–1919) was a highly respected naval officer who served not only at sea but also led the Office of Naval Intelligence and the Naval War College. He wrote a definitive history of the causes of the Civil War.

Chapter 13. The "Conversation"

Read *The Assassin's Honor* to find out what exactly happened at Tampa in 1892 and how it altered world history.

Chapter 14. The Army

Maj. Gen. William Rufus Shafter (1835–1906) served with distinction in the Civil War. In 1895 he was retroactively awarded the Medal of

Honor for his actions at the Battle of Fair Oaks in 1862. After the Civil War, he fought in many of the Indian Wars, where he was given the nickname "Pecos Bill." By the time of the Spanish-American War in 1898, he was a brigadier general and in very bad physical condition, weighing more than three hundred pounds and suffering from gout and other diseases. He was chosen to command the U.S. Army's Fifth Corps and the invasion of Cuba primarily because of his lack of political ambition or liability. Shafter was precisely the wrong man for large-scale combat in a tropical jungle, and he ended up spending a large part of his time in Cuba sick in bed. Fort Shafter, Hawaii, is named after him. To understand more about him, read *Honoring the Enemy*.

For a detailed description of the Battle of Santiago and the battles preceding it, read *Honoring the Enemy*. Wake was in the midst of it all.

The Fifth Corps, which consisted of 20,000 men in two infantry divisions and one cavalry division (which was mainly dismounted in Cuba), assembled and trained at Tampa, Florida. Most of its troops were regular Army veterans, but it also contained the legendary 1st U.S. Volunteer Cavalry—Theodore Roosevelt's "Rough Riders." On the corps' chaotic time in Tampa and in Cuba, read *Honoring the Enemy*.

Shafter's comments about the Spanish reinforcements are indicative of his disdain for the Cuban army, which though outnumbered and outgunned by the Spanish, almost succeeded in stopping them before five thousand Spanish troops reinforced the defense of Santiago.

Maj. Gen. Nelson A. Miles (1839–1925) had a very good reputation for organization. In 1892 he was retroactively awarded the Medal of Honor for his actions at the Battle of Chancellorsville in 1863. By 1898 he was the commanding general of the U.S. Army. He'd asked to command the invasion of Cuba but was kept in Washington by President McKinley. When Shafter's invasion turned into a siege, Miles was sent to Cuba with reinforcements. He later commanded the invasion of Puerto Rico. After the war, he was promoted to lieutenant general and commanded the Army until his retirement in 1903. At the time of his death in 1925, he had been the last surviving general officer from either side of the Civil War.

"Unacclimated" in those days meant without immunity to local diseases.

Chapter 15. Waitin' for the Fevers

Theodore Roosevelt (1858–1919) had been Wake's good friend since 1886. Here, Roosevelt has been promoted to colonel and is in command of the regiment. For more about the relationship between Wake and Roosevelt, read *The Darkest Shade of Honor, The Assassin's Honor, An Honorable War,* and *Honoring the Enemy.*

Maj. Gen. Joe Wheeler (1836–1906) was a Confederate cavalry general in the Civil War and afterward an Alabama congressman. In 1898 President McKinley placed him second in command of the invasion of Cuba, with the concurrent command of the Fifth Corps' cavalry division. Wheeler was a feisty commander and a favorite of his troops. He famously forgot which war he was in at the Battle of Las Guásimas in Cuba when he yelled to his troops, "Go git 'em boys, we got them Yankees on the run!" He stayed in the U.S. Army after the Spanish-American War and served in the Philippines and the continental United States.

Richard Harding Davis (1864–1916) was a journalist, war correspondent, and the author of thirty-eight books. An old friend of Roosevelt, Davis ensured that he got very positive press coverage during the war.

Edith Carow Roosevelt (1861–1948) was Roosevelt's second wife. (His first wife, Alice, died days after giving birth to their daughter Alice.) Edith and Theodore had a warm and loving marriage that produced five children. Edith and Wake's wife, Maria, are dear friends.

Chapter 16. A Different Sort of General

Secretary of War Russell Alger (1836–1907) served in the U.S. Army as a volunteer officer in the Civil War and afterward became a successful businessman and politician. President McKinley made him secretary of war in 1897. Alger did not emerge from the Spanish-American War with a good reputation for efficiency, however. He failed to get the Army ready for the conflict or to efficiently lead it once the war began. Roosevelt despised him.

Chapter 17. Humiliating García

Major General Calixto García (1839–98) fought for Cuban independence for thirty years. When Wake knew him, he had a terrible scar on his forehead from a .45-caliber wound received in 1873 that gave him constant headaches for the rest of his life. He was humiliated by Shafter at Santiago but in December 1898 led the Cuban Commission to Washington, where he was treated with the respect and appreciation he deserved. He died in Washington shortly after arriving and was buried with full military honors at Arlington National Cemetery. Later his casket was taken back to Cuba with full naval honors on board the cruiser *Nashville*. He was considered a soldier's general and a brilliant tactician and is revered among Cubans everywhere today. For more about Wake's friendship with him, read *Honoring the Enemy*.

Major General José Toral (1832–1904) was second in command of the Spanish army in the Santiago area. The commander, Lieutenant General Arsenio Linares (1848–1914), was wounded in the battle, and Toral took command, surrendering Spanish forces two weeks later. After the war, Toral was reviled by many in Spain. He gradually went insane and died in an asylum six years later.

García's July 1898 letter of protest to Maj. Gen. William R. Shafter is reprinted from *The Spanish-Cuban-American War and the Birth of American Imperialism*, Philip S. Foner (1972).

Chapter 19. Maria

Maria Wake (formerly Maria Abad Maura, of Spain) married Peter in May 1893 in Key West. Widow of a Spanish diplomat, she is the mother of two sons: a Franciscan priest who was murdered in January 1898 by Wake's longtime nemesis in the Spanish secret police in Havana,

Colonel Isidro Marrón, and a young Spanish reserve army officer whom Wake captured in battle at Isabella in May 1898. Wake and Maria found each other later in life and share a passionate and mutually supportive love, but the war's heavy toll on Maria is mounting.

Matthew Arnold (1822–1888) was one of the most famous poets in Victorian England. His father was headmaster of the renowned school at Rugby, England.

Chapter 22. Orders

Francis J. Higginson (1843–1931) served in the U.S. Navy from the Civil War until 1905, when he retired as a rear admiral. He enjoyed an intriguing career and good reputation.

Torpedo boat–destroyers were the prototype for modern destroyers, a term that came into use shortly after the Spanish-American War.

Whitehead torpedoes were the first self-propelled torpedoes. They were designed and sold worldwide by the English engineer Robert Whitehead (1823–1905) starting in the 1870s. In 1898 they had a range of 900 yards and speed of 15 knots, and carried a 60-pound explosive charge.

Schwartzkopff torpedoes were designed by the German engineer Louis Victor Robert Schwartzkopff (1825–1892) in the 1880s and 1890s. They traveled in excess of 20 knots, had a range of 700 yards, and carried a 44-pound explosive. Since his torpedo was similar to Whitehead's (except for the speed), there has long been debate whether Schwartzkopff used stolen plans of a Whitehead torpedo.

A barque-rigged ship is a type of square-rigged ship.

Chapter 23. Into the Black Beyond

Compañía Transatlántica Española was the most famous Spanish passenger and shipping line from its beginnings at Havana in 1850 until 1994, when it began to go bankrupt. By 2012 the courts had dissolved the company.

Chapter 24. Smoke in the Rain

Hontaria made large-caliber guns for the Spanish navy.

Chapter 26. Sunrise

That smoke haze is still over Haiti, caused by charcoal cooking fires and slash-and-burn farming, which has led to severe soil erosion.

Chapter 27. A Silent Ship

"Wig-wag" was turn-of-the-century sailors' term for semaphore flag signaling.

Chapter 32. The Enchanted Isle

Capt. William H. Whitney (1866–1949) was Miles' chief spy inside Puerto Rico and a true hero of this war. A West Point graduate (1892), Whitney was an expert in mapmaking and spoke Spanish. He first disguised himself as a journalist, then became the English sailor H. W. Elias (whose identity he had stolen), and then a kerosene salesman. Whitney did a brilliant job of reconnoitering the Spanish defenses across the island while eluding the secret police, who were searching for him. Whitney's information convinced Miles to change the invasion plan, thus saving many American lives that would have been lost at Fajardo. He later served in the Philippines, against Pancho Villa on the Mexican border, and on the western front in World War I, retiring as a brigadier general in 1920. In 1918 Whitney was awarded the Distinguished Service Cross for his perilous mission twenty years earlier in Puerto Rico.

No-see-ums are tiny biting midges common near water, especially at dawn and dusk.

Chapter 35. Invasion

Richard Wainwright (1849–1926) came from a family of famous political leaders and naval officers. He graduated from the Naval Academy in 1868 and in early 1898 was a lieutenant commander and executive officer of the battleship *Maine* when she was destroyed at Havana. He was then given command of the gunboat *Gloucester* (the former yacht of the financier J. P. Morgan), in which he had a very active and successful combat tour on the coasts of Cuba. The rest of his career was also filled with action, and he retired in 1911 as a rear admiral.

The lightweight Navy M1895 Colt machine gun issued to Navy and Marine Corps units—the U.S. Army had a similar version—could fire up to four hundred 6-millimeter Lee Navy rounds per minute. They were used extensively in the Spanish-American War. Theodore Roosevelt's Rough Riders had some but didn't like them—they broke down too often. This machine gun was used worldwide until the end of World War II. The last known use of one was in the 1962 Yemeni civil war.

Chapter 36. Honor Satisfied

The Spanish Mauser Model 1893 fired 7-millimeter smokeless rounds from five-round box magazines. In the Spanish-American War, it proved far superior to the American Army's Krag-Jørgensen rifles. In 1903 the U.S. Army replaced its Krags with the Springfield rifle, which was copied from the Spanish Mauser. The Springfield served as the standard U.S. infantry rifle for thirty-three years.

Agustín Barrenechea, Vicente Ferrer, Juan María Morciglio, Simón Mejil, Salvador Muñoz, Cornelio Serrano, and Pascual Elena did much to ensure a peaceful U.S. military occupation during 1898–99 when they served as civic leaders for the area. Mejil became the constable.

The king of Spain in 1898 was twelve-year-old Alfonso XIII (1886–1941), whose father died while his mother, Queen Maria Christina of Austria, was pregnant with him. The real powers in Spain were the queen regent and the various prime ministers of that period. Alfonso XIII ascended the throne in 1902 at age sixteen and stayed there until Spain fell into complete chaos and civil war in 1931, when he fled to Fascist Italy. He died in Rome in 1941. The current king of Spain, Felipe VI, is Alfonso's great-grandson.

Chapter 37. In All Their Glory

Lieutenant Colonel Francisco Puig commanded a combined Spanish–Puerto Rican force at Yauco. Faced with overwhelming odds at the Battle of Yauco and with several men killed or wounded, he executed a skillful withdrawal, at one point causing panic among the men of the 6th Massachusetts Infantry that later led the senior officers of that regiment to resign. Fearing that the loss of his artillery at Yauco and his failure to destroy a rail junction would lead to a humiliating court-martial back in Spain, Puig committed suicide on 2 August 1898.

Brig. Gen. George Garretson (1844–1916) graduated from West Point right after the Civil War and served in the Army for a few year. He then went into civilian life as merchant and banker in his home state of Ohio. He later joined the state militia and rose to senior rank. He was well connected in Ohio and in 1898 was given a general's commission by President McKinley, another Ohioan. Garretson was Puig's opponent at Yauco.

Chapter 38. A Calculated Risk

Aspinwall was the old American and British name for Colón. It was named for William Henry Aspinwall (1807–1875), a successful businessman and shipping line owner who founded the Panama Canal Railway in the 1850s. The town of Aspinwall was the Caribbean end of the railroad that crossed the Isthmus of Panama. That name fell into disuse as the French began their effort to build the canal and used the locals' name, Colón, which is still the name today.

The Leewards and Windwards are the curving arc of smaller islands forming the eastern edge of the Caribbean, from Grenada north to the Virgin Islands.

Chapter 40. Captain "Perhaps"

Alfred Dreyfus (1859–1935) was a Jewish artillery officer in the French army. In 1894 he was falsely accused and convicted of betraying secrets to the Germans and was sentenced to life imprisonment at Devil's Island (Île du Diable) in French Guiana, South America. He was in that hellhole from 1895 until 1899, when he was convicted again—in spite of evidence proving he was innocent—and then pardoned by the French president. In 1906 he was finally exonerated of all charges, promoted, awarded the Legion of Honor, and returned to a command in the army, where he served with distinction until the retiring at the end of World War I. Drefus is still considered a French and Jewish hero.

The ONI *Ports* book is the Office of Naval Intelligence's periodically updated and fascinating reference work: *Coaling, Docking, and Repairing Facilities of the Ports of the World.* Every U.S. Navy ship carried the latest version until the 1970s. Now they use computers.

Chapter 41. As Fate Would Have It

From 1807 to 1830 Simón Bolívar (1783–1830) led the independence movements in what are now Venezuela, Colombia, Ecuador, and Peru. The movements spread across the Western Hemisphere until all Spain's imperial colonies were free, Cuba and Puerto Rico last of all. He is revered from Mexico to Argentina as a great hero and Master Mason.

Chapter 43. Gonna Be Big Trouble, Sure as Hell!

The Nouvelle du Canal de Panama didn't last long. The United States bought the company and all its assets for $40 million in 1902.

Chapter 44. A Caribbean Lady with a German Accent

SMS *Greier* was a modern, well-armed German gunboat. Wake had had dealings with her in the past. In World War I she was taken by the U.S. Navy and renamed USS *Schurz.* She sank in a collision in 1918 off North Carolina, and the location is now a popular dive site. The SMS prefix stands for "Seiner Majestät Schiff," the Imperial German Navy equivalent of the British HMS.

The Hamburg South American Steamship Company was economically and politically very powerful in Latin America. One estimate has it carrying 60 percent of the European cargo trade to and from Latin America in that period.

Chapter 46. Politics and Crime

Pedro Prestan was either a bandit or a revolutionary, depending on whom you ask. He led a rebellion at Colón in 1885 that burned the town and held hostage some ex-pat Americans and U.S. sailors from the cruiser *Galena*, which was visiting the port at the time. A joint U.S. Navy–Colombian army force restored order by capturing Prestan and his followers, who were executed by the Colombians.

Chapter 49. Alone

Matusalem & Company was founded in 1872 at Santiago de Cuba by Eduardo and Benjamin Camp of Spain. Using the ancient solera process, they created a premier sipping rum and became the main competitor of Bacardí. Both companies left Cuba after the communists took over in 1959, with Matusalem taking its cane stock to the Dominican Republic. *Matusalem* is Spanish for "Methuselah," signifying the distilling process is "as ancient as Methuselah." In my not-so-humble opinion, Matusalem is the finest Cuban-genre sipping rum in the world. It's available almost everywhere and is the drink of choice for many Wakians.

Chapter 50. Lunacy

Wake intentionally drowned Lieutenant Moreau, his Spanish secret police enemy, near the Statue of Liberty on its dedication day on October 1886. Moreau had tried to kill Wake's family in Florida six months earlier and had returned to kill Wake. Read *The Darkest Shade of Honor*.

A master-at-arms is a petty officer who is a warship's policeman. The U.S. Navy still has them.

Chapter 51. The "Conversation"

Guerre de course is the age-old naval strategy of raiding an enemy's commercial ships on their global trading routes. Rear Adm. Raphael Semmes (1809–1877) of the Confederate States Navy was the master at it, roaming the Atlantic, Indian, and Pacific oceans in the legendary cruiser *Alabama*. To this day, he holds the world record for the most enemy (Union) ships captured by an ocean raider: eighty-six. His memoirs, written after the Civil War, were required reading for American and most European naval officers.

Chapter 55. Battle Stations

A pelorus is a compass-like instrument on a pedestal that allows compass bearings to be ascertained on other ships or landmarks ashore. Almost all ships' bridges have at least one.

Bradley Fiske (1854–1942) was a brilliant naval officer and scientist who invented many instruments that greatly assisted naval seamen. His stadimeter was an instrument used to determine the range to an object. He also worked on torpedoes, optical sights, and navigation equipment. He retired as a rear admiral but kept working on inventions to help the Navy for the rest of his life. He is considered an American naval hero.

Chapter 56. The "Conversation"

The General Board of the Navy was a planning advisory group formed in 1900 by Secretary of the Navy John Long and chaired by Admiral of the Navy George Dewey until his death in 1917. It continued in operation until it was deactivated in 1951. It had various senior officers as standing members, along with temporary adjunct members, including the Navy's brightest minds.

Chapter 58. Only for a Year . . .

William Allen White (1868–1944) was a Kansas newspaperman and Progressive and the author of twenty-two books. He and Theodore

Roosevelt were close friends for twenty years, frequently staying at each other's homes. White once explained their long friendship this way: "Roosevelt bit me and I went mad!"

Joseph Bucklin Bishop (1847–1928) was a newspaperman and author of thirteen books. He met Roosevelt in 1895 when the latter was commissioner (and great reformer) of the New York City Police Department. They became the best of friends, and Bishop was an enthusiastic supporter of America building the Panama Canal.

William S. Cowles (1849–1923) was a career naval officer who married Theodore Roosevelt's older sister Anna (called "Bamie" by family and friends) Roosevelt (1855–1931) in 1895, when they were both in their early forties. Cowles served as a naval aide to President McKinley and President Roosevelt and retired as a rear admiral.

The American Anti-Imperial League (1898–1920) was against America's acquisition of overseas colonies and the ensuing subjugation of their people. Mark Twain, former president Grover Cleveland, Andrew Carnegie, William Jennings Bryan, and many other prominent businessmen, civic leaders, and statesmen belonged to the movement. Peter Wake is not a member but does sympathize with their ideas.

Cuba became an independent country on 20 May 1902. José Martí, Wake's dear friend from 1886 until Martí's death in battle in 1895, frequently warned about American economic and political dominance over Cuba. Wake promised Martí in 1893 that he would work for Cuba's independence. For more about their friendship, read *The Darkest Shade of Honor*, *Honorable Lies*, and *The Assassin's Honor*.

Alfred Thayer Mahan (1840–1914) was a lackluster naval officer involved in several negative incidents with ships he commanded, but who later became widely admired for his ideas on naval strategy. His 1890 book, *The Influence of Sea Power on History: 1660–1783*, was a bestseller and is still highly regarded today. In many navies it was, and still is, a mandatory read. From the mid-1880s Mahan stayed ashore, writing and lecturing about his ideas and enjoying his many famous friends, including Theodore Roosevelt. Unlike most in the Navy, Wake wasn't impressed with Mahan.

Chapter 59. Bamboozled

"Boss Platt" was Thomas Collier Platt (1833–1910), a lawyer, business-man, and politician who became the most powerful (many thought him the most corrupt) man in New York state and city politics in the 1880s and 1890s. While Theodore Roosevelt was governor of New York (1899–1900), he and Platt sparred over many issues. In 1900 it was Platt who, resenting Roosevelt's crusade against corruption and inefficiency in state and city government, got Roosevelt out of New York and into the do-nothing job as President McKinley's second-term vice president. When McKinley was assassinated September 1901 and Roosevelt suddenly became president, Platt's influence dropped very quickly.

Delmonico's has been a famous upscale restaurant in Manhattan since 1837. Opened by the brothers Peter and John Delmonico, over the years it has been in eleven different locations but has always retained a reputation for fine food and an elite clientele. Many legendary dishes were invented there, including Delmonico steak, baked Alaska, lobster Newberg, wedge salad, Manhattan clam chowder, and eggs Benedict. Wake first met Roosevelt there in 1886 (see *The Darkest Shade of Honor*). Nowadays, Delmonico's is located near its original site in Manhattan, at 56 Beaver Street, down near the Battery. Wake loves going there but can't often afford it.

Chapter 60. Silver Stars

Admiral of the Navy George Dewey (1837–1917) was the highest-ranking officer in the history of the U.S. Navy, after being promoted to five-star admiral for his stunning 1898 victory at Manila Bay. As a commander in 1883, he rescued Wake and Rork from an island in the South China Sea (see *The Honored Dead*). Dewey and his General Board of the Navy helped prepare the U.S. Navy for the twentieth century.

Rear Adm. John Grimes Walker (1835–1907) helped to modernize the Navy in the 1880s and 1890s. As chief of the Bureau of Navigation in the 1880s, he was also the overall superior, and great supporter, of the fledgling Office of Naval Intelligence (and thus of Wake) and the Naval War College. After retiring in 1897 he chaired the Isthmian Canal Commission to determine which route across Central America—Nicaragua or Panama—was the best one for a canal. On 16 November 1901 (a month after Wake's promotion party), Walker's commission recommended Nicaragua, because it was easier to build a canal there and also because the French canal company in Panama was asking the exorbitant price of $109 million for its rights, assets, and equipment. Two months later, the French lowered the price to $40 million, and Walker changed his recommendation to Panama. In 1903 Panama became independent from Colombia, the United States acquired the Canal Zone, and the work began. The Canal opened for business in 1914.

The Sampson Medal was introduced in March 1901 for naval personnel who served at the Battle of Santiago. Wake and Rork were at the battle, but as prisoners of war on a Spanish cruiser while Wake's son, Sean, was a gunnery officer on the battleship *Oregon* and shooting at them. Their Sampson medals will long be a source of amusement for all three men.

Bibliography of Research Materials

U.S. Naval Operations and Maritime Events in the Caribbean

The American Steel Navy, Cdr. John D. Alden, USN (Ret.) (1972).

Battles and Capitulation of Santiago de Cuba (War Notes, nos. 1–8: Information from Abroad), Office of Naval Intelligence (1899).

A Century of U.S. Naval Intelligence, Capt. Wyman H. Packard USN (Ret.) (1996).

Characteristics of Principal Foreign Ships of War, prepared for the Board on Fortifications, etc., Office of Naval Intelligence (1885).

Coaling, Docking, and Repair Facilities of the Ports of the World, Office of Naval Intelligence (1909).

Conway's All the World's Fighting Ships 1860–1905, Robert Gardiner, editorial director (1979).

Cruise of the U.S.S. Dixie, W. C. Payne (1899).

Dictionary of Admirals of the U.S. Navy, vol. 1: *1862–1900*; vol. 2: *1901–1918*, William B. Cogar (1989, 1991).

"King Alonzo Adams Arrives," *New York Times* shipping news from Boston (July 1909).

The Naval Annual of 1891, T. A. Brassey (1891).

The Naval Aristocracy: The Golden Age of Annapolis and the Emergence of Modern American Navalism, Peter Karsten (1972).

"The Naval Base at Key West in 1898," Cdr. Reginald R. Belknap, USN, U.S. Naval Institute *Proceedings*, 41/5/159 (September–October 1915).

Navalism and the Emergence of American Sea Power 1882–1893, Randy Russell Shulman (1995).

The Office of Naval Intelligence: The Birth of America's First Intelligence Agency 1865–1918, Jeffry M. Dorwart (1979).

Rear Admiral Schley, Sampson, and Cervera, James Parker (1910).

"Record of the *Oregon*," *New York Times* (June 1900).

Rocks and Shoals, James B. Valle (1980).

The Spanish-American War: Blockades and Coast Defense (War Notes, no. 6), Office of Naval Intelligence (1899).

Spanish-American War Documentary Histories, Naval History and Heritage Command, U.S. Navy (2016).

U.S. Cruisers 1883–1904, Lawrence Burr (2008).

U.S.S. Olympia, Herald of Empire, Benjamin Franklin Cooling (2000).

With Sampson through the War, W. A. M. Goode (1899).

U.S. Army Operations in the Caribbean

The American Army Moves on Puerto Rico, pts. 1 and 2, Mark R. Barnes, Senior Archaeologist, National Park Service.

"The Capture of Santiago," Maj. Gen. William Shafter, U.S. Army, *Century* (February 1899): 612–30.

Cuba in War Time, Richard Harding Davis (1897).

The Cuban and Porto Rican Campaigns, Richard Harding Davis (1899).

From Yauco to Las Marias, Karl Stephan Herrmann (1900).

In Cuba with Shafter, John D. Miley (1899).

"Incidents of the Operations around Santiago," *National Tribune* (30 June 1898).

Marching with Gomez, Grover Flint (1898).

Puerto Rico 1898: The War after the War, Fernando Picó (2004).

Puerto Rico: Its Conditions and Possibilities, William Dinwiddie (1899).

"*Seneca* Passengers Free," *New York Times* (23 July 1898).

Serving the Republic, Nelson A. Miles (1911).

The Spanish-American War, Albert A. Nofi (1997).

Under Three Flags in Cuba, George Clarke Musgrave (1898).

United States Army Logistics 1775–1992, vol. 2, Charles R. Shrader (1997).

War Map and History of Cuba, Ebenezer Hannaford (1898).

The War with Spain in 1898, David F. Trask (1996).

The Cuban Commanders' View

Larry Daley, Spanish-American War Centennial Website.
Major General Calixto García's July 1898 letter of protest to Maj. Gen. William R. Shafter, in *The Spanish-Cuban-American War and the Birth of American Imperialism*, Philip S. Foner (1972).
The Official War Report of Major General Calixto Ramón García Iñiguez, translated by

The Spanish Commanders' View

Admiral Pascual Cervera's Report to the Spanish Ministry of Marine of the Battle of Santiago, La Correspondencia (August 1898), translated and printed by U.S. Government Printing Office (1899).
En Guerra con Estados Unidos: Cuba 1898, Antonio Carrasco Garcia (1998).
Guerra de Cuba: Atlas Ilustrado, 3rd ed., Juan Excrigas Rodríguez (2012).
La Guerra del 98 y Mayaguez, Federico Cedó Alzamora, Historiador Oficial de Mayagüez, Puerto Rico (2014).

Theodore Roosevelt in the Spanish-American War and His Presidency

The Arena, vol. 95, no. 2, Newsletter of the Theodore Roosevelt Association, March/April 2015.
The Autobiography of Theodore Roosevelt, 1920 ed., Theodore Roosevelt (1913).
The Bully Pulpit: Theodore Roosevelt, William Howard Taft, and the Golden Age of Journalism, Doris Kearns Goodwin (2013).
Colonel Roosevelt, Edmund Morris (2010).
Grover Cleveland: The 24th President 1893–1897, American Presidents Series, Henry F. Graff (2002).
Imperial Cruise, James Bradley (2009).
New York Times, 1897 and 1898 newspaper articles, http://spiderbites.nytimes.com/free_1897/articles_1897_02_00001.html.
President McKinley: Architect of the American Century, Robert W. Merry (2017).

"The Right of the People to Rule," 1912 Roosevelt campaign speech recording (recorded by Thomas Edison), Vincent Voice Library, Michigan State University.

The Rise of Theodore Roosevelt, Edmund Morris (1979).

The Rough Riders, Theodore Roosevelt (1902).

Theodore Rex, Edmund Morris (2001).

Theodore Roosevelt's Naval Diplomacy, Henry J. Hendrix (2009).

The True Flag: Theodore Roosevelt, Mark Twain, and the Birth of American Empire, Stephen Kinzer (2017).

William McKinley: The 25th President, 1897–1901, American Presidents Series, Kevin Phillip and Arthur M. Schlesinger (2003).

Maps, Charts, and Sailing Guides

Chart of Old Providence Island (1885–1912), British Admiralty.

Chart of Swan Islands (1974).

A Cruising Guide to the Caribbean and the Bahamas, Jerrems C. Hart and William T. Stone (1976).

Cuba, a Cruising Guide, Nigel Calder (1997).

Eastern Coasts of Cuba, British Admiralty chart no. 3865 (1939).

Gulf Stream: Caribbean, Gulf of Mexico, Atlantic Ocean, Lt. Mathew Fontaine Maury, USN, U.S. Office of Coast Survey (1852).

Map of Colón, Panama (1911), Isthmian Canal Commission.

Map of Lighthouses in Puerto Rico (1885).

Map of the Bay of Guánica, Puerto Rico (1898).

Map of the Island of Puerto Rico (1898).

Map of the West Indies and Caribbean (1899).

Sketch Map of Puerto Rico, war correspondent Edwin Emerson (1898).

Southeastern Bahamas and Eastern Cuba, British Admiralty chart no. 1266 (1889).

Straits of Florida and Northern Cuba Coast, U.S. Office of Coast Survey (1895).

Upper Caribbean Sea and Gulf of Mexico, American privately published chart with U.S., British, French, and Spanish survey data (1860).

About the Author

Robert N. Macomber is an award-winning author, internationally acclaimed lecturer, Department of Defense consultant/lecturer, and accomplished seaman. When not trekking the world for research, book signings, or lectures, he lives on an island in southwest Florida, where he enjoys cooking the types of foreign cuisines described in his books and sailing among the islands.

Visit his website at www.RobertMacomber.com.